A RIVER OF GOLDEN BONES

ALSO BY A.K. MULFORD

THE FIVE CROWNS OF OKRITH

The High Mountain Court
The Witches' Blade
The Rogue Crown
The Evergreen Heir

THE OKRITH NOVELLAS

The Witch of Crimson Arrows
The Witch Apothecary
The Witchslayer

A River of Golden Bones

BOOK ONE OF THE GOLDEN COURT

A.K. Mulford

HARPER Voyager
An Imprint of HarperCollinsPublishers

A RIVER OF GOLDEN BONES. Copyright © 2023 by A.K. Mulford. Excerpt from THE AMETHYST KINGDOM © 2023 by A.K. Mulford. All rights reserved. Printed in the United States of America. No part of this book may be used or reproduced in any manner whatsoever without written permission except in the case of brief quotations embodied in critical articles and reviews. For information, address HarperCollins Publishers, 195 Broadway, New York, NY 10007.

HarperCollins books may be purchased for educational, business, or sales promotional use. For information, please email the Special Markets Department at SPsales@harpercollins.com.

Harper Voyager and design are trademarks of HarperCollins Publishers LLC.

FIRST EDITION

Designed by Angie Boutin
Title page background © Moolkum/shutterstock.com
Chapter opener illustration © Mari Muzz/shutterstock.com

Map design by Nick Springer / Springer Cartographics LLC

Library of Congress Cataloging-in-Publication Data has been applied for.

ISBN 978-0-06-329142-3

23 24 25 26 27 LBC 5 4 3 2 1

To those trying to discover themselves in a world that can be unyielding and unforgiving, this book is for you. May this story remind you that the answers you seek are not beyond you but buried within. Keep unearthing the brilliance and beauty that is you.

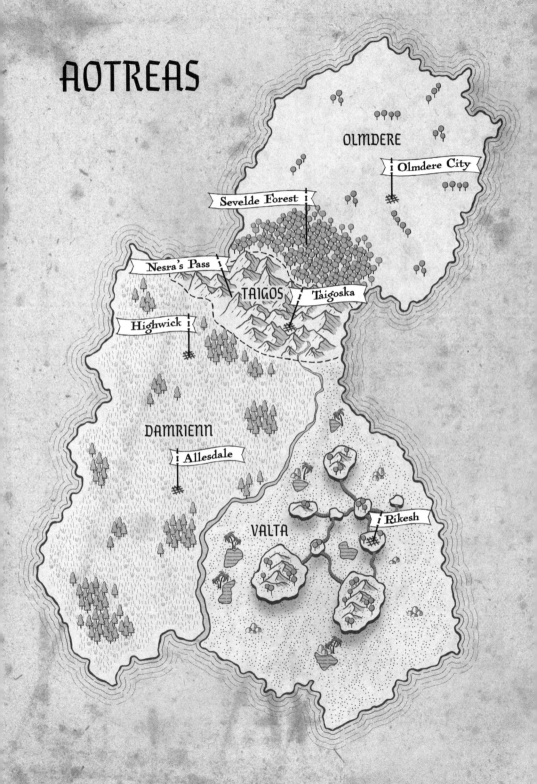

AOTREAS

OLMDERE

Olmdere City

Sevelde Forest

Nesra's Pass

TAIGOS   Taigoska

Highwick

DAMRIENN

Allesdale

VALTA   Rikesh

Map by Nick Springer, copyright © MMXXIII Springer Cartographics LLC

A RIVER OF GOLDEN BONES

ONE

THE GOLDEN CARRIAGES KICKED UP DUST AS TOWNSFOLK rushed to the streets, packing every window and stoop. They waved their handkerchiefs at the two coaches, craning their necks, trying to get a peek at the crown prince. The villagers didn't know why he was there, but I did, and it made my heart leap into my throat with excitement. I knew tomorrow I'd be leaving town in one of those gilded carriages back to his castle.

A rook cawed above me, iridescent wings shimmering as it landed on a maple branch. I scowled at the midnight bird—a bad omen. Sawyn's army of cloaked guards brandished the same moniker. And now, whenever I saw them, my stomach turned sour, sobering me from the thrill of the encroaching carriages.

With a frown toward the rook, I leapt from my trusty perch. I didn't need any bad omens today of all days. My gut lurched as the wind rushed around me and I landed in a crouch. I did a quick scan of the clearing, though I knew no humans were nearby. Their scent would've carried easily through the dry summer forest.

I peered back at the maple tree, but the rook had disappeared into the dense foliage. I tucked my amber necklace back under my neckline and dusted the leaves off my threadbare dress. Sticks snapped under my bare feet as I darted downhill. My dress snagged on a thicket of thorns and I pulled it free, grimacing at the sound of fabric tearing. Vellia would have to mend it again. I hated dresses, but Vellia insisted I wear them when I ventured from the cabin, as wearing tunics and breeches would only draw more attention.

As if I wasn't stared at anyway, being one of the two strange girls who lived in the wood.

I shielded my eyes from the glinting sun as I ran—not from the rook, though it still had me a bit spooked, especially with who was coming, but toward the road. My bare toes clung to the rough bark of a fallen tree as I crossed the narrow creek, rushing toward the royal procession. In one of those carriages was Graemon Claudius, the crown prince to the Silver Wolf kingdom of Damrienn. My friend had returned at last.

My heart drummed in my ears. I wondered if he looked the same. We'd still been pups the last time I saw him, only thirteen years old. Full moons were the only time his father, King Nero, permitted him to visit us here, and only ever as a Wolf—it was too risky any other way. For if anyone discovered a Gold Wolf in this village, the news would surely spread to Sawyn . . .

I glanced up again, to see if I could spy a rook spying back on me.

When no birds caught my eye, I cleared the forest with a swift leap. My bare feet slapped against the dusty cobbles as I raced toward the throng of well-wishers. It was with a sense of mischievous contentment that I knew I would be watching the world through their human eyes one last time, pretending to be just another among them. My lungs panted sweet air as I pushed my legs faster. I rushed past broken carts and bags of spoiled grain, my hair whipping behind me as I steered toward the main road.

I skirted down a shortcut and heard the crowd roar. I turned my head toward the sound, not watching up ahead, and slammed into an unyielding object. My feet slid out from under me as I bounced off what I realized was a cloaked figure. Arms wheeling, I braced myself for the hard thump onto the stone when two powerful hands grabbed me midair and hoisted me back to my feet.

"Apologies," I blurted out, even as I scrambled for the paring knife in my dress pocket. Vellia wouldn't let me bring my dagger, but I could justify a paring knife for foraging.

The figure chuckled—a deep, throaty laugh that made me still my hand.

"Hello, little fox."

The familiar rasp of his low voice made my eyes go wide. My stomach somersaulted at the sound of my nickname. Brushing the curls off my face, I narrowed my eyes, peering into the darkness of his hood. Only one person ever called me that name—and that person I hadn't seen in seven years.

Someone who should be in one of those carriages instead of standing before me.

"Grae?" I dropped my hand from my knife's handle.

He pulled back his hood, and the sight of him rattled me more than colliding headlong into him had. This was not the boy I had known. No, this was not a boy *at all*. I'd never seen a more stunning man. He had classic Damrienn features—obsidian hair pulled to a small knot at the crown of his head, golden brown skin, and hooded umber eyes. But he was also twice my size, towering over me, the peak of shoulder muscles from his neckline denoting a warrior's physique. He was gorgeous, and yet still wolflike even in his human form, with glinting canines and a hardened jaw. His angular cheeks dimpled as he smirked down at me.

"Wh-what are you doing out here?" I asked, scanning the vacant backstreets.

"We're visiting, of course."

"I mean what are you doing *here*, in this alley?" I said.

His grin widened. "I wanted to see the village where you

grew up without being noticed." His voice was an octave lower than since last I'd heard it. "Maybe a bit too unnoticeable, seeing as you ran straight into me."

That voice. Gods, help me. His Wolf voice had spoken into my mind during his visits, but we had been thirteen then. Hearing it now was . . . distracting.

"Briar and Vellia are waiting at the cabin for you," I whispered. It was all I could think to say as my gaze hooked on his face, dumbstruck.

How was it possible *this* is what Grae looked like?

His dark eyes twinkled, making the hairs on my arms stand on end. "Walk with me?"

My lips parted, and I followed him down the alley and onto the wider back road. Cheers and whistles bounced off the stone as we walked across the worn cobbles. My heartbeat thrummed in my ears. He was really here.

I cleared my throat. "How did you know it was me?"

Grae's cloak flapped behind him as he peeked at me. Every time those red-brown eyes landed on me, it felt like the ground gave way.

"Your hair."

"My hair?" I snorted, grabbing a brown ringlet and pulling it straight. "I don't have curly hair in my other form."

Immediately my eyes darted to the curtained windows and closed doors. No one was around to hear me, but I still said *other* instead of *Wolf*. Sawyn would pay handsomely for the last Gold Wolves' location, and no matter how pretty the man next to me was, I was always on guard. We had kept our secret these many years through dogged vigilance, not even whispering the word "Wolf," and that wasn't about to change.

"Not the texture of your hair." Grae chuckled, the sound making my toes curl against the rough stones. "The scent of your hair."

"My scent?" Most humans smelled the same to me, like rising

bread and tilled earth, but each Wolf had their own scent, like a fingerprint special only to them.

And he remembered mine.

Grae took a deep, slow breath, making me blush. His nostrils flared as he seemingly tasted the air and let it out again. "Like lilies in summer sunshine and a hint of spice . . . cinnamon perhaps?" He murmured each word as if savoring it.

Pinpricks covered my lips up to my ears, and I knew the creeping blush had probably turned my cheeks bright red.

Yes, he knew me—and I knew Grae's scent, too. He'd always smelled like . . . damp earth and woodsmoke—a bonfire after a rainstorm. Powerful and elemental, disparate yet whole. The echoes of his essence flooded back to me, along with all those childhood memories. I still heard our laughter, that giddy glee of chasing each other through the nighttime forest. And when we were tired from our runs, we'd sit by the river and he'd tell me stories from every corner of the realm.

Closing my eyes, I breathed deep through my nose. As a Wolf, I could smell the pies cooling in open windows, the fresh hay being carted off to the town stables, and the wildflowers in the meadow beyond. I imagined the wind in my hair was blowing through my golden red fur instead as I realized that with Grae here, it possibly meant the end to our hiding, and my Wolf could finally be free. That thought made me giddy, and I hoped the forests in the capital would be larger. In Allesdale, I had to run in circles to run at all. The eastern wood surrounding our little cottage took only ten minutes to cross on all four paws. I'd learned every fallen log and muddy creek by heart and was beginning to feel like the dogs kept tied up outside the butchers.

After today, though, I'd no longer feel trapped.

Grae tipped his chin toward my bare feet, and his cheeks dimpled. "Your feet must be as tough as your paws." His laugh had changed since we were young. Now it was a rolling thunder that emerged from his chest only to be felt deep in my own.

I checked over my shoulder again to see if anyone had heard him, but the streets were empty. Soon the carriages would roll out the other end of town, and people would return to work, but for now they were entranced by the spectacle.

"You should be more careful," I muttered, instantly regretting that I had just rebuked the crown prince. I mean, I was royalty, too . . . but if Briar were here, she'd scold me for my lack of decorum. Grae was not the playful pup chasing bunnies in the eastern wood anymore.

"When we get to Highwick, you'll never again have to whisper about what you are," he promised. The sincerity in his voice made me press my lips together. "You can be proud to be a Wolf." He lifted his chin up to the Moon Goddess. "You can be exactly as you are, little fox."

I huffed. Exactly as I am? That wasn't saying much. Briar was "the Crimson Princess," with her ruby red hair and long, lithe frame. The Moon Goddess designed her perfectly for royal life. Me . . . I was Briar's opposite in every way, the other side of the same coin. No one would ever guess that we were twins. Only a handful of people even knew who I was—Grae and his father being two of them. I was a whole head shorter than Briar and twice her size, with rounded curves that belied the muscles I'd spent years of combat training honing. Even in my Gold Wolf form, I was lacking compared to my twin—small and scruffy next to her, with a hue of rust to my golden fur. It was why Grae called me *little fox* . . . and it was also why his promises that I could be myself felt nothing but deflating.

The words spilled from my mouth before I could stop them. "Who I am is no one."

Grae's footsteps faltered at my muttered confession. He sidestepped me so quickly I almost walked straight into him . . . again. Blocking my path, he spun to face me. His stare felt like a weight pressing down on me. His calloused pointer finger touched the tip of my chin, lifting until my eyes met his dark ones. Holding his gaze felt thrilling and familiar all at once.

"You will have a home in Highwick, too, little fox." His breath brushed my cheek. "You will stand on the dais as the royalty you are once your sister and I are married. There will never be any mistaking that you are truly someone."

My racing heart plummeted into my gut. Not at the promise, but at the reason why he could make such a promise:

Once your sister and I are married.

That was why he was here. On the full moon, it would be our twentieth birthday, and they would finally fulfill the marriage that had been arranged since before our births. The Crimson Princess would marry the Silver Wolf of Damrienn for the good of the pack.

Shame burned inside of me at my bitterness. Neither of us were children anymore, though I still preferred climbing trees to rouging my cheeks. I knew we all had a role to play. I reminded myself of Vellia's words, the ones she told me and my sister over and over again. That the fate of our kingdom depended on this marriage and the money and soldiers that came with it. With the might of the Damrienn army, we could reclaim the fallen Gold Wolf kingdom. This was how daughters of kings gained power—through marriages and alliances. Briar would rally support through tea parties and balls, and, as her guard, I'd muster it with my sword. I was definitely getting the better end of the deal, training in secret to be a killer instead of a dainty, poised princess.

It was the whole reason we had hidden ourselves in this quiet village.

The realization still hit me like a blow, however.

As if on cue, a rook cawed overhead, taunting me, and I pressed on. Grae fell into stride beside me.

"I'd still prefer we don't discuss these things until we are in Highwick," I muttered.

Grae chuckled. "As you wish, little fox."

Little fox. He kept saying it, and it kept sounding different now, even though it was the only nickname I'd ever had. Briar

wouldn't even appreciate how good it felt to be noticed by someone like Grae. I clenched my fists as we walked, knowing I should
focus more on the coming battles than on the handsome prince
beside me. The pack was more important than my desires.

I looked around to distract myself. The streets began filling
with people as the royal carriages wheeled out of Allesdale. Only
Grae and I knew they wouldn't be rolling into the next town,
but veering off toward Vellia's cabin in the woods. Grae and his
guards would stay the night, and we'd leave at first light for our
long journey back to the capital.

Grae pulled his hood up again, hiding his visage in shadow
as I scanned the dreary stone buildings. I wouldn't miss this
drab little town. The haggard faces of villagers watched us as
we climbed the hill. The townsfolk had always been wary of
Vellia, and Briar and I by association. An old lady living alone in
the woods garnered rumors she was a sorceress. Little did they
know, Vellia was indeed magical, but she was no witch.

The road inclined, steeper with each step. I welcomed the
pleasant burn of my muscles as I hastened to keep up with Grae's
long legs. I savored this last moment together, just the two of us.
I peeked at him, unable to see his eyes from the shadows of his
hood, but somehow knowing he looked back at me. Despite all
my eagerness to leave, I would miss this—two friends without
titles or grand destinies. That daydream would end as soon as
we reached the hidden cabin in the woods where his betrothed
waited.

We hurried along, yet all I wanted to do was linger. I couldn't
do that, though. Not to Grae. Not to Briar.

All things must come to an end—even if it's just a walk
through the woods.

TWO

THE DENSE CANOPY HIGH ABOVE US CAST COOL SHADOWS down the forest trail. My fingers brushed over the moss dripping from the trees as we fell into easy conversation. We crunched through the leaves, following the thin rivulets the carriage wheels carved down the path. Grae told me the latest news from Damrienn. Drought had hit the farms over the summer and his father was even more surly than usual, but the city had the upcoming wedding to buoy their spirits. News had apparently spread like wildfire that the Crimson Princess was not only alive but also about to marry their crown prince.

Rumors had swirled for years that the last of the Gold Wolf line yet lived, that the Marriel princess named Briar had survived the fateful night of her birth . . . but no one whispered about another named Calla. The world had searched for my twin sister these twenty long years, but I remained a shadow behind the dream of the Crimson Princess. After two decades, we would finally be able to reveal our secret: not one Marriel survived that night, but two.

Not that I thought the world would care all that much—they'd still focus everything on Briar, as they should. I was very content to let her bear all the scrutiny of court life while I watched—and plotted—from the shadows.

Grae reached out and hooked his finger along the chain of my necklace. He pulled until the amber stone lifted above my neckline and smiled. "You still wear it."

"Of course I do," I said, my skin tingling where his knuckle grazed my collarbone. "When a prince gives you a protection stone, you wear it."

His cheeks dimpled. "Does Briar still wear hers?"

"Yes."

"Liar." He chuckled, snapping a budding white flower off a low branch and passing it to me. "I can smell the lie on you as easily as I smell the perfume in the trees."

I scanned through the summer forest, resplendent with flowers. The woods surrounding our cabin were filled with as many memories as the cabin itself. Every full moon of our youth, Briar and I would prowl into the dark forest, hoping Grae would appear. That was seven years ago . . . I still had his last correspondence in my dresser drawer. Along with his letters came two necklaces—a ruby for Briar and an amber for me. I had wondered if Grae had selected the stones for the shades of our hair every time I had read my now-crinkled letter. Briar's letter was two pages long, but mine was only a brief paragraph:

> *My father has sent me to Valta for schooling. I will be*
> *unable to visit for the foreseeable future, but I'm sure*
> *I'll have even more stories to share when I do. This is a*
> *protection stone. Wear it always. I'm sorry, little fox.*
> *Don't forget me. G*

I toyed with my delicate amber pendant along its thin gold chain. How could he think I would forget him? He was my first and *only* friend I hadn't shared a womb with. Seven years since I'd seen him or heard his tales of magic and monsters. Seven years since we'd chased each other through the forests or shared our hopes for the future. It had hurt more than I'd liked to admit that no more letters came . . .

The summer's swollen moon, hidden in the clear blue sky, pulled on me. Soon it would be full, and the urge to transform would overwhelm me once more. Most of the time I could control it, but the days leading up to the full moon set every Wolf on edge . . . and that was before my current rarefied state.

"Do you remember the story of the necklace?"

I swirled the stem of the flower in my hands. The cloying, sweet aroma wafted around us as we ambled through the woods. "It was your great-grandmother's dying wish that her children be protected from harm. A family heirloom now." As I remembered his recent tragedy, I rested a hand on Grae's forearm, the feeling making my whole body buzz as I said, "I heard about your mother's passing. I'm so sorry."

"It was many years ago." His eyes scanned my face before he stepped out of my touch.

My heart ached at that little movement. I knew it meant he didn't want to talk about his mother. The baker had told me that Queen Lucrecia had died a week after our necklaces arrived. I'd wanted to flee to Highwick and find Grae the second I'd heard, and probably would have if Briar hadn't hugged me so close, whispering soothing words into my ears. I was devastated for him.

"Do you remember any of my other faery stories?" Grae asked, changing the subject.

"All of them," I murmured. I cleared my throat as his cheeks dimpled. "The cleaved peak, the ever-sailing ship, the gold mines of Sevelde . . . of juvlecks and ostekkes and other monsters that even the myths and songs seem to have forgotten."

Of course I remembered them all. I had pestered him to tell them over and over, always begging for another story. And, in the long years since I last saw him, I repeated them in my mind, imagining the sound of his voice.

I tucked the white flower behind my ear. "What do you remember of your visits here?"

He sighed, closing his eyes. "Games of chase, the sound of

your laughter in my mind." His grin widened. "And your many secret words."

"Code words," I corrected. "In case we need to flee."

"I think shouting 'run' would be just as effective." He chuckled, clasping his hands behind his back and slowing to a creeping pace. Maybe he didn't want this moment to end as much as me.

"I don't think shouting 'run' is particularly stealthy." I teased, tapping my forefinger to my chin in mock contemplation. "Our current one is 'quiver,' by the way."

He barked out a laugh. "How would one stealthily work the word 'quiver' into a sentence without being detected?"

"I'm sure we'll come up with something." I winked at him, and he nearly walked smack into a sapling, dodging it at the last moment. This was the playful Wolf I remembered.

GRAE PULLED UP SHORT, STARING AT THE SPOT WHERE THE trail ended in dense forest. "Where's the cabin?"

With a laugh, I pointed to a thin seam of warped air. The image of the forest bent as if looking through steam on a hot day. "For all the faery stories you tell, you haven't seen a glamour before?"

Quirking his brow, Grae reached out and touched the bending air. His mouth dropped open as his fingertips disappeared.

I snickered and looped my arm through his; the contact making my cheeks burn as I tried to hide it with bravado. "Come on," I said, tugging him through the glamoured air. "Vellia will delight you with her magic once we're inside."

Stepping through the seam, cool air rushed over my skin and the cabin appeared. What was once an empty forest was now a sprawling acreage, complete with gardens and stables. Two golden carriages parked in front of the house, the horses already unhitched and grazing in the grassy gardens beyond our home. I dropped my hold on Grae's arm, flustered at that buzzing contact between us, and clenched my hands by my sides.

I really needed to stop touching him.

Grae's eyebrows shot up. "This is the *cabin*?"

Vellia built the three-story house from giant redwood trunks. Garlands of wooden beads hung from the rose-colored shutters, vivid summer flowers filled the window boxes, and a bright blue door greeted us. A faery clearly designed the home.

"Do you like it?"

"All these years running in the woods together, I'd imagined you were returning to a one-bedroom hovel," Grae jeered. "I should've known better." Shaking his head, he followed me up the steps to the front door.

"Did you *want* us to live in a dilapidated shack?" I teased.

"No, no—of course not. It's just . . . this," he said, gesturing at the house.

"Dying wishes make for powerful magic." Before he could reply to that—and before my fingers could reach the handle—the door opened.

Vellia stood in a sage green dress that made her pale gray eyes seem to glow. A matching scarf wrapped around her silver hair, fluttering as she dropped into a low curtsy. "Welcome, Your Highness."

"Thank you for receiving me," Grae said in a princely tone that sounded so different from the easy one that had just flowed between us.

Vellia took another step backward, opening the door with a flourish to grant him entry. She gave me a wink. This day was a victory for Vellia. Upon my mother's deathbed, Vellia granted her dying wish: protect my daughter until her wedding day. The power of that wish had filled Vellia with immense amounts of magic. I always wondered if my mother would have changed her wish if she had known I was about to arrive a moment later. The elderly faery seemed to think so, and so Vellia had protected Briar and me both with a ferocity that would make any mother Wolf proud.

The cabin ceiling rose high above us as we spilled into the

grand entryway. A towering gray stone fireplace bisected the room. Boughs of evergreen covered rough beams of wood, and an antler chandelier flickered with hundreds of magically lit candles. A circle of guards stood beside the fireplace. They all had the same thick black Damrienn hair, angular faces, and light golden-brown skin. Wearing thin plates of silver armor, their hands rested on the hilts of their swords as they laughed, listening to a joke from the elegant woman in the center of their circle.

Briar.

She wore a dusty rose dress, covered in delicate lace that billowed around her willowy frame. She probably had Vellia conjure it for her this morning. Her red hair was braided back at the temples with wispy white flowers circling her head like a crown. She flashed the soldiers a broad smile, drawing attention with ease—born to be in the center of any circle.

Spotting Grae over her shoulder, she sauntered over. Her hair swished in rhythm with her hips. She dropped into a bow and murmured, "Your Highness."

"Your Highness," Grae said in return, inclining his head to her.

I blanched, realizing I hadn't addressed him by his title. Maybe I would've remembered to bow if I hadn't run smack into him.

"I trust the journey from Highwick was not too harrowing?" Briar already spoke with the grace of a queen holding court.

"Not at all." Grae played along with her courtly act. "It's an easy day's journey, and the countryside is lovely."

Briar demurred, lifting her lashes to look up at him. She barely had to incline her neck, the top of her head reaching his eyes. She would look perfect standing beside him. My lips thinned as I hid my frown. It was such a waste. Briar knew she would never love him—had said as much to me in secret moments. But love had nothing to do with royal marriages. Love was for humans. If Briar had been born a boy, she could've avoided all this peacocking and laid claim to Olmdere herself. Sometimes I wished I could've been born a boy for all the ease and permission it would've granted me. Sometimes I wished I didn't have to play a role in order to be valued. But this was how Wolf bloodlines stayed strong and how the four kingdoms maintained their peace. Ruling a pack meant sacrifice, and we all had a part to play.

They held each other's gazes for a moment longer before Briar said, "I can show you all to your rooms. You'll probably want to wash up before dinner."

A strand of black hair fell around Grae's face as he nodded, and I had the terrible urge to brush it behind his ear. I balled my hands into fists until my fingernails cut into my palms.

"Thank you." Yet he didn't look at her; instead Grae's eyes found mine, and he gave me a half-smile.

Briar led them up the winding steps to the upper balcony. I watched them disappear around the corner, only to realize Vellia was still standing beside me. Her eyes crinkled with knowing mischief.

I narrowed my eyes at her. "What?"

"Nothing." Vellia shrugged, drumming her fingers on her cheek. "This day has been a long time coming for us all." The clink of the knights' armor rang down the hall. Vellia looked me up and down. "What do you want to wear for dinner? A periwinkle blue to match your sister's rose?"

Wear? What did she mean? Then I frowned at my crumpled brown dress, touching the fresh tear from the thicket. It was perfect for the village, plain and unremarkable. I huffed, as if what I wore now mattered. I could traipse through Allesdale in a ballgown and, if Briar were by my side, no one would notice me.

"I'd rather dress like the knights," I said. "A tunic and leathers, nothing too fancy—"

"Nothing too fancy?" Vellia tutted, rolling her eyes. "You are dining with the crown prince of Damrienn tonight."

"And *I* am a royal of Olmdere."

"Then act like it," she snapped.

"I'm not meant to be noticed." I scowled. "The guards don't even know who I am."

We would keep the secret of my parentage until the King of

Damrienn decided otherwise. In his letters, he had promised once Briar married Grae he'd reveal the truth . . . until then, I was to remain a secret. Their wedding fulfilled a contract forged before our birth, and the future of Olmdere hinged upon it. Our position was too precarious to argue, and this could put that all in jeopardy.

That's what I was telling myself, at least.

"It's Briar who must dress like a queen," I said.

Vellia tugged on the lobe of my ear. "As you noted, you are a Marriel, too, Calla."

"But I'm fine with being a shadow." I'd decided long ago to make the most of my obscurity. If I couldn't be a queen, then I'd be a warrior. We needed both roles to regain our homeland, and it suited me more anyway. "It will be much easier to sneak up on Sawyn that way. I will be there when they avenge my parents . . . and I won't be wearing a fancy dress."

It was something I had learned from my endless hours of training. I would never win from brute strength, but from cunning and surprise. I gripped the knife in my pocket, imagining dragging it across the sorceress's throat. It was my own ancestors who'd rid the world of monsters and sorcerers—the promise we made to the humans who placed crowns upon Wolves' heads. I would carry on that legacy, defeating dark magic once more.

Vellia released a long-suffering sigh. She was a faery who lived to dote on us, and I made it rather tough. Fluttering her fingers at the stairwell, she shooed me away. "Go bathe, at least. Your outfit will be waiting."

White magic sparked from her fingers, floating up toward the high ceiling, and I knew a hot bath waited for me.

I was one foot up the stairs when Vellia's voice called after me.

"It will be all right, you know, Calla."

Her reassurance was anything but comforting. I had never been fearful of something so mediocre as "all right"—I had a kingdom to resurrect and parents to avenge. My sister would marry and make allies and sign treaties, and *I* would be the nameless Wolf who won back our throne.

THREE

AS PROMISED, MY OUTFIT WAS ON MY BED WHEN I CLIMBED OUT of the bath. I inspected the silver brocade along the tunic's neck and sleeves, a smile tugging on my lips. Vellia had outdone herself yet again. It was the most decadent fabric; the shoulders cut wide to make me seem more muscular, the stone-gray trousers designed to curve over my rounded thighs. But the true gem of the outfit was my freshly shined—and sharpened—dagger. The golden hilt gleamed in the candlelight, the etchings along the silver scabbard clearly defined once more. My eyes skimmed over the symbols of Olmdere—stag's antlers over a pawprint, a crown in the center pad. Vellia had gifted me the weapon when I was ten years old. It had been far too big and heavy then, but with time came ease, and now, it felt as familiar to me as my own hands.

I traced my finger along the carved metal symbols and sighed. What would it have been like to grow up under these banners? To stand beside my family sitting on their thrones? Vellia had conjured little drawings of my parents over the years—maps of their kingdom and their ethereal castle in the center of a lake. Briar and I would incessantly nag her for more, for her to describe the details of a life we never knew. But some things even faery magic couldn't conjure. I would never know the sound of my mother's voice, the warmth of my father's embrace, or the confidence of who I could've been with their guidance. A part of me would always be missing, and that made me grip the handle of the knife all the tighter.

The sound of footsteps grew and then faded as the guests passed my bedroom door, heading to dinner. I sheathed the knife, then dressed, cinching the thick black belt that covered my entire midsection and stretched from my hips to under my breasts. My thick belt kept the knife from tugging my trousers down, the tight leather also making me stand straighter. The fitted material smoothed my curves. Even so, I was shaped more like a rectangle than like Briar's hourglass figure. It suited me, though—my body looked powerful this way. I stared at my reflection, straightening my shoulders. I liked the warrior who watched me in the mirror. She was strong and soft, masculine and feminine, threatening and enticing, all at once. Briar knew how to be a princess, but this . . . whatever this was . . . I could be.

My eyes tracked down my reflection—my brown curls, my green eyes, my skin a shade darker than Briar's pale rose, the dagger resting on my wide hips. And a little voice whispered inside me: *good, but not enough.* How could I ever feel like enough when Briar was perfection personified? I tried to carve my own path, but I didn't know how, not with her shadow looming over me. Something I couldn't put my finger on just never felt quite right. So I pushed that feeling away and focused my energy on training instead. I'd trained my entire life against every possible foe Vellia could think to conjure. The dizzying pendulum of thoughts swung back the other way: *I have the skill. I am ready,* I assured myself for the hundredth time. I just needed to act like I believed it.

Gods, I didn't know how people did that—be all the things they felt inside.

I picked up my discarded towel and squeezed my ringlets one more time, catching the last drips. Casting a final long look at the image in the mirror, I tried to summon an ounce of the confidence that oozed from my twin. Fake smile, shoulders back, eyes shining . . . but none of it felt real, and I slumped once more. No mask I wore felt right—there was always a piece missing. I sighed, painfully aware of that missing piece as if it were a chunk taken out of my side. Could everyone feel it as much as I could? I wondered if Grae could see it—see that I was incomplete.

I rolled my shoulders back again and opened the door, trying and failing to push my swirling thoughts away. Of all people, I hoped Grae didn't think of me as incomplete.

LAUGHTER DANCED THROUGH THE DINING ROOM AS I CROSSED the threshold into the gilded chamber. Grae shot up from his chair as his guards moved to do the same. He was immaculate— like the prince I had always imagined he would become. He wore a double-breasted black jacket and tails; golden buttons dotted down the smooth fabric, and golden epaulettes hung from his shoulders.

But it was the way he looked back at me that made my heart skip a beat. My eyes darted to the high neck of his collar that grazed his sharp jawline, up to his parted lips and wide eyes. The rest of the room faded away as I held his dark gaze. I wished I could bottle up that awed expression and take it with me always.

If nothing else, it made me stand a little taller.

Briar's voice broke the spell between our eyes. "You look splendid, Calla."

I swallowed. I didn't want to look *splendid*; I wanted to look strong, something my sister had never understood. Looking at Briar, I bit down on my snicker as I replied, "As do you, Your Highness."

My twin had changed into a voluminous burgundy gown that matched Grae's sash. Long satin gloves covered her forearms, and a golden necklace of stag's antlers draped over her collarbone. She wore her hair twisted up in an elegant bun, a little tiara at the front. Our parents would be proud—the perfect daughter to marry off to a dashing prince.

Briar stood at the head of the table, Grae to her right, and the rest of his guards took up the remaining seats, leaving the one at the far end vacant for me. Ducking my head, I sat as Briar gestured to the others to do the same. I begrudged my sister many things, but I was grateful to not be the one hosting. I would rather be eaten by an ostekke than take her place at the head of the table. This was the first time we had guests in . . . well, ever, and Briar made it look effortless. All those games of pretend that she forced me to play as a child were finally paying off.

As I sat, my crystal goblet filled with golden liquid. I grabbed the glass as I looked around the room to find where Vellia was hiding. It took me a moment before I spotted the wallpaper in the far corner bending. I winked at the warped air where Vellia hid, watching over our dinner. At least there was wine.

"I'm Hector," the guard to my right said, and I hoped he didn't think I'd lost my mind for winking at what appeared to be a vacant corner of the room.

Hector looked older than Grae, with sharp eyes and a toothy grin.

"A pleasure to meet you, Hector."

"And this is my little sister, Sadie," he gestured to the guard to my left.

"You've got to stop introducing me as your *little sister*," Sadie snarled.

I chuckled, looking between them. They had the same wide-set eyes, broad noses, and slender arched brows. Sadie wore her short hair braided back and scowled at her brother under her straight black bangs.

"Are you twins?" I asked.

"No." Hector laughed, taking a sip of his wine. "She's two years younger."

"A year and a half," Sadie corrected. She flicked out a knife from her belt and snicked a white rose in front of her place setting. She had a pinched, morose expression as she surveyed the flower, her long bangs falling into her eyes.

"You see what I have to put up with? It devastated me when Grae picked her for the royal guard." Hector grinned in a way that told me he wasn't disappointed in the slightest.

He pointed to the last guard sitting beside Briar. "That's Maez. She's Grae's cousin."

All three guards wore matching pewter tunics with half-moon chest plates etched in the crest of Damrienn—a phoenix with its wings spread and a crescent moon through a crown above it.

Hector. Sadie. Maez. Too many names. I folded my arms, nodding as I tried to remember, but knowing I'd forget. Names were the least memorable thing about a person. I was far more interested in what caused that scar on Maez's top lip, which side Sadie would duck to in a fight, and why Hector twisted at the waist when he looked at me instead of turning his neck.

"You don't need to remember," Sadie said, as if reading my thoughts. "You can just say 'hey you' and we'll respond."

"Save that energy for the King's courtiers," Hector added with a knowing chuckle. "They won't give you such leniency."

I shuddered. Soldiers I could understand, but the smiling, simpering nature of courtiers was something Vellia could never truly prepare us for. They were the highest ranked Wolves— apart from the royal family themselves—with the guards below them, and then the rest of the Wolf families. The pack hierarchy was rigid. Wolves lived and died by their rank, and we were the fortunate ones at the top. Vellia had told us Wolves worked their whole lives to earn the King's favor and raise themselves within the ranks, and we were already there through virtue of our birth. But until our new pack knew of my birth, my rank was unknowable, and I couldn't imagine those of the upper echelon taking too kindly to a sudden upstart joining their cohort. Where would I fit within this new world?

"Welcome to the life of a royal guard." Hector concluded, seeing my dismayed expression and clearly thinking of some courtier in particular.

I could see myself falling in with this group of soldiers—

wearing the pewter tunics and chest plates that suited Sadie and Hector equally. They seemed easier friends than the ones Briar was bound to attract.

"That is a gorgeous dagger." Hector tipped over the edge of the table to examine the silver scabbard.

"Vellia made it for me," I replied, resting my hand on the gilded hilt.

"It must've been wild to grow up here with a princess," he mused. "You two must be like sisters."

I bobbed my chin. "Something like that."

"But can you use it?" Hector asked, mirroring my pose with his own sword. I cut him a sideways look, my expression saying everything, and the guard snorted. "Aye, she can," he said to his sister. "You should come train with us in Highwick. I want to see that dagger in action."

"I'd like that," I said, giving him a nod of thanks. Vellia's conjured monsters and foes were all of her own design. They made fine training partners, but they only moved one way, thought one way. They were all controlled by Vellia's mind, and she wasn't of the martial spirit. I needed new opponents with minds of their own if I were to improve my skills.

"I still can't believe it," Sadie said, swiping her short braid over her shoulder. Leaning in, she looked down the table at Briar. "The Crimson Princess is alive after all these years. When the King told us, we were all stunned. We thought the rumors were just that . . . and Grae knew the entire time." She snorted as she lifted her goblet. "Explains why he's kept all the swooning ladies at arm's length. He had a princess waiting for him."

I glanced up from the table, leaning past the tall stem of the candelabra to see Grae talking with Briar and Maez.

"Do you think they're fated mates?" Sadie asked, snapping my attention back to her.

"It's said that the King and Queen Marriel were fated mates," Hector said, swirling his goblet.

It was a good question—and strangely one I hadn't ever really thought about. Lots of Wolves took a mate. Some married, others had many lovers over their lifetime, but fated mates were something special. There was a magic to their bond that existed beyond this realm, weaving through time. That magic superseded all others, a most rare and respected gift from the Moon Goddess herself.

Some said it was like two bodies existing with one soul. Most thought it was beautiful, but I only thought it was tragic. When my father died, my mother died, too, so strong was their fated bond. The bards wrote ballads about their love, but all I felt was their absence. Tying two souls together didn't seem like a gift . . . it seemed like cruelty.

Probably why I never considered it for Briar.

"Maybe Grae and Briar are, too," Sadie mused, shaking her head so that her bangs moved out of her eyes. "Maybe it was the Goddess who made their parents arrange their marriage."

"All royals arrange these alliances if they have daughters instead of sons," I said.

"But why Damrienn?" Sadie asked. "Why not one of the other kingdoms?"

I shook my head, setting down my glass. "Taigos has no male heir and Valta's male royals are either too old or too young."

Of the four kingdoms of Aotreas, each was ruled by a different pack, protectors of their human kingdoms. The Gold, Ice, Silver, and Onyx Wolf packs ruled over the continent, with my kingdom at the very north and the floating islands of Valta at the southernmost tip.

"It would explain why Grae's been keeping this secret," Hector replied. "Didn't want one of the Valtan princes to swoop in and propose to her, too old or not."

Sadie twirled her knife. "I can't image the Onyx Wolves attempting to rule a kingdom so far from their own. They'd need to cross Damrienn and Taigos to even oversee it."

"It needed to be a secret." My goblet refilled, the candlelight flickering at the magical act. "To protect her from Sawyn." Even whispering the sorceress's name felt wrong. Her magic seemed to darken every room.

Sadie rolled her eyes. "Sawyn is probably a withered old crone by now."

"Sorcerers are immortal, as is the gift of their dark magic," Hector countered. "Everyone knows that."

"Maybe she's not a very good one, then," Sadie snapped back. "No one has seen her in a decade. Olmdere might be flooded with her Rooks, but any fool with a sword could take that throne."

"Then why haven't you?" Hector japed. This seemed to be a conversation they'd had before. "If Sawyn isn't a threat, then why hasn't *anyone* taken Olmdere?"

"They were probably waiting for her." Sadie hooked her thumb at Briar. "King Nero needs a Marriel daughter before he can name his son King of Olmdere."

And there it was, laid out on the dining room table. I bit back on the bitter taste in my mouth. My kingdom would no longer be ruled by Gold Wolves, and all because Briar and I hadn't been boys. Grae and his father would get everything, having won their titles and thrones the moment the midwives peeked between their legs.

I scowled at Briar, trying to wish away the pain of that truth. She leaned across the dining table, in deep conversation with Maez. I clenched my teeth, forcing myself not to roll my eyes. It'd been only a few minutes and Briar had already lost interest in entertaining Grae, preferring the company of the guard. Grae and Briar had always been amiable, but they'd never really been friends . . . not like us.

Grae's eyes lifted to meet mine, one cheek dimpling. That bloody grin turned me into a melting idiot. I grabbed my wineglass and dropped my eyes, shifting back in my seat so the candelabra blocked my view of the handsome prince. I wasn't a swooning dame. Leave the fans and coy smiles to Briar.

With a flicker of shimmering light, the empty plates on the table filled. The greasy scent of spiced meats lifted into the air as the guards gaped at the sumptuous meal before them. I picked up my fork and speared a balsamic-glazed carrot.

Listening to the guards' banter, I ate in silence. Briar was magnificent as she regaled our guests with story after story of our magical childhood, spinning our sad tale into something worthy of a song. But every story took place in the same cabin in the same forest. That sameness became nagging no matter how magical, and it kept reminding me that we were both like caged animals, ready to bolt from a trap. Tomorrow, all that would change. I didn't care if the food was rotten and my clothes were the itchiest wool. I was ready for something more.

FOUR

I STUMBLED OUT OF THE DINING ROOM, THE GOBLETS OF HONEY wine rushing to my head. I couldn't believe how many times Vellia had refilled my cup over the course of the evening. On wobbly legs, I somehow made it across the entryway. The chandelier above me still glimmered with half-melted candles. A fire roared to life beside me, despite the balmy summer air. Vellia seemed determined to make this home seem grand, using up every last drop of her magic before our departure tomorrow.

The night had droned on until the genteel voices became drunken howls. The guards became more boisterous with each hour that passed, endearing them to me even more. Vellia had kept the food coming, dish after dish, until the third round of desserts. At that point I was so stuffed I thought I might be sick and had finally excused myself.

"Little fox," a mirthful voice called after me as I reached the stairs.

I certainly didn't feel like "little" anything at that moment, and I practically froze with the thought that he could see how the butterflies in my stomach had nowhere to go. I turned anyway, and the impact of seeing his figure in that uniform again made me suck in a breath. The wine had loosened my limbs, along with my good sense. I scanned him from head to toe, permitting myself to appreciate his glorious features for one more night. Those muscled thighs, lean hips, and broad shoulders. My eyes roved up his angular cheekbones to his hooded bedroom eyes.

"Your Wolf form is magnificent, Grae," I murmured, waving my hand at him. "But you are quite the dashing prince in this outfit, too."

Ebarvens kill me, had I said that out loud? I grimaced, gripping my hands together as Grae chuckled.

"And you look like a warrior—beautiful and mighty," he said with a grin, taking a further step toward me.

My eyes dropped to my hands as I picked at my fingers, feeling his eyes upon me as his shined black boots came into view. I had a hard time believing his words. Because with them, I knew he saw the same person I did when staring in the mirror. He saw me.

"Calla," he whispered, his breath in my hair. I loved the way he whispered my name, wished I could hear the resonance of that sound every day of my life. "I need to talk to you."

The tips of my ears tingled as I looked up at him. His storming eyes met mine, and I had to wring my hands together to not reach out and touch him. I couldn't handle being this close to him as his bonfire scent wrapped around me. That golden wine hummed in my veins.

"Why didn't you visit?" I asked before I could stop myself. "You didn't even write. They sent you south for school, but surely there were holidays and breaks. I . . . I missed you."

His eyebrows knitted together, a pained expression crossing his face. "I missed you, too, little fox." His fingers skimmed the chain of my necklace. A mindless touch.

"Then why didn't you visit?"

"I was afraid of what would happen if my suspicions were true," he murmured, dropping his fingers to take my hand. "Now, I'm certain that they are."

The feel of his warm, rough hand in mine made my whole body tremble. I prayed my palms weren't too sweaty as I struggled to steady myself.

"What suspicions?"

Grae opened his mouth to speak as his three guards stumbled into the entryway, Briar two steps behind. At the sound of their drunken arrival, I dropped Grae's hand and retreated a step on instinct. To the others, I was Briar's guard and nothing more. There would be a lot of questions if they caught me holding hands with the princess's betrothed. I wished the floor would swallow me whole. What in the world was I thinking?

I raised the back of my cool hand to my burning cheek, trying to snap myself out of this magical spell. I blamed the wine.

"Come on," Maez said, sweeping her arms as if herding sheep. "To bed with you lot. We've got to wake up in only a few hours."

Briar reached my side and looped her arm through mine, swaying on tipsy legs as she dragged me up the stairs. I looked back at Grae, who tracked my every step under heavy brows. Whatever he had to say would have to wait. I curled my fingers into my palm, remembering the feeling of his rough grip on my own. The sensation burned into my mind. Gods curse me. Did Grae hold hands and rumble whispered promises to all his friends? I couldn't allow myself to answer that. Either way, it would only hurt me.

THE PULL OF THE WAXING MOON BEGGED FOR MY WOLF. THE silvery light kissed my skin from where I stood between the gauzy curtains. I was so ready to shed my chemise and shift, to run through the midnight trees. That would make me feel steady again, instead of the jittery mess who couldn't get the feeling of Grae's hand out of my head. But my fur in the wind and my paws on the earth would have to wait one more night. We were leaving for Highwick in the morning and I couldn't go gallivanting off into the forest.

The Moon Goddess smiled down on me from the twinkling stars as I promised her, "tomorrow." I was so close to the end of this—a pacing wildcat ready to be unleashed. Twenty years of waiting would come to an end. I'd finally have a pack and new forests to explore.

The latch on my door clicked, and I whirled to find Briar shutting the door behind her. On bare feet, she padded toward my bed and slipped into the sheets.

She grinned at me. "The moon is too bright and I'm too excited."

With an exaggerated sigh, I walked to the bed. "Shove over."

"Thank you," Briar whispered, shuffling to the side.

I turned to look into my sister's large blue eyes. "Will you still be climbing into my bed when you're the princess of Damrienn?"

Lifting her chin with a smug smile, she said, "Possibly."

I huffed. A sudden painful thought swept into my mind: Would she be sharing a bed with Grae? My stomach tumbled. They'd be sharing a lot more than a bed. That's what these marriages were for, not only alliances and land treaties, but siring future Kings. Bile burned the back of my throat. I knew this day would come, I told myself. It was the price of being part of a pack; traditions must be upheld, sacrifices made, but in exchange we'd finally have a family.

It didn't mean I liked it, though.

"You should be sleeping," a warm voice called from the corner.

Vellia appeared, a rocking chair with her. She glided back and forth, smiling at us. Our whole life she appeared the same: a warm lined face and silver hair, but the lines never deepened, and the strands never whitened more than their grayish hue. She seemed stuck at the age she was when she granted our mother's dying wish. I wondered if tomorrow she'd age again.

"We can't sleep," Briar grumbled, just as she had when we were children. "Tell us the story."

Vellia chuckled at us—her two grown wards. "It has been many years since you've asked for a bedtime story."

"Not just any story," Briar corrected. "*The* story."

Our story.

Vellia's eyes crinkled as she bowed her head in acquiescence.

"All right," she said in her hushed voice. "Seeing as it's the last story I will tell you."

Sorrow stabbed through me at that confession. I knew Vellia would leave us and we'd journey to the capital alone—it was always to be that way. Even so, a life without her felt unfathomable.

"It was a beautiful summer's night," she began, as she always did. "Queen Rose Marriel's belly was as swollen as the full moon. The night of her babe's birth had arrived. As the Queen labored, the King called forth the rulers of every Wolf kingdom to celebrate the birth of his heir. The Silver, Onyx, and Ice Wolves all came, and just before the clock struck midnight, a beautiful baby was born. The castle celebrated, their cheers heard throughout the entire kingdom. This child was a manifestation of the greatest love the world had ever known."

Every child in Aotreas knew my parents' love story—of how Sawyn cursed my mother to a deep sleep and locked her in the tallest tower in her keep. But my father had found her, and his kiss had broken the spell. *The Sleeping Queen*. The story was told in every corner of the continent—a cheerful story of true love conquering dark magic. That's where the songs and poems ended. But life, as it always does, carried on. I nestled my head into my pillow and watched Vellia's rocking falter, just as it did every time she told the tale of our birth.

"But on the twelfth tolling of the bells, as the new princess took her first breaths, the sorceress Sawyn appeared." Briar gasped in faux surprise. "Sawyn snuffed out every candle until only her eerie dark magic glowed from her haunted eyes. She stormed up to the King, demanding he bow to her power. King Sameir looked her dead in the eyes and said, 'You will never be queen.'"

I mouthed my father's damning words along with Briar. My sister thought our father's condemnation was brave, but I thought it was pure arrogance. He sneered in the face of a powerful sorceress, and look what happened. Whether it was bravery or arrogance, my father's words were his death sentence.

"Sawyn struck down King Sameir with a bolt of her power. She pointed a crooked finger to the circle of onlookers and professed, 'The line of Marriel ends tonight. Now, bow down to the Queen of Olmdere.' One by one she knocked down every Gold Wolf who sprung to the King's aid. And so the other rulers fell to their knees, groveling for salvation from the sorceress's wrath."

"Cowards," Briar muttered.

I snorted. Cowards, perhaps, but survivors, too. They all still had crowns on their heads, and we didn't even know if our parents received a burial, let alone the rest of the Gold Wolf pack who died protecting them. I wondered what would've happened if they had all attacked. Would it have been enough to overtake Sawyn? Her magic couldn't hold them all at bay . . . could it?

"After all those many years, Sawyn finally got what she had always wanted," Vellia said. "To be queen."

I'd never understood this part of the story. Why would Sawyn reappear after so many years? What was it about our birth that made her demand the throne from our father? Why Olmdere? There had to be more reasons for her actions. Briar didn't seem to mind, but I always felt like we were missing part of this story. Vellia would simply say that dark magic was a hungry beast, always wanting more. It knew when to stalk its prey, and when to strike.

"What Sawyn didn't know was that Queen Rose had another surprise in store," Vellia carried on, casting a quick look at me. "The guards rushed to tell her what had happened, but the Queen already knew. She had felt the mating bond snap, and, as Sawyn stormed toward the birthing chamber, Queen Rose made one last wish. A beautiful faery appeared to grant it." Vellia brushed her silver hair over her shoulder, puffing out her chest, and I heard Briar's soft laugh behind me. "The Queen wished for the faery to protect her child until her wedding day. With one foot in the afterlife, her belly clenched again. The pains grew more frenzied until the arrival of a second child, another baby girl."

"You and me," Briar whispered. She hooked her arm over my side, resting her chin on my shoulder. I closed my eyes, feeling the comfort of her warmth radiating onto my back. We'd heard the tale so many times, it stopped feeling real—just another bedtime story. Yet being here, on this night, with my sister . . . it felt just a little bit more tangible.

"The faery was astonished." Vellia winked at me. "The wish had already been made, but the faery couldn't leave the second babe to suffer the wrath of Sawyn, and so she disappeared with them both. Even the sky mourned, pouring for months on end, the Goddess saddened to lose that most magical of bonds. Sawyn was furious, razing half of Olmdere in her rage. She scoured the continent to find the Crimson Princess, but never found her, returning to the abandoned castle on the lake. To this day, she hides in wait for rumors of the Crimson Princess whispered on the wind, sending her scouts to every corner of Olmdere, hunting for her."

Over the years, Sawyn had become a ghost story. The children in the village would dare each other to step out into the forest and whisper "I am the Crimson Princess," thinking one of the sorceress's Rooks might hear. But the rage with which she searched for Briar had simmered into nothingness, and I wondered if she even cared at all anymore. Perhaps reclaiming our castle would be as easy as opening the door.

I watched Vellia's gentle rocking, a mix of emotions filling me as I asked, "Are you sure you can't come with us?"

Briar laughed even as her arm tightened around me. "Hasn't she done enough? She's kept us safe for nearly twenty years."

"The magic of your mother's wish is waning," Vellia said. "I can feel the last dregs being spent."

"Then I could make another wish," I offered.

She shook her head, straightening the knot of her kerchief under her chin. "A faery wish is a desperate sort of magic, Calla." Vellia had said the same thing a dozen times before. "Powerful, yes, but it's the ultimate sacrifice and will cost you everything. Your mother's essence fuels my magic. She paid for your safety with her soul."

My shoulders slumped. There was no way to wish for Vellia to stay with us. When my mother's wish finished, Vellia would disappear, waiting in the ether until another dying wish was made.

Vellia stood, placing her smooth hand on my cheek.

"I will miss you two," Vellia whispered. "But my magic will always be with you. I will be close even when I feel very far."

I swallowed, nodding my head.

Vellia drew the curtains, moonlight fading to shadow. "Get some sleep. You wake at first light."

Briar groaned, already unhappy about the idea of waking up. I took a deep breath as Vellia flickered out of sight, off to another part of the cabin.

"Do you remember that traveler who came to town with those spun sugar treats?" Briar's voice was a low hush.

"Yes." I craned my neck back at her. "Why?"

"I bet they have them in Highwick."

I chuckled and settled back into my pillow. "I bet you'll be able to request any treat your heart desires, *Your Highness*."

"You will, too," Briar said. "We will finally be able to go out and explore and meet people and be a part of a pack . . ." She sighed. "It's going to be great, Calla."

"With Nero's aid, we'll be able to save Olmdere," I murmured, feeling sleep tugging me under.

"That too." Briar chuffed. "You and me, we'll take over the continent . . . so long as we can eat some spun sugar treats first."

"Agreed." I nuzzled my face deeper into the feather pillow, feeling my sister's warmth behind me radiating through the duvet. As my heavy eyes shut, I smiled. She was trying to cheer me up, and it was working. Sorrow mixed with exhilaration, and I fell asleep dreaming of a new promised adventure.

FIVE

THE GLOWING DAWN BLED INTO THE DARKNESS AS THE STARS blinked out of the sky. My head pounded. I was never drinking wine again. We only drank on special occasions, and last night had been overly extravagant. I scowled at my sister. Briar somehow looked fresh-faced and buoyant while I looked as haggard as I felt.

I pulled my traveling cloak tighter around my neck. The guards raced about, hitching the horses to the carriages. Their faces were sleep-addled, but they moved at great speed, seemingly less affected by the many drinks and little sleep.

Vellia clasped her hands as I stared down at the dusty front steps. This would be the last time I would ever stand here. I tried to remember every detail, every scent and sound, pressing each sense into my memory so I could hold on to them. This day had felt so far in the distance, and then suddenly it was upon us—there was no in-between.

Vellia squeezed my elbow as if knowing all the aching parts of me warred between excitement and sadness. I didn't know how to say goodbye to her. Tears welled as I watched the guards load our bags. Grae and Briar chatted at the front carriage, my sister breezy as ever, while I tried to keep tears from falling.

"Oh, you." Vellia chuckled, even though her voice was tight

as well. She gripped my cheeks in her weathered hands and promised, "I will see you again one day, my dear. Take heart in that."

I nodded, blinking back tears. How far away would "one day" be?

"Don't live out your years with your tail between your legs." Vellia leaned closer, pinning me with a look. "Whatever it is you want from this life, Calla, I hope you have the stubbornness to take it."

"What if I don't know what I want?" Staring at her, I pressed my lips together so tightly I was certain they had turned white.

"Then I pray you have the courage to look deeper." Her pale gray eyes roved my face. "That will be a harder challenge than swinging any sword."

Vellia had always been loving, but hard. She'd trained me to be a warrior with the same fervor she'd trained Briar to be a princess. My appreciation for that now bubbled out. Briar's tittering laughter filled the air as I wrapped my arms around Vellia, giving her one last hug.

"I'll try," I whispered. "Be well, Vellia."

"Be brave, my dear."

I swallowed the lump in my throat, my shoulders straightening as I marched down the stairs. It was time to prove my worth to my pack.

A shadow appeared over me. "You okay, little fox?"

I lifted my wet lashes to find those gleaming brown eyes. "Yes."

Grae's lips curved. "Liar." He lifted his knuckle and wiped a stray tear from my face. My cheeks burned. I hadn't realized I'd been crying. "I'm sorry you have to leave your home. I hope you'll be happy in our new one."

Our.

Grae's heavy stare weighed on me.

Briar stuck her head out of the open carriage window. "Calla, let's go," she said, straightening the hood of her cloak.

I noticed the golden door of the carriage in front of us waiting ajar. "You're not riding with us?"

"Briar said you got little sleep last night. It's a long journey to Damrienn. You two should rest," Grae said, pausing when I didn't reply. "Unless . . . you'd like to ride with me?"

My heart faltered at his question. A whole coach ride with just the two of us. I was about to open my mouth to agree when Briar popped her head out of the carriage door again.

"Cal, come on," she demanded.

I rolled my eyes. It would've been a terrible idea, anyway. I felt embarrassingly out of control around him, and now I wouldn't have the wine to blame.

Grae grinned at my sister's antics, giving me a wink that made my whole body tingle. "I'll speak with you after we arrive in Highwick?"

I nodded, cringing at myself as Grae strode away. I climbed into the rounded belly of the carriage, sitting on the crushed velvet bench beside my sister. Satin cushions sat on either end and gold filigree papered the walls. It was the most opulent space I had ever been in . . . and this was just the carriage.

I adjusted the neckline of my cloak as Maez's face appeared in the window. She had short-cropped hair, light golden brown skin, and a mischievous twinkle in her hazel eyes. Her lips twisted into a smirk.

"Ready, Your Highness?" she asked Briar, casually leaning her forearms through the open window. Her eyes lingered on Briar before she peeked at me. "It'll be about six hours."

Briar pursed her lips, pulling Maez's attention back to her with ease. "Are you driving the carriage?"

"No, Your Highness, I'm just riding with Hector."

"Why don't you ride with us?" Briar offered, gesturing to the empty bench.

I cut my sister a look that I knew she was ignoring. She'd told Grae we wanted to sleep and now she was inviting company into our carriage? Briar waited for Maez's response with innocently raised eyebrows.

"Oh." The guard's eyes widened as a grin stretched across her face. "Okay, I'll grab my satchel."

As she retreated from the carriage window, I elbowed Briar in the ribs. "What are you doing?"

"Ouch," Briar snapped, though we both knew I hadn't injured her. "I just wanted some entertainment on the long ride."

"I thought you were going to desist with that form of *entertainment* now that Grae is around."

"Can you blame me? Look at her! Besides—" Briar shrugged. "Grae and I talked last night."

"When?" Mouth agape, I glared at my sister. "What does that mean?"

The door opened.

"It means we talked last night," Briar muttered out of the corner of her mouth.

Plastering that queenly smile back on her face, she greeted Maez.

As the guard sat across from us, my mind spiraled. What had Briar and Grae talked about? What agreement had they reached, and had it something to do with this mysterious suspicion of Grae's? My nerves were as tight as a bowstring, ready to snap.

"Did you grow up in the capital?" Briar asked, breaking into light conversation.

"All the Silver Wolf families live in Highwick," Maez replied. "Grae and I are cousins on his father's side."

I racked my brain for note of the King's siblings, but whoever Maez's father was, he must've passed long ago. I couldn't recollect his name in any of our classes, though Vellia's tutelage had been more focused on the living royal lines.

"I entered my apprenticeship with the royal guard at thirteen," Maez said. "And Grae invited me into his personal guard about . . ." She looked at the ceiling, silently counting. "Four years ago?"

"Impressive."

Maez shrugged. "It spared me from my uncle marrying me off to another kingdom. I pledged my sword to the crown prince, so I'm not a threat to his line."

I pursed my lips, considering Maez. It was a smart move. She'd been confronted with the possibility of an arranged marriage and she'd found her own way out. I respected her more for it—her charming swagger suddenly more understandable, that bravado hard won. She knew what she wanted from life, and she'd taken it, just like Vellia had bid me to do.

"How old are you?" Briar asked.

I glared at her again, knowing she was shamelessly interrogating the guard for her own purposes.

"Twenty-four," Maez said, cocking her head at Briar, a mischievous fire in her hazel eyes. "And you will be twenty at midnight tonight."

Briar scanned the guard from head to toe, playing along with her game. "And do you have any . . . sweethearts in the capital?"

Goddess, I wished I could fade into the cushions and disappear from this conversation. I nudged Briar with my knee, but she moved her leg away, merely blinking back at Maez with her blue doe eyes. Briar and I didn't need to say a word to have an entire conversation. She knew I was warning her to behave, and I knew she was ignoring me.

The carriage lurched forward, and I leaned out the window to wave goodbye to Vellia. The cool morning air tousled my curls as we rode down the forest path. My godmother waved her white handkerchief to us in farewell. Once, twice, and on the third time she disappeared, a trail of glittering stardust left in her wake. Another breath, and the cabin disappeared, too.

I squinted, trying to find the seam of warped air, the glamour hiding the edifice . . . but there was none. It was simply gone. All evidence that we had ever lived there—the place that held every one of my childhood memories—had vanished.

My eyes welled again, and I kept my head half out the window to let the breeze stymie my tears. I hated that the tears came so easily. Warriors weren't meant to cry.

My excitement dampened, I stared at the morning sun rising through the trees. I felt the absence of Vellia's magic more with every turn of the carriage wheel. We had to make it on our own now.

"Hardly." Briar's voice pulled me back into the moment. I leaned back beside her, not hearing a word of their conversation as I watched the vacant spot where our home had once been. "I don't know why anyone would fancy men, Moon help them."

I pointedly cleared my throat.

"Calla likes men and women," Briar said to Maez in a conspiratorial whisper. "We'll forgive her for that."

"You're about to marry a man, might I remind you?" I gritted out.

There was nothing Briar could say that would untie the knot in my stomach. I didn't know if it would make it easier or harder if Briar loved Grae . . . probably harder. But Grae deserved someone who adored him, someone who got butterflies in their stomach every time they looked at him. *Someone like me.* I grimaced at the sharp pang of that train of thought, and instead tried to shift it to why Briar would be an excellent mate for him. For one thing, he needed a consort who was regal and elegant, too, someone who commanded a room just by entering it, someone who could be his queen. Briar would be perfect for that, and that made this arrangement make at least a modicum of sense. None of us had chosen these lives for ourselves, but the future of Olmdere was at stake. All Wolves sacrificed for their pack, and for princesses, that meant marriage.

"These things are never love matches." Briar waved her hand, giving voice to my churning thoughts. "Our kingdoms have an alliance. With Damrienn's backing, we will help save Olmdere and, in return, they'll get access to Olmdere's gold mines and natural resources." Briar glanced longingly back at Maez. "What happens outside of that is no one's business but ours."

I hated that answer. I had heard it so many times over the years. But Briar was willing to sacrifice to uphold our parents' wishes. The least I could do was stay out of her way.

I knew love matches were rare in the Wolf world and fated mates were even rarer. Humans had much more freedom to marry who they wanted, *be* who they wanted, and all the Wolves got was to rule over them.

"Tell us more about the capital," Briar urged, making Maez grin.

She bowed her head and launched into her tales of the sprawling silver city of Damrienn, of the moon temples and marketplaces, the theaters and bakeries. It sounded magical. I listened to Maez's soothing baritone as my eyelids grew heavy, the lack of sleep catching up to me. As the carriage swayed, my head bobbed until I couldn't hold it up any longer. Leaning my head against the backrest, I left my sister to indulge in her conversation with the attractive royal guard.

AS THE DIRT ROADS SWITCHED TO COBBLESTONES, I JOSTLED awake. Rubbing my hand down my face, I squinted at the gilded door frames and elegant wallpaper.

"We're here," Maez said, as Briar threw back the velvet curtain.

My mouth fell open as I stared out at the sprawling city of Highwick. I knew it would be bigger than Allesdale, but it was gigantic, twenty times the size at least. Steepled rooftops stretched into the clouds, silver pennants waved from tall windows, and doves flitted from glinting temple spires. We rolled through the towering iron gates, soldiers watching us from high parapets guarding the western road.

The majesty halted at the overwhelming scent of fish and

filth. Gagging, I withdrew from the window. Piles of rubbish and buckets of fish guts filled the streets as we wound our way through the markets. Fishmongers removed their woolen caps in silent greeting while others waved from arched windows. People crammed the streets, an overwhelming press of bodies.

Briar propped her elbow on the window ledge, waving back to everyone with a practiced smile, while I fought the urge to tuck my nose into my tunic. Children with soot-smeared faces paused their play in the streets to gawk at the golden parade, while some of the older townsfolk ignored us, probably used to seeing processions every time the royals moved in and out of the city.

We passed through a rundown square where the human temples circled a trough overgrown with algae. My eyes trailed the symbols carved over the archways and the small altars filled with melted candles. The humans had a god for just about everything. Wolves prayed to nature: the moon, the sun, the earth, and the sea. But the humans prayed for things: love, wealth, courage, children, vengeance, health . . . dozens and dozens of amorphous concepts, so many I couldn't keep track. They even prayed to us Wolves, for all we had done to rid the world of monsters at the dawn of Aotreas. Our people had driven out the beasts and fought back the sorcerers, bringing peace to the continent. It was why we ruled each of the four kingdoms. We were the protectors of the realm.

That didn't mean they loved us. Some humans outright scowled at us as we passed crammed dwellings and streets filled with debris. Not all humans saw us as protectors anymore. I frowned up at a sign in a high window reading *No Skin Chasers*. It was a slang term for Wolves with a predilection for human company. It didn't matter that the vast majority of Wolves stuck to their pack and didn't mix with humans. It always ended badly. Though humans and Wolves of each kingdom spoke roughly the same language, their cultures were entirely different. The names humans used, the foods they ate, the things they valued—all different to those of the Wolves.

The stench of the fish markets ebbed as we carried on, giving way to the scent of sunbaked limestone and fresh summer flowers. The city morphed into elegant townhouses and neat rows of pink, blossoming trees. A giant fountain sat in the center of the Wolf quarter. Carved Wolves decorated the silver facade, spitting crisscrossing arches of water. I hung halfway out the window to gawk at the fountain as we passed. It was like nothing I'd ever seen before, large enough to be a lake. More and more Wolf symbols covered the public spaces as we ventured through the heart of the city. The most elegant buildings had paw prints carved in the stone railings and banners of Wolf silhouettes flapping in the breeze. They must belong to important Wolf families, the courtiers who served the king—my future pack mates.

The further we pushed into the vast metropolis, the taller the buildings grew, until we reached the soaring stone castle. It had seven silver spires that shot like needles into the sky. Stone wolf heads howled above sculpted stone windows, and flying buttresses held up the giant palace that gloriously reached into the clouds. But it was something beyond the castle that made me suck in a breath.

A lush summer forest stretched out toward snowcapped mountains on the horizon. The rolling, verdant greenery beckoned me. It would take a lifetime to memorize every tree and stream in that wilderness, and I couldn't wait to do exactly that. The itch to shift and go explore grew with each turn of the carriage wheel. Vast forests circled all four of the capital cities for their Wolves to run in, but I couldn't imagine any forest being larger than this one. *Soon*, I promised myself. Soon I'd be able to run in the forests of Highwick.

The castle gates opened with the squeal of grinding metal and we passed through the pointed archways carved with the phases of the moon. I lifted my chin high in the air in gesture to the Moon Goddess, and Maez and Briar followed. It felt like her silvery magic touched every corner of this place.

As the carriages pulled to a halt, I adjusted my soldierly

garb. I wore a simple jacket over a tan tunic, a black leather corset buckled down my bust, and matching leather trousers that hugged my thighs. The golden buckles of my corset matched the gilded hilt of the dagger strapped to my hip. Knee-high boots finished my outfit, complete with a knife I'd hidden down the back. I looked like what I was meant to be—the personal guard to the Crimson Princess.

I eyed my twin. Briar's delicate scarlet dress didn't have a single crease from our long journey. She pulled a wisp of her red hair back into her braid and pinched her cheeks. It didn't matter that I looked plain beside her. It would feel far worse to have an entire city's eyes upon me, judging me as their future queen. The thought of that much scrutiny turned my stomach to acid. I'd rather have an ostekke suck my heart out through my rib cage than be her right now. Thank the Moon I got to be a shadow.

"You look stunning, Briar," I whispered, and Maez nodded in agreement. "You look like a queen."

Briar took a deep breath, reaching over and giving my hand a squeeze. This was it—the moment she'd prepared for her whole life.

Maez clambered out of the carriage, opening the door and holding her hand out to Briar. "Ready, Your Highness?"

With one last smoothing sweep down her skirts, Briar stood. "I guess I have to be." She took Maez's hand and stepped out of the carriage. I clumsily clambered out behind her, pins and needles tingling my stiff legs.

As I craned my neck toward the dizzying steeples, Grae and the other guards approached. My heart fluttered as he prowled toward me. His hand lifted ever so slightly, and I had the sudden urge to reach out and take it. He opened his mouth to say something, but Briar cut in between us.

Circling her arm around his elbow, she said, "Your home is beautiful, Your Highness."

Grae smirked at her, glancing an apologetic look to me. "I hope it will come to feel like home for you, too, Your Highness."

I snorted, toeing the gravel with my boot as I muttered, "Yeah, right."

The palace was a city unto itself, nothing homey about it.

Sadie nudged me with her elbow and I looked up to see Grae and Briar already walking toward the open entryway, Hector and Maez trailing behind. I hustled to catch up.

"Prepare yourself," Sadie muttered as we crossed the threshold.

"For what?"

"For His Majesty," she said, shaking her bangs out of her eyes.

My stomach dropped. I had wondered for many years if King Nero was anything like Grae, but, judging by Sadie's odious tone, I guessed not. Currying the favor of a king was an art form in and of itself, and, in that moment, I was once again glad I was spared from the pack's attention. That job would be Briar's alone.

SIX

THE INSIDE OF THE PALACE WAS ANOTHER WORLD, WITH HIGH vaulted ceilings, sparkling chandeliers, and stained-glass windows. Our footsteps ricocheted off the stone, my body feeling light in the entryway's vastness. I wanted to stop and take in each column and alcove, press each gilded image into my mind, but the group was marching ahead. I took in the mosaics along the walls and frescoed ceilings. The stories Grae told me as a child were painted in every corner of his home. The snow snakes of Taigos; the curling, whip-like tongue of the juvleck; the many-tentacled ostekke of Lower Valta—images of our ancestors fighting back the monsters of old. They painted the glory of our people in one long story along the hallway, and it was inspiring to now see it depicted like this.

At the dawn of Aotreas, dark magic plagued the realm. Monsters and those turned evil by dark magic rained chaos over the continent . . . all apart from the Wolves, our packs strong enough to fight back any foe, even dark magic itself. The earliest humans pled with the Wolves of old, begging for their salvation, and the Wolves answered their prayers. The four Wolf leaders risked the safety of their own packs to fight back the scourge of dark magic and save the humans. When the last of the sorcerers fell and the Wolves forced the monsters to the very edges of the realm, the humans rejoiced. They split up their human lands to the four pack leaders, placing crowns on their heads and erecting temples in their honor.

I glanced up to the carved, curving passage in the arch above my head: *The saviors of Aotreas. The power of the pack.*

The sounds of hushed voices grew as we reached the closed doors of the grand hall. My sister adjusted her posture, shoulders further back and chin held higher, if that was possible. Grae bent to whisper something in her ear, and she smiled. The sweet moment made me ache, and I knew it made me the worst sort of person. Our lives weren't our own. We belonged to the pack, the ones who defeated the monsters now so poetically painted along the halls of this castle.

But, oh, if that weren't the case . . .

The prince nodded to the doormen, and, with a creaking groan, the doors opened. Eager faces greeted us, leaning over each other and lifting on tiptoes to get a peek at the woman they long thought was dead. A sea of satin gowns and velvet jackets, intricate hairstyles and glittering jewelry—each one looked as if they could be royalty themselves. I wondered what the Silver Wolves would look like in their wolf forms. Gooseflesh rippled across my forearm at the thought. Hundreds of Wolves running through the forest . . . It had only ever been a dream.

Awed whispers echoed in the vast hall as they appraised Briar. The pack's nerves thickened the charged air. Briar had been a ghost story to these people until this moment, and now she was flesh and blood—a beautiful promise of what could be.

The crowd parted to form an aisle, revealing a dais. A carved silverwood throne sat in the center, and upon it, the King presided over the crowd. King Nero Claudius was younger than I had expected, his black hair only graying at the temples and peppered through his short beard. He wore a silver chest plate carved with his phoenix crest. It molded to his torso, giving him perfectly shaped muscles that I doubted matched his actual flesh. Everything in his attire seemed designed to make him look more formidable—wide shoulder plates, silver cuffs along his forearm, and a razor-sharp crown atop his head. It worked.

His cold eyes scrutinized Briar, examining her as she and Grae proceeded down the aisle. I bit down on my lips, wanting to snarl at his leering assessment. Instead, I kept in line with Sadie, a few paces behind the other guards. Knowing I'd do something rash if I kept observing the King's hungry gaze, I looked around, spotting gnarled faces in the crowd—one missing an eye, another with a long scar snaking down his jaw. I wondered at their injuries—were they perhaps the result of ranking challenges? Or maybe punishments for sedition?

The latter would not surprise me—I had heard stories that skin chasers received the worst punishments, debasing themselves by indulging in human flesh. I glanced back at the one-eyed man, his lone eye staring vacantly at Briar. What was his crime? Had the King been the one to dole out his penalty?

King Nero shifted in his chair and the pack bristled, finely attuned to his every breath and action. The pack turned to face their leader, silence blanketing the room until the only sound was Grae's and Briar's shoes walking down the aisle.

"The Crimson Princess, Briar Marriel, daughter of the last King and Queen of Olmdere." King Nero's deep voice carried easily over the crowd. His many silver rings clinked against the wooden armrests as he pushed up from his throne. "The tales of your beauty don't do you justice, Your Highness."

Briar dropped into a deep curtsy, holding it until the King descended from the dais. My stomach jittered, knowing whatever nerves I felt, Briar must've felt tenfold. I focused on the air pulling through my nostrils, filling my lungs as I fought the urge to be sick. I'd never needed Vellia's calming techniques for her conjured monsters, but this . . . there were more people in this one room than I'd met in my entire life. The fate of my fallen kingdom hedged on this going well.

More, this was my sister, my *twin*. Subject to scrutiny and expectation, and all I could do was watch. I sucked in another steadying breath. I couldn't ruin this moment. I had to trust that Briar's training would see her through.

The King took Briar's hand, making her rise as he lifted her knuckles to his lips. "Your parents and I had spoken joyfully of this union long before you were even born. Sameir and Rose would be so proud." I pressed my lips together at the sound of my parents' names. "Welcome to my court, Princess." He placed his other hand on top of hers and looked out at his pack, addressing them directly. "The day has finally come. Together we will reclaim Olmdere and join the kingdoms forever."

Clamorous cheering erupted, making me flinch. Some even howled to the skies.

"The Gold and Silver Wolves have always been close," the King continued, dropping Briar's hand to pat his son on the shoulder. "But with this union, we will be one pack."

"For the pack!" More howls echoed around the room.

The King leaned past Briar, his eyes landing on me. I rocked back on my heels at the full force of his stare. Was it time? Was he going to tell everyone who I was? Sadie cleared her throat beside me and my senses came back to me. Dropping my eyes, I bowed.

"The Princess's personal guard," King Nero said, flashing his canines as he grinned. "The only other Gold Wolf to have survived Sawyn's wrath. Not much of a warrior, by the looks of you."

The crowd tittered, their stares pressing in on me as my cheeks burned. Spots clouded my vision, and I pushed against the dizzying feeling in my head. Just get through this one moment and then I could fade away into the background again.

Grae took a half step toward his father, his voice lighthearted as he said, "I wouldn't underestimate her."

King Nero cut him a sharp look and Grae dropped his eyes. I prayed to the Moon that my face hadn't turned an unseemly shade of green. A painful awareness of my body made me clench my jaw. I felt their eyes wandering over me, taking in everything from my dark curls to my large hips to my diminutive stature. Nothing lithe or graceful about me. Nothing forceful or menacing, either. I forced myself to stare at the crowd, challenging each of their mocking glances. My body might not look like that of a killer, but my expression did. One by one, their eyes dropped, and I straightened my shoulders.

The King looked me up and down again, a twinkle in his eyes. He knew who I was.

"Perhaps we will need a demonstration of this skill at some point." He laughed, and the crowd echoed the sound. Bile rose in my throat as he turned back to Briar. "But for now, we have a wedding to prepare for. Tonight, when the Moon Goddess is full in the sky, we shall fulfill the Marriels' ultimate wish to bind our families together forever. Olmdere will have a king once more!"

A king. Not a queen. Briar was a kingmaker—that was her true value to them. Without her, Grae couldn't be king of Olmdere. My fingernails dug into my palm as I watched the smiles shared between father and son, king and prince. As I watched my sister's trueborn self seemingly vanish before our very eyes.

Cheering broke out again as King Nero waved his hand, dismissing our traveling party. Grae joined his father on the dais as the rest of us bowed in unison and hastened to a side door. I cast one last look at Grae, finding his dark eyes already upon me. I couldn't read his steely expression as his eyes tracked me out of the room.

In the forests of Allesdale, I thought I knew him. But here, in this world, he was another person. And I wasn't sure if this version of Grae would ever be friends with someone like me.

My ears rang in the hallway's silence. The air was cooler, smelling of silver polish and fresh paint. Servants rushed past the narrow space, carrying trays of silverware and baskets of linen napkins, racing to prepare for the wedding feast.

The one that was apparently happening *today*.

The King hadn't revealed who I was. Worse, he let everyone

laugh at me. I clenched my hands to keep them from shaking as a million thoughts battled in my mind. Maybe he didn't want to take away from the excitement of the wedding? Or maybe he was embarrassed by me. Gods, the way they laughed. I looked nothing like Briar. There was nothing regal about me. Maybe he took one look at me and realized I didn't belong in his pack. Perhaps he would announce it once the ceremony was over . . . My worries popped up faster than I could assuage them.

"It's okay. You were perfect," Maez whispered from up ahead.

I leaned past the guards twice my height to find Briar's reddened face, panting as her eyes welled. I shoved my embarrassment aside and rushed to my sister. She looked like she might throw up, too. Her vacant eyes scanned the ground as I pulled her into a hug.

My embrace seemed to snap her back into reality, and she buried her head in my shoulder.

"Your beauty and poise awed every single one of them, Briar." My voice was muffled in her hair as I swept soothing circles over her back. I knew it's what she needed to hear. "You couldn't see their excitement, but believe me, they were joyous."

Briar nodded into my shoulder. "I'm okay," she breathed, pulling back and looking me in the eye. "We're okay."

We'd rehearsed that moment in our minds for twenty years and still it had felt overwhelming. The vaulted ceilings, sparkling jewelry, and press of so many people . . . nothing could have prepared us for it. The world was different when we were being watched. No longer did we exist as ourselves, but rather a projection of their own assumptions and beliefs—Briar the beautiful princess, and me the lowly guard. It made me stand differently, move differently, trying to contort myself into who I thought they expected me to be.

"Let me show you to your chambers," Maez offered.

Briar and I took a simultaneous deep breath, making the guards chuckle. Whenever we acted in unison, it seemed to elicit the same response. We appeared like complete opposites, but in many things, we were the same. I released my sister from our hug and grabbed her hand. It was as sweaty as my own.

"We're okay," I echoed to her as we followed Maez into the heart of the palace.

SEVEN

MY FEET DANGLED THROUGH THE BALUSTRADE, FLOATING IN the open air as I ate my lunch. The doors to Briar's bedroom sat open at my back, welcoming the warm, perfumed air from her chamber. From my vantage point, I could see the entire city of Highwick—the rolling forests bordering fine townhouses and out further to the crammed human quarter. Thin trails of smoke curled into the air from the many smokestacks, the wind carrying them away from the Wolf part of town.

The sound of a string quartet floated up to the fourth-floor balcony where I sat. They'd play and pause, tuning their strings, breaking into jaunty melodies, and pausing again. I recognized this current song from its very first notes.

"'The Sleeping Queen,'" I said with a huff. "A little on the nose, don't you think?"

Briar sauntered over from where she stood by the mirror, trying the same two earrings back and forth as if the fate of our kingdom rested on her selection alone. "It's a famous song about our parents. Why wouldn't they play it at my wedding?"

I pulled my head back through the railing and gave my sister an incredulous look. "Because they died?"

"I think it's nice to remember them on my wedding day. We're in a foreign kingdom with different customs than our own pack. It's nice to have this little part of Olmdere." She shrugged. "And our parents loved each other. We should still celebrate that, even though it ended."

I didn't know if my heart could take hearing it in full. I'd heard it around Allesdale before—hummed by washwomen hanging clothes on the line, trilled by a lute in the local tavern, but to hear a proper rendition . . . Something about the joyful notes scratched against my ears. The song was about their happily ever after, about them defeating the sorceress who ultimately killed them. It was a lie preserved in melody.

"It should be a sad song," I muttered. Every time I heard those notes, they'd cling to me for days, turning my mood sour as I remembered all we had lost. Every vibrato and dip, every pause and crescendoed note was a mocking sound that haunted me over and over.

"They *were* happy though," Briar said, leaning against the balcony door. "They had happiness for a long time before Sawyn returned."

"Which only makes it more cruel." I leaned back on my hands, my eyes following the lines of smoke as they blurred into the clouds. "Why did Sawyn wait so many years after father broke the sleeping curse to return? Why didn't she just retaliate instantly?"

"She's filled with dark magic," Briar said, as if that could excuse everything. "Who knows what that twisted power does to a person? Maybe she needed time to regain her strength. Maybe that compulsion for violence builds slowly, festering over years."

"But—"

"No one knows, Calla," Briar snapped, clearly getting frustrated. "How many centuries has it been since the last sorcerer? We don't even know what compelled her to turn toward the darkness in the first place. The only people who might've known are long dead."

I twisted around to look at Briar. Her cheeks were flushed, her eyes wide, as if she, too, had wondered about these things.

But Briar had the good sense to hide it. Before the rise of Sawyn, monsters and sorcerers were myths of the past—things that didn't exist in the world anymore. We knew little about Sawyn. There wasn't a single note of where she came from or who she killed to turn herself into a sorceress.

That was where the dark took hold: the first kill. It was a teetering precipice anyone who killed could fall into, one that soldiers trained to withstand. Those with enough of it in their souls could turn just as we could turn into Wolves. It was a one-way shift, a magical change, that the world knew little about. Lean into the darkness and forever be consumed.

Sawyn had been swallowed whole, and then turned her dark hunger on my family, my pack, my kingdom.

Why, why, why?

The strings started playing again and I was relieved it was a different tune. Even so, the brand of "The Sleeping Queen" burned into me. I was glad I didn't have to hear those final sweeping notes, but the lyrics looped over and over in my mind, replaying before reaching the final refrain—the happy ending that never came.

I LOUNGED ON MY SISTER'S BED, A BOWL OF CANDIED ALMONDS tucked beside me, as I watched the seamstresses fit Briar into her wedding dress. Briar's room took up an entire wing of the palace. As her personal guard, I had been appointed a room within the wing, connected through an internal door to her bedchamber.

Sumptuous jewel-toned fabrics decorated my sister's suite. The wealth of Damrienn was clear from the silver-framed mirrors to the gem-studded jewelry box on the mantel. It was decadent and, compared to what I had lived with my entire life, ostentatious. I reminded myself again, though, that with these fanciful riches also came an army of Silver Wolves, who would help reclaim our kingdom.

With only a moment to splash water on our faces, a team

of dressmakers had arrived at Briar's door. It had been a long journey to Highwick and, though I'd slept, I'd hoped we'd get some rest. It hadn't dawned on me the wedding would be the moment we arrived. And now the evening was nearing, and the ceremony would take place at exactly midnight—the time of our birth. Symbolically it made sense. And the more I thought about it, politically, too. A good warrior should be prepared for an ambush, and I had totally missed this one.

Not that it mattered all that much—it was inevitable, so better to get it over with. Instead of dwelling on it, I thought about what midnight would bring. I loved that Briar and I had different birthdays even though we were only born minutes apart. Today Briar was twenty years old and tomorrow I would be, too. We each had a full day to be celebrated by Vellia as children, and I realized this was going to be my first birthday without her. The faery's absence hit me anew.

"Ouch." Briar frowned down at the seamstress prodding her with needles.

The seamstress merely rolled her eyes, not the least bit apologetic.

"Stay still," I called, chuckling at her squirming.

"I am," Briar growled, eyeing me in the full-length mirror. "Shouldn't you be getting fitted, too?"

"They left a very fine silver jacket hanging in my wardrobe." I shrugged. "And a ceremonial sash to match the other guards."

"I think you look better in gold." Briar always had a better sense for clothes. I was happy to let her pick my attire often and let her mold the image of myself.

"I'll wear what they tell me." My voice fell into a murmur. "Since I'm a guard of Damrienn now . . ."

My sister paused, watching my reflection. "Could you give us a moment?" she asked the two women pinning the hem of her dress.

They rolled their eyes but nodded as if used to being dismissed by royalty.

"Just don't sit down," the one with pins in her mouth muttered. "We'll be back."

"Ten minutes," the other said and shut the door behind them.

Briar hiked up her flowing lace skirts and stepped off her pedestal. She looked like a painting of the Moon Goddess, billowing white and silver skirts that cinched in at her narrowed waist, long lace sleeves, V-shaped neckline, and silver buttons down her back. Once the crown waiting for her was on her head, she'd be the perfect picture of a queen.

"You look gorgeous, Briar," I said, stuffing another almond into my cheek, trying to let the act of chewing relieve how tightly I clenched my jaw. "I wish our parents were here to see it."

Briar sighed. "I wish they were here, too." She walked around the bed and put her hand on my forearm. "I'm sorry the King didn't announce who you were straight away. Maybe he's waiting until after the ceremony?" Her worried thoughts mirrored my own. "Once I'm married to Grae, it will solidify his claim to Olmdere . . . he'll probably share the news then."

"We'll see."

Briar smiled. "You'll be a princess and a knight, Calla. You'll be formidable. While I'm holding high teas and birthing pups, you'll be galloping off into battle."

Birthing pups. I shoved the bowl of almonds away, suddenly sick to my stomach. The roles of man and woman were so rigid, so constraining, completely controlling who we could be and what we would do with our lives. Everyone around me seemed so willing to play these parts, even Briar. Some even seemed like they *wanted* them. And while any mandatory role wouldn't be one I'd choose for myself, the desires of an individual meant nothing in a pack. There was no point even considering them.

I glanced at my bedroom door, wondering when the siring of pups would commence. Gods, would Grae come here? Would I hear them together? My soul left my body imagining those sounds. My cheeks heated, my skin prickling as I swallowed back the panic. I scanned the room for wine, intending to get rip-roaring drunk at the wedding feast. There were only so many things my soul could take, and this moment had been one I'd been trying to reconcile for the last seven years.

I toyed with the amber stone hanging around my neck. "Are we sure we want to do this?" I asked Briar for the hundredth time, placing the cool back of my hand to my flushed cheek.

"We don't have a choice. You think we can defeat a powerful sorceress all on our own, Calla? And even so, what then?" This had been an ongoing battle our whole lives. Briar's countenance soured. "We have no brothers and even if we did, we'd *still* need these alliances. Our parents knew the importance of allies or else they wouldn't have arranged this union. It was our mother's dying wish for Vellia to see me to this day."

"I just wanted to give you one more chance to back out, Briar," I whispered. "If you didn't want this, I would break you out of this castle myself."

Briar bobbed her head. "I know you would." She squeezed my hand. "But I have accepted my fate. Grae and I may never love each other, but we have agreed to be friends and work together to save Olmdere. It is the right thing to do. It's what our parents would've wanted. For the good of the pack."

"For the good of the pack," I muttered.

"You'd save us all if you could, Cal." Briar wiped at a tear under her eyes with a laugh. "You're proud, stubborn, and single-minded."

"If I were a man, you'd be praising those qualities."

Briar rolled her eyes. "Let me do this. Let me honor our parents by honoring our traditions."

My eyes softened. For possibly the hundredth time in the last few days, I had to remind myself that being part of a pack meant sacrifice.

"Fine," I relented, though my stomach still churned. "But I'm telling you now: I don't care for King Nero. He seems like a power-hungry oaf."

Briar chortled. "We'll steer clear of him as much as possible."

She turned toward the stained-glass windows that peered out over the lush summer forests. "The wedding and feast will be boring, but then we can run through the trees with our new family. The best way to celebrate our birthday."

I smiled, staring out toward the sun setting through the endless sea of trees. The tightness in my chest eased at the thought of running, not having to circle the same patch over and over, but actually being able to roam.

The sunset cast long beams of colorful light across the room as a light rap sounded on the door.

"Let's get on with it, then." Briar sighed, giving me one last wink.

I clambered off the bed, expecting to find the seamstresses, but instead finding two guards.

The older one with a zigzagging scar down his cheek spoke. "The King has requested to speak with the Princess's guard."

"What?" Briar called from behind me.

We swapped bemused looks. "Will you be okay in here?"

I didn't like the idea of leaving her. Everything felt on tenterhooks in the lead-up to the ceremony.

"Go, go." She nodded. "I think I can handle being pricked by a few more needles while you're gone."

"So much for steering clear of the King," I muttered. I balled my hands into fists at my side, steeling myself for another encounter with the Silver Wolf King.

EIGHT

MY BOOTS SCUFFED ACROSS THE STONE AS I FOLLOWED THE two guards through the labyrinth of hallways. We arrived at a carved wood door, another two guards stationed beside it. I rested my hand on the hilt of my dagger as I entered.

The smell of old books hit me as I stepped onto the ornate rug. King Nero leaned back in his chair behind a painted maplewood desk. Over his right shoulder stood Grae. Arms folded across his chest, he stared daggers into the back of his father's head as if he didn't even notice me. I narrowed my eyes at him, observing that his right eye was swollen, a purpling bruise along his cheekbone. What had happened? My pulse thrummed in my ears as I bowed.

"I'm sorry it came as a surprise that I did not reveal who you were." The King's voice was a scratchy wooden note as it bounced around the study.

I glanced at Grae but couldn't read his hard expression as he stared everywhere but at me. Fire churned in my chest at the bruises on his face. Who had he been brawling with?

"I feel it is best you remain a secret, Calla," King Nero continued.

I opened my mouth to protest, but he raised a hand, silencing me.

His countenance darkened. "You think I'd let you undermine the future your parents and I worked so hard to plan? You'd steal your sister's legacy right out from under her, wouldn't you?"

"What are you talking about?" I furrowed my brow and folded my arms tightly across my chest.

The King's eyes widened at my casual, biting tone. Clearly, no one questioned the King. He was the leader of the pack, equal to the Gods themselves. But he was the one who was being inappropriate, threatening me with such accusations.

"Two daughters of Olmdere. Pity Sameir didn't have a son." He gestured toward the giant tapestry behind him displaying a detailed map of the Wolf kingdoms.

Olmdere sat to the very north with ocean surrounding its three sides. The mountains of the Ice Wolf kingdom of Taigos separated Olmdere and Damrienn with a thin white line. To the south sat the kingdom of Valta, homeland of the Onyx Wolves.

I had stared at the map of Aotreas so many times as a child, wondering what the other kingdoms might be like. It was said that Taigos was blanketed in permanent snow, the pack living in the high alpine peaks. Valta was said to be dotted with cerulean lagoons and floating islands covered in teeming jungles rarely visited by the other Wolf kingdoms.

The three other kingdoms of Aotreas seemed to carry on as if nothing had happened twenty years ago. If Vellia's story was to be believed, they were there that night, too. They had watched my father die and his pack slaughtered in their attempts to protect him. It was what made a pack so strong. They would do anything for each other, willing to run into certain death to protect one another. But the rulers of other kingdoms had no such allegiances to our pack, only to their own. They had turned a blind eye to Olmdere, and now our supposed ally was staring daggers into me.

"You were born under the same moon as your sister. You are equally the eldest child," King Nero snarled. "If you chose to ally with another kingdom, war would break out over who was the rightful king," he fumed, as I stared blankly at him. "Answer me."

"You haven't asked me a question," I said, baffled by the surprised look on his face. I darted a glance at Grae, who stared straight at his boots.

"Your parents wanted nothing when it came to you." The King's mirthless laugh made me grit my teeth. "You were never meant to exist." His eyes scanned my body again and his lip curled. "Why would I give you a piece of anything? But seeing as you're here, I will do the gracious thing and give you a choice: remain the princess's guard, or reveal yourself and, as a father-figure of sorts, I shall arrange an advantageous marriage for you to prince Tadei of Valta."

"Tadei?" I blanched. "He's forty years older than me."

"Princess Briar understands her place in these plans, a pretty thing on my son's arm." He tipped his head to the prince, and Grae still didn't look up at me. I took a shallow breath. I couldn't believe he wasn't saying anything. Had he known this all along?

"If you think I'm such a threat, then why not just kill me?" I snarled, finally pulling Grae's eyes up from the floor.

"I've considered it." The King huffed. "Believe me, girl, it is still an option. But a secret such as yours could come in handy in the future, should something happen to your sister." Grae shifted on his feet, shoulders raising.

"Is that a threat?"

"You tell me." The King leaned forward, pressing his lips to his steepled fingers. "Think reasonably. Grae and I are the only ones who know who you really are. You could howl that you are a Marriel until you're blue in the face, but no one would believe you." He narrowed his eyes at me. "I've waited twenty years to mine Olmdere of her gold and I will not let you threaten what's mine." *What's mine.* "In the olden days, we used to kill off the runts." The King's lip curled. "I see that soft-hearted faery didn't have it in her."

My eyes beseeched Grae to say something, but he remained

woefully silent. I didn't know this man at all. His betrayal slammed through me. He'd led me into this trap. Had he befriended me those many years ago so that I would submit? To win me over to his side? Grae had let me believe his father would reveal my true identity, and now I didn't even know if my sister and I would be safe. I clenched my hands into fists, wishing I could claw his eyes out.

King Nero lifted a paper off his desk, seemingly bored with the conversation. Finally, he muttered, "You are to remain a humble servant of the Crimson Princess and honor your pack or you'll be sent to Valta. Is that understood?"

I steadied my voice. "Yes."

"Then you are dismissed," the King said, eyeing me as a wicked smirk twisted his lips.

I knew then that he'd do it—that he'd kill me, or worse, if I didn't play along. This was the leader of our pack, the father to us all, and he'd just admitted to wishing me dead.

I bobbed my head in a halfhearted bow and left. I tried to steady my breath and failed. Gods, I'd been so naive. I wanted to ram my dagger straight through King Nero, but with four guards waiting at the door and Grae at his back, I couldn't do it.

My thoughts spiraled as I walked down the narrow servant's corridor back toward my sister's chambers. No guards followed me this time. No torch guided me through the windowless halls as the darkness filled me. Thoughts darted through my mind too fast to hold on to . . . apart from one: I had to protect my sister from that monster of a king. Briar was my only pack now.

Footsteps echoed behind me and I knew who followed by his telltale gait. It sounded the same on four paws, quick and lumbering, like a bear barreling through the forest.

"Little fox," Grae's voice pleaded.

"Don't you *dare* call me that." I sped up, turning down another darkened corridor, unsure if it was the right way.

"Please. Talk to me."

"You didn't seem to want to talk when your father called me a runt," I snarled, racing across the gray stones. "Or when he threatened to hurt my sister and *kill* me."

Grae's hand grabbed for my elbow and I whirled. Faster than he could lift his hand, I punched him hard in the jaw. My knuckles barked in protest, but I wasn't done. I lashed out again, but he caught my forearm, trying to spin me back against his chest. I moved, pretending he was overpowering me so that I could kick him in the knee. He dropped my arm as he pivoted to keep me from breaking the joint and I dropped to the ground, landing in a crouch and snatching my knife from my boot.

Thank the Gods for Vellia and her training—I never carried just one weapon. Grae stooped as if to help me up and I lurched forward, making him stumble back into the wall as I pinned him in place with my knife.

His eyes went wide as he held up his hands. The tip of my blade bit into the flesh of his neck. With the slightest pressure, I knew the skin would break. With more pressure still, he'd be dead.

His surprise morphed as his lips parted into a smile and his eyes scanned my face. "Only you would dare put a knife to my throat."

He was the son of the King, the second rank in our pack, and I was threatening to slit his throat. If anyone caught us, it would be enough to have me killed, or at the very least scarred like those Wolves in the great hall. No one threatened the pack . . . apart from its king.

Grae's cheeks dimpled, and my eyes snagged on his mouth before my simmering rage pulled me back.

"You knew. This whole time, you knew, didn't you?" I hissed, searching his eyes for an explanation. My gaze caught on the purpling bruise along his cheekbone. "Is that what you were trying to tell me?"

"No, I—"

"No, you weren't going to tell us of your father's true intentions?" I pressed my knife lower against his windpipe. "That the truth of who I am would live and die with me?"

Grae didn't respond—couldn't—the knife digging into his throat. I knew I should run away. This was a quick and dirty move, not one for having a conversation. He could easily overpower me if he was fast enough, but Grae didn't move. I eased the pressure from him and he took a gasping breath.

"Thank you," he rasped, touching a hand to his neck as I retreated to the far side of the hall.

I kept my blade aloft, pointed at him. "Why didn't you tell me?"

Grae shook his head, his face filled with regret. "I didn't think he'd deny you like this."

"Really?" I scowled. "Because I've known the man for a handful of minutes, and none of this surprises me."

"I wanted to tell you, Calla, I did, but . . ."

I raised my eyebrows at him. "But?"

He rubbed a hand down his face. "I . . . I've always felt protective of you and I worried—"

"Well, you've done a great job protecting me." The hilt of the knife bit into my clenched fist. "I didn't need a protector, Grae." I nodded to the red mark on his neck, flipping my knife over in my fingers and sheathing it back in my boot. "What I needed was a friend."

I refused to let him see the tears welling in my eyes. Damn those tears. He *had* been my friend, but only for a few dozen moons as a child and nothing more. I'd become blinded by his handsomeness and charm, but now I saw him for what he really was: his father's son. I stormed down the hallway, not waiting for his response, the walls feeling more and more like a prison with each step. Grae didn't follow.

I DIDN'T RETURN TO BRIAR'S ROOM. SHE COULD HANDLE A FEW seamstresses on her own. Instead, I veered down a covered walkway and out to an open courtyard. The simple bench seats and weapons racks told me enough—these were training rings. If the space was for royalty, there'd be flower beds and fountains, but there was only a patch of dirt, marred by the divots of many boots.

The space was blissfully empty.

I shielded my eyes as I stared up the ivy-clad walls to the sun high above and ran my other shaking hand through my curls. Taking deep gulps of air, I paced back and forth, following the tread of boots along the dusty earth. This panic would help no one. Marching to the weapons racks, I pulled a heavy wooden sword from its hooks. My muscles strained as I swept it left and right, testing it in the air. If I couldn't slow my racing heart, then at least I could work with it.

My boots carved a pattern in the dirt as I practiced my footwork. Block, block, strike. Block, block, strike. The steady rhythm focused my mind as the memories of the King's office flashed through me. I should've known better, shouldn't have believed that Gods-forsaken faery for all her wishy-washy promises. A pack, a family . . . No, this was just another type of cage.

My cheeks flushed, a mop of sweat breaking out on my brow as I swung the heavy sword. I'd been so hopeful—too hopeful—and for what? Even if King Nero had embraced me with open arms, the shadows I once reveled in were now my ultimate trap—unable to lead an army, unable to save my fallen kingdom like I'd trained for my entire life, watching as my twin and Grae married, started a family, and found some kind of happiness.

The sword whipped through the air faster, my shoulders burning as I pushed harder. Grae was the part that hurt most of all. I wished he'd never visited us, never wrote those letters, never pretended to care. It was the worst kind of cruelty—pretending to be kind—and I'd been the fool who'd fallen for it.

The sound of heavy footsteps made me whirl, and the three guards on the walkway halted. Sadie, Hector, and Maez glanced at each other and back at me. My boots were now caked in dirt, sweat stained my tunic, and I was certain my face was a startling shade of red. Whatever surprise was on their faces vanished in a blink.

"Oh good," Sadie said, as if she were expecting me. "Now we can pair off."

They must've known—must've seen the pain bleeding from my every breath—but they ignored it, and I was grateful. I wondered how many times each of them had found solace in a training ring. How many times did they find peace at the tip of their blades?

Hector unclasped his cloak and hung it on a hook. "I don't suppose you had many sparring partners in Allesdale?" he asked, rolling his shoulders.

"Only the ones Vellia could conjure," I replied, resting the tip of my heavy sword on the ground.

Maez's eyebrows shot up. "Now that I would've liked to see."

Hector rolled up the sleeves of his tunic. "What kind of creatures did she conjure?"

"All sorts," I said with a shrug. "Snakes, soldiers, creatures of her own making."

"But if they were conjured, could they actually land a blow?" Maez asked.

I pulled the neckline of my tunic wide over my shoulder, where three raised scars clawed over the joint and down my chest.

"Gods," Hector breathed. "What did that?"

"A mountain cat," I said, quirking my brow.

"And shifting didn't heal the wound?"

The magic of changing forms could heal almost any wound, if done quickly enough. Every time we shifted into our furs and back again, our bodies were rebuilt, wounds healed, sore muscles eased. It was why Wolves lived nearly twice as long as humans; the shift seemed to fend off old age. There was something sacred about that moment between one form and the next—when we were both and neither. That was the magic the humans prayed to—the magic of change.

"I didn't shift for two weeks," I finally said, meeting their gaping expressions as I pulled my neckline back into place. "I wanted this one to last."

"I think I'm going to enjoy having you on our crew," Sadie said with an approving grunt, unfolding her arms and heading to the weapons rack. "Here." She tossed a wooden dagger to me and I caught it in midair. "That sword is too big for you."

"I know." I scowled. "I was just building my strength. I didn't know you'd be here."

"Come to vent?" Maez asked with a knowing smirk. "We've all had those days. I can't imagine meeting King Nero helped."

"Indeed," I said, causing them to chuckle.

Sadie selected a matching dagger from the rack. "Did Grae not tell you what the King was like?"

She unbuckled her belt and placed her actual weapons on the rickety bench. Steel weaponry was expensive. They wouldn't dent and blunt their most powerful tools, hacking away at each other in a sparring match.

"Grae didn't tell me a lot of things," I muttered, stretching my neck from side to side as Sadie approached.

Maez turned toward Hector, readying her stance. "My cousin has reasons for his silence."

It was all she said, though I knew there must be more there. The other guards seemed to agree. What did they know that I didn't? *I've always felt protective of you.* Betrayal swarmed my senses. Why had he said that?

I beckoned Sadie to attack, needing a distraction from my swirling thoughts. She was fast, her movements sharp and unfamiliar, but I was faster. I darted and ducked out of each of her strikes, landing a blow on her hip with my practice blade.

She panted a heavy breath. "Nice."

I bowed my head, receiving the compliment. "Vellia trained

me as best she could, but I'm glad to have living sparring partners now."

Even as I praised her, I seethed at the fact that Vellia had done us a disservice by making the Silver Wolves seem like family. She should've been harder on us, prepared us for their disdain and manipulation. I thought I'd be welcomed into a new pack, but instead, I was a pawn in the greedy King's ministrations.

Sadie attacked again, her dulled dagger slicing my arm at the same time I held the tip of my blade to her side. It would've been a killing blow.

"You're welcome to train with us whenever you like." Sadie's lips twisted up as she scanned me from head to toe. Pride bloomed in my gut at the impressed look she gave me. "Seeing as Grae and Briar will be together most of the time. I think our little trio will soon become four, anyway."

I waited until she was ready and lurched forward again. She blocked each of my strikes, each of us trying to make the other pivot, trying to find the upper hand. It felt glorious. Like a battle and a dance all at once. Block, strike, duck, spin. Again and again, the dull clank of our wooden daggers filled the space.

Sadie's eyes darted over my right shoulder, only a split second, but with her focus diverted I found my opening. Lunging forward, I hit her hard in the ribs, and whirled to whoever she spotted behind me. The bite of steel halted the sweep of my dagger, a hand grabbing my wrist to stop my strike, and Grae's storming eyes stared down at me.

NINE

I TWISTED OUT OF HIS GRIP, TRYING TO LAND A PUNCH TO HIS side, but Grae was faster. He blocked my strike and I retreated a step, kicking at his knee while swiping my wooden blade. I blinked at him—at his speed and skill—and realized how easily he could've disarmed me in that hallway. He let me think I had the upper hand, but he could've pried that dagger from my grip at any moment.

I scowled at him, slicing my weapon through the air. He ducked under it, narrowly avoiding the strike to the head. Lunging forward, he tried to knock me off balance, but I was right there, forcing him to circle around me like a predator stalking prey.

A man behind him, watching our exchange, clapped slowly. I squinted, noting he was the guard who'd led me to the King's office.

"She's got claws," he said with a chuckle.

"Aiden," Grae snapped, using his friend's name as a reprimand. He sheathed his sword and held up his fists. "Trying to make it fair," he murmured.

"It wasn't fair the moment you brought us to this place." I chucked the dagger at his feet. "You've blindfolded us with your smiles and fake friendship."

Grae paused, lowering his hands at my words, and I struck like an asp, punching him across the jaw.

Aiden guffawed, and the rest of the guards paused from their training. I thought they might attack me for that—for taking a cheap shot at their prince—but they snickered as if hiding their delight.

Grae held a hand to his bruised cheek. "I suppose I deserved that."

"What happened to your eye?" I asked, still holding my clenched fists aloft.

"Are you going to even it out?" Grae turned his face, offering me his unbruised eye.

"We got a little rowdy training before," Aiden said, walking up and clapping Grae on the shoulder.

Grae smiled—a fake smile—and I knew it was a lie.

"It doesn't seem like you're too concerned about the prince's bruises, though." Aiden chuckled, inspecting Grae's jaw. "Seeing as you've given him another one. Come." Aiden gave me a wary glance. "Let the girl train in peace. You've got a wedding to prepare for."

I curled my lip at the word "girl." I had always hated being called *girl*, even when I'd been the right age for the word, though I resented being called *lady* just as much now. Why call me such trivial things when I could be called a warrior, a Wolf, a royal?

Grae turned back to me, words dying on his lips. Whatever he was going to say, I didn't care anymore. I didn't want to hear any more of his lies.

"Go," I gritted out. "Your bride awaits." I hated how petty it was. I hated how bitter I sounded.

Taking a step closer to me, Grae lowered his head until his breath brushed my hair, making my skin ripple. "You say that as if you care, Calla."

I forced myself to look up into those beautiful, dark eyes— the ones that bewitched me the moment I first saw them—and said, "I don't."

"Why not?"

My mouth dropped open. Why not? What in the Moon's name was that supposed to mean? Why would he want me to care about something I could never have?

Aiden dropped his hand on Grae's shoulder and steered him toward the doorway. "Come on. Let them train," he said.

My body felt boneless as I watched him walk away, steered by his father's guard like cattle through the archway.

"This wedding has made him broodier than a snow snake with a fresh kill," Sadie muttered.

"That's rich coming from you," Maez said, making the shorter guard frown. "You're as gloomy as they come, Sads."

Sadie rolled her eyes. Standing from the bench, she circled the splintering dagger in her hands. "Everyone is edgy around the full moon."

"Then your world must be full of full moons," Hector taunted.

Maez hit him in the hip with the broadside of her training sword.

Sadie stooped to where my discarded dagger lay in the dirt and picked it up. She flipped it over, holding the hilt out at me. "Again?"

I took the weapon, grateful for the distraction. "Thanks."

"Few people understand the mind of a warrior." Sadie shrugged. "We get you."

Hector and Maez returned to sparring. The thwack of their wooden swords brought a steadying rhythm that slowed my pulse. There was sanity in training, the repetition pulling us back in on ourselves.

Sadie advanced again before I could think on it. I fell back into that dance, my mind honing down to each footstep and blink. For so long I'd tried to understand Briar, to put myself in the shoes of a princess, but it made as little sense to me as trying to understand the shoes I should be wearing. Here, though, with these guards, they understood. They understood the calm of training, the confidence born of discipline, the calloused hands and sore muscles and minds that only worked when in motion. And even when the world felt like it was crashing down around me, I'd have this, and I knew these three would help me blunt the sting of what was to come.

I SCRATCHED AT THE ITCHY FABRIC OF MY CEREMONIAL TUNIC. The look in Grae's eyes played over and over in my mind.

Why not?

I had been such a foolish pup, regaling him with stories of how I would defeat Sawyn, of how I would reclaim Olmdere for my sister Queen . . . and now I wasn't sure if I'd ever see my homeland again.

Frowning at the silver carpet beneath my feet, I felt his eyes upon me. The rest of the congregation ignored me, but his eyes were like a leaden weight. Maybe Grae desired Olmdere for himself, like his father. The gold mines lay just over its border. King Nero made it clear he was going to use this marriage to ferry gold into his kingdom with impunity, not even getting close to Sawyn in the capital. Gods, I'd longed for this day my whole life, and now I felt bribed into silence. The threat of being married off to a stranger and being separated from Briar forever loomed over me.

I scowled at the delicate wedding decorations—a constellation of paper stars and crystal baubles. What a sham. They had transformed the grand hall into a white wonderland over the course of the afternoon. Long wooden pews now lined the space, the voices of well-wishers reverberating off the vaulted ceilings. The string quartet from earlier now sat in the corner, bows resting in their laps as they waited for the ceremony to begin. A trail of white flower petals ran the length of the aisle, up to the dais where King Nero sat. I had the urge to take the knife in my boot, slice it across his smug face, and stain the petals red.

A full moon priest stood at the bottom step of the dais. He held a heavy tome in his hands, waiting for the far doors to open.

His flowing stone-gray robes were embroidered with silver images of the moon's phases, and he had long obsidian hair with a matching scraggly beard, looking more like a woodsman than a priest. I could already picture exactly what he would look like in his Wolf form—matted fur and beady eyes.

A circular window high above the throne perfectly captured the first silvery streak of moonlight. The crowd all lifted their chins in unison. Soon they'd all be in their furs, howling at the moon.

"The Moon Goddess smiles upon us this night," the priest said, holding one hand up as his fingers cast shadows through the glowing light. "When the veil between land and sky is thinnest and the Goddess can hear our prayers. We ask her to bless Damrienn and all her allies."

All her allies. I glared sideways at the king, who looked out over his pack. King Nero didn't care about his allies, he cared about power, and with each heartbeat, it felt more and more like we were sacrificing Olmdere to his greed. This had nothing to do with the good of *my* pack, that was for damn sure. I stole a glance toward Grae, staring straight past him to Maez. His cousin wore a silver jacket and sash that matched my own, but I could make out the crown prince's sharp expression from my periphery. This all would've been easier if he hadn't been . . . Grae. My Grae. My friend. He'd made me think it'd all be okay somehow. At least King Nero had shown his true colors the moment we met.

The priest dropped his hand.

"Moon Goddess, bless us this night." The crowd murmured the hushed prayer in unison.

I whispered the same, one step behind the rest. Despite my anger and worry, I couldn't help but be awed by being a part of all this. We'd lit candles and said our prayers every full moon . . . but I had never experienced a true moon ceremony before.

The priest wandered over to a chunky candle on a pedestal beside him. "In the light of the moon . . ."

"Our truth is revealed," the crowd replied.

I felt the pull to shift deep in my belly. That wild part of me stirred as the full moon rose higher. The feeling churned deeper in my chest at the call and response of the pack. This is what it felt like to have people, to be one of many. Yet what should have been joy right now felt nothing like the belonging I'd always dreamed of. It felt like fear, like desperation, like if I didn't blend in, I'd be cut down.

That fear made my muscles coil, and I pushed away the yearning to shift, stretching my neck to the side.

"We pledge ourselves to our joined fate, stronger together than apart," the priest said, sweeping a hand through the candle flame.

"We pledge ourselves to the good of the pack," the crowd murmured.

"For we may die."

"But the pack lives on."

At the final whispered prayer, the string quartet started a slow, sweet tune. The crowd stood, twisting to see the far doors open. Soft "oohs" escaped their lips as Briar walked down the aisle.

In only a handful of hours, they had perfectly tailored the dress to fit her lean body. A diamond tiara sat atop her braided red hair and a long veil flowed in a river of lace behind her. She maintained a gentle smile as she walked with deliberate slowness. Pride filled me as I watched the control in her movements. It was a dance to her, just as sparring was a dance to me—a role she performed beautifully. I was certain she captured every Wolf's heart as she glided past.

Good. It would be easier to pivot out of King Nero's jaws if the pack adored her.

And how could they not? It seemed as if the very moonlight stretched up the aisle to greet her. Resonant melodies flowed around us, and my chest tightened. As she stepped into the glowing moonlight, she cried out, eyes flying wide.

The bouquet of white flowers slipped from her hands, and the crowd gasped as it hit the floor. Briar doubled over and clenched a fist to her gut. On instinct, I unsheathed my dagger, searching for any threat in the stunned crowd. The pack sucked in a collective breath as my mind tumbled into panic. Was she poisoned? Was it an arrow so fast I couldn't see?

I took a step toward Briar but her eyes flashed gold, the reflective light of her Wolf eyes making me halt.

She wasn't injured.

Magic shot out from her, a silver beam that flew across the room, landing on the chest of another.

Maez's eyes flickered a matching metallic gold. Her hand hit her gut and she panted as if the moonlight had knocked the air from her lungs. When her eyes locked on Briar's, I knew for certain what it meant.

The word began echoing around the room: *Mates.*

I gaped in stunned silence.

Briar and Maez were fated mates.

"What is the meaning of this?" King Nero boomed, rising from his throne and growling at the priest. "Fix it."

The priest held up beseeching hands to the furious King, gesturing to my sister. "I cannot control who the Moon Goddess chooses."

"This must be a sick kind of joke," Nero snarled. "Mates or not, she is my son's betrothed."

Rogue growls rang through the room. The magic of mates was the most sacred of all Wolf magic. The only thing that superseded King Nero's power was that of the Goddess herself. He sneered at his pack, promising trouble to whoever questioned him, and his followers fell in line, their snarls dropping back to murmurs. But even his most loyal wouldn't be fully cowed.

The King's gaze slid to mine, and the moon rose higher as if in response. His brow arched at me, and I could see him contemplating it: replacing me with Briar as if swapping shoes and not living people.

The light crept down the aisle until it shone upon the entire room. The moment that sacred light touched the back of my hand, gooseflesh rippled across my skin. Like a punch to the chest, the air whooshed out of my lungs. The muscles in my stomach clenched until the building intensity of magic threatened to burst out of me. Immense pressure built behind my eyes, making me screw them shut. The Gold Wolf inside me growled, a snarling deep sound. I gritted my elongating teeth as I struggled to regain control, half-shifting from the force within me.

I heard Grae shout my name as footsteps raced over to me. I somehow knew they belonged to him.

His glowing golden eyes beamed down at me, his stare crashing into me like a tumbling wave. I could *hear* his heartbeat, I could *see* the thin slits of his golden eyes dilate as he watched me, and his smoky earth scent carved into my bones.

Howls broke out around us, human and wolf alike, as the moonlight refracted through the hall. They all felt it, this magic that overcame us.

"Calla?" A panting, breathless voice was in my head. *His voice.*

And I knew instantly what it was, this magic that bound us inextricably together. It felt like a burning rope tied around my rib cage, pulling me toward the low thunder of that voice.

"Two matches on the same night?" the full moon priest asked, his soft, awed voice too loud to my sensitive ears. "After decades with none."

"It's impossible," King Nero spat.

"Songs will be sung of this moment and this moon for centuries to come," the priest said and the noise of the crowd swelled in response. "The Goddess smiles brighter than ever down upon us."

"Curse this fickle moon," King Nero barked in reply and the gossiping voices of the crowd hushed again. I looked up through squinting, pained eyes as he leered down at me. "Perhaps there is a use for you after all, girl."

Every heightened sense overwhelmed me, nausea roiling in

my gut. The whispers were deafening and the flickering candle-light blinding. Sweat beaded on my brow as I peered at my sister through bleary eyes. Briar stood stock-still, staring at Maez.

A figure to my left took another step toward me and I knew without looking it was Grae. I could sense it was him, as if a part of me existed within his body. That keen awareness tipped me over the edge of panic.

Without another thought, I turned and dashed down the aisle, fleeing the ceremony and the judging eyes of the Silver Wolf pack. I heard Grae's voice calling my name again and I shoved away the sound, pushing him out of my head. I darted for the nearest doorway and stumbled into the moonlight. Fresh air hit my lungs, but I didn't stop. I raced toward the back gate, darting past open-mouthed guards and into the woods. I bolted as if the Moon herself chased me.

TEN

MY LUNGS BURNED AS I PUSHED MY ACHING LEGS HIGHER AND higher toward the snowcapped peaks in the distance. Whatever joy and freedom I thought I'd feel in this forest evaporated during that ceremony. I couldn't think, couldn't breathe.

Grae was my mate.

As I dashed through the filtered beams of moonlight, my Wolf howled inside me until I couldn't take it anymore. The only thing I needed to do was stop denying the change and it began. The sharp twist of pain racked through me as my bones twisted and hair grew. A building strain, like a seized muscle, increased more and more until it vanished with a pop. Bone and sinew settled back into place. I swished my rust-colored tail.

The breeze blew through my copper red fur and I pawed the mossy earth. Even in my Wolf form, I was different from Briar. She was a stunning golden Wolf, from her molten ore eyes to the tip of her gilded tail, whereas I was a shade of faded bronze . . . just another way I didn't belong.

I peered far into the distance of the shadowed forest, spotting a trail my human eyes hadn't seen. Shredded clothes lay discarded beside me, along with my dagger. The only thing that had remained intact was the amber stone still around my neck. I released a frustrated breath. I should've remembered to take them off. Now the chain dug into my fur, an ever-present collar that reminded me of him: my mate.

Snarling at the discarded pile, I dismissed the concern of having no clothes. How could I possibly return to that place, anyway? Would the king even accept me if I did? Would he expect me to play the role of princess in the same way Briar had? He had all but said so when he announced maybe I had a use after all.

A low growl escaped my maw. I wouldn't be holding tea parties and dressing in ball gowns. And I certainly wouldn't let King Nero put me on a leash.

My ears twisted toward the sound of leaves rustling. I sniffed the air. A deer walked the trail up ahead, and beyond it I smelled the rushing water of a stream.

The sounds of the forest normally soothed me, but even in my Wolf form I couldn't escape the white-hot dread in my chest. I wondered how disappointed Grae was. He had planned for Briar and now he was stuck with me. My paws chewed up the earth as I dashed up the mountainside. What was I going to do? The second I stepped foot back into that castle, King Nero would tell everyone who I was . . . and then he'd force his son to marry me. I'd spend a lifetime being called "the wrong sister," "an embarrassing mate," and I'd have to simper and smile as Grae toyed with my feelings, pretending to care for me one moment and acting against me the next.

I groaned, a rasping howl toward the sky, pushing my muscles harder until I reached a clearing. I breached the trees and collapsed into the tall meadow grasses. In my grief, I shifted back into my human form and buried my head in my hands. Salty tears dropped through my fingertips as the rough grass swayed around my naked body. I looked up to the bright night sky and cursed the moon.

I was prepared to be a shadow in Damrienn, my only focus on saving Olmdere. I was prepared to stand by, bite my tongue, and suffer the sight of them together, all for Olmdere. Now, if I ever returned to that castle, I might never even see Olmdere. The second I returned, they'd trap me in a marriage that would justify King Nero's lust for gold and I'd be even less than a shadow. Briar easily replaced with me.

I thought of the map in Nero's office. Beyond the snowy summits of Taigos in the distance, my kingdom called to me. It was tempting, yet my shoulders trembled against the chill. I probably wouldn't survive a trek over those jagged peaks.

I couldn't run and I couldn't stay.

The hours passed on and my tears didn't ebb. I sat crumpled, paralyzed by my lack of options, each one more heartbreaking than the last. This wasn't what my life was meant to be.

A twig snapped behind me and I whirled.

Briar stood in her wedding gown, the white fabric glowing in the darkness. She offered out a bundle in her hands, a simple brown tunic, and said, "I found your clothes in the forest and figured you'd need some new ones." She marched over and crouched beside me. "Are you okay?"

"How could I possibly be okay?" I gritted out, snatching the tunic from her and bunching the fabric in my hands. "What even happened back there?"

"Maez became my fated mate," Briar said, a secret smile pulling on her lips. "And Grae became yours."

My voice wobbled. "*How* did this happen?"

"Our parents were fated mates, too. We are both a product of that true love. Perhaps it's in our blood." Briar shrugged as if what she was saying wasn't world changing. As if what she was saying wasn't *impossible*. There was nothing in any story that remotely alluded to something like this happening. Yet here she was, practically shrugging it off as she sat back on her heels. "Maybe it's part of our destinies. Maybe that's why I found Maez so . . . distracting."

My sister seemed so light in that moment, joyful even. I felt none of it.

"And I got stuck with a liar," I snarled, picking a stalk of golden grass and twisting it in my fingers. "Who is probably also mourning the fact he got stuck with me."

Briar snorted. "If you think he feels that way, you're even more of a fool than me."

I glared at my sister. "How can he not?" I waved a hand over my bare figure. "I'm a *runt* compared to you."

"That's not true." Briar leaned her shoulder into me. "Look, Grae made me promise not to tell you this, but he should have known that I would, anyway."

"Tell me what?"

"That night, when I said we talked?" Briar looked sideways at me. "He told me he was sorry and that our marriage could only ever be a symbol of our alliance, that we could only live as friends and nothing more, but that I couldn't tell anyone, especially not King Nero."

"He said that?" My heart leapt into my throat. "Why?"

"Because he was in love with someone else," she whispered, her smile widening. "It's you, obviously, if that wasn't clear." My mouth fell open and Briar chuckled at my disbelief. "I wonder if he knew you were fated mates. I think he may have suspected for a long time."

"Oh. My . . . " I groaned, burying my face in my hands again. "He knew. He *knew*?"

My mind flashed back to those moments when he had tried to talk to me. He had said he needed to tell me something, but things kept getting in the way. And then in his father's office, he'd seemed upset about a potential marriage to Tadei. He said he felt protective of me, but . . .

I clenched a hand to my stomach. "I think I'm going to throw up."

"Why?"

"Because he loves me."

Briar laughed as she stroked a soothing hand down my cold skin. "Put this on," she insisted, nudging the woolen tunic squashed in my hands. "It's colder in the mountains than in Alles-dale."

I begrudgingly pulled it over my head. It must've been a servant's tunic she nicked from the wash line. The fabric drowned me and itched against my skin, but it eased the chill. "He lied about everything, Briar, all of it." My voice wobbled again. "The King never intended to reveal who I was. He never wanted to help save Olmdere."

"That doesn't surprise me," she said, which *did* surprise me. She went on. "Grae is not the same as his father," Briar said. "You know that. And one day he'll be king."

"He didn't say anything to stop him—"

"His father's the pack leader and a *king*!" Briar's exasperated breath swept across the grasses, making them sway. "You think Grae can just openly disagree with him? The pack would tear out his throat for one ill-spoken word. The King might order you to stay, but if you wanted to ride to Olmdere tomorrow, do you think Grae would really stop you? Our Grae?"

"He isn't *our* anything," I snapped.

"No," Briar whispered. "He's *your* mate, Calla. He is your everything, as you are his. Your lives are tied together now. I don't think he would deny you anything."

"I don't care," I hissed. "He lied to me. I walked into that office like a fool and one word from him could've prepared me. If he was on our side, he would've told us as much."

My chest clenched again.

Briar brushed her hand in circles down my back. "He didn't say anything at all?"

"Not in the King's office," I said. "He followed me afterward ..."

"And?"

"And I put a knife to his throat."

Briar doubled over, cackling. "Of course you did."

"It's not funny," I growled.

"It's a little funny," she wheezed, trying to stop the giggles by pressing her lips together. She wiped her eyes. "Oh, Goddess,

I love you. Maybe he would've explained himself better if you weren't trying to slit his throat."

A laugh bubbled up from my chest. The sound of my twin's cackles was infectious. Like two mischievous children, we chuckled there in the tall grasses. Briar always had a way of replacing my tears with laughter. I'd given her plenty of occasions to hone that skill.

"You're right. I should probably have a conversation with Grae without my weapons." I sighed.

"That's probably a good idea." She smiled warmly, plucking a weed from between the meadow grasses. "He's your mate now. Killing him would end your life, too. You need a better plan."

"You're not mad?" I held my sister's pale blue eyes. "You planned your whole life to be a queen. I'm taking that from you."

"I never wanted to be a queen."

"What?" My brow furrowed as she twirled the dried weed in her hands.

"Nobody ever asked me what I wanted." She blew on the featherlike seeds and they scattered into the air. "I was only ever told."

"What do you want?"

"A quiet life with someone I love." She stared up at the stars. "A cottage in the forest, a little stream to bathe in, a garden patch to grow food . . ."

"You never told me this," I whispered. "You tell me everything."

"Not everything. Some things are too precious to even whisper." Briar's eyes welled as she grinned. "Especially when there seemed no chance of it ever coming true. But now that I've met Maez, I want to shout it to the moon. Gods, I feel like I love her already. How can that be? Do you feel it, too?" She pounded her fist against her stomach. "That burning ember inside you?"

I looked up to the moon, wishing I could lie but instead saying, "I do."

"Of course you do—you've felt it forever."

I flushed, because even though I had kept *that* secret from her, of course she knew.

"I know you never planned on this, Cal," Briar said. "And I'll be here to help you do all those courtly things, but this is the first and only thing I ever truly wanted for myself. Love." Her brows knitted together as her voice cracked. "And the Goddess's blessing means no one can take it from me now."

She had hid that deepest wish even from me. I had thought Briar wanted the crown more than anything, and I felt the pang of her choice to marry Grae all the keener. She had wanted none of it, but she'd done what she thought was best for our people, knowing she'd never have the kind of love she craved . . . just as I would deny myself that love in favor of her.

She placed a gentle hand on my forearm. "You'll make a better ruler anyway, Cal." I opened my mouth to protest, but she carried on. "Wolves don't need diamonds and lace. They need strength and smarts. And you have more of that than anyone I know. You'll find a way to defeat Sawyn without King Nero's aid. That's what matters to our people, our legacy. And I will help you with the gowns and rouge."

I huffed, my lips pulling to the side. We stared up at the twinkling stars as fireflies danced around the meadow. My thundering heart settled. We'd find a way forward together, as we always did. Somehow, it would be all right.

"You should go back to the castle," I murmured. "Be with your mate."

"I can stay if you want—"

"No," I said, wiping a hand down my face. "I'm not ready to return just yet."

"But you *will* return, yes?" she asked, concern in her voice.

"I'm your shadow, Briar. You can't go far without me," I quipped.

But she leaned down once more, pulling me into a fierce hug. "You're not my shadow, sister. You're my twin, the other half of my coin. I'm so sorry you ever felt that way."

I didn't know what to say to that, so I just sat there and hugged her back as the crickets chirped their nighttime chorus around us. Eventually she stood up, looking down at me with love in her eyes.

"Maez will be introducing me to the pack in the grand hall if you want to join us," Briar said, kissing the top of my head. "It'll be okay, Cal. We'll deal with the King. He may think we're just pretty, mindless girls. But you and I both know we are more than that. Vellia trained us well. We can handle him. There are worse things in this life than finding your one true love."

I grimaced as my sister walked off. *One true love.* I should be as light and happy as her, but all I felt was trepidation. If Grae were a baker or a farrier, maybe I wouldn't feel this white hot poker in my gut, but he was the crown prince. I'd be the center of his pack's scrutiny, and I was certain King Nero would try to make my life miserable because I was more than a submissive, pretty thing. I pursed my lips together. Part of me wanted Grae, had *always* wanted Grae . . . but, seeing who he was in Highwick, could I trust him?

I stood with a sigh, trailing my fingers through the tall meadow grasses. I plucked a cornflower, its petals fluttering away in the breeze. The hem of the tunic swished around my knees as I paced from one end of the meadow to the other. I ruminated over every worry again and again, circling through my options and always coming up short. I knew there was no getting out of returning to the castle. At some point, I'd have to face him.

Taking one more turn around the spans, I steeled myself for what was to come. I turned back toward the city and something caught my eye. I froze.

Leaning against a tree trunk, watching me, was my fated mate.

ELEVEN

HIS DARK EYES REFLECTED GOLD IN THE MOONLIGHT AS THAT predatory gaze tracked me. My mate. The only part of him that moved was his eyes as he leaned against the tree, and he was all the more menacing for it. Birds cawed in the distance and my heart hammered so loudly I was certain he could hear it. The knot in my gut tugged me forward, and I was grateful that I didn't have a knife on me still.

"You should've told me about your father's plans," I said, stopping a few paces away from him, knowing I needed the distance to think.

"Yes," he gritted out, his voice filled with regret. "I thought I had convinced my father to acknowledge you, but I should've known better. He lied to me, too. That is why I remained silent in his office. He already knew how much you meant to me and . . . and I was one breath away from snapping his neck."

My mouth dropped open. Even in the depths of the forest, he shouldn't have said such things. Our Wolf magic thrived on these powerful bonds, to our kings and our mates. Hurting the pack leader was a death sentence, heir or not. And I knew then that if he had stood up for me in that office, it would've ended badly for both of us, and yet, the less logical part of me hated that he didn't. Judging by that suspicious bruise on his eye, I wondered if he was punished for sticking up for me in the grand hall. I hated that I understood the reasons for his silence now. It would've been easier to just stay mad at him.

"What he said . . ." I gulped, reliving the moment in the King's office. "That my parents should've—"

Grae pushed off the tree, the action silencing me. In a split second, his hands bracketed my face and he pulled me into a hot, burning kiss. My arms instinctively wrapped around him, the way they had yearned to a million times before. His mouth claimed mine and his fingertips dug into my neck, holding me to him. I tried to leash the desire to thread my hands through his hair, but as his smoky scent filled me, my restraint snapped. A groaning snarl escaped his mouth as his tongue lashed my own, skittering shocks of lightning shooting through my body at the contact. I barely had time for my lips to respond before he broke our kiss and rested his forehead on mine, leaving me reeling.

His eyes scorched into me as he said, "I've been wanting to do that since you nearly bowled me over in Allesdale, little fox."

The immensity of what this was came flooding back into me—the power of fate, of magic, of bonds that stretched into immortality coursed through my veins.

I took a hasty step backward, out of his grasp. "Why didn't you tell me?"

Grae cocked his brow. "Why didn't I tell you I was completely bewitched by you?" His voice was a low rumble that made my toes curl in the soil. He tilted his head, eyes trailing down my figure. "Why didn't you tell me the same?"

"I-I . . ." I pressed the heel of my hand into my eye. "You're assuming that's true."

"It is." Grae's canines glinted as he flashed a wolfish grin, and the sight of those sharp teeth made my stomach flip. "I know you felt it as much as I did when the moonlight touched your skin." He reached out and ran his rough, calloused hand from my collarbone, over my amber necklace, and up my jaw until he cupped my cheek. My eyelids flickered at his soft touch. "You're my mate, Calla. You and I were always meant to be."

I shuddered at those claiming words, turning my face into him until my lips skimmed the inside of his wrist. It felt so right—his scent, his touch, my name on his lips.

He smoothed back his thick hair, watching me with hooded, wanting eyes. "I'm sorry I didn't tell you sooner. I was afraid of what my father might do if he knew."

"And Olmdere?"

"I never wanted to stop you from helping your homeland. Believe me," Grae said, his eyes filled with pleading. I wanted to believe him—I wanted to believe in every inch of him at that moment—but the events of the day had shredded my faith in everything I was raised to believe: the pack, our duty, the family that we'd have. Grae dropped his hand and a pained longing made me want to reach for him again. The need to touch him—to always be touching him—filled me to the core. "One day, I pray to storm the castle by your side and watch as you retake your parents' throne."

"But?"

Grae hung his head. "But my father is a dangerous man, more than you could ever know, and I fear what will happen if you stand between him and his plans."

Kings and their plans—for gold, for power—it was a hungry, bottomless pit, not so different from what Vellia had told us of dark magic. What was the difference between a greedy King and an evil sorceress? All they both wanted was more.

"He can't kill me now that we're tied together," I whispered, hating that my voice wobbled. "But he'll make the pack hate me." My gaze dropped to my feet. "Everyone will call me runt behind my back. They'll think you're shackled to me. And there are no other Golds to come to our aid—it's just you and me . . . and Briar."

With my sister's name, I prayed to the Gods to have even half of Briar's composure. My emotions always seemed bigger than hers, as if the well ran deeper within me. The slightest look or ill-spoken word could swing me from one extreme to the next. Briar seemed immovable compared to me, steady, easy, calm—words never used to describe me. It's what would've made her a beloved queen . . . when there was nothing easy to love about me.

Grae's long finger lifted my chin until I met his storming eyes. He held my gaze for a moment, as if hearing all the worried thoughts in my mind. "You have no idea, Calla, not one bit." I bit my lip as he said my name like a prayer. "It is you and me—and that's all I've ever wanted. My whole life, you have been my best friend, little fox." My eyes welled, a burning lump in my throat, my emotions so beyond my control now. "I counted the days until the next full moon because I was so eager to see you. And when circumstances kept us apart, it broke me."

His confession stole the air from my lungs. He brushed his thumb over my bottom lip, and I stared up at his perfectly angular face and intense eyes. Breathless, desire flamed anew, and it blasted away all my doubts. The rest of the world faded away when Grae looked at me like that. My fears could wait. Nothing mattered in that moment other than him and the way he stared at my mouth.

"You are brave, and smart, and vicious," he said, "and so breathtakingly beautiful that it hurts not to touch you."

I reached out and pressed my hand against the center of his chest as though I could feel the ache inside him. Grae reached up and covered my hand with his own, holding my palm to him.

"Then touch me."

My soft plea unleashed him, his hands snapping to my waist and hoisting me up. I wrapped my legs around his narrows hips, the soft flesh biting into his belt as my mouth met his. My heart exploded from my chest as his tongue skimmed the seam of my mouth and I opened to him. That hot, branding kiss made my thighs clench tighter to his sides, my hips tilting of their own volition.

He groaned and spun until my back collided with a tree trunk. I gasped as he pinned me there, the rough material of my pilfered dress doing nothing to keep the bark from scratching my back, and I rubbed against it and him, wanting more of any sensation caused by Grae.

I opened my eyes for a second to see nothing but feral lust in his gaze. It was a magic unlike any other, one that burned me up with wanton need, wanting him to press into me until I couldn't tell where I ended and he began. That mating bond begged to be fulfilled in every way, the moon practically screaming at us to realize our fate.

I pulled Grae's face back to mine, delighting in the carnal smile on his lips. His hands slid up the fabric of my tunic and he growled as he skimmed my bare backside. His fingers kneaded my ass as he pulled me harder against him, the outline of his erection straining against his trousers. I arched into his touch, heat pooling in my throbbing core, as I rocked against him. I had done nothing like this before, and yet, nothing had ever felt more right. As if by magic, I knew exactly what I wanted—*needed*—how I was desperate for him to touch me, fill me, cry out my name, and make me come undone.

My hands dropped to his belt buckle as a crack rent the night sky. We both jolted, looking up to the eerie green clouds that blocked out the moonlight. A trickle of fear traced down my spine.

"What in the . . . " I murmured as Grae set me back down on my feet, any disappointment vanishing as my warrior instincts kicked in.

Without a word we ran into the clearing, gazing out toward the tallest spires of the castle peeking above the tree line. Bolts of green lightning shot down upon the castle as swirling storm clouds spiraled above. Acid rose up my throat as I stared at the verdant light. Rooks cawed overhead and emerald flames licked toward the sky.

"Sawyn." Another bolt of lightning zapped from the sky, its

crack echoing through the mountainside. "We've got to go help them." I swallowed the thick lump in my throat and took off into a run—not toward the castle, but deeper into the woods.

"Where are you going?" Grae called, easily keeping pace beside me.

I glanced over my shoulder at him. "To get my dagger."

WE RACED INTO THE SILENT HALL, SHOVING THROUGH A WALL of darkness. Trails of smoke swirled from snuffed-out candles. Heavy clouds obscured the windows, leaving only the eerie green glow haloing one figure.

Sawyn, sorceress and unlawful ruler of Olmdere.

She was surprisingly young, appearing to be even younger than me, even though the earliest stories of her were from when my parents first met many decades ago. She had a tall, slender posture with smooth skin as pale as starlight, and bloodred hair. Her eyes glowed an unearthly green as flickering emerald magic seeped from her. Luminous tendrils of power reached out toward the cowering crowd. Her obsidian robes floated on an invisible breeze as she slowly stepped toward a person at the far end of the hall.

Everyone crouched and shielded their eyes apart from the object of her attention, frozen in a trance in front of her.

Briar.

My sister's eyes filled with magical light, a shimmering, vicious green. Briar's expression was utterly vacant as she lifted her hand out to Sawyn.

A scream tore through my chest and I unsheathed my dagger, blindly running. Grae charged forward by my side. Sawyn looked over her shoulder, her thin brow arching into a peak. With a flick of her hand as if shooing a fly, we flew across the room. My stomach lurched. That iridescent magic circled my legs and wrists, slamming me into the unyielding stone wall and pinning me there. I thrashed against her bindings, but they did not budge.

Sawyn let out a throaty laugh. Her voice was elegant and deep, like the woody notes of a lute. "Ah, Prince Grae, I wondered where you'd scuttled off to. Such a heroic entrance, you should take notes, Nero." She darted a glare between me and where the King hid behind his throne. "Even your servant has more spine than you."

Servant. She didn't know I was a Wolf, let alone the child of her sworn enemies. Her ghostly eyes scanned me from the muddied hem of my plain brown tunic to the amber stone hanging from my neck. "A protection stone." Her eyebrows lifted in amusement. "We shall see."

She turned her attention back to Briar, whose hand froze in midair, waiting for Sawyn to return. Desperately flailing, I tried to break my restraints as I bellowed my voiceless screams. Whatever magic held me to the wall had silenced me. The harder I strained, the more my eyes blackened.

I darted pleading glances around the room to the pack, but not a single one moved.

Cowards! I wanted to scream. If they all charged forward at once, they could overtake her. Her magic couldn't keep them all at bay. Would they have fought if it was their king standing before the sorceress instead of my sister? But Briar wasn't their leader, only a token, a symbol—and not even that, anymore, was she? Regardless, a symbol wasn't worth dying for. I thrashed against my magical bindings. Why wasn't the King giving orders? Why wasn't he even trying to save her?

In that moment, I wondered if my father had felt the same way before he died. It was like a strange familiarity of a memory that wasn't my own. We'd lived this moment before—Sawyn striking down the Gold Wolf line, and the other Wolf packs doing nothing to stop it. King Nero had been there the night of my birth. Had he cowered behind his throne then, too? I was certain I knew the answer. It highlighted all the lies he told, the facade of a life he built. Welcoming his new Gold Wolf daughter was nothing more than show. Once again, the Silver Wolves would not lift a finger to help my pack.

Sawyn ignored my voiceless screams as she took Briar's hand and flipped her palm up. With one long, sharpened fingernail, she traced a symbol on Briar's palm.

"Tell me," Sawyn purred. "Who is your one true love?"

Without looking, Briar lifted her free hand and pointed into the darkness.

"Ha! Come." The sorceress laughed as Maez walked forward, her eyes filled with that same hypnotic glow. "So not your prince, after all." She grinned up at the empty throne and the king behind it. "I suppose my magic was wrong, Nero. I thought a Marriel princess was the mate of your son . . ." She sneered over her shoulder at Grae, who remained pinned to the stone beside me. She didn't even bother to look back at me—the Marriel princess who was his fated mate.

"All the better for me." Sawyn snickered. With a flick of her hand, the throne toppled over, revealing more of King Nero's hunched figure. "You will never have a claim on Olmdere, Nero. Your lust for gold has made you too brash, but you're nothing more than a weak, pathetic little puppy. Who was the last Wolf king who actually deserved his throne? I bet we've lost his name to time. This little Gold Wolf will serve as a reminder of who the true power on the continent is. If you do not wish to befall the same fate as her, you will stay out of my kingdom."

With that promise, she pricked her fingernail into Briar's finger and held up a single droplet of blood. Casting her glowing eyes to Briar, she commanded "Sleep, " and Briar dropped like a stone.

My voice shredded as I watched my sister fall, blood vessels bursting in my eyes, and yet no one heard and no one saw.

Once again, I was just my sister's shadow.

"I will be taking your niece with me," Sawyn declared, grabbing Maez by the upper arm. "Just in case you get any ideas about breaking this curse." Spots clouded my vision as the ten-drils of magic retracted. "All that you have, Nero, is because *I* allow it. Remember that."

Darkness pulled in on Sawyn, and, with a whoosh of air, she and Maez vanished.

The moment they disappeared, the magic pinning me to the wall snapped. I collided with the ground, my head cracking on the hard stone. I faintly heard Grae screaming my name over the roar of rushing blood in my ears. I wanted to say something, but my throat was used up. I wanted to go to my sister, but I had no strength. I wanted . . .

The scent of earth and smoke circled me as the darkness pulled me under.

TWELVE

THE SOUND OF WHISPERED, BICKERING VOICES ROUSED ME. A throbbing pain exploded behind my eyes as I squinted into the bright morning light. With a groan, I tenderly touched my bruised temple. Adjusting my thin nightgown, I propped myself up on my elbow. I was in Briar's bed, the one I had lounged upon eating candied almonds less than a day before.

Briar . . .

I gasped, bolting upright and scanning around the room. The horrors of the night before came flooding back to me. Where was Briar? I needed to find her.

My ears rang, a high tinny sound as two growling voices crept from beyond the bedroom door. Blood drained from my face as I identified them—Grae and King Nero.

"There is no way to break the curse," the King snarled. "Maez is either locked in a tower or under a spell herself. The only reason we know she's not dead yet is because the other one lives. There will be no retrieving her."

"She is your niece!" Grae hissed.

"And I grieve her along with the rest of the kingdom."

"We have to go get her," Grae insisted. "We can't just leave her to that sorceress."

"You step one foot in Olmdere and Sawyn and her Rooks

will kill you, Grae," Nero growled. "You are not going. What's done is done. We can still mine the outer reaches of Olmdere in secret. The pack won't question it once you marry that girl."

My hands shook with unrestrained rage. I shot out of bed, snatching the charcoal gray robe hanging over the back of Briar's chair and belting it. I threw open the door and the two men paused.

"Calla," Grae breathed, relief washing over his expression as his eyes narrowed to the bruise on my head.

I glared at the King. "You were never going to help Olmdere, were you?"

Nero chuckled, rolling his eyes. "Why would I do such a foolish thing?"

"Because you swore to my parents." I stormed forward and Grae took a half step between us, putting a steadying hand on my shoulder. "You were meant to be their ally!"

"My allies are dead," King Nero snarled. "The only thing left of their kingdom worth keeping is the gold mines."

I blanched.

"Careful, father," Grae warned.

"Or what?" King Nero lifted his chin with the arrogance of someone who knew they had the upper hand. "I am your king. I've let your leash grow too long, Grae." His cold eyes slid from me to Grae. "Remember your lessons. Remember what I can do." Grae shifted another step in front of me, a growl rumbling in his throat. "Olmdere is gone and so is Maez. The Crimson Princess will never wake from her slumber. You will marry the other one and we will take what is left of our *ally's* resources."

Grae balled his fists, taking a swift step toward his father. I was certain he was about to strike him, threats be damned. I grabbed him by the crook of the arm, forcing him to look at me.

"I want to stab him as much as you," I whispered, holding his eyes as his wrath cooled. "But if you hang, I hang, remember?" I turned to Nero. "Now, where is Briar?"

"We've put her in a room in the eastern tower," the king answered. "Far out of the way."

I gritted my teeth but held Grae's eyes. "Take me to her."

He bobbed his head, giving one more warning look at his father before heading off down the hall.

Tightening the belt on my robe, I followed Grae through the labyrinth of winding halls and spiraling stone staircases. The castle was quiet, the haunted memories of the night before still filling the dreary passageways. Higher and higher, we climbed up the eastern tower until we reached a dusty wooden door.

Grae paused, hand on the handle, as he looked at me. "We will find a way to break this curse."

The door creaked open and tears instantly pricked my eyes at what I saw. Briar lay in her wedding dress upon a stone tomb. Her red hair was still perfectly braided atop her head, her veil flowing over the hard stone. Her lifeless hands clutched her bouquet of wilting white flowers.

My eyes welled at the rise and fall of her chest. She was alive. Numbness spread through my limbs as I drifted toward her.

"Briar," I whispered, resting a hand on her cold cheek. "Wake up." I shook her shoulder. "Please." Tears slipped down my cheeks. "I don't know how to do this without you."

My sister's cold body moved, limp as a rag doll, as I shook her again. It was like looking down upon a piece of my soul, and I remembered what Briar had said in the forest. She and I had always been opposites, but of the same coin. One didn't exist without the other. Her being gone took a part of me, too, and I didn't know who I was if not Briar's twin. Briar would've been the one to know what to do right now, as well-versed in the dances of politics as she was in the waltz. Guilt swarmed through me. I'd failed as her protector. Goddess in the sky, I needed her to wake up.

"How do I fix this?" I cried, shaking her harder, her veil falling askew. "I can't do this without you." My rage boiled over as a sob racked through me and I smacked her hard across the face. My palm stung. "Wake up!"

Strong arms wrapped around me, trying to haul me back. I spun on Grae, shoving him away. He held up his hands as I shoved him harder, ready to absorb all my pain. I shoved him again, his back colliding with the wood door, his face a steely neutral. My hands fisted in his shirt and I slammed him against the door again, and I knew he'd let me shove my grief into him all day long if I needed to.

Another silent sob shook through me and I dropped my hands. As I hung my head, Grae was there, wrapping his arms around me and pulling me into his warm body. I buried my head into his hard chest, shoulders shaking. With each pained cry, he drew me further into him. The moment stretched on as that smoky scent filled my lungs and wrapped around me as tightly as his arms.

"I've got you," he whispered. "We will fix this, Calla. I swear it to you."

My breathing slowed as I curled my arms around him.

"We have to go after Maez," I murmured into his chest. His burgundy tunic stained with tears. "She can break this curse. Sawyn wouldn't have taken her otherwise. We have to fix this."

"We will go after Maez," Grae assured. "But I need time to convince my father that it is the right plan. Rally the rest of the pack to this cause."

"We don't have time." How long would Briar survive like this? A day? A year?

"Time might be all we do have. Maez *is* alive," Grae insisted, glancing over my shoulder. "Sawyn could have just killed her, but she didn't, and that means she's not planning to. But we can't rescue her on our own."

I turned back to my lifeless sister, a fresh bout of tears springing to my eyes again—a well of sorrow that would never run dry. "We can't leave her like this."

"Give me time to work on my father."

Those words snapped the final tether to my rage. Work on his father? He said it as if he'd been successful in the past. But, judging by my icy reception, King Nero would never be swayed by his son.

I pushed off Grae's chest, stepping out of his hold. "I have waited twenty years—my entire life—for promises that your father never intended on upholding." My voice wobbled as Grae reached to wipe my tears. I smacked his hand away. Enough of this charade. "I don't want your comfort."

"To disobey him is more dangerous than you understand," Grae said, some fear-tinged heat in his voice now. "You don't know what you're asking, and I can't do it."

"Can't or won't?"

"The answer is no, Calla." Grae's face was stone. "One day you'll understand I'm doing this to protect you."

Why would I need protection, though? Protection from what? A king who doesn't even recognize me as someone with a name? A witch who doesn't even know of my existence? I didn't need protection—I needed allies. And it was clear there were none to be found amongst the Silver Wolves.

No, nothing would happen, nothing would change, unless I forced it into being. I knew then for certain what I had always known: I'd have to carve out my own path in the world, because no one would clear the way for me . . . not even my mate.

I huffed a bitter laugh, grabbing the amber stone from around my neck and yanking the chain free. "I have no use for your protection nor a mate who's a coward." I threw it at him, watching his shock morph into devastation as it fell to the floor.

I pushed past him and left without another word. He didn't stop me.

Storming through the castle, my heart thundered in my rib cage. I was sick of waiting for the promises of men. I threw open the door to my chambers and hastened to my wardrobe. It was time for me to take charge. I donned my battle leathers and belted my dagger to my waist. I put some changes of clothes into my backpack and looked around to see if there was anything else of use.

Who knew how many days my sister would last before she withered away like the flowers in her hands? How many weeks would the sleeping curse preserve her life without food or drink?

I pushed through the adjoining door to Briar's room, straight to her gem-studded jewelry chest. I grabbed out a pouch of coins from the bottom drawer and a handful of trinkets, shoving them into my heavy pack. That should be enough.

Rescuing Maez would take stealth . . . and the one thing I seemed to be good at was being ignored. The only one who might have tried to prevent me from going was Grae, and I was unsurprised that he chose to obey his father like an obedient little lapdog rather than actually help the person he purportedly loved.

Pulling my hood up, I strode through the castle toward the back gates, not a single servant stopping to question my movements.

THE HAUNTING IMAGE OF BRIAR'S LIFELESS FACE CHASED ME through the forest. My heavy pack bounced with every step and its thin leather straps cut into my shoulders. I heaved ragged breaths, pushing my burning legs to move faster. I needed to get far from Highwick by nightfall.

Doubling back on my steps and passing through the rivers would slow down their hunt—and there was no doubt that when the moon rose in the sky, the pack would come for me. I was the mate of their prince . . . and a deserter. Wolves didn't leave their pack. Desertion was usually a death sentence, but at least I knew they couldn't kill me since I was tied to Grae. Nero needed me, too, to legitimize his theft of Olmderian gold.

They'd track me, though. Drag me back to Highwick, stuff me in a wedding dress, and once the vows were done, they'd lock me up in that castle and never think of me again except maybe to let Grae try to sire some litters with me. I shuddered at the thought of him even touching me now. This is the only role I'd be allowed, my whole being reduced to my ability to give the King heirs. I gritted my teeth wondering how many years would Grae promise and plead to fix things before he gave up? How long before the fire inside him died?

I slogged through another murky creek. My boots hung by their laces from my pack, my trousers rolled up to the knee. Barefoot, I could sense the earth below my feet. It also meant I could keep my boots dry for when I reached the next town.

The white summits of the Stormcrest Ranges towered above me, signaling the Taigos border, home of the Ice Wolves. This northern part of Damrienn was a mystery to me. I had never thought to study the little towns scattered throughout the forests here, since I always assumed I'd go straight from Damrienn to Olmdere. That wasn't an option now—I needed some distance and needed to go in the least likely direction. But I knew the Stormcrest Ranges were vicious, with icy gales and unpredictable blizzards. There would be no going straight over them into Taigos. I needed to get through the mountain pass before the Silver Wolves did or they'd block my only way through.

The wind whipped through the trees and the hours wore on at a slow human clip. My Wolf would've made quick work of this terrain, but then I'd have to leave my backpack behind. I could carry a few things in my mouth for a short distance, but I wouldn't make it to Olmdere in my Wolf form. All Wolf palaces had changing rooms for travelers—stocked with spare clothing. They considered it Wolf hospitality, making it much easier to travel the realms than on foot or by horse. The royals and richest Wolves sent their servants ahead with their belongings so they wouldn't need to borrow clothes. But I wasn't going anywhere near a Wolf home, so I'd be stranded naked if I shifted.

I imagined Briar shouting at me even now: What in the Gods' names are you doing?

"I'm saving you . . . and our kingdom," I said aloud to the quiet forest.

I stared down at my dagger. If I stayed, Briar would be locked in that room forever while Grae's father pilfered gold from my homeland. I couldn't go back, couldn't exist in the world without her if I knew there was a chance she could be saved.

That kiss Grae and I shared buzzed through my mind, and I hated the traitorous thought, especially since I couldn't dismiss it. It had almost been more than a kiss. I cringed, thinking of how I'd let that lust override my logic. The Wolf in me wanted him, I told myself, that was all. It was the magic of the mating bond that made me dizzy every time he was near. He might care for me, love me even, but it was all just magic. Love wasn't born from moments of passion, or whispered promises, but from actions. Grae's vows of love meant nothing if he was willing to watch me rot away in that castle. Doing hard things, making hard choices—that was love.

Putting distance between us made me feel stronger and weaker all at once. I snarled at the Wolf who kept playing over and over in her head what that kiss could've turned into. The way he snarled into my mouth when his hand skimmed my ass . . .

"Get a grip," I growled to myself, startling the birds from the trees.

My eyes caught on the kicked-up leaves beside me. The little dips perfectly placed into the stride of footsteps. A human had been in these woods. I followed the steps, sniffing the air.

There. The scent of worn leather and musk—a woodsman of some sort. He didn't have the distinctive smell of a Wolf, not that I'd expect him to. Wolves kept to their packs . . . except for me, but the Silver Wolves were never truly my pack. My only pack-mate was half dead in a foreign castle.

I followed the woodsman's trail. The scent of smoked meats filled the air as a thin track appeared. My stomach clenched, a rumble of hunger shaking through me. The trail opened up into a small clearing with a log cabin in the center. The cabin was unkempt, shutters hanging on by one nail and the weeds climbing the walls. Were it not for the trail of thick smoke billowing from the chimney, I would've assumed it was abandoned.

Clothing flapped on a line strung from a window to a nearby ash tree. Perfect. I'd need some less conspicuous clothing. Wearing my shined battle leathers would draw too much suspicion. I crept up to the line—mostly sheets, but I snagged the wool socks before the front door snapped open. I ducked down behind the swaying curtain of blankets.

"Alice? Is that you?" a crotchety voice called.

I peeked up at the swaying aprons and worn dresses. So this woodsman wasn't alone. I waited until I heard the door shut and nicked the woman's clothing off the line. I grabbed a coin from my pocket and left it on the ground, hoping they'd find it.

I stood tiptoeing back toward the safety of the forest when I heard the faint scratch of a bowstring being tightened. I whirled to find a pair of brown eyes watching me in the woods.

"You must be Alice," I murmured, taking in the middle-aged woman and the bow in her hands. I smelled the blood before I spotted the kills at her feet, the brown fur popping up from where she dropped them in the leaves. Rabbits, I suspected.

"And you must be a thief," she hissed, pulling her bowstring tighter.

"Wait! Wait," I pleaded, dropping her clothes and holding up my hands. "I left a coin and-and . . ."

"Leaving coins doesn't mean you can just steal from me." Her eyes scanned me from the top of my head to my bare feet. "You've been stealing from the capital, too, I see." She chuckled at the royal brocade on the sleeves of the tunic beneath my leather vest. "You can't fool me into thinking you're a Wolf just because you wear their crest."

I narrowed my eyes at her. Maybe I didn't have to try so hard to rid myself of these clothes after all. No one believed who I was anyway. Wolves were tall and lean and elegant . . . I was none of those things.

I trained my eyes back to her arrowhead. "I'm sorry. I didn't know what else to do."

She paused and lowered her weapon, clearly thinking I wasn't much of a threat. "Who are you running from?"

"Someone I can't let find me" was all I said, still holding up my hands.

"Aye. Skin chasers." She pursed her lips and I didn't correct her. "I've been there myself when I was your age."

"Who is this?" the man's voice boomed from the doorway.

I didn't turn to look at him, still watching Alice and her fingers stroking the fletching of her arrow.

"It's just a lost girl," Alice called to him.

I bit down on my snarl at the word "girl." Correcting someone who was about to shoot me with an arrow seemed like a bad idea.

"Lost all the way out here?"

"I'll point her the right way, Logan."

She put the arrow back in her quiver, and my stomach dropped, thinking of Grae and our secret words. *Quiver.* I almost wanted to laugh at my naïveté, thinking we could carry on like we had when we were young. I felt the loss of that childhood friend all over again.

"She doesn't want to come in for supper?" Logan offered.

"No," Alice snapped. "Go on inside, Logan." The door shut again and Alice folded her arms. "If you had just knocked on the door, we would've helped you, but I can't blame you for thinking otherwise. Sounds like you've been given plenty of reasons not to trust."

Her eyes drifted over my face, landing on my bruised neck where Sawyn's power had strangled me and my temple where it had cracked into the stone floor. She'd come to the wrong conclusions, but she wasn't entirely incorrect. Grae's father had given me plenty of reasons not to trust him.

"Follow the path." She hooked her thumb behind her. "You'll reach a wider trail with red markers. Ignore the white ones, those will lead you astray. Follow the red to Pinewood Valley. There's an inn there called The Broken Fiddle." She untied a bit of fletching from her arrow, passing the indigo feather to me. "Tell them Alice and Logan sent you, and they'll give you a room for the night."

I twirled the feather in my fingers, reaching into my pocket to grab another coin. Alice's weathered hand covered my own, staying my movement.

"Take the clothes and keep your coin," she said.

I furrowed my brow. "Why are you helping me?"

"Because no one did when I was you," she murmured. "Just do me a favor? If it ever comes down to you or them. Make sure it's them."

I blinked at her. She spoke with an undercurrent of pain I felt as acutely as my own.

We stared at each other for one more moment—strangers, only sharing a handful of minutes together. And yet, I was certain I would never forget her face or her gruff sort of kindness.

"I promise."

THIRTEEN

I CHANGED INTO ALICE'S CLOTHES BEFORE JOINING THE WIDER trail, shoving my leathers into my bag. I doubled back in the wrong direction to discard my silver sash, hoping it might throw the pack off my trail . . . but if they had followed me that far, they would surely search Pinewood Valley. I hoped the pack wouldn't descend on Alice and Logan's home, that I hadn't inadvertently put them in the line of attack. It was an actual worry—no one got between a Wolf and their pack. But there was nothing to be done for it now.

Pinewood Valley was just as its name suggested—the little town nestled between two steep hills of evergreen trees. The long, narrow line of houses led up toward the Stormcrest foothills. With steep sloping roofs and houses perched on stilts, this town clearly weathered heavy snow in the winters. I squinted up toward the sun setting over the mountain peaks. When I reached the summits towering above, it would be winter still.

I paced down the trail into town, the wear of grueling winters evident even in the midst of summer. Wildflowers grew in a blanket down the lane, beautiful shades of reds and yellows, making the most of the brief summer months. The shadow of the mountain crept across the town as the evening sun fell from the sky. As I ventured into the shade, I felt that strange pull toward

the snowy peaks and what lay beyond them. This was the closest I had ever been to my homeland. Beyond the snow-covered
ranges of Taigos, Olmdere waited, a ghost kingdom for twenty
long years.

A few townspeople stopped to give me a quick look before
carrying on. In Alice's dress and apron, I seemed like just another
traveler passing through—probably a bar wench or laundry girl
moving to the next town for work.

The Broken Fiddle sat at the end of the main road next to a
battered stable and paddocks of burnt yellow grass. I entered,
and my eyes strained to adjust in the dimness of the windowless
room. It wasn't the boisterous banter I expected from a tavern
based on the stories Vellia told us. No roaring drunks sitting at
the bar or clamorous music bouncing off the low ceilings. Rather,
a few small groups gathered around tables, their hushed conversations stalling as they looked up at me.

"You looking for a meal or a room?" the barman called. He
threw a towel over his shoulder and walked to the end of the bar.

I warily approached. A few patrons craned their necks to look
at me. I felt all their leering stares, wishing I could evaporate into
the air.

"Both, if possible." I held out the indigo feather to him. "Alice said to give this to you."

His eyebrows raised as he looked between me and the feather.
He rubbed a hand over his bald head and said, "All right then."

Simple as that. I looked at him, unsure of what to do. Is this
how all humans treated each other? They wouldn't be so kind if
they knew I was a Wolf.

"What would you like to eat?" he asked, pocketing the
feather.

"Um . . ." What did Vellia always say the taverns served? "Do
you have stew?"

The barman chuckled, pointing to the board behind him.
"The menu's up there."

My cheeks burned as I glanced up at the chalkboard. The

tavern in Allesdale only served one thing, and if you didn't want it, you didn't eat. I was woefully underprepared for this journey. How was I going to defeat a sorceress when I couldn't even order food?

"Sorry, it's been a long day." I rubbed my forehead.

"If you've come all the way from Alice and Logan's then you must be exhausted," the barman mused. It was probably a big trek for humans, but my body was stronger and faster, even in this form. Yet I *was* tired, so I was glad for his empathy in the moment. He turned and grabbed a key off the hook, sliding it across the bar to me. "Go rest. I'll have them send something up. A pretty thing like you shouldn't be around these oafs anyways."

My cheeks burned as I dropped my eyes. It was equal parts compliment and warning.

"Thank you," I said, picking up the key.

I tried to ignore the looks from the patrons as I hastened toward the stairs. They were probably just curious, but my heart hammered as if each one might discover I was a Wolf. Nero would pay for my location—Sawyn, too, if she knew I existed.

The floorboards creaked as I treaded down the shadowed hall. I peeked at the number 8 on my key and the corresponding numbers on the doors. The key would probably match the door, at least that bit made sense. One puzzle solved, there still seemed to be so many things that people knew how to do that I'd never been taught.

Arriving at the eighth door, a sense of dread made me peek back over my shoulder . . . but no one was there. I entered the small room and turned the lock, checking it twice before stepping toward the bed. My bag landed on the floor with a thunk and I collapsed onto the hard mattress, barely taking in the humble dwelling. Days without sleep made me feel boneless and hollow. The nerves and panic finally ebbed, forced into the back of my weary mind. I needed to rest before I could even begin to process the roiling storm of emotions brewing inside me. Before, falling asleep had always been a choice, but now it was a deep-seated need.

A light rap on the door made me groan. I didn't want to get back on my feet after hours of trekking, but I forced myself up. Stabbing pains shot through my tired feet. I hobbled to the door and opened it, finding a maid with a tray.

"Your food, ma'am," she said, holding out the tray without looking me in the eye.

I muttered my thanks, resting the tray on my forearm and relocking the door. Setting the tray of food on the bed, I lay down beside it. The silence pushed in on me and my body demanded rest. I only managed to eat a few bites of bread before sleep claimed me.

I WOKE UP IN A POOL OF DROOL. RUBBING MY HAND DOWN MY wet cheek, I glanced at the tray of cold food. Moonlight filtered in through the window, the pull of the moon rousing me from my stupor. I had barely shifted on the night of the full moon. My Wolf still owed the Goddess her prayers, and the demand for payment tugged on my soul.

Shifting under the full moon was remittance for our gifts. We had strength and speed, incredible senses and quick healing, but the moon required penance. I moved to the edge of the bed, skirting the tray of abandoned food. I popped a cold roasted potato into my mouth and grimaced. It would have to do. My legs throbbed from the long hike and the blisters on my toes stung against the cool air.

I stumbled toward the windowsill and stared up at the moon. If I shifted, my legs would heal, and I'd be ready for the long journey when the sun rose. I needed fresh air and moonlight more than ever. My Wolf was strong. She'd know what to do.

I pulled up the window and stared down at the ground below. Wildflowers and brambles covered the back of the tavern, spilling into the forest. I leapt from the window into the bushes; the rush making my stomach drop. The sensation made me miss my favorite oak tree in Allesdale. Briar would've laughed at me—to miss a tree, of all things.

The rest of the second-floor windows were dark. No one peered out onto the overgrown patch of earth behind the inn where I stood. Rowdy chatter rang out from the front of the building, along with the tunes of a flute and drum. The inn must've come alive while I slept. There seemed little to do in this town at night other than drink and gather with friends.

I crept into the tree line, welcoming the darkness. Trekking through the underbrush, I got far enough that the faint lights of the inn faded away, until only the light of the moon guided me.

Sniffing the air, I checked one last time that no one was near. All I smelled was damp earth and pine. I sighed, whipping Alice's dress over my head and hanging it on a low branch. My undergarments clung to me with dried sweat. I peeled them off, wrinkling my nose. There were more pairs in my pack. I'd wash these in the next town, since they wouldn't dry in time before I would need to be on the move again. I couldn't wait for things like laundry, though. Making it through the mountain pass was my highest priority. Once I got into Taigos, I could disappear until I was ready to go after Maez and save my sister.

The evening air swirled around my cool skin as I stepped into a pool of moonlight. The change racked through me the instant the light touched my skin. I groaned as though stretching a sore muscle, feeling the familiar pop and strain as my spine twisted and I dropped to all fours. My groan morphed into a low snarl as my paws hit the earth. Strength and calm radiated through my limbs. I didn't feel outside the world anymore.

I prowled off into the pine forest, a slow walk at first as I investigated my surroundings, then breaking out into a sprint. I raced up the hillside. The thrill of my pumping muscles and the wind in my fur made all my sorrows feel as distant as the twinkling lights of the village below. I thought about the stale meal on my bed and decided I'd hunt in my Wolf form tonight instead.

If I had a pack, I could probably take down a stag, but on my own I'd settle for a hare or squirrel. I just needed to fill my belly and make my sacrifices to the moon. The search didn't take long, the creatures of this forest unused to being hunted.

As I licked the blood from my maw, I felt a strange spark within me. My ears twitched, searching for the sound as the rest of me went still.

"Calla?" a voice whispered.

I whirled, but no one was there. The voice echoed in the recesses of my mind. My gut clenched. It was Grae's voice.

"How?" I asked. How close was he that he could speak into my mind? As Wolves we used to test it, see how far we could go before that bond would snap. The last time I'd tried with him, it had only been the length of the Allesdale woods before his words grew so faint I couldn't hear them anymore.

Now, I couldn't smell or sense him in any other way. Had he followed me this far already?

"Thank the fucking Moon." I could feel the relief in Grae's voice rattle through me. "Are you okay?"

"How are you in my mind?" I began trotting back down the hillside, unsettled by this connection. Maybe he'd be able to use it to find me.

"You're my mate," Grae rumbled, his claiming words making a thrill run through me even as I ran from them. "Our Wolves are linked always."

My heart sank. Even my Wolf wasn't an escape anymore. I couldn't pretend to leave it all behind with Grae still in my head.

"Where are you?" he asked.

So he didn't know. Good. I raced faster back toward the inn, needing to get rid of him. I couldn't go back.

"Don't come after me."

"Calla—"

"Don't," I snapped. "I'm going to fix this on my own. I'm gone, Grae."

"Then let me go with you," he pleaded, his voice edging on panic.

I leapt over a fallen log, hurdling downhill so fast I nearly stumbled even on my stealthy Wolf paws.

"No," I said. "You are a prince. You have a duty to your pack—"

"Fuck my pack."

I sucked in a breath at his reckless proclamation. No one said that. Ever. The pack was all that mattered. Individuals died, but the pack lived on, and now Grae and I both were flirting with that very dangerous line.

"You don't mean that," I said.

"I do," he seethed. "I should've said it before. You're my *mate*, Calla. Nothing else matters without you. If you die, I die. My life is your life. We are one now."

The lights of the inn flickered through the dark forest. I was getting close. "You'll drag me back to Highwick."

"I'm not my father," Grae gritted out. "I would never do that to you. To anyone."

"But *he* will," I insisted. "He will force your hand, Grae. You can't help me and stay loyal to him. He is your *King*. He'll kill us both for your disobedience."

That was if I hadn't signed our death sentence already by fleeing myself. I was meant to pledge my loyalty to King Nero that night, but I ran. If Grae came with me, he'd be picking sides. I'd take away his family, his pack, and ultimately his life.

I didn't trust him in the moment, but I also couldn't bear to think of him dead, either.

"Twenty years, little fox." His voice filled with barely leashed restraint. I could feel him in every corner of my body, straining to control it. "I didn't want the crown or the glory or any of it. There's only one thing that ever mattered to me, and now I finally understand why."

My chest heaved. I pictured his tortured expression, knowing exactly the crease of his forehead and slope of his eyebrows. Even in my defiance, I wished I could soothe away that torment.

But I couldn't go back.

Olmdere lay in ruin under the wrath of a sorceress, and Briar lay alone in that tower. I couldn't go back and live out my days as if she wasn't there. I refused to walk by the stairwell that led to her room day in and day out until time and practice made me stop caring that she was there. I wouldn't abandon her like that.

I spotted my discarded dress on the tree in front of me. My paw hovered in the air as I debated what to say. Tell him he always mattered to me, too? That would only spur him on. But I couldn't lie to him, either.

Pain lanced through me again as I began to shift. "Goodbye, Grae."

"No!"

FOURTEEN

THE SOUND OF GRAE'S SHOUTS DISAPPEARED AS THE BOND SEV-ered. My hands trembled as I returned to my human form. The things he had said . . . they hurt. My blisters were healed and my legs felt strong, but my heart still ached. Nothing in me felt right.

I snatched the dress off the branch and pulled it over my head with a huff when the snap of a stick made me freeze. I peered over at a tree at the edge of the forest. A man leaned against it, reliev-ing himself as he whistled. I curled my lip as I crouched down behind the sparse bushes.

He wouldn't spot me in the shadows. His eyes were still trained to the bright tavern lights. I waited as he buttoned his trousers, ignoring the rustle of leaves behind me until it was too late.

"What's a fair maiden doing alone in these woods?" a deep voice called from above me. I shot up, turning to see two men emerging from the other side of the clearing. This drunken man hadn't been alone.

"Waiting for a lover?" the larger man behind him jeered.

They were both incredibly tall, nearly twice my size. Their faces hid in shadow, but I could make out their silhouettes. I stumbled, my back colliding with the tree trunk. As the third man approached from the other side, the three of them circled me like wildcats.

Think. I could shift and outrun them easily, but that would reveal my identity, and then Grae would be back in my head. Within an hour, everyone would know there was a Wolf in the village . . . and then King Nero would come looking for me.

No. I'd have to fight them in my human form.

I wished I had thought to bring my dagger or even my knife into the woods. In my exhaustion, I hadn't thought about anything but shifting. I wasn't as helpless as I might have looked, though. I pushed a little of my Wolf magic into my muscles. My eyes dilated and I could make out their shapes in finer detail.

"Go back to the tavern," I said, trying to sound neutral. It was a delicate balance with drunken men, one I'd only had a few occasions to practice in Allesdale. Be too aggressive, and it would provoke them. Be too sweet . . . and it would provoke them. They were just as temperamental and brutish as the Wolves in that regard.

"I think we could have more fun out here," the tall one said, taking another step toward me.

"I can promise you, you won't," I snarled. "Look, I've had a really bad few days and I have no patience left."

The first man chuckled, reaching out for me. The second his hand landed on my shoulder, I grabbed it and twisted, forcing him to drop his face forward until I could smash my forehead into his nose.

"You bitch," he hissed as the two other men rushed toward me.

"You have no idea." I laughed, kicking one in the knee and elbowing the other.

The one behind me snatched the waist of my dress, yanking me to the side. I stumbled, throwing out a punch but missing as I caught myself. Beefy arms circled around me, pinning my arms to my sides. I threw my head back, hoping to hit his nose, but it only smacked into his chest. He coughed but didn't let go.

A fist collided with the side of my face, then another hand smacked back in the other direction. My ears rang, their laughter muffled as I kicked out. My foot landed on the leg of the man in front of me, shifting his weight enough that it blunted the force of the next blow to my mouth.

I spat blood. Enough of this. I needed to stop fighting like a human. I turned my head into the bicep that snaked around me and bit down.

The man screamed as I thrashed my head back and forth, shredding his clothing and pulling muscles from bone. With a yowl of pain, he released me, and I dropped to the ground. I sprang forward, taking out the legs of the tallest man. He landed hard, head smacking into a rock. I didn't wait to see if he survived the blow as I barreled into the man with the broken nose, snarling as I pummeled my fists into him.

"Help!" he shouted as blood poured from his nose.

I was about to help him learn a lesson he'd never forget.

It didn't matter how big or tall he was when he was lying flat on the ground. My knuckles split, but I didn't stop, the pain urging me onward. I thought hunting would fix it, but my Wolf's rage wasn't sated.

The one I had bitten grabbed me again, trying to pry me off his barely conscious friend. The other lay lifeless, blood trailing down the rock beneath his head.

I whipped around as the last man hauled me back to my feet. He flinched, lifting his one good arm in surrender. The stench of urine stained his trousers.

"Who are you?"

I panted, wiping the blood from the corner of my mouth and smiling. I knew he could barely see my outline, but with my vision I saw the whites of his wide frightened eyes.

"I am a monster lurking in the shadows," I purred. "Worse than any ostekke or ebarven. And if you ever think about laying a hand on someone again, I will be there. Tell your friends to think twice . . . if they survive."

I spat more blood onto the ground and stalked off around the side of the building. Throwing back my shoulders, I raised my chin, trying to be as regal as Briar. I'd be swollen with bruises, but I didn't dare shift again—not here, anyway. That was a much closer call than I'd let on. I needed to grab my things and find a way out of this town before people came looking for who did this to them. If I was lucky, their pride would get the better of them and they'd say it was a bear attack. Either way, I couldn't stick around. No more foolish mistakes.

I WIPED MY NOSE WITH THE BACK OF MY HAND. DRIED BLOOD stained the front of my dress brown . . . and it wasn't only my blood. I'd left the inn through the window once more and headed up the main road out of town. The crickets and hooting owls silenced as I passed, waiting until I prowled away before striking up their nighttime chorus. I felt the moon's watchful eye, seeing my grimy garments and hair clotted with blood. With each step uphill, the air thinned, growing frostier by the minute.

My backpack tugged on my shoulders, my briefly healed feet blistering again on the dusty road. How could humans stand being so fragile, I wondered tiredly. I didn't know how many hours I had slept at the inn. Not enough.

My throat was scratchy and my eyes swollen as I stared up at her—the mother Goddess in the nighttime sky who hears us all.

"Do you still watch over Briar?" I whispered to her. "Do you still speak to her in her dreams?"

A tear slipped down my cheek, the salt stinging my cuts.

"Those white roses are probably brown now." I sniffed, wiping my scratchy woolen sleeve under my eyes. The thoughts that had swarmed my mind came spilling out even as I choked on my words. "I wish it was me. Briar deserves to be a part of this world. She was *meant* to be a part of it. I was never planned, never wanted. It should be me lying cold on that tomb." Cold air slid over my bottom teeth and I gulped a pained breath. "She would've had a plan. She would've told me what I needed to do to fix this." I stared up through watery eyes at the glowing moon. "I can't just fight my way out of this. But that's all I know. What do I do now?

"Who am I supposed to be without her?"

Tears trailed over my lips as I tried to regain my composure. It was true. I had always taken my cue from Briar. Whatever she was, I was the opposite—if she liked sweets, I only wanted savory. If she wore pastels, I wore earth tones. If she wanted to be the center of attention, I wanted to be a shadow. I always knew how to be by looking at her. Who would I be if I had to decide on my own? I couldn't put my finger on why, there were no words to describe it, but none of my options felt right.

I imagined Briar walking beside me, her breath fogging the evening air as we both stared out at the dark forest. If she appeared right now, I wouldn't question it—it would only feel right. She was supposed to be here with me.

I reached out with my senses as if I might be able to feel her. I always knew when she was close, but now I felt nothing.

Just me. Only me.

A building appeared on the side of the road, and my eyes widened.

No, not a building, a wagon.

It had giant wheels, taller than me, and a towering canvas roof. I crept closer, not seeing a single flicker of candlelight. Whoever owned this monstrous wagon appeared to be asleep. Colorful ribbons streamed along the side windows in a riot of color. Carved wood wrapped around the back door leading into the wagon's back cabin. Painted musical notes danced along the wood.

What strange sort of traveler lived here?

It didn't matter, so long as they were leaving town.

I snuck to where two dusty leather trunks hung on either side of the folded-up stairs. With deft fingers, I raised the rusting latch and lifted the heavy lid. I placed my pack in first, wedging it between stacks of balled fabrics and leather bags. I clambered in and pulled the hessian cover back over my head.

It was a strange load of wares. Clothiers perhaps? The thick wad of canvas beside me felt more like tenting fabric. Maybe they were stall holders at a country fair? Judging by the cobwebs, these bags didn't get taken out often, and I hoped their owners would ride out of town without checking them.

Curling into a ball, I settled my swollen cheek against the rough fabric. I felt for the front pocket of my pack, untying it and grabbing out my knife.

"Goddess, bless me this night," I whispered. "Grant me safe passage through the mountains."

I lifted my chin to the sky beyond the sealed lid, and the cuts along my neck stung at the movement. I prayed that the night was calm and that I could get a few more hours' sleep to prepare for whatever lay ahead. I clutched my knife to my chest as my eyes fluttered closed.

FIFTEEN

I HELD IN ANOTHER SNEEZE. THE WHEELS KICKED UP SO MUCH dust it was unbearable. I jostled back and forth, being shoved side to side as the wagon bumped over the rocky terrain. We'd been riding uphill all morning. My legs shook from bracing myself against the trunk's side. My ribs smarted with each bounce and shudder. Finally, I relented and just let the wagon tousle me about.

The rocking slowed, the driver called to someone, and then the wagon halted. I clutched the hilt of my knife tighter. My ears strained, still ringing from the attack the night before.

"All right then," a warm voice said. They spoke in Valtan, the language of the Onyx Wolf kingdom. But the accent was distinctly human, not as formal or lilting as the Wolves' tongue. "Who are ya?"

The lid lifted and the hessian above my head peeled back. Shielding my eyes, I squinted against the bright sunlight. The human hovered over me, cocking their head like a curious pup. Their eyes scanned my face, widening at my wounds. It must've looked pretty bad then.

"Hello," they said, touching their fingers to their forehead. "What's your name?"

"My name's . . . Calla." I considered lying, but no one knew that name.

My Valtan was a garbled mess. Vellia had trained us in all four languages of the continent, but the Onyx Wolf kingdom's language was the hardest to comprehend.

"Beautiful name," they said. "I'm Ora, palizya of this home."

Palizya. It roughly translated to "owner," but the Valtan word was reserved for those who were neither man nor woman, and used the -ya endings to their titles. Though the humans spoke the same languages as the Wolves in their kingdoms, they had many more words that Wolves were forbidden to use. Valta had eight different words for gender, but the Onyx Wolves, like all Wolves, only ever used two. It was just another way the Wolves and humans were different, even when they lived in the same lands.

"Hi," I said, grimacing as I sheepishly lowered my knife.

Ora swept their maroon scarf over their shoulder and extended a hand out to me. I'd seen no one like them before. They had dark hair that fell in waves around their shoulders. Permanent smile lines etched into their brown skin. Kohl lined their dark bronze eyes, red paint covered their lips, and dark stubble covered their jaw.

I took Ora's hand and stepped out of the luggage compartment. Dusting myself off, I looked warily at them, wondering if they were going to strike me or scold me.

"Don't worry." Ora chuckled. "You would be far from the first to stow away on this wagon. That's how we found half our crew."

I furrowed my brow, looking through the open doorway to the high fabric ceiling of the wagon. I hadn't had time to appreciate the sheer size of it the night before, and that's when I had even first mistaken it for a house. It was easily two stories high, taller than any tavern I'd seen. Rows of shelves and ladders lined the walls. A loft sat at the far end and below it were cushion-covered trunks circled around a table turned into a makeshift seating area. To the right, curtains sectioned off the back half of the wagon. Not a single spot was bare, the space crammed with trinkets, plants, and exotic fabrics.

"Welcome to Galen den' Mora." Ora waved their hand around the space and I realized I was still gaping.

Galen den' Mora. It meant "a wandering song."

"You're musicians?" I asked, spotting the hard leather cases on one shelf beside a tray of resin and baskets of broken strings.

"What gave us away?" Ora smirked. "Do you play? We're heading up to Nesra's Pass. I'm guessing you're headed toward Taigos, too?"

My lip stung as I gave a half-smile and nodded. I'd have to pass through the Ice Wolf kingdom to get to Olmdere, and now it seemed I might have a way to do that.

"You can ride with the rest of us in the lower cabin." Ora beckoned, their jewelry clinking together with each movement. "Unless you prefer to ride in a trunk?" They smiled wide as I shook my head no. "Didn't think so. Let's meet the others— Navin is driving the oxen in the front."

I clenched my hands in my pockets. I wanted to trust them, but after the past few days, the feeling of my knife comforted me. Ora led me into the wagon, pulling back the curtains to the sunken seating area.

Two sets of gray eyes watched me under thick, long lashes.

"Ha!" The one on the right barked out a laugh, throwing cards down onto the chest. "I knew we'd get a stowaway in Pine-wood."

The one across from her wore a matching red satin dress, both with low-scooped necks and a thin golden belt under their busts in the Rikeshi style—the largest of the floating islands of Valta. They each had thick brunette hair tied back with red ribbons, bright gray eyes, and brown skin. Mirrors of each other, they even sat in the same position.

"This is Mina and Malou." Ora gestured to them. "The newest additions to Galen den' Mora."

"We've been with you for three years." Malou scoffed. "There's nothing new about us. We've been everywhere on the continent together."

Mina put her finger to the corner of her mouth in gesture to her sister.

"Ah yes. Nearly," Malou said, nodding to her twin. "Once we get to Olmdere, then we can claim that."

My ears perked up as I dropped onto the couch beside Malou. "You're going to Olmdere?"

"Haven't you heard?" Ora's voice dropped to a whisper as they leaned across the chest. "Sawyn has found the last Gold Wolf."

My heart punched into my chest. "What?"

"We found out last night," Malou said, her lips stretching into a mischievous grin.

The news had spread that fast?

"They say she placed the Crimson Princess under a sleeping curse," Ora said.

"How wicked," Malou added with a chuckle. "The same fate as her mother. Though I doubt true love's kiss will save this Marriel."

I frowned at her. It was just a bit of gossip to them. Sawyn's actions were just stories to tell around a campfire. The tales of the sorceress had once felt that distant even to me, but now . . . The image burned into my mind of Briar's vacant face as Sawyn's magic cursed her. Those same bolts of power had killed my father, I knew, but it hadn't felt real until that moment. These weren't some tall tales. Dark magic was real and real people were hurt by it.

"So you're going to Olmdere because she cursed the princess?" I tried to hide the haunted hollowness in my voice. Maybe they'd think it was just nerves, being in this strange new space.

"Sawyn is planning weeks of festivities to celebrate her victory." Ora leaned back against the patchwork of colorful cushions. "The borders to Olmdere are finally open. Entertainers from all over will flock to the capital. And seeing as we're heading through Taigos anyway . . ." They grinned at me.

"Who better to play for the sorceress with mountains of

gold?" Malou asked, tossing her ponytail over her shoulder. "I doubt there are any talented musicians left in Olmdere. It has been a wasteland these last twenty years. There will be no competition."

My stomach soured. The curse had just been cast and Sawyn was already planning her victory celebrations. I squeezed my palm around my knife in my pocket as I glanced between the three musicians. Her arrogance was astounding. Why had the sorceress made the demise of my family her personal joy? Why not Taigos or Valta? Why did Olmdere have to bear the brunt of her dark magic?

"Are you looking for another player?" I asked, watching Ora's face light up. Maybe sneaking into my family's castle would be easier than I thought.

"Ah, so you do play," Ora said. "I can always tell."

"I don't know any instruments, but I can sing," I offered. "I've always wanted to see Olmdere . . . and there's nothing for me in Damrienn."

The three of them exchanged knowing glances. It wasn't a lie, but I'd let them come to their own conclusions.

Malou leaned her elbows onto her knees. "They say the trees in the Sevelde forest are made of solid gold."

Mina rolled her eyes, signing back to her sister.

"They could be!" Malou turned to her. "Have you ever been to Sevelde? No. How many gritas if I'm right?"

"It won't matter how many gritas if the trees are truly made of gold," Ora guffawed. The rings circling their fingers clinked as they clapped their hands together. "A single branch would make us rich as kings . . . but then, we would've seen at least one of these gilded leaves around Aotreas by now. I'm fairly certain the trees are simply of a golden hue."

"Even if Sawyn pays us a few gold crovers, it'll be enough to feed us for a year." Malou lifted her mug of tea in mock salute. "We don't need the trees at all, not in the capital of the Gold Wolf kingdom. It is said the Marriel castle was built on an island of gold coins, that they flooded the basin around them so that none would discover their treasure. Perhaps we should go for a swim in that lake to find out?"

Mina signed something again and I quirked my brow at her, realizing I wasn't as well-versed in the languages of Aotreas as I thought. Why had we never been taught this one?

"You better keep in line," Ora said, nodding in agreement with Mina. "Sawyn's Rooks are a vicious lot."

"Have you seen her Rooks before?" I asked.

"They're rife in Taigos," Malou replied. "Queen Ingrid lets them roam through the Ice kingdom just as they do in Olmdere. They don't seem to follow any codes other than what their sorceress commands."

"Why does the Ice Wolf queen let them in her kingdom?"

"Maybe it's easier than trying to keep them out." Malou shrugged. "Maybe since her kingdom borders Olmdere, she knows that the other kings will use her as a buffer to Sawyn's wrath and she is smarter than to fight Sawyn alone."

I bit the inside of my lip, and Ora patted me on the shoulder.

"Keep your head down, love, and you'll do just fine." They gestured up to a line of velvet curtains. "That bunk is empty or the one over the kitchen."

Mina gestured to the one above her.

"Yeah, take that one," Malou said. "The one by the kitchen always reeks of cooking."

"*Delicious* cooking," Ora said with a feigned scowl.

I chuckled, nodding to the curtained off bunk built into the stacks of shelving. "That one it is."

Ora stood, bracing a hand against the cabinets to keep from wobbling. "You'll get your sea legs, too." They winked at me and climbed the steps to the upper level. Tossing a look over their shoulder, they said, "Welcome to Galen den' Mora, Calla."

"THIS IS DELICIOUS," I HUMMED, EATING ANOTHER SPOONFUL of spiced lentil stew. "I've never seen orange potatoes before."

"Jara," Ora said. "They're native to Valta. Sweet and keep for months."

"These are great, but next time don't overdo it on the spice trying to impress the newcomer." Malou chuckled, tipping her head to the spice rack behind her. Dozens of jars filled the shelf, a rainbow of powdered spices and herbs. "We won't be able to restock until we head southward again."

Ora waved their hand. "Olmdere has plenty to flavor food. Honey, rosemary, ginger . . . We will be fine."

Sitting between Malou and Mina, I gulped down my breakfast . . . or maybe it was dinner? My stomach growled in protest regardless, being stretched full after days on lean rations. Malou reached for the pot in the center of the table and ladled another helping into my bowl.

I studied Ora from across the table—their maroon scarf, their high-waisted trousers that ballooned out in colorful brocade, the fabric-covered buttons that trailed down their billowy shirt . . . Everything about them seemed so free, so unencumbered by the rules with which I'd lived my entire life. I didn't even know someone was allowed to be this way—not that humans needed to seek permission to be all the things they felt inside. I continued shoveling more jara into my mouth but kept peeking at Ora, feeling like a key was being placed in a lock that I was too afraid to turn.

The wagon rattled along the road. Ribbons hanging from the bronzed chandelier swayed above us like prairie grass. I reached up and touched a finger to one ribbon, each one stitched with a trail of little badges in various shapes: suns, swords, animals, food . . .

"What are these?" I traced a finger over the embroidered badge in the shape of a candle.

"There's one for each of the people who have called Galen den' Mora home," Ora said, rubbing their thumb over the nearest ribbon. "You should think about what you want your badge to look like. A songbird perhaps?"

"You'd have to pick a new color." Malou huffed, dipping a

piece of flatbread into her stew. "We've already had a red, green, yellow, and blue songbird. What colors do you like?"

"I don't know."

"You don't know what colors you like?" Malou's eyebrows shot up, and Ora gave her a look.

"Besides." I grinned. "You haven't heard me sing yet."

"Ten gritas says she's good," Malou said, giving me a wink. Mina signed to her sister with a mischievous smile. "Deal."

"What happened to all of them?" I asked, admiring the hundreds of little badges trailing above the dining table.

"Most of them moved on to other lives," Ora said, eyes softening. "Some passed away. Galen den' Mora has been traveling for longer than I've been alive. I was born in this very wagon." They waved around them. "This place was my grandmother's dying wish. A home for any traveler with a song in their heart. The wheels never break and the oxen never tire. Galen den' Mora rolls on forever. Life and death, a whole world, within this rolling home."

"That's beautiful," I murmured.

"It's part of a song I wrote." Ora smirked. "'The Traveling Bard of Hallisville.'"

"You wrote that?" I'd heard it before. "Though it was called 'The Wolf of Hallisville' when they performed it."

"Must've been a servant at some Wolf fete, then." Ora huffed. "The Wolves always steal our songs and make them their own."

Mina signed something I guessed was about Wolves and Ora chuckled. I looked at Malou to translate.

"Esh," Malou muttered. "The Wolves killed a few monsters hundreds of years ago and now they think everything belongs to them."

"The humans granted the Wolves their sovereignty for their protection against monsters and magic wielders," I said, garnering a snort from the twins.

"I didn't realize the humans of Damrienn cared for their Wolves so much," Malou jeered. "If the Wolves were our protectors, they would've dealt with Sawyn, but they all turned a blind eye to the suffering of the Olmderians," she hissed. "Because it didn't affect their crowns or their gold."

Ora shook their head. "Maybe their ancestors had good intentions, but the Wolves haven't cared a crover about the humans in a long time."

I bobbed my head along in agreement, trying to blend in. This was how humans talked. I sounded too much like a Wolf—an unwelcome guest in any human troupe. I made a note to be more careful with my words and reactions.

Mina stood, bringing her empty plate to the basin.

Malou nodded. "Go swap with Navin before the stew goes cold."

My eyes tracked Mina as she climbed toward the front of the wagon, and I realized I'd only seen a small part of this giant structure. "Do the oxen never stop?"

"They don't need to," Ora said, "but we like to give them time to rest and graze anyway."

"That's how you joined us," Malou said, laughing.

I laughed as well, then whispered, "This place is amazing," looking around the space again. Little details covered every corner—buttons and velvets and potted herbs. I could spot influences from every kingdom, from the dented copper bowls and colorful rugs of Valta to the fur-trimmed hats of Taigos.

"You haven't even seen the best part yet," Malou said. "You want to have a wash?"

"A wash? On a moving wagon?" I dropped my spoon into my empty bowl with a clang.

She pushed back from the table and beckoned me to follow. "Come on. I'll show you."

I bowed my head to Ora. "Thank you for this delicious meal . . . and all of your kindness."

Ora bowed. "It's a pleasure, Calla."

They said it with genuine warmth . . . and it still befuddled me. Why would anyone be nice to me when I had nothing to give them in return? Surely humans weren't this kind to strangers. Unless they had some sort of ulterior motives . . .

I would keep my guard up, just in case.

I followed Malou toward the back of the wagon. Twisting down the narrow corridor, I had to shuffle sideways to fit. She reached a low cabinet door and opened it, revealing a hole with a ladder.

I gaped. "What in the Gods' names?"

"There's a water basin that sits under the firebox. It keeps the water warm for a little while after dinner. If you go now, it'll be lovely," she said. "There's soap and towels down there already. You'll have to duck down. It's pretty crammed, but it's something."

"It's amazing," I whispered again. I reached up to my bunk above and grabbed out my spare chemise.

She gave me a wink as I slid feet first into the hole and down the little ladder. I crouched into a squat, waddling forward off the landing and onto an open grate. Cold air rushed up through the floor as the heat from the metal box above my head radiated downward. I watched the road whizzing by between the slats in the metal. Beyond the grating were rows and rows of wooden dowels, washed clothing hanging on them.

They made use of every inch of Galen den' Mora. Built along the wall were baskets of soap and hand cloths. I picked up the first square of soap and smelled it—citrusy and fresh.

The wagon rocked and I tipped forward onto my knees, laughing despite myself. How did they not topple over all the time? What had Ora called them?

Ah, yes: sea legs.

I hung my clean chemise on a hook by the footwell and disrobed. Leaving my dirty clothes below me, I turned the little spigot above and warm water sprayed out. The fine misting was perfect, just enough to wash without wasting the entire basin in one go. I selected a cloth and scrubbed myself clean, rivers of brown water and dried blood tracing down my bare skin. I raked my fingers through my hair and squeezed the dirty water out of my clothes.

As the warmth washed over me, that tight knot in my chest eased, giving way once more to sorrow. The quiet moments were the hardest. When I was safe, warm, and fed, I couldn't ignore what had happened. I had abandoned my pack, my *mate*, in order to save my sister. I had thought I knew loneliness before, but I had no clue. It felt like my soul was bursting out, desperately trying to pull that feeling back into me, and I knew I couldn't go on this way.

I scuttled back to my bunk, deflated, murmuring a quick good-night out to the wagon before climbing onto the thin mattress. The bunks weren't stacked one on top of the other, but rather scattered throughout the wagon, creating little nooks. Mina slept between two shelves of books and folders of sheet music. Malou slept above her to the right, where another bunk notched above storage cupboards. Each one had a thick velvet curtain that pulled across to give the sleeper privacy.

Soft candlelight peeked in as I stroked my hand down the curtain. The sheets were smooth, the pillow soft, and I thanked the Gods I was exhausted enough to be given a reprieve from my churning thoughts.

I closed my eyes, thinking of what badge I would want to hang on the ribbons above the dining table. My gut clenched, thinking of what they had said, because I couldn't even pick a color, let alone an object that symbolized me—mostly because I didn't know any of those things about myself. Briar would have a badge in mind in a heartbeat, but me? How do you depict a shadow? Would they even let someone have a blank black badge? Besides, if they knew what I truly was, they'd kick me out, or worse. No, there'd be no badges, no memory of me. I'd travel with them to Olmdere and then become a shadow once more.

SIXTEEN

THE SEASONS SEEMED TO CHANGE OVER THE NEXT TWO DAYS—
summer fading into blustering winter. Higher and higher the
wagon crept into the Stormcrest Mountains, crossing the border
into Taigos. We slowed to a stop in Nesra's Pass and I finally got
to step out of the wagon for the first time in days. This was it.
Once we got through this narrow mountain pass, the vastness of
Taigos would swallow us up, making tracking me nearly impossible.

I followed the twins and Ora down the ladder and onto the
bare road. Wind whipped my hair across my face, the air smelling of impending snowfall. I stared out over the rolling pine forests far below. Down there it was still summer, but in Taigos, the
land was blanketed in perpetual snow. My legs wobbled beneath
me for a moment, unused to the solid ground. The wagon nestled
against one side of the road, finding a break from the squalls.

Nesra's Pass appeared more of an outpost than a true village.
No taverns or inns, only three buildings lined either side of the
gray gravel road. Behind each row of buildings, cliffs shot up into
the clouds. The town cut through the mountainside, the road a
steep ascent into the ranges.

I'd always wondered what the Ice Wolves of Taigos looked
like. If Vellia's paintings were to be believed, they were pure white.

Olmdere's neighboring pack to the south, their kingdom was hidden above the clouds and under the snow and ice. I craned my neck up toward the thick blanket of gray and shuddered. What cities lay hidden in the murky skies?

"Here," Ora said, offering me a woolen blanket. They pulled their shawl tighter around their lean shoulders. "We won't be doing much camping in Taigos." They huffed. "But if the weather's fair in Olmdere, we can set up our tents or sleep under the stars. It's nice to get out of that wagon every now and again."

Navin turned the corner, leading by the halter two creatures I'd never seen before.

"What is that?"

They were bigger than a normal ox, taller than a horse, with shaggy copper red hair and curling horns.

"You've never seen Taigosi oxen?" Navin grinned, stroking a hand down the beast who stood shoulder height to him. The oxen seemed built of solid muscle, slow but strong, perfect for hauling the monstrous wagon. "They're harmless."

Navin was a lanky man with short twists of black hair and long, slender fingers that looked perfectly designed for plucking strings. He wore a blue velvet vest with a mishmash of different buttons and a flowing white shirt with ballooning sleeves. I looked from Navin to Ora to the twins. Not one of them dressed like I'd ever seen before, with faint nods to the different kingdoms, but unplaceable by attire alone.

"This is Opus." Ora patted Opus's flank. "And that one's Magnum."

"Very clever," I said.

"My grandmother named them," Ora said. "I think their names tell you plenty about her spirit."

We exchanged smiles. "She sounds like she was an incredible person."

"And a fine musician, too." Ora nodded, gazing up at their home. They'd painted songs around each of the boards. A whole evening's worth of tunes etched into Galen den' Mora's sides.

Navin looked over his shoulder as he led Magnum down the trail. "We'll see you in twenty."

Ora gave him a quick wave before tucking their hands back in their shawl.

"There are some tussocks beyond the ridge to graze the oxen," Ora said, as we watched Navin head down the switchback trail. "You can go with the twins to stretch your legs if you'd like." They gestured to Mina and Malou, who were peering into a darkened window across the street. "But Nesra's Pass is full of ne'er-do-wells, so stick together."

I bobbed my chin in thanks and scuttled off to join the twins. We meandered to the end of the road, which was only a few paces, and peeked into the general store window.

Mina's breath fogged the glass. There was something in the store she wanted, though I didn't know quite what. I'd figured out some of her language over the past few days. She was patient with me as I practiced it with her. It didn't help that she signed in a Valtan form of the language, and so I had to translate it twice over in my head, but I was getting there. Another language I could eventually add to my repertoire. I'd noted that Mina could hear what people were saying and preferred people to speak to her while she communicated back through sign. But whatever she was signing now was lost on me.

"Come on, then." Malou tugged on her sister's sleeve.

"You'll spend all our coins on sweets," Mina signed, even as she followed.

I huffed. That I understood.

"What's the point of traveling the kingdoms if we can't sample all the sweets in Aotreas?" Malou grinned as the bell above her tinkled.

We navigated down the dusty, sparse shelves. Wicker baskets lined the far wall, picked nearly clean apart from a few rotten apples. Strings of dried lemon and bundles of dried mint hung from the windows to ward off the bugs. In the corner sat a table of glass jars filled with colorful boiled candies.

"Have you ever had aniseed candies before?" Malou asked, lifting the jar and scooping out a dark round ball.

She offered it to me and I picked it up off the spoon, giving it a sniff. It smelled sweet, with an undercurrent of spice that reminded me of cloves.

"Just try it," Malou snickered, taking a candy for herself and popping it in her cheek. "Don't chew it though, not if you want to keep your teeth."

Mina slipped one in her mouth and I followed. The flavor made me grimace, and the twins burst out into laughter. It was strangely smooth yet bitter, spicy yet sweet. I swallowed, the taste of it coating my mouth. I rolled the candy across my tongue, getting used to the bizarre tang that lit up my taste buds.

"Okay." I bobbed my head, beginning to understand the appeal.

"Is there anything else you need?" Mina signed, her tongue clicking as she sucked the candy.

I surveyed the bare room.

"Save your money," Malou said. "They'll have better wares in the capital city of Taigoska."

We ambled down the shelves anyway, taking our time to be out of the wagon. The syrupy flavor of the candy coated my tongue as it shrunk into the size of a pebble in my mouth. We had nearly wound our way to the back of the shop when I noticed a tipped-over sack. Grain spilled onto the hardwood floor. The hairs on my arm stood on end as I glanced over the back counter to an upturned chair. My ears strained, but I couldn't hear a sound.

"Hello?" I called, waving the twins over.

Why hadn't I thought to question it when no store owner appeared? We'd eaten their candy and perused their shelves for several minutes.

"Hello? Anyone here?" Malou shouted toward the cracked-open door that led to the back of the shop. "We're from Galen den' Mora." The Taigosi words flowed easily off her tongue.

"Are you all right?" I called.

"Aye," a gruff voice shouted back. A weathered-looking man with a long beard shuffled out from behind the back door and we collectively sighed. He looked unscathed, a bottle of amber liquid clutched in his hand. "Just waiting for the Rooks to pass."

"Rooks?" I glanced between the twins.

"How long ago were they here?" Malou asked.

"Ye just missed them." The owner pointed out the back window.

Malou chucked a copper coin onto the countertop and spun around. "We need to get back to the wagon."

"You think they spotted us?" Mina asked.

"If they weren't above the cloud line," Malou said, looking at the steep road through the windows. "They would've seen us riding uphill."

"Come on." Mina grabbed my elbow and steered me out of the shop.

I rushed back out onto the street, nearly colliding with Malou's back when she halted.

"Shit," she hissed.

I leaned past her, staring down the road to see a mob of seven black cloaks. They wore black scarves that covered their mouths and noses, their eyes shadowed in the depths of their hoods. Obsidian feathers covered their shoulders, shimmering with iridescence.

I'd never seen the weapons they wielded before. The blades curved like a scythe around the knuckles of their gloved hands. One flipped it over and back, spinning the blade by its hook. I assessed the claw-like weapons, expecting they'd use them like an extension of their own fists. I made a note to not let any of their blows land. Normally, I could get away with absorbing a few punches, but not if a blade sharpened them.

They crowded around one figure and my pulse doubled its speed when I realized it was Ora.

My feet were moving before I could stop myself. "Hey!" I shouted, drawing a few of their gazes.

"Calla," Malou hissed. "What are you doing?"

"Go get help," I called over my shoulder. Neither of them looked like they knew how to fight, and I didn't need to be worrying for them when I needed to be focused on fighting. The best thing they could do at that moment was stay out of my way.

I clenched the handle of the knife in my pocket, glad I had placed it there out of habit that morning. It wasn't my dagger, but it was better than nothing.

Three of the Rooks turned, guffawing as they sized me up. I knew I looked pathetic with the paring knife in my hand. Good. They wouldn't fight me like they would a soldier.

"Calla, run!" Ora shouted when they spotted me. Their wide, panicked eyes undercut their warning. I wouldn't leave them to this wild pack of Sawyn's lackeys.

"Listen to your friend," the nearest Rook said in Taigosi. I could tell from his tone that he was smiling, even though I couldn't see his mouth.

A few more Rooks stepped away from the wagon. Perfect. If I could train all their eyes on me, then it would give Ora a chance to flee . . . one I hoped they'd take. With any luck, Navin would return any minute and then maybe the tides would turn. Navin wore a dagger on his belt and I prayed he knew how to use it. Three against seven was far better odds.

"Are you afraid to lose to someone like me?" I fluttered my lashes, pretending to be demure like Briar did so well. I dropped into a mock curtsy, the gesture egging them on.

I remembered the wide, wary eyes of the men from nights before and my lips twisted into a wicked grin. My smile alone made the first Rook stall and I chuckled as the rest charged.

They were fast. I'd give them that. I ducked under the swinging claws of the first attacker and stabbed my knife into the back of his knee. In, then out. I shot back away from him before he could lash out. He screamed, falling to one knee, as I whirled on the next Rook. My blade snagged on his cloak but didn't connect. I thanked the Moon they didn't wield long swords, but even just the reach of their arms was far greater than mine.

I heard Vellia's voice in my head: *No high strikes. The cloaks would get in the way. Aim for the legs.*

The boot of another Rook connected with my hip and I twisted, trying to keep them all within my line of sight.

Don't spin. Don't give them your back.

I blocked a sweeping blow downward with my knife.

Lock your guard. Straight arms.

Two charged me at once and I dropped to one knee, too low for their scythes to reach. Fast as a striking snow snake, I stabbed my knife into one's calf and the other straight through the Rook's boot. Before I could rise, another boot collided with my back, stomping me to the ground. I barked out a pained cry as my chin collided with the gravel and my teeth clacked together. The flesh split as the dusty stones pressed into the open wound. I blindly swung my hand backward and my knife nicked the attacker. He lifted his foot off my back to avoid my blade, and I rolled. The slope of the hill made it easier to get out from under him as he tripped backward. Crouching, I watched the hesitation cross their faces.

I tilted my head, letting my Wolf speak for me. "Not the opponent you were expecting?"

I goaded them forward. Three more charged and I slashed my knife in tight arches, controlling the group and only allowing one to enter my striking range at a time.

"Fun's over," a mean voice growled and I whipped my head to see the Rook that had Ora pinned to the wagon unsheathe a dagger from his hip.

Shit. So they did have other weapons.

Ora's eyes widened as they stared at the dagger. Without thinking, I threw my knife. A sickening, wet thunk sounded as it pierced through the attacker's ear into their skull. His shrieks died on his lips as he fell forward.

A walloping blow to the back of my legs toppled me, gravel biting into my knees. I had thrown away my only weapon and given them my back.

Breathe. Think.

Bile rose in my throat as I stared at their glinting scythes. The dropped dagger was only a few paces behind me, crimson blood pooling beneath it. If I could get to it, I'd have a fighting chance. But as the Rook's fist came crashing down, all thoughts left my head. I twisted on instinct as the scythe smashed into the gravel beside my ear. I glanced over to see a few locks of my hair sliced off.

Too close.

A boot stomped on my sternum, knocking the air out of me, and I grabbed a handful of gravel, whipping it up into my attacker's eyes. The pressure on my chest lessened, and I twisted the boot, hoping to snap the Rook's ankle. I didn't feel the pop, but he hopped backward, nonetheless. I scrambled back to my feet, turning toward the dagger on the ground.

Don't turn your back.

In my desperation I'd forgot the most important rule: defenses up, always. I felt the whoosh of a nearly missed kick behind me and then a scream. I didn't look back, racing to the dagger and snatching it.

Yes.

Another scream rang out as a feral growl rent the air and I clenched my jaw. I knew that sound. I whirled around and the sight of the carnage blasted through me.

Seven mutilated bodies lay scattered across the road, and standing in the middle of them was Grae.

SEVENTEEN

HE LOOKED LIKE A GOD IN OBSIDIAN LEATHERS, HIS HAIR TIED in a knot atop his head, and blood splattering his face. The sight of him made my whole body pulse like a war drum. His chest heaved as he stared down at the bodies with brutal wrath . . . and I knew it was because of me. The Rooks had attacked his mate and he'd shredded them apart for it, Wolf taking over.

More than all that?

He'd found me.

Grae sheathed his sword, and the look in his midnight eyes broke me. Both our expressions warred between anger and relief. So many unspoken words floated in the dusty air between us. So much pain, but even when it was directed at him, I knew the only person I wanted to comfort that torrent inside of me. Grae. Always Grae.

In two strides, he was before me, pulling me into a tight hug. That bonfire scent wrapped around me as he pulled me tighter into his hard leather. The action cracked me open, the sorrow bleeding from me worse than any wound.

His lips dropped into my hair and he murmured, "Are you okay?"

I nodded into his warm chest, my arms snaking around his back despite myself. I'd lost my sister, I'd lost him as my friend, and now that his arms were around me, I indulged in that brief moment of comfort, of relief, before the reality coursed through me again. "I could've taken them."

"I know." His voice was thick as he gave me a final squeeze and released me. Examining my face, he scowled. He held my chin between his thumb and forefinger, his eyes skating over my older wounds—my bruised eye and split lip, both clearly not from this fight.

His growl was a feral promise. "Who did this to you?"

I stepped out of his touch and his hand lingered in the air before dropping to his side. I remembered that moment in the forest again. *It hurts not to touch you.*

"I handled it," I said, taking another step back as if the distance might settle the burning urge to reach for him again.

His lips twisted up. "I'm sure you did."

"Who are these people, Calla?" Ora's voice was a shaken whisper.

I looked between Ora and Grae, realizing Sadie and Hector stood amongst the bodies as well. They didn't wear their royal uniforms, no crest carved into their weapons. Instead, they wore simple black fighting leathers, though they were still armed to the teeth. Their clothing told me enough: they weren't here at King Nero's behest.

"This is, um." I glanced at Ora. "This is Gr—"

"Graham," Grae said, extending his hand out to Ora. "Calla's husband."

My eyes flared for a split second before I schooled my expression. Of all the lies he could come up with, of course he picked that one.

"And them?" Ora nodded to the others.

"They're part of our troupe," I said, frantically grasping for an explanation. If the others knew we were Wolves, it would mean trouble. "I sing, um, and they . . ."

"Play music," Hector offered, wiping his sword on his leg and stepping over a body with such a casualness that Ora's mouth fell open.

They scanned him from head to toe, eyeing the belts of daggers around his meaty thighs. "Oh? And what instruments do you play?"

"I'm a . . . flautist," Hector said.

Sadie snorted, and her brother gave her a glowering look.

Ora raised their brows at me, waiting for a better answer.

"Okay, fine," I said with feigned exasperation. "This is my crew. We were planning on meeting in Olmdere because we heard there were crovers to be made for anyone good with a sword."

Ora chuckled. "Now *that* I believe."

My shoulders dropped at the sound of that laugh. They'd believe a lie as long as it was a carefully crafted one. We didn't look like musicians, but mercenaries . . . I looked at Sadie, picking her bloodied fingernails with her throwing knife. *That* was a credible lie.

"We got separated along the way and I decided to head toward Olmdere on my own." I shrugged. "I'd hoped I'd find them there."

"Holy ebarvens," Navin's voice called as he dashed up the trail. "What happened?" His haunted face scanned over the bodies.

"Nothing holy at all. Rooks," Ora said, picking up my discarded blanket and dusting it off. They wrapped it back around my shoulders and Grae took a half-step toward me. "Calla saved me."

Mina and Malou darted across the street, holding armfuls of rocks. "This was the best we could do," Malou panted. "By the time we got back, it was clear we weren't needed." The rocks thudded to the ground around her feet and she clapped me on the shoulder. "You're a beast, Calla."

"We helped a little," Sadie added. Everyone's eyes turned to her and she sheathed her knife back in her belt.

"That's Sadie." Hector tipped his head to his sister. "I'm Hector. We're part of Calla's crew."

Calla's crew. I liked the sound of that.

"We can't stay here." Ora frowned at the bodies strewn across the road. "More Rooks will come swarming through Nesra's Pass when they hear what happened."

"Curse the Gods," Navin grumbled, wandering through the carnage. He stooped and pulled one Rook's mask down, looking upon their face for a long time before moving to the next one. His body seemed to float from one to the next, hollow and vacant.

"Why are you doing that?" Sadie asked as he crouched before the last Rook. A strange sort of sorrow clouded his expression as he stared at the last Rook's face.

"They were people," Navin murmured. "Desperate people, but people still. They deserve to be laid to rest."

Sadie paused, considering him for a moment, before walking over and grabbing the feet of the Rook she had just killed. "Come on. It'll be easier than you dragging them."

Navin's eyebrows shot up as he regarded her. "Thank you."

He grabbed the Rook around the shoulders and they carried the body to the side of the road.

"Hector," Sadie snapped, his name a command, and her brother joined in.

They piled the bodies in the ditch carved into the road by heavy rains.

"Are you still riding with us?" Ora asked, turning to me.

"Yes," I said at the same time Grae said "No."

I glowered at him and he returned the look—an entire conversation passing between our eyes. I knew he thought traveling with humans wouldn't be safe, and I knew we'd be safer with them.

"We can give you a ride into Taigoska," Navin offered, giving Sadie a soft smile as he dusted his hands down his vest. "You saved Ora's life. It's the least we can do."

Malou scanned up and down the steep road, landing upon their three leather backpacks. "Where are your horses?"

"We came on foot," Grae said.

"On foot?" Malou's cloudy gray eyes widened. "You were planning on crossing the Stormcrest Ranges *on foot*?"

"Yes." Grae narrowed his gaze at me. "We were eager to catch up to Calla."

I fought the urge to roll my eyes. I'd told him not to follow me. Their grueling trek this far was their own damn fault.

"I'm not walking across the ranges when we have the offer of a ride," I gritted out.

Pushing Grae felt like walking a knife's edge, and I knew one more little nudge and he'd relent. I glanced back at Galen den' Mora. It was filled with warm beds, good food, and curiosities from every stretch of Aotreas. Hiking to Olmdere would be exhausting and take ten times as long.

"May I speak with you privately?" Grae rumbled.

"No, you may not," I snapped back.

"They're definitely married," Malou murmured to Mina.

"Fine," Grae relented, not breaking my stare. "We'll ride with you out of Nesra's Pass and then we'll break off on our own tomorrow." He was about to take a step when he begrudgingly added, "Thank you."

I bit my lip to keep from smiling, and Grae's eyes darkened. If only King Nero could see his son thanking a group of humans. I couldn't help but drop my eyes to the muscle that popped from Grae's jaw when he was angry. Goddess, that muscle had a magic all its own. How could I want to run from him and have his lips on mine all at the same time?

The general store owner stumbled out onto the street, looking at the blood-stained road with an unsettling indifference. These sights were probably common in Nesra's Pass.

"Ye better get on before more come," he shouted. "Snow's coming and the high roads will be blocked." He looked at the group of them—a strange mixture of artists and warriors—and quizzically back at the wagon. "I never saw anything. Get on before you make me a liar."

"Thank you," Ora said, placing their hand on their chest with a bow. "Let's go."

MY MIND KEPT TURNING BACK TO THE BODIES BURIED IN A shallow roadside grave. They'd kicked some rubble over them and moved on and it was still more kindness than those bastards deserved. A terrible thought echoed through me: they were Olmderians. Those Rooks, cursed by Sawyn's magic or no, were citizens of my kingdom. I was meant to be going to Olmdere to save it, but so far I'd only added to the body count.

We rode three more hours, the path a straight shot into the mountains. It took me an hour before I realized that no one drove the oxen. With towering cliffsides on either side of the road, the magical beasts were able to navigate the road unguided, their stamina seemingly endless.

Images of those cloaked bodies plagued me the rest of the ride. How many had I killed? I'd gotten my knife in most of them, but it was probably Grae and the others who ended all but the one I'd thrown the knife into. I shuddered, thinking of the fury on his blood-splattered face the moment I heard that growl and knew he was there.

I sat with the Wolves in stilted silence. We needed to speak with each other, but couldn't do it in front of the others. I dutifully avoided Grae's eyes from where he sat across from me. Mina and Malou fell into easy conversation with Sadie and Hector, both parties seemingly excited to have someone new to converse with. I sat listening as dread pooled in my gut. The lies came so easily to them: now that the borders were open to Olmdere, the most *creative* businesses would be the first to get in, and those businesses tended to need people skilled with a sword. I hated that cover. It made us no better than the Rooks, but it was conceivable enough to mask our more wolflike traits.

Sadie and Hector already knew how to sign, dropping in and

out of Mina's language with ease. Shame heated my cheeks. I'd prided myself on knowing every language on the continent, but this one had been left out.

"A sorceress Queen," Malou huffed, brushing her thick brown hair over her shoulder and putting her slippered feet on the table. "How many hundreds of years since the last one of those?"

"The Wolves have gotten lazy," Navin said. Sadie's eyes darted to him. "Sawyn was around for decades before she took that throne. Why hadn't the Marriels sent out their armies to defeat her sooner? Where were the other kingdoms?"

"What good are kings and queens if they don't protect their people?" Malou asked.

"Yeah," Hector added halfheartedly.

Sadie took out the throwing knife from her belt and flicked it back and forth.

"Why aren't we sorcerers?" I asked, drawing everyone's gazes. "I mean, sorcerers are created by death magic . . . we've killed, too."

"Their killings were cold and calculated—a clear and unprovoked choice," Hector said. "They welcome dark magic. It bleeds them of all feeling until they can only care for themselves."

I shook my head. "It seems a small difference."

"That pain you're feeling right now is the difference," Grae murmured, finally making me look at him. "You can turn toward that darkness or push away from it. The pain you feel about it is what keeps you whole."

Sadie twirled her blade. "Who did Sawyn kill to turn her?"

"A great many people," Hector said. "Though I don't know the first. Probably some poor farm boy from whatever village she sprouted up from."

"A storm is coming." Ora swayed down the narrow hall. "We're going to shelter in the forest once we breech the pass tonight. If the snow's not too deep, we should reach Hengreave tomorrow."

"The Lord can wait another day for his songs," Navin said, waving a hand, and it made me wonder how many times they'd played for the Lord before.

"I sleep up in the loft, but we only have six bunks," Ora said, looking between us.

"The married couple can share a bunk," Malou said with a shrug.

My eyes darted to her. The bunks were small. We'd barely be able to lie shoulder to shoulder without toppling out, which meant we'd be on our sides.

"Unless you want a tent," Ora said, searching my face. "It's more space, but it's so cold out—"

"A tent will be fine, thanks," I cut in. Wolves could survive the cold.

Ora glanced at Grae and back at me. "Okay."

"Want some privacy?" Sadie snickered beside me and I elbowed her. Hard.

My stomach dropped to my feet. That's probably what they all thought—not that I wanted to put distance between Grae and me, but between us and everyone else.

The wagon rocked as we veered off the trail; the oxen pulling us unguided into the forest.

"I'll make up some gloftas," Ora said, their bangles clanging as they moved back toward the galley. I thanked the Gods they spared me from the awkwardness of replying to the tent comment. "We can roast them on the fire."

"Ooh yes." Malou smirked, lifting her thick lashes toward Hector. "Have you ever had them before?"

Hector shook his head. "I've never been to Valta."

"Lucky for you, Valta is coming to Taigos tonight," Ora called out.

The group chuckled, and once again the warmth of the troupe warred with the coldness I felt knowing I was lying to all of them.

"Is it true the islands of Valta really float in the sky?" Sadie asked.

"Yes, hundreds of them." Mina nodded. "We only play for the main cities, though."

"How does a wagon travel to a floating island?" Sadie quirked her brow.

"Ever heard of a bridge?" Malou grinned.

Navin shook his head. "It's pretty harrowing riding over thin air."

"I can't imagine," Sadie muttered.

Navin twisted his head, looking down at Sadie with a wink. "If you stick around, I'll show you."

Hector kicked his feet up onto the table with a loud thud, pulling everyone's focus toward him. "We're only going as far as Olmdere." He scowled at Navin, crossing his arms. I never had a brother, but I could imagine what he was thinking right now.

The wagon lurched to a halt, throwing us all sideways. I braced my hand out as Sadie fell on top of Navin. His hands bracketed her waist and he stared up at her.

"We'll go get firewood," Hector snarled, jumping to his feet. He tapped his sister on the arm. "Let's *go*."

She grimaced but followed, an inevitable lecture waiting the moment they were out of earshot.

"I'll see if Ora needs help." I jumped to my feet, my eyes flitting to Grae and then falling away. "You go set up the tent."

My ears burning from the awkward exchange, I turned before he could reply. I'd called him a coward. I'd thrown his necklace at him and ran away. How was I meant to speak to him after that? I hated that he'd found me, and I hated even more that I was glad he did. It was too much, but I knew at some point I'd have to speak with him.

Probably in a tent.

Alone.

Gods, help me.

EIGHTEEN

ON A SPARSE PATCH OF ICE-COATED FOREST, WE DISEMBARKED to set up camp. I felt Grae's eyes tracking my every step. He would be ready to chase me if I broke off into a sprint—I was certain of it. I'd run away from him once before, and though I was certainly justified in doing so, I didn't see why he'd trust me now. Yet I had no plans on running. I just didn't have plans for talking to him—and telling him that—either.

I skirted away from him the rest of the evening, helping with the fire while Grae set up our tent. The pine forest provided some shelter from the icy alpine winds, but we were so high up the trees were scraggily and far apart. It wasn't an ideal place to rest, and an even worse idea to sleep in a tent, but at least it was far enough off the main road that more Rooks wouldn't come looking . . . hopefully. It wouldn't end well for them regardless, now that Grae, Sadie, and Hector were there.

"We don't have much in the way of a meal with four more mouths to feed than I rationed for," Ora said to the group as I watched Grae string up our tent between lean pine trees. "Not if we want to eat tomorrow before we reach Hengreave. Gloftas will have to do."

"That's all right." Hector stepped out into the clearing, holding an armful of kindling to his chest. "We've brought our own provisions."

"He has incredible hearing," Ora murmured to me. They prodded at the burgeoning fire, coaxing it to life.

"That he does," I replied, frowning at Hector. He obviously spent little time pretending to be a human. It took practice to not move too quickly or show too much strength . . . or show off his other heightened senses.

"I'll make a warming brew." Ora tipped their head back to the wagon, parked between a wind break of scrawny trees. "I'm going to get cleaned up for dinner. Why don't you do the same?"

I glanced over at Ora and realized I'd been standing stock still while the campsite sprung to life around me. I shifted the pack on my shoulders. Grae left the tent to help Sadie move logs into a circle for the fire, which meant I had a moment to change in privacy.

Ora squeezed my hand, making me look at them. "Thank you for saving my life today."

"Of course!" I waved if off as if the fight was as effortless as lending Ora some flour.

"No—not of course. It was incredibly brave of you. Foolish, perhaps, but brave. So, please—accept my thanks."

My eyes softened. "You're welcome."

That's why they thought I was frozen—the horror of the attack, not because I was afraid to speak to the warrior who had rescued us. Who they thought was my husband.

Who was, in fact, my mate.

I waited until Grae was on the other side of the clearing and hastened over to the tent. I planned to change quickly and get back out in the open before he could corner me. That's what he'd do, scolding me for leaving once he had me trapped, and I didn't want to be demeaned and chastised for doing what I knew was right. I was the one who took action, who fought, and I wouldn't be shamed for trying to save my sister, whether it was against the king's wishes or not.

The tent was tall enough that I didn't need to duck my head, only the center bowing down where it wasn't tied to the slack line. Rough canvas covered the ground and a single bed mat lay on the floor with a fur blanket folded at the foot. I sighed, dumping my pack. Out of the cold, I felt all my bruises more acutely, numbness fading back to aching pain. My stomach and back throbbed from where I'd been kicked and my chin stung with each unconscious movement of my mouth. I lifted a hand to my bloodied jaw and hissed. The cut was deeper than I thought. At least it wasn't still bleeding, but it felt gritty with sand and debris. I slid the neckline of my tunic wider and pulled one arm out, surveying my skin mottled with swollen bruises.

A smoky scent wafted in that I knew wasn't from the fire. I thrust my arm back into my sleeve and turned to find Grae standing half in the doorway, his arm frozen, lifting the tent flap. His eyes brimmed with rage as he stared at my exposed skin. He tracked every bruise and my heart hammered in my ears, my skin dimpling with gooseflesh everywhere his eyes landed.

"I should've killed them more slowly," he said, somehow fiercely quiet, stepping into the space and closing the tent flap behind him.

He walked over to his pack against the far fabric wall and pulled out a brown glass vial. "This will help with the wounds for now, but you need to shift to fully heal."

"I know that, Grae. But I can't shift here, not with so many people around." My eyes darted to the tent flaps. If they spotted a Gold Wolf, they'd either try to kill me, sell off the information of our whereabouts, or at the very least, kick us out.

"Just do it in the tent tonight. No one will know."

"And you don't think my wounds magically disappearing would tip them off?"

He shook his head in frustration. "Tomorrow night then, once we get further into Taigos," Grae said, prowling over to me. I felt each step right in my core. "Until then, this'll have to do. Sit."

"I can do it myself." I grabbed for the vial and Grae lifted it slightly higher.

I grimaced, unable to lift my arm above my head. The bruises down my back shouted their displeasure. He raised his eyebrows at me as if I'd just proved his point.

"Goddess, you are so bloody stubborn," he said with a smile that belied the anger in his eyes. "You can't even see where your bruises are." He took another step, his chest brushing against mine as he stared down at me. "Please?"

I frowned at his *please*. Princes didn't say please. They didn't ask at all—they demanded. I knew he used it like a weapon to get me to acquiesce . . . but it worked.

"Fine." I sat, wrapping my arms around my knees and pinning the front of my tunic in place as the laces loosened down my back.

He crouched beside me, uncorking the vial. Dabbing a thick liquid on his finger, he swiped it over my eyebrow. I hissed at the sting.

"Sorry," Grae murmured, moving more slowly.

"No, you're not."

He chuckled. Grae had been right. I hadn't even realized there was a cut over my eyebrow, the one on my chin hurting so much that I couldn't focus anywhere else.

"Now your chin." He said it like a warning and I braced for the pain.

His other hand reached out and threaded his fingers through mine, squeezing as he dabbed his finger along my chin. The sharp sting made me screw my eyes shut, inhaling a rough breath through my nose. I clenched my jaw harder, refusing to cry out in pain even if it meant cracking a tooth instead.

"I'm sorry," Grae whispered again, blowing across my skin and drying the salve. The skitter of his breath on my face made my skin ripple.

"I'm fine," I gasped out, trying to focus on his breath and not the endless burning.

"You don't always have to be, little fox," Grae whispered.

That name made my eyes snap open, finding Grae's gaze inches from mine. That nickname had always made me feel like someone special. It brought me back to who we were to each other before all this. Before he was a crown prince, before he was my mate, he had simply been my friend, and we'd cared for each other. Whether lies and titles and time had irrevocably changed that, I didn't know, but I knew that much to be true.

I knew that *had* been true, at least.

The look in his eyes made me break our gaze, as if he was feeling every one of my thoughts in his mind.

Grae hung his head. "Can I see your back?"

I gave a brief nod, dropping my head in my hands, careful not to touch my sticky wounds onto the fabric of my trousers. Grae adjusted his footing, moving toward my back. His rough calloused fingers made quick work of the strings that ran down my shoulder blades. Whatever Grae saw made him snarl.

"That bad?"

His fingers traced the stinging balm over what must have been a giant bruise along my spine. So that explained why it felt like I was being kicked by a horse every time I breathed.

Grae's fingers lingered in the middle of my back. His warm forehead pressed against the cool skin of my neck.

"When you were attacked last night, I *felt* it." His voice was a pained whisper. Without thought, I reached back and threaded my fingers though his hair, holding his head to me. "And again today . . . I thought I might not get to you in time." His lips skimmed the skin along my neck. "It was a horrible, helpless feeling, Calla. To know you were in danger but not be able to find you."

I wouldn't apologize. "I had to go."

"Why?" Grae snapped, pulling away.

My hand dropped back to my side. Here it was—the argument I'd been bracing for since we got back in the wagon.

"What do you mean *why*?" I grabbed the blanket and wrapped it around my bare back, uncaring as the fibers stuck onto the salve. "You *know* why."

"I know the reason, but not the rationale. What exactly is your plan beyond killing Sawyn?" Grae corked the vial and threw it back toward his bag. "What is your plan to *kill* Sawyn? She has an *army* of Rooks. Even if you do manage to kill her, do you really think they'll just let you take her throne?"

"You think that's what I'm doing here?"

"Isn't it?"

"My sister is dead!" My chest cracked open and that festering pain flowed out in my poisoned words. "She's gone, Grae. Never to wake again. Not unless I do what I'm doing. The only chance at saving her is in Olmdere." I flung my hand toward the wall and the mountains beyond. "All I care about right now is finding Maez and breaking Briar's curse. I can't live knowing she's still on that tomb. Sawyn, Olmdere, the throne, *you*—everything else can wait."

Grae swallowed, steadying his breath. He seemed relieved by my answer, though he flinched a bit at the "you" part.

"My father didn't want me to help my cousin, his niece," he murmured. "In fact, I'm certain he has his soldiers out looking for us right now with orders to bring us home. I tried to convince Sadie and Hector not to follow me, but they wanted to rescue Maez as badly as I did."

My eyes slid across his face. His eye was no longer swollen like it had been in his father's office. He'd probably shifted to heal it.

"What will he do when he finds you?"

Grae's fists tightened. "Whatever punishment he doles out, it'll be ten times worse for them."

The Wolf in me snarled, fighting the sudden urge to tear my

teeth into King Nero's throat. He could kill Sadie and Hector for disobeying him, or take an eye or hand like those Wolves in his palace. Part of me knew he had to, to preserve his place at the head of the pack. Part of me *needed* him to, to preserve what it meant to be a Wolf. Questioning one rule would break me open to questioning them all, and I was terrified what I might discover if I followed that line of inquiry too far. As much as I hated the idea of the king's punishments, it was also ingrained in me, and it was very hard to shake.

"Is that why you're not in the Damrienn uniform? You're hiding from his scouts, fleeing his soldiers to save Maez?" I asked, eyeing his unadorned leathers again.

Grae nodded. "We have the same goals, little fox."

"Only because I took action," I snapped. "Tell me, would you be here right now venturing to Olmdere to save your cousin if I hadn't left first?"

Grae didn't answer and my lip curled. Maybe he would've . . . eventually. But we both knew my decision was what forced his hand. Would he have let me live my days, dying a little more inside with each passing season, until only the shell of a person remained? I'd hoped not, but I wasn't certain, and that seed of a doubt spoke volumes about how much I trusted Grae right now.

I ran my hand across my collarbone. That protection stone would've come in handy over the past few days. Better that Grae have it though, one less way we were tied together. It was his grandmother's necklace after all. It was meant to be his . . . A sudden thought made my eyes snap up.

"Why didn't Briar's protection stone work against the sleeping curse?" My brow furrowed, remembering how it seemed as if Sawyn wanted to crush my windpipe but couldn't quite do it. "Why did Sawyn's magic work on Briar and not on me?"

"I gave her that ruby necklace for its beauty," Grae said, rubbing the back of his neck. "Only your necklace had a protection stone."

My heart thundered. "And you gave it to *me*? Not your betrothed?" Grae didn't answer. "What about yours and Briar's future?"

His eyes softened. "You still think its hers and mine?"

No. I didn't. The Moon Goddess had made that much very clear. But Grae hadn't known we were fated mates when he gave me that necklace years ago, which meant . . . I'd always been important to him, even when I was just a little fox in the woods. He could only protect one of us, and he'd chosen me. The thought made my chest heavy.

"So we're hiding from Damrienn and Olmdere alike? Great." I changed the subject, touching a hand to the sticky ointment along my jaw. "The eyes of two kingdoms will be searching for us. I think we should stay with Galen den' Mora."

"No."

"It's a better cover than us traveling on our own," I insisted. "The four of us look like what we are—Wolf warriors. Your father's guards won't be searching for a traveling group of musicians. They'll probably be hunting our scents on all four paws and won't be tracking wagon wheels. Sawyn wouldn't suspect them either if she catches wind of your plans."

"We risk revealing ourselves if we stay with them." Grae twisted toward his pack and grabbed a cloth. "You saw Hector and Sadie. They have probably revealed to the whole camp that they're Wolves by now."

"They'll learn. They can handle it," I said, watching as he tipped his skin of water onto the cloth. "You just need to remind them. Why would they suspect we're Wolves? Wolves don't leave their packs."

"No. They don't." Grae scrubbed the cloth down his blood-stained face. "They don't abandon their mates, either, but I guess we're breaking all the rules now, aren't we, little fox?"

My cheeks burned.

"They aren't going to help Sawyn," I insisted. "Look at what just happened to them."

"Exactly—look at what happened. We also risk endangering

them by staying." Grae stared at me as he scrubbed along his neck.

"I still think it's a better idea to fade into a human troupe than to travel to Olmdere on our own."

"And I still think it's too big a risk." Grae chucked the cloth onto his bag, his voice dropping an octave. "Listen . . . can we talk about us for a second?"

"There is no us." The words came tumbling out of my mouth before I could second-guess them. "Not while my sister is lying on that tomb, forgotten in your father's castle. I won't forget her the way the world has forgotten me."

Grae's eyebrows knitted together. "I never forgot about you, little fox." He stared at me for a long time and I could tell words were on the tip of his tongue, but he didn't speak them.

My tongue couldn't even move.

He turned toward the tent flap. "I'm going to check on the others and make sure they haven't revealed our secrets already."

"Fine."

Grae took one more step and paused, looking back over his shoulder at me. "You're my best friend, Calla. You always have been." His eyes scanned me up and down. "Would it really be so bad? To be mine?"

My eyes dropped to my split knuckles. The pain of his crestfallen face stung worse than any wound. Is that what he thought? That I didn't want to be his mate? But maybe that was the case after all. Maybe I didn't . . .

Gods, I'd messed this all up. I didn't know how much of me was running from him and how much was running toward Olmdere, but this was Grae, *my* Grae, and he was mine if only I'd let him be.

"No," I whispered, though he was already gone. "It wouldn't."

NINETEEN

WE GATHERED AROUND THE OPEN FIRE, SKEWERING THE SAVORY breads Ora made onto sticks and cooking them over the flames. It was a lean meal but better than the dried meat and hard cheese that the Wolves had brought with them. I sat between Hector and Sadie, staring into the flickering orange flames and holding my aching fingers out to the fire. The cold crept deeper into me as the sun fell below the horizon, my joints stiffening and needle pricks covering my nose and fingertips.

Grae tapped Sadie's shoulder and she shifted down the log. He squeezed in beside me, our arms and thighs brushing together. Sadie passed him a mug of ginger tea.

"Thank you," he murmured, placing his elbows onto his knees and leaning toward the fire, his shoulders too broad to fit sitting up.

I pondered that *thank you*—how easily it was uttered by him—and I wondered if those words weren't actually for show. Maybe he really did speak to his soldiers this way. Perhaps even his kindness toward the humans wasn't a ruse.

"To our saviors," Ora said, lifting their mug in the air. "We are forever grateful you were there in Nesra's Pass. May the Gods grant you all the blessings in this life that you so rightly deserve."

"Hear, hear," Malou said, lifting her mug.

I had always found that human prayer odd—that their Gods only granted the blessings that someone deserved. We had just killed seven people. We didn't deserve any of the Gods' blessings.

"We've been thinking," Grae said, drawing the attention of those sitting across the fire. Their images warped from the twisting flames. Grae's eyes shifted to me and then back to Ora. "The Rooks are rampant in Taigos and I'd imagine even worse in Olmdere. Maybe our crew could join you, seeing as we're traveling the same way? We could offer you some manner of protection on your travels?"

My mouth dropped open as I blinked at him.

He'd listened to me.

"I was just about to suggest the same thing," Ora replied, giving Mina a grin. "We're a little on edge after what happened today. Having some people who are good with swords on our side would be most welcome."

"Guards to the musicians," Hector said, raising his mug again. A log cracked and embers danced into the darkening sky.

"I'm assuming it's not just generosity that made you offer such things." Ora pursed their lips, rotating their glofta around the licking flames. "You need to keep a low profile, too?"

The four of us froze. What did they know?

"Yes," Grae finally answered for us. "In our line of work, it's best to go unnoticed."

"Until the sword's in your belly," Hector said with a laugh that he cut off as soon as Sadie elbowed him hard in the ribs.

"That must be very difficult," Navin said, his eyes meeting Sadie's.

Flirting aside, he had no idea. The people we were trying to avoid were our own pack. Now that Grae was gone, too, we were certainly being hunted even as we sat here. We needed to stick to the fringes of town, the human quarters, if we wanted to keep hidden. For all the pomp and circumstance, a musical group would actually draw the least suspicion. Wolves didn't learn the faces and names of humans, they were window dressing, servants, entertainers, and nothing more. The Silver Wolves hunting us wouldn't think we'd affiliate with lowly humans. That arrogance would be our greatest cover.

"What are we going to tell people when they ask about them?" Malou asked Ora.

"Hmm." They considered each of us. "They could help with the setup, or maybe we could say they know how to repair instruments? They could broker performances for us or . . . Calla, you said you can sing?"

"Oh." My eyes dropped. "Not really."

"Will you sing for us?" Mina signed. She grabbed a piece of spiced bread her sister passed to her and popped it into her cheek.

"No, no, no, no." The words came spilling out of my mouth. It would've been embarrassing before, but now that Grae and the others were here . . . my face heated, the icy sting of the evening air gone. Hector shook beside me with restrained laughter and I elbowed him.

"Will you both stop elbowing me!"

"Not anytime soon," Sadie muttered.

"That is four nos." Ora laughed, looking at me.

"When we have the instruments out," Malou insisted, "you can sing along then, and if it's bad we'll just drown you out so no one will know."

I snorted, adding a mocking, "Thanks."

We all stared into the fire, watching the flames dance between us.

"Any good stories from wherever you've come from?" Ora asked. "I think we've heard twenty different versions of every tale in the land."

"It sounds like you've traveled to every corner of Aotreas," Hector said. "Your accents are hard to pick."

"You'd never guess it." Malou chuckled, nodding to her companions. "None of us look like the kingdoms we were born in. Take Navin." She hooked her thumb at him. "He looks like he'd be home in Valta, hey?" Navin leaned forward and steepled his fingers against his lips, hiding a grin. "But say something in Valtan."

"*Inge asha astanne carrasrostrom.*" He barely got the words out before he burst into laughter.

It took me a second to realize he was even speaking the native tongue of Valta, the words were so jumbled. I thought he'd meant to say: hello, how are you? But it was nearly impossible to decipher. Everyone cackled with laughter.

"Eight years traveling with us and it hasn't gotten any better," Ora wheezed, wiping tears of laughter from their eyes.

"You must be from Damrienn, with the way you roll your *R*s," Sadie said.

"Wrong."

"Taigos?" Hector guessed.

Navin shook his head again.

"We're running out of kingdoms." Sadie chuckled, picking at the seed heads on the flowers beside her. "If you're not from Damrienn, Taigos, or Valta . . ."

"Olmdere," I said, as Navin's golden-brown eyes found mine.

His cheeks dimpled and he nodded.

"I've never met someone from Olmdere before," I whispered. Besides Briar and myself, I'd never met a single Olmderian. Other than the Rooks, of course.

"Not many people have," Navin said, his eyes hardening.

"Will you tell us about Olmdere?" Sadie asked. "What's it like there?"

"You'll see for yourself soon enough," Navin said, though his expression morphed to one of sorrow. "I was young when the Gold Wolf throne fell to Sawyn. I don't really remember a time before her Rooks patrolled the streets, before our grain was her grain, before our lives were her lives."

I bit the inside of my cheek. This was the side of the story I'd never heard before. I'd heard about the night I was born, but never about the aftermath. And definitely not about the humans.

Vellia always told us that Sawyn closed the borders to the kingdom and sent her Rooks out to scour the continent for Briar,
but . . . I'd never heard the tale of what had happened to all the
people who survived within Olmdere.

"It wasn't easy," Navin murmured. "We were cut off from all
trade within the continent and could only survive off what each
village could grow itself. When the blight came twelve years ago,
I escaped. There are a few secret ways out of Olmdere, through
the abandoned mines."

He sighed, scrubbing a hand down his face. I didn't even
know about the blight, nor any of the troubles my kingdom faced
while I grew up safe in that cabin in Allesdale. Beyond the Stormcrest Mountains, our people had been starving to death and I
had no idea. I picked at my fingernails, trying to distract myself
from my hitching breath. Those were my people, my parents'
people. And they'd been left to starve.

Grae's knee pressed into mine, and I wondered if he could see
the pain seeping out of me like the bending air above the fire's
flames. Did he know it hit me the same way I felt the blow of a
fist or kick of a boot? But this was a pain deeper than all others,
too—loss, hopelessness, shame.

"I still can't believe you made it out the other side," Malou
huffed, shoving more food into her mouth.

"Most didn't," Navin whispered. "It was an act of desperation. People who crossed the border like that had no other
choice. A slow death awaited us if we stayed . . . unless we pledged
ourselves to Sawyn. It's why my brother became a Rook."

We all froze, exchanging nervous looks between each other.

"That's why you pulled down their masks," Sadie murmured.
"You were searching for him?"

"I don't know what happened to the rest of my family who
remained," Navin murmured, neither confirming nor denying
Sadie's suspicion. "My father attempted to cross with me . . ."

Bile rose up my throat. This was my family's failure, and I felt every ounce of that shame. Grae's warm hand reached over and took my trembling fingers. He didn't look at me as his calloused palm squeezed my clammy hand.

"I'm sorry," Sadie said softly.

"I think you'll find most of us have sad stories to tell," Ora said, looking up to the milky constellation of stars. "When we get to Taigoska, we'll play them for you."

"Play?" Hector asked.

"Our stories." Ora added another log to the fire, embers spraying up from the ashes below. "We could tell you what happened, but a song will make you feel it. It's been the only thing I've found healing."

"That sounds beautiful," I whispered.

"One day." Ora looked at me. "We'll write your song."

Grae's hand clenched around mine and I dropped it.

"That would be nice," I said, standing up and feigning a yawn. "It's been a long day. I think I'll retire now."

"Good night," the group called. "Sleep well."

I was halfway to the tent when I heard Sadie say, "What about Valta? Any stories from there?"

Ora replied something I couldn't quite hear and they all erupted into laughter. It hurt hearing that laughter, and I wasn't sure why. They were all able to enjoy the bittersweetness of life while I only felt overwhelmed by it.

I couldn't let it be. The world wouldn't change if I accepted those stories of Navin's family as just another part of the rhythms of existence. That anxious thought filled me, not knowing what action I needed to take, but knowing I must act. I couldn't let Navin's life be just another story. What they said about Wolves not caring about humans anymore . . . if I did nothing, it would prove them all right.

I entered the tent and kicked off my boots, sighing as I peeled off my woolen socks. I wiggled my bare feet against the chilly canvas. The moon was bright in the sky, but the space was dark, the heavy shadows leaching the color from the room. I stared at

Grae's single bed roll and blanket. We could both fit better than the bunk for sure, but it would still be snug . . . I'd sleep on the floor.

I opened the front flap of my pack and felt for the glass jar that held my tea light candles and flint. I lit only one and placed it beside my pack, just enough light to see as I searched for any clothes I could use as a blanket.

The canvas swayed as the tent flap opened behind me, and I didn't need to look to know it was Grae.

"Are you okay?"

I hated that question. I pushed down the feelings threatening to rise up to the surface.

"Thank you for asking to travel with them," I said instead.

"You were right. It's a better plan to hide amongst them." Grae's discarded boots thudded to the floor, and his socks appeared beside me as I rifled through my pack. His gentle hand on my shoulder stilled my movements. "Talk to me."

"I'm just tired," I said, yanking out my cloak and laying it across the floor.

"Take the bedroll," Grae insisted.

"No—"

"I'll sleep by the door. Take it, you've had a worse few nights than me." I could feel his eyes lingering on my bruises. "I promise to take a turn tomorrow night if that'll convince you."

I sighed, still not looking up into those dark eyes. "Fine."

The air was too cold for me to undress. I'd sleep in my clothes. I crawled onto the bedroll, pulling the fur up to my shoulder and tucking my wounded chin over the top. It wasn't a bed in a palace, but it was far more comfortable than being directly on the ground.

My eyelids drooped, the warmth of the furs tugging me down toward sleep. I listened to Grae's ruffling, wondering what sort of makeshift bed he had constructed for himself but too exhausted to lift my head and look.

His deep voice carried easily across the silent room. "What Navin said . . ."

"Don't," I cut in, blowing out the candle flame flickering in front of me.

I screwed my eyes shut, as if the act alone could force me to sleep. I didn't want to talk to him about Navin's story or how many other Olmderians had similar tales to tell. What would my parents think? I felt the mounting weight of it all crushing down on me. Compared to the plight of humans, I had no sad song to sing. If I didn't help fix their world, I didn't deserve to mourn it. As I yielded to the warm tug of sleep, I tried to imagine what my song would sound like, but all I heard was silence.

TWENTY

THE ICY WINDS WHIPPED THROUGH THE TENT AND MY EYES cracked open. Seeing it was still nighttime, I wasn't sure how long I'd been asleep. My whole body trembled, the furs unable to fend off the chill as the storms picked up in the night. My fingers ached, curled so tightly in my blanket. Ostekke gut me, I was a fool. We were Wolves, we'd survive, but the bunks would be nice and warm right now . . . especially with Grae beside me.

"Grae?" I whispered, teeth clacking together.

"Yeah?"

"Are you awake?"

"I am now." His voice was husky with sleep. "Why?"

I shuddered, curling tighter into a ball. "Are you cold?"

"Freezing."

"Me too," I whispered, craning my neck up to see his shadowed figure lying across the threshold of the tent. The blustering wind rustled through the canvas. I couldn't make out the details of his face, but I knew he was watching me. "Well, get over here."

"Thank the Goddess," he rasped. "I thought we might both die from stubbornness."

I held my breath as he prowled over to the bedroll. He lifted the side of the blanket and I gasped at the rush of cold air.

"Sorry." He shuffled in.

I rolled to my side, facing him, and he wrapped his arms around me, pulling me into him so that we both fit. I tucked my face against his warm chest and sighed.

"Better?" he asked, and I nodded, folding further into his warmth. His arms tightened around me and my trembling eased.

"Thank you," I whispered.

I'd tried to push him away but couldn't, even as my anger at him for trying to stop me prevailed. There must be reasons for what he said in that tower. I could taste it even now—fear. He'd feared me leaving for reasons I didn't understand, had tried to make me stay because of that fear, but it made it harder to hate him for it. He was here now, his warmth reviving me, and the only thing that still felt right in this awful world was him and me.

"Thank you for taking pity on me." Grae chuckled, his warm breath in my hair.

"I did it for myself," I muttered, thinking of Navin's story again. "It seems Marriels only ever consider themselves."

Part of me wished I had never known about the horrors of Olmdere, but it also fed the fire deep in my belly. I knew with even more certainty I couldn't turn back. My people had suffered in ways I hadn't ever known. But now that I knew, I wouldn't turn a blind eye to it. I had wanted to defeat Sawyn to avenge my parents, to fulfill our own legacy. Those goals felt hollow and selfish now. I hadn't considered how much my people might need me—people my ancestors had vowed to protect. Sticky black shame filled me. It tarred my bones.

"I'm sorry for what has happened to Olmdere," Grae murmured, placing his hand on my cheek, careful to avoid my cuts. He tipped my head back, making me look into his eyes. A knot tightened in my throat as my eyes welled, letting him see my shame. "I know you care, Calla. You wouldn't be this upset if you didn't, but what Navin said is not your fault." I shook my head, trying to look away, but he held my face as a tear fell down my cheek and he swept it away with his thumb. "What happened to your kingdom is not your fault. None of this is your fault, little fox."

The dam broke as tears came spilling down my cheeks. Grae dropped his hand to pull me into him again. Tears stained his shirt as I sobbed. He ran a soothing hand down my back as it all rushed out of me. I felt rudderless in a fierce and unrelenting storm, thinking of all the things I should have done. All the ways I could have prepared.

I should've protected my sister. I should've helped my kingdom sooner. I should've demanded more of this world, and listened harder when it was demanding more of me.

My parents were gone, my sister cursed, my kingdom in ruin, and I was the last Marriel who could save it. But it wasn't just Briar's life that hung in the balance. An entire population had suffered devastating losses. It was too much. Before, my destiny had just been daydreams, and now, it was real and raw and vicious.

I fisted my hands in Grae's tunic as I wrung out my grief, clinging to him with desperation—the anchor in my storm.

"I've got you," he whispered, arms tightening around me. That tenderness broke me further. "I'm here."

I allowed myself to fall apart in his arms, knowing he would hang on to me. I purged that sorrow from me, that festering pain that threatened to swallow me whole, some of it building within me my whole life. My sobs slowly morphed into sniffles, riding over the sharp cliff of pain and tumbling down into exhaustion. The tension in my body eased and finally I could take a deep breath.

With each slower breath, I saw the road ahead with new clarity. I'd defeat Sawyn and spend the rest of my life making it up to them. No more people would risk their lives fleeing my kingdom. I'd give them something I'd never truly felt myself—home.

"HOW LONG HAVE YOU TWO BEEN TOGETHER?"

I lifted my eyes to meet Malou's assessing silver gaze. Grae bristled beside me, sitting a little straighter at the question. The back of the wagon was packed with the twins and Navin on one bench and all four of us Wolves across from them.

"It depends when you're counting from," Grae said. "Some might say we've been together our whole lives."

Mina smiled dreamily. "That's so romantic."

I coughed, trying to cover my laugh. She seemed more besotted with my mate than I did at that moment. My eyes scanned down her satin half-shirt, a sheer top over it revealing the peeks of skin on her shoulders and belly. It tucked into a pink pleated skirt, the fabric billowing at her feet. The garment was designed for hot Rikeshi summers, not the brisk air of Taigos, but she didn't seem to mind, her long thick hair wrapping around her back like a shawl.

I'd always wondered how people knew what to wear. The colors and patterns Mina wore now suited her perfectly—everything from the way she styled her hair to the golden rings on her fingers to the hue of her painted lips. I wished I could feel that way—so steady in my appearance. My clothes never looked right on my body, the shade of the fabric, the cut—it was always just off, as if my clothing was as confused about what I was trying to be as the rest of my soul.

"Where's your ring?" Malou nodded to my hand and I folded my arms.

"Lost," Grae and I both started at once.

Sadie and Hector snickered, and Grae gave them a look like a tutor scolding children.

"Are you going to get her a new one?" Malou looked between the two of us.

"It depends," Grae said.

I twisted toward him before he could carry on that sentence, worried he'd reveal something about who we were. I placed my hand on his knee and that seemed to catch him off guard.

"Shall we go ring shopping in Taigoska?" I cocked my head, putting on a honeyed tone that I knew he'd know was fake.

He dropped his hand on top of mine, holding it there, calling my bluff.

"Splendid," he said with equal charm. He leaned in and kissed my cheek, whispering, "Why haven't you looked at me all morning? Are we back to that?"

I blushed, pretending what he had said was a sweet nothing murmured in my ear. I batted him away playfully, but forcefully. "Oh you," I tittered, trying to sound like Briar. I had no clue how to play these cat and mouse games.

His observation cut, though. I hadn't been able to meet his gaze after our shared moment in the tent. That storm within me was too raw to relive in the daylight. I couldn't look at him without falling apart all over again. He probably thought it was directed toward him, but it was me I was protecting. That moment was too delicate to touch without it falling to pieces.

"I can't believe it's summer in Damrienn, and look." Sadie tipped her head to the half-moon window at the back of the wagon.

Flurries of snow danced in through the open window, melting before reaching the ground. With the insulated walls and press of so many occupants, they'd needed to open the window even in the blizzard. Galen den' Mora seemed to flex with each changing season, contort to the weather and the temperature, as if the magic applied not only to the oxen and the wheels but to the comfort of the occupants inside. I, for one, was grateful.

"Are you cold?" Navin asked, standing and turning to the bench before Sadie could object. He flipped up the wooden seat to reveal a compartment filled with pillows and blankets. "Here." He opened a blanket and leaned over to place it on Sadie's legs, but Hector snatched the corner, pulling it over both of them.

"Thanks," he said, covering his and his sister's legs with it. I pressed my lips together. Now he was just being childish. "Will we reach Taigoska tonight?" he asked, clearly having paid little attention to our many conversations about our travel plans.

"We're stopping in Hengreave," Malou replied. "We're scheduled to play for the Lord. We'll spend the night there and leave for the capital the following day."

Navin looked at Hector's pinched expression. "How long did you expect it would take to traverse an entire kingdom?"

"I don't know," Hector murmured, his shoulders rising to his ears as he stared. I could almost see his Wolf in the way he looked at Navin—hackles raised, snarling maw, vicious golden eyes. But, to Navin's credit, he kept his unwavering, open, kind face as he stared back.

"He's just eager to see Olmdere." Sadie covered for her brother, shifting her weight in front of him to break their stare down.

"It's a big climb into the Stormcrest Ranges, even for magical oxen," Malou said.

It felt like time we didn't have, yet the choice seemed out of our hands. Not with King Nero's hounds and Sawyn's Rooks out there looking for us.

Thinking of Nero, I released my hand off Grae's leg as if it were burning me, suddenly regretting the weakness that I showed him. I shouldn't have let myself go like that—shouldn't have cried in his arms. A life with him would mean being under King Nero's control, whether Grae wanted it that way or not. And if he promised me he'd stand up to his father this time, I still wouldn't believe him. There was just too much evidence to make me feel otherwise. And that little seed of doubt in his promises and actions was enough to undo any hope rising in my heart. I couldn't be happy with someone I didn't trust.

Grae cleared his throat as though trying to ignore my action. He lifted his arm and rested it across the back of the bench.

"There's not much to do in Hengreave," Malou said. "The tavern's halfway decent if you need somewhere to entertain yourselves while we're rehearsing, but . . ."

"We might hike the crater," Grae said. "Rumors say its waters have magical healing properties." He tipped his head toward me, and I felt keenly aware of the bruises on my face. "Worth a try."

"You've been to Hengreave before?"

"A few times," Grae hedged.

I'd imagined Wolves had invited him to all the important houses and towns in neighboring kingdoms as an ambassador. But Hengreave was a human town, ruled by a human Lord . . . it wouldn't make sense for the heir of Damrienn to be visiting there.

"I wouldn't hike up that crater for a thousand griftas," Malou said. "But suit yourself."

"It'll probably take you all day." Navin stretched his fingers out in front of him. "And that's if you're fast."

With a sudden rock of the wagon, my chest moved forward and slammed back into the unyielding wood bench. Grae's hand slipped from the backrest and caught my head just before it smacked into the wood.

"Esh! Fast reflexes there," Navin said.

I glowered at Grae. He should've just let me take the knock. It would've been fine, maybe the smallest bruise on my body at that point. My spine still ached from being stomped on by the Rooks, though Grae's salve had helped. It's the longest I'd ever remained wounded for, but I still didn't want to risk shifting.

"Maybe you should go lie down," Mina suggested.

Exhaustion hit me as though she had conjured it into being with her words. My limbs felt heavy, my head fuzzy, and I knew all of my energy was going into healing the many injuries covering my body.

"Good idea," I murmured, rising on shaking legs.

The wagon rocked again and I tumbled to the side. Grae's hands shot out, grabbing my hips and steadying me.

"I'm fine," I snarled, shoving his hands away when he didn't let go. No one seemed to notice the way I pushed him away, or, at the very least, didn't find it strange. I was too tired to act like his wife.

He just said "Mmhmm," and the next thing I knew Grae was standing before he scooped one arm under my legs and the other under my back. He lifted me with ease, climbing the steps up to the second level.

"They're adorable." Malou's voice dripped with sarcasm.

"Put me down," I hissed.

"You're not used to being this injured," Grae whispered back, echoing my own thoughts. The warmth of his chest radiated into my cheek. My limbs betrayed me as they wrapped around him, hypnotized by his warmth. "The last thing we need is you falling and cracking your head open. Plus, I'm supposed to be your doting husband, remember?"

"Fine," I snapped, and he chuckled.

We reached my bunk and Grae gently set me down. He pulled away only an inch, his warm breath skirting over my cheek.

His eyes stormed with intensity as he said, "You must be tired."

"Why?" I breathed.

His hand slid up my arm toward my fingers, still wrapped around his neck. "You can let go of me now."

"Right." My cheeks set on fire. I hastily released him and turned away.

"Sweet dreams, little fox," he whispered.

"THANK THE MOON WE DON'T HAVE TO SLEEP ON THAT WAGON again." Hector shucked his boots and set them beside the roaring fire. The rocky ride had taken its toll on him and he still looked peakish.

I stared out the window, chill seeping from the pane. Below, the village of Hengreave was buried in snow. Mounds of grimy brown ice lined the streets, the steep rooftops dusted in white. How deep was the town submerged? I couldn't see the cobbles or the bottom steps that led down from the raised houses.

"You should ride up front with Ora," Sadie said, swinging her feet from the top bunk.

Grae had bought out the entire room, so we didn't have to share with travelers. Two bunks, a seating area, and a giant clothes rack around a hearth to dry snow-sodden clothes. I was grateful that he hadn't tried to get a suite for just the two of us. I didn't think I could handle another night alone with him.

"I've got to keep an eye on you," Hector replied, tilting his head and staring up at his sister. His shortly cropped hair was growing long enough to stick up at odd angles now and he brushed down his stubbly hair.

"I don't *need* you to keep an eye on me," Sadie retorted.

"I've seen the way that human looks at you." Hector glanced at Grae. "Right?"

Grae laughed and continued unpacking his bag. "I'm staying out of this."

"He doesn't look at me like anything, and his name is Navin, not *that human*," Sadie growled.

"It wouldn't work out, Sadie." Hector stretched out on his bed, placing his hands behind his head. "He's not one of us."

"I *know*—"

"Enough," I snapped, my breath fogging the glass. "She gets it, Hector. Back off."

"Not all halflings have cheerful stories like Lord Hengreave," Hector muttered. "If the Silver Wolf pack hasn't disowned us already, this would definitely do it."

"Wait—" I whirled. "Lord Hengreave is a halfling?"

"You didn't know?"

"I can't imagine gossip was a part of her lesson plans," Grae noted, laying his jacket over the wooden slats of the clothes rack.

"It's one of those things that everyone knows, but no one talks about," Sadie said, combing her fingers through her hair. "Lord Hengreave is the illegitimate son of the late Taigosi king and half-brother of the current queen."

"What?" My eyes widened. "I didn't think it was possible to conceive a half-wolf."

"It's possible," Hector muttered, tucking his hands under his head. "But rare."

"The Taigosi king gave his son a lordship out here, away from the city and the Ice Wolf pack." Sadie shook her head. "The late Queen was none too pleased."

Vellia had taught us all about the different royal families, but I'd never heard this part of the Taigosi history before.

"Don't get too comfortable," Grae said, switching the subject. "We're hiking up the crater today."

"Do we have to?" Sadie groaned.

"No one will be up there." Grae kept his back to us, laying his gear across the top bunk. He'd brought a slew of weapons with him and an extensive kit of elixirs and remedies. No wonder his bag dropped like a stone whenever he set it down. "We need to shift."

"*We* don't need to shift." Sadie raked her fingers through her bangs, pointing her foot at me. "She does."

"I'm fine," I said with little conviction. I'd slept the rest of the day and through the night in the wagon and still didn't feel fully revived. Sleep seemed like the only thing I could do, and it wasn't enough. "I'm healing."

"At the pace of a human." Hector looked me over. "That wound on your chin hasn't even fully scabbed over yet." He pretended to gag and I scowled at him. "How the humans handle it, I have no idea."

"I'll survive," I muttered, narrowing my eyes at him. I unlaced the leather strapping holding my pack closed and pulled out the tincture Ora gave me.

"And if we suddenly get attacked by Rooks again?" Hector asked. "Is that salve going to help us fight a mob? Think like a soldier, Calla."

Grae nodded. "Exactly."

I groaned as I sat beside my bag and rested my head against the peeling wallpaper. "I have been thinking."

Sadie unsheathed her knife from her belt and twisted it in her hands. "That's not ominous at all."

"If you two turn back now—"

"No," the siblings said in unison.

"I've already tried, little fox," Grae said, selecting a dagger to add to his belt. "They may squabble endlessly, but on this they agree."

"You could blame us," I pleaded. "Say that we made you and you had no other choice."

"King Nero would still skin us alive," Hector said. "We disobeyed him. And to disobey him is to turn our backs on the pack."

I ground my teeth until my jaw muscles ached. "That's a stupid rule."

"It's one your ancestors benefited greatly from," Hector reminded, crossing his legs and staring at the slates above him. "The Wolves became Gods to the humans, and the Kings became Gods to the Wolves."

"Even without Grae," Sadie cut in, "we'd still have come. Maez is like our sister. She's our family. And if Princess Briar is still alive, that means Maez is still alive, too, and I won't let her rot away in a dungeon, even if it means being killed for saving her."

I rubbed my hand down my face, grimacing as my fingers skated over my bruised jaw. "I'm sorry."

"You didn't put us in this position, Calla," Hector said. "But maybe when you're Queen of Olmdere, you can pardon us."

My eyes darted to Grae. "You told them?"

"That's your story to tell." Grae shook his head. "But they guessed it."

"It seemed far more likely than that faery finding another random Gold Wolf pup the exact same age as the princess and deciding to raise them together," Hector said, tipping over the side of his bed to look at me. "They say the Marriels had green eyes and red hair. Your sister got the red hair and you the green eyes."

"And then you and Briar both finding fated mates on the same full moon. It's so obvious now that I think of it." Sadie chuckled. "I don't know why we hadn't guessed it before."

"No wonder King Nero didn't want us to rescue Maez," Hector said. "He traded one Gold Wolf Princess for another, and the mate of his son, no less. He doesn't need Briar anymore."

"That's all we're good for," I snarled. "Being married off to princes."

Grae's fingers stilled on the laces of his boots, but he didn't reply.

"I've been thinking," Hector said, no subtlety in his change of subject. "We should try to find some nitehock while we're in the capital."

"Stealing poisons?" Sadie leaned over to look down at her brother. "You can't be serious."

"They're said to nullify dark magic." Hector glared back at her. "And we honestly need all the options we can think of. Does anyone else have a better plan? How are we meant to kill Sawyn with her full power turned on us? You saw what she did in Highwick."

"If a few more Wolves tried to fight her off, it could've gone differently," I noted, and Hector had the good sense to look ashamed. They'd been there and they did nothing.

"But there won't be a few more Wolves," Hector countered. "Just us four, maybe five if we free Maez and she's in a good enough condition to fight . . . that's not exactly an army."

"We won't find nitehock in the human quarter, not prepared at least," I said. "Maybe the seeds, but even then we'd have to find an illegal trader. And it's too risky to go near the Ice Wolves."

"They wouldn't look twice at us if we were with the humans. We could slip in and out of the palace through the servants' quarters undetected. Wouldn't you feel better storming into your castle knowing you had a weapon that could actually defeat the sorceress?" Hector looked between Sadie and Grae for support, but neither of them looked convinced. "Galen den' Mora is playing in the capital in two days' time. We could go with them. It's the perfect cover."

"I'm with Calla," Sadie said, laying back in her bunk. "It's too dangerous."

"So is going into Olmdere without any way to defeat Sawyn," Hector snapped.

The whole room stiffened. Hector had a good point. We needed every advantage, and if we were too afraid to steal poison from the Ice Wolves, how well would we fare killing a powerful sorceress once we reached Olmdere?

"Maybe—"

"We should get a move on if we want to be back before sunset," Grae cut me off, changing the subject once more. This wasn't exactly the room for finished conversations.

"You two should go," Sadie said. "We'll hang back. I want to listen to their rehearsals."

Hector snickered. "You just want to watch Navin play."

"If you want to hike up a mountain on our day off, Hector," she suggested sweetly, "I won't stop you."

"Especially if you decide to throw yourself off," she muttered.

"Good point," Hector said, and I was pretty sure he hadn't heard that last part. "I'll hang back and keep an eye on things here." Hector looked at me and then pointedly up to the bunk above him where Sadie was sitting.

"I already told you there's nothing to keep an eye on," she said, leaning forward and glaring down at her brother.

He shrugged, feigning innocence. "Then it won't matter that I keep my eyes open anyway, right?"

I bent and pulled back on my boots. "I'm ready to go," I said, marching to the door. "I can't take any more of the sibling bickering."

"Agreed," Grae said, giving the pair one last stern look. "Keep a low profile and stay out of trouble. We'll be back by sunset."

"Aye, aye captain." Sadie gave a mock bow.

"Insufferable fools," Grae muttered, pushing out the doorway.

"You picked them to be your personal guard," I pointed out, following him out the doorway.

"That's because I'm a fool, too."

TWENTY-ONE

OUR BOOTS CRUNCHED THROUGH THE ICE-CRUSTED SNOW. I panted whorls of steam as each footstep squeaked beneath my feet. We walked in stilted silence, climbing toward the crater high above us. My lungs burned in the thin Taigosi air, my brow slicked with sweat.

"Nearly there," Grae breathed as he climbed toward the ridge. "Do you remember the story I told you about Herren's last wish, little fox?"

"Why? Are we going to freeze to death?" I clenched my jaw, bracing against another gust of wind. Was it possible for eyelashes to freeze?

He grinned. "So you do remember."

"Of course I do, it was a good story." I wheezed. "Herren's family was trapped up a mountain, attacked by ebarvens and freezing to death. A faery appeared to grant his last wish. He wished that his family stay warm until help arrived."

"The faery cleaved the mountain in two, drilling into its hot core." Grae carried on the story, just as he had when we were young. "And Herren's family survived in the hot springs, keeping warm and hiding from the ebarvens until aid came."

I glanced back at the town of Hengreave. We'd climbed so far from the village that it was only a dot in a sea of white. "They built a town at the base of the mountain, believing the land was blessed."

Grae stumbled the last few slippery steps up to the peak. "And the waters are still believed to be magical, even to this day."

I gasped when I saw the turquoise water come into view. Steam curled from the lake and a faint sulphuric scent wafted in the air.

"It's beautiful," I whispered, staring at the rivulets of ice that melted into the lake at the center. Giant icicles dripped down from hollow caverns like the teeth of a frozen beast.

"This is one of my favorite places," Grae murmured.

I tore my eyes away from the sweeping vista and found Grae staring at me. Wisps of his hair whipped across his forehead. His cheeks and nose were wind-chapped, his lips parted.

My eyes widened, the memory flooding back to me all at once. "This is it, the place from your stories?" His cheeks dimpled and I gazed back out at the steaming lake, remembering the stories he told me when we were pups. He'd told me about how he'd run in the fresh powder and swum in the hot pools—that it felt like another world and . . .

"You promised to bring me here one day."

"I did." His gaze lingered on my face. "I didn't think it would be like this, though."

I shifted my feet, uncomfortable under his stare. Like this— with me being wary, distrustful of him, without the easy joy and laughter that used to be what our friendship was built of. That tension still hung between us, and I knew at some point, some- how, it would all come to a head.

"Come on," he said, staving off that moment while trudging down the side of the crater. "We'll change in the caves."

Hengreave disappeared as we dipped below the lip of the cra- ter. I followed Grae toward a curling tunnel of ice. It looked as if one mighty ocean wave had smashed over the side of the crater, frozen in motion. Such a bizarre structure—a long, hollowed-out cavern at the center of the spiral. Grae trudged into the tapered passage. The room seemed made of glass with dripping icicles of the palest blue. The image of the crater twisted and distorted as I stared through the translucent ice and our footsteps echoed across the bright space.

I ducked into an alcove to change, putting a wall of ice between Grae and me. The walls flowed in waves of beautiful crystal as if they melted and froze and melted again, hundreds of times. I traced my finger over the cold ripples, lost in this other world.

Grae's movement to my right made me turn my head, and what I saw made the ice burn beneath my fingers. His image was so warped I could hardly make out his shape, but instead of charcoal clothes, I saw only his golden brown skin. He reached to the knot of hair on his head and untied it, black now cascading down to his shoulders. He turned away from me, facing the opposite wall, in what I assumed was an act of modesty for me.

"Are you getting changed, little fox?" he asked.

I hastily unclipped the latch of my cloak and let it pool around my feet. "Yes."

"Or am I distracting you?" I could tell by his infuriatingly attractive voice that he was smiling.

"No, nope," I said, whipping my tunic over my head and unbuttoning my trousers.

"Good, because if you kept staring at me like that, your Wolf would probably combust and shred off all your clothes."

"I wasn't looking at you," I protested, yanking down my trousers.

Stepping out of them, I looked up to see Grae watching *me* through the ice. My nipples peaked against the chill. How much could he see? We stared at each other, my shallow breaths steaming the air. Both of us bare. Only a thin layer of ice stood separating his naked form from mine. Part of me wished I was bold enough to walk around the wall, confront him like this. I knew from his form-fitting leathers that his body would be glorious.

Gods, I wish he didn't make me feel like such a puppy.

Grae turned and left down the passageway before I could summon the courage to move.

"I'll see you outside."

Part of me was excited when Sadie and Hector hung back, but now, being along with Grae . . . There was too much there between us, too many unsaid things. It made me feel unsteady, second-guessing my every word and action. And I wished then that I had some of Briar's confidence. She'd have known exactly how to act.

An impatient howl echoed into the cavern.

The sound called to the most primal part of me, and the shift took me by surprise. With a sweet pain and sharp release, I fell onto all fours. I whirled in a circle, looking at my swishing red tail. Never had something triggered the shift in me like that. It had come on so fast I couldn't even think, the Wolf in me instantly reacting to his howl. I loved and hated it all at once, that my body could react to him so acutely. I felt out of control and a strange belonging all at the same time. All those contradictory feelings battled within me, trying to make sense of this white-hot burning in my gut.

I shoved it all down. I'd make sense of it later. Right now, I needed to run.

I bolted out of the wave of ice, shooting like an arrow through the powder. I didn't stop to look at Grae as I zoomed around the lip of the crater, leaning into the slope with delight, letting gravity propel me faster.

"You think you can outrun me, little fox?" Grae's playful voice whispered into my mind.

The connection between us now felt stronger than ever. I felt him in every cell of my body—his voice, his scent.

"You might be bigger, but I'm faster," I taunted, zipping through the swirling steam from the hot pools.

Grae's chuckle skittered through me and I felt him pick up the pace as if it was my own legs burning. I pushed harder into my haunches. The feeling of the wind in my fur and the powder beneath my paws was something close to ecstasy. The bruises and weariness from the battle in Nesra's Pass lifted and the sudden absence of pain was euphoric. This moment—there was a rightness to it all. Grae chased me just as he had when we were young. A giddy laugh filled me as he drew closer, nipping at my ankles. His muzzle knocked me in the side and I lost my footing, tumbling into the snow.

"Oh, you are so dead," I teased, his laughter filling my mind. I whirled on him as he bolted in the opposite direction.

In five strides, I caught up to him and sank my teeth into his flank. Yelping, he turned to get me back, but I was already dashing away.

"You're faster than a snow snake," he panted, taking off after me again.

My muscles grew heavy, filled with a pleasant burning as I raced through the snow. My heart thundered in my chest. On and on, the minutes stretched by with nothing but my panting breath and the snow beneath my paws. With each passing moment, I felt Grae fall a little further behind.

"Time to slow down, little fox," Grae panted. "You're going to pull something and I don't want to have to carry you down this mountain."

Our Wolves could walk for days on end, but we weren't distance sprinters. Our bodies were designed for short bursts of action and long stretches at a slower pace. But I pushed myself right to the brink of pain, relishing the all-consuming feeling of it. In my Wolf form, everything else felt miles away. I was so in my body and out of my mind. I ran as if my troubles were chasing me—Briar, King Nero, even Grae.

"Don't be a puppy," I jeered, pushing harder, zigzagging along a patch of slippery ice before plunging back into the snow.

"Seriously, Calla."

I ran faster, as if I could avoid his words, and I knew he chased after me in earnest then. I couldn't stop. The comedown was not something I wanted to face. Let me pretend nothing else existed for a little while longer.

Grae barreled into me, knocking me into a deep snowbank. I growled as I shook the powder from my fur. I met his golden eyes and finally really looked at him.

His fur was a brilliant shade of silver, tipped with black. Obsidian ears and a muzzle and tail that faded to a shade of midnight. He looked regal even in his fur. He had always been that breathtaking, even when we were young. But his lanky body had bulked out in muscle just as his human form had. He was in his prime now, his presence more dominating, his scent more alluring.

"I thought you might never look at me again." His voice was a whisper in my head. "You are just as stunning in your furs as you are in your skin, little fox."

"Thanks," I breathed.

"I wish you believed it," Grae murmured, cocking his head at me. "You can't help but pull me in, though I know how hard you try not to."

Reality caught up to me then. Not even my Wolf could outrun it. My sister was cursed, and a kingdom riddled with Rooks stood between us and her salvation. I was fated to the son of a greedy king and expected to take my sleeping twin's place on her throne.

"I'm just trying to survive," I whispered into his mind. "That's all I can do."

Grae hung his head. "Let's go for a swim," he said. "Maybe there's a few more miracles in these waters."

I huffed, grateful he hadn't pushed me any further. My paws were growing cold. Even my Wolf form couldn't comfort me forever. I trotted after him down toward the lake. Grae's front paws entered the water. He got as far as his chest before shifting back into his human form.

My heart lurched as I gaped at his muscled back, the water lapping low around his hips. He was a perfectly sculpted warrior, better than any painting or statue. I studied the three long scars trailing down his back. They must have been brutal to not have been healed by shifting.

He waded in deeper, up to his chest, and dipped his head back, slicking the hair off his face. He glanced over his shoulder at me and I snapped shut my gaping maw. My gaze dropped to the swirling turquoise water and I took another step, wondering if any magic was left below its surface. I looked back at Grae's muscled physique and gulped. I needed whatever magic I could get.

TWENTY~TWO

THE WATER WAS THE WARMEST BATH THAT NEVER GREW COLD. I swirled my arms around, mindlessly drifting around the lake with my eyes shut. The water was so buoyant, I barely needed to paddle to stay afloat.

"Your wounds look much better." Grae's voice made me open my eyes.

I ran my fingers along my chin, feeling for the gash, but it was smooth. It was still tender, but vastly improved. My back and chest didn't ache from the kicks anymore. I felt lighter than I had in days. The ringing in my left ear finally gone.

I met Grae's hooded eyes. "Thank you for bringing me here."

"I promised you I would."

Plumes of steam whorled between us like little clouds. I wiggled my toes into the silty bottom of the hot pools, wondering if the story about the lake's creation was true. Faery magic was a powerful thing. Vellia hadn't torn down a mountain, but she'd raised us for twenty years. Food, clothing, shelter—it probably took even more magic over that long span of time. It didn't look as epic as a massive crater in a mountain, but she had given us both a life, all because my mother wished it so.

Not everyone got to make a last wish. The Goddess came too swiftly for most, reclaiming them to the earth, but for those lucky souls who lingered with one foot in the afterlife, sometimes a faery would appear and grant one final wish. I wondered what my father would've wished for if he'd had the chance.

"Have you ever thought about what wish you'd make?" I peered from the dunes of snow back at him. "Your last wish?"

Grae's brow furrowed. "Sometimes a person's only wish is for it to end."

I blinked at him, rolling his words around in my mind. It was clear he was speaking of someone, though I didn't know who. There was a sorrow in his words that surprised me. I wanted to ask more, but he carried on.

"I suppose I'd wish for you." His words were so low I strained to hear them. Those umber eyes drifted down my face to my lips. "I'd wish to break the mating bond and let you survive without me."

Pain stabbed through my chest. My body responded as if our bond was being threatened, even by that confession. It felt so unsettling, so wrong. I didn't know what it was I wanted from Grae, but I knew for certain it wasn't that.

I could barely get the words out. "I pray you never have to make that wish."

His hands swirled idly by his sides. "Me too."

I stepped closer, dipping lower, even though I knew he couldn't see my breasts beneath the cloudy water. "Do you ever wish we could go back in time? To when we were just Calla and Grae?"

"We are still just Calla and Grae."

"No. We're not." My voice thickened. "Not like then."

I squinted as the thick clouds parted, sunlight brightening the snow until it was nearly blinding.

Grae slicked a wet hand over his hair. "Who we are to each other is infinite. Our bond will only ever grow and strengthen. It will always be you and me. Always."

"You don't know that."

His fingers touched my chin, lifting my gaze as water dripped from his hand. "I do." The certainty and stillness in his words made me shudder. "I know it more than my title, or my pack, or even my name. I know I was meant to be yours."

My hands trembled as I reached up to touch his cheek, searching his eyes. The words I wanted to say were so close to the tip of my tongue. My thumb skimmed his bottom lip and his mouth parted. It would be so easy to claim him, with my words, with my body.

I lifted up, shoulders breaching the surface of the water as my breasts brushed against Grae's chest. His hand curled around to the back of my neck and he watched my lips with hooded eyes, waiting for me to bridge the distance between us.

A keening howl rent the air.

Our heads snapped toward the sound.

"Is it—"

"It's not Sadie or Hector," Grae whispered, instinctively gathering me tighter to him as we both lowered deeper into the water. The brush of my skin against his was electrifying, even as my ears strained toward the sound.

"Ice Wolves?" I whispered as another baying howl echoed across the crater.

"No," Grae growled. "They're Silver Wolves—Hemming, Soris, Aiden. They're my father's guards."

"Shit." I wrapped my arms around him tighter, remembering those guards from the palace in Damrienn.

He tilted his head toward the sound and we watched as five dots darted across the lip of the crater and past to the far side of the mountain.

"They're not going to Hengreave?"

"They probably don't think we'd stop in a human town," Grae said, staring at the horizon as if they might reappear. "I'm guessing they're heading to Taigoska to speak with the Queen."

We both remained still, watching the ridge line. Another howl echoed up, more distant than the last.

"I think we're safe," I whispered, though I didn't release my grasp from around Grae's neck. His arms remained tight, holding me flush against his naked body.

"For now. We should head back to warn the others," Grae murmured, his eyes drifting back to my mouth.

"Yes." I nodded breathlessly.

His arms loosened around me, letting me go, and a flicker of disappointment flashed through me.

Before I could give it a second thought, I tightened my grip around his neck and lifted, my mouth landing on his. He didn't miss a beat, hauling me back against his muscled chest, his lips meeting mine in a hot, burning kiss. I claimed him with my tongue, the frenzy building in me as he groaned into my mouth. The hard outline of him pressed against my belly, spurring me on.

A deep hiss circled the hot pool.

I released Grae at the sound, searching the crater for the telltale line of mounded snow. Ice creaked as we scanned for the monsters, probably driven back over the mountain by the thundering pack of Wolves. I hadn't spotted any ebarven burrows on the trek up, but this would be a perfect place for the snow snakes to hide. I shuddered, thinking of the paintings of their long white bodies and beady blue eyes.

"We really should get back," I whispered.

"Yes," he said, watching me with wanton eyes.

I smiled, planting one last chaste kiss on his swollen lips, and he hovered there, leaning in as if he couldn't pull away.

"We've got curses to break and kingdoms to save."

"I thought you wanted to be just Calla and Grae?" He rubbed a wet hand down his face, trying to regain his composure.

"Maybe we can be everything: rulers, friends . . ."

"Mates?"

I took another step back to keep from throwing myself at him. I needed the distance with that hopeful look in his eyes.

My voice was barely a whisper. "Maybe."

His eyes darkened as he trailed his finger along my collarbone, to the spot where his necklace used to sit. "Maybe." He hummed. "I can work with maybe, until I can prove myself worthy of more."

He turned away, striding toward the shoreline before I could reply. The memory of me throwing my necklace back at him flashed into my mind. I thought he wasn't going to help me and I had done the thing that I thought would break him the most. It was a cruel, childish thing to do—to make him hurt the way I hurt inside. But he was here now, not telling me to turn back or change my course. How far would he let me push? The answer whispered in my mind: as far as I was willing to go.

I watched as the water flowed down his torso and he shifted again before I could admire his figure any further. The Silver Wolf didn't wait for me as he walked back up to where we had stashed our clothes.

I wanted to shout after him—to tell him he was already worthy of me. He was worthy the moment he chose to be my friend all those many years ago. But instead, I silently trudged out of the warm water and back into the stinging snow.

A MELODIC CHORUS OF STRINGS SANG DOWN THE ALLEYWAY. A sign across the back door of Galen den' Mora read *Rehearsing* in four languages. Climbing up the steps, we peeled back the curtains to reveal the quartet huddled around the table. They didn't pause to look at us, all focused on the song they were playing.

Malou held something akin to a fiddle, though longer and narrower. Mina played another stringed instrument with her fingers, a deeper, resonant sound carrying across her twin's melody. Ora played a long wooden lute, and Navin plucked a beautiful, gilded harp. Their notes flowed at a sweet, slow pace that made me feel a churning nostalgia in my gut.

I'd always loved this tune: "The Lone Rose." It was a perennial favorite at balls and soirees, according to Vellia. It was also an easy, slow song to learn to dance to. Vellia had conjured these tunes for Briar and me, and we'd take turns being the leader and follower of the dances. I heard the sound of my laughter as I stepped on Briar's toes as readily as I could hear the notes now. Briar had taken it so seriously, and her frustration had only made me laugh harder.

Grae put his arm around me and pulled me into his side, kissing the top of my head. He did it with mindless ease, as if it was something he'd done a thousand times before and would do a thousand times again. I welcomed his smoky scent and comforting warmth as the sweetness of my memories turned to ash, replaced by the image of Briar on that cold tomb.

Sadie leaned forward, her head in her hands, listening with the ever-present scowl on her face. To an outsider, it looked as if she wasn't pleased to be there, but her stare never seemed to veer from one player in particular.

The song crescendoed to a flourishing close, the trilling lute singing its last sonorous notes. The group didn't pause, flipping the sheets of music on the table and adding little notes in the margins. It was impressive, not only to see their skill but also their diligent preparations for that night's performance.

Grae seized the opportunity to whisper to Sadie, "Where's Hector?"

Sadie reluctantly broke her gaze from the harpist. "At the pub. Why?"

"We spotted some . . . people heading east."

"Shit," she hissed. "Do you think they're going to Taigoska?"

Grae bobbed his head. "That would be my guess."

"Good," she hedged. "When they get there and the Queen has seen no sign of us, they'll move on. Meanwhile, we'll be rolling into town."

"Let's hope so," Grae muttered.

"So long as we stay with the troupe, we'll be fine." Sadie unsheathed a knife from her thigh strap. I narrowed my eyes at the movement, her bravado undermined by her nervous habit of playing with her weapons.

"I'm going to find Hector and let him know. I could use

a drink." Grae's arm dropped off my shoulder. "You want to come?"

"Nah," Sadie said, even though Grae was asking me.

"Quiet in the wagon, please," Ora called in a singsong voice, as if scolding small children.

I gave Grae a little nod, threading my fingers through his. He seemed instantly relieved that I agreed to come. After what had almost happened between us in that lake, I didn't want to be away from him. It felt like any distance might undo the steps we'd made.

I know I was meant to be yours.

The hair on my arms stood on end. I'd relived those words again and again with every step down the mountain. I tried to tease apart all my thoughts like a ball of poorly wound twine, but they were too knotted together, and I prayed a drink at the pub would help.

TWENTY~THREE

"AREN'T YOU WORRIED YOU'LL BE RECOGNIZED?" I ASKED, shuffling along the wooden bench beside Grae.

We found Hector at a rundown pub that reeked of old ale, sitting in a far shadowed booth.

"No one in Hengreave knows what the Damrienn prince looks like." Grae blew out the candle in the center of the table. Even in our skin, we could see better than most humans and it would fend off any prying eyes. "Not unless they've traveled to the palace in Taigoska, and I doubt anyone here would've garnered an invitation."

I twirled my fingers through the twisting trails of smoke. "You've been to the crater before, though?"

"From the opposite side of the ranges, the same way the Silver Wolves went. I'd stop there on my way to Taigoska."

I pursed my lips. "But you were careful in Allesdale, when you came to collect me and Briar?"

Drunken laughter erupted from two men at the bar and I jolted. It was a quiet evening, half the tables empty.

"Allesdale is part of my kingdom," he whispered. "I've traveled through Damrienn far more extensively, and more humans work in our castle."

I cocked my head. "You don't think a human from Hengreave could've traveled to Highwick?"

"Most humans don't have the luxury of ever leaving the town they were born into." Hector snorted into his tankard. "And those with enough coin to travel the realm aren't coming to a place like this." He took another long swig and gestured around the seedy, dark room.

A barmaid dropped three plates on the table. "Here ya are. Three fry ups." She set down two cups for Grae and me, one filled with golden liquid, the other maroon. We hadn't ordered them, and I guessed they were probably whatever drinks they had left.

Grae peered into the two glasses and swapped them, moving the golden one in front of my plate. I arched my brow.

"You still prefer the honey wine?"

He'd remembered.

Eight years . . . it was eight years ago that I'd told him how Briar and I would sneak drinks from the local tavern and that the only one I could stomach was the honey wine.

"Yes," I whispered. He'd really remembered my stories as well as I remembered his.

I took a sip of the sweet honeyed wine, staring at the food swimming in a soupy gravy.

Hector chuckled at my frown. "It's no roast pheasant, but I reckon it tastes better."

I picked up my spoon and scooped up a bite of mashed potatoes. The buttery, salty flavors lit up my tongue. A hint of rosemary and sage.

"See?" Hector said. "The worst-looking places always have the best food."

As I took another bite, I hummed my pleasure and Grae's hand slid under the table to my knee. I never knew a hand on a knee could feel so intoxicating. I took another long swig of my wine, letting it burn down my throat as I darted a heated glance in his direction. His eyes darkened, his fingers pressing in on the flesh of my knee, and I knew exactly what he was thinking about.

Our heated gazes hooked into each other. We'd left that moment in the crater unfinished between us. It made me agitated and antsy to actualize what we'd started. That taunting kiss. The feel of his naked body . . .

Hector coughed. "Should I leave?"

"Yes," Grae said at the same time I said, "No."

Hector snickered. "Mates."

Grae's hand left my knee and he took a long, frustrated breath that made me smile around the rim of my wineglass.

"I can't believe Sadie would rather listen to music than come drink with us," Hector said through a mouthful of food.

"I don't think it's the music that's motivating her," Grae said, scooping up a spoonful of peas.

I tried to shoot him a warning look, knowing how Hector would take it, but Grae seemed intent on his food and drink.

"So it's not just me, then?" Hector raised his eyebrows. "You think she fancies Navin?"

"We shouldn't be talking about her like this," I scolded the two of them. "It's her business. Let her handle it."

"It's not just her business," Hector said, slopping a piece of bread into his gravy. "She's a Wolf, he's a human. If the pack found out, they'd call her a skin chaser or worse. It's pack business."

"Pack business?" I asked. "The same pack that you're defying just by sitting here?"

Hector's gaze dropped back to his plate. But he wasn't wrong. They'd move Sadie down the ranks if the rumors spread. She'd lose her standing in the pack and her reputation would be tarnished. Navin would probably be fine. Humans would judge him for it, but since he was already a traveler, he'd probably not be stuck with any small-town gossip for long. There would be no prying villagers for him, but for Sadie, she could lose everything.

But I was just doing the same thing as Hector: clinging to the pack like I was actually a part of it. Contorting and breaking everything I was to fit their mold. Giving the idea of the pack so much faith when I'd receive none of their loyalty in return. Why did I grab on to the pack's rules so tightly even as I fled them? Like they hadn't already forced me to make a choice.

The light beyond the fogged windows dimmed as the sun set beyond the rooftops.

"We should go back soon. They'll be heading to the Lord's manor for their performance and I don't want to leave Sadie alone," Hector said, swigging the last of his ale.

"We'll meet you back there," Grae said, taking another bite of his food. He gestured to Hector's already empty plate. "Not all of us eat like wild animals."

Hector shrugged. "See you at the wagon," he said, grabbing his cloak folded over the back of the booth.

As Hector walked away, my heart began to race. The closeness of Grae, alone, in this dark booth made every sense feel heightened. That kiss in the crater was an unfulfilled promise, and now my body craved him like something I'd never known before. All I could smell was his scent. All I could hear were his steady breaths.

I took one more bite of potatoes and pushed the plate away. Leaning back against the hardwood, I folded my arms.

My eyes flitted to his. Just looking at him made me want to combust. In the shadows, his cheeks and jawline were sharper, his features more wolflike. The depths of my yearning made every muscle tense. I gritted my teeth, angry at myself for how all-consuming this feeling was. It was something I'd never done before, but all I could think about was the desperate need for Grae to help me find that release.

"You're not hungry?" Grae asked.

"Not for food."

A feral growl boomed from Grae's chest as he dropped his

spoon and it clanged onto his plate. His hand was back on my knee. That touch alone made my lips part.

"Gods, if you keep looking at me like that, I'm going to take you right here on this table," he rasped.

His hand slid up my leg and I parted my thighs, arching, so lost in that desperation for his hand to drift higher.

"You'd let me do it, wouldn't you? You'd let me fuck you right here?" His fingers dug into my fleshy thigh and he let out a deep chuckle. "You want me that badly?"

"Yes," I breathed, that magical desperate yearning making my eyes flutter closed as he planted a kiss on my neck.

He pulled away and I opened my eyes to find his heated gaze on me, filled with the predatory stillness of a wolf stalking his prey. His hand lifted off my thigh and my skin begged for the warmth of his dominating grip.

"Not here," he whispered.

I swallowed, ice dousing my flames. Goddess, what was I doing? I was trying to seduce him in the middle of a sordid pub. My eyes glanced to my half-empty glass of wine. I couldn't blame the drink for my salacious actions. Shame burned my cheeks as I dropped my gaze to my hands. I was such a fool.

"Ugh, I'm sorry," I murmured, wishing the ground would swallow me whole.

"Hey." Grae's fingers gently turned my face back to him. "Don't think for one second I don't want you just as desperately. Every ounce of me is fighting the beast inside me that wants to claim you in every way." His eyes were molten umber, burning into me. "But when I have you, I'm going to make you moan my name so loud even the moon will hear." My breath hitched as heat pooled in my core. "And then the Goddess will know for certain that she was right for giving me to you."

His words ignited my soul, a white-hot need devouring me. My mind raced with all the ways he might fulfill that promise. I bit my lip so hard I thought it might bleed, trying to steady myself. A wicked grin spread across his face as he watched what his words did to me.

I cleared my throat. "Let's take the long way back," I muttered. "I think I need the fresh air."

He chuckled. "Me too."

THE COOL TWILIGHT HELPED TEMPER THE FEVERISH RUSH IN MY veins. That quick-burning fire slowed into something more warm and steady. Grae kept his arm around my shoulders as we strolled across the packed snow. Villagers moved briskly to and fro, hastening back to their houses and out of the cold. No one paused to watch us. No one bowed. Why would they? To them, we were just two humans on an evening stroll.

We passed the town square, where little shrines and rundown temples to the human Gods circled the open space. Dozens of them lined the square. The carvings above the archways denoted the different deities: a sword for the God of War, a coin for the Goddess of Abundance, a paw print for the Wolf Kings. A giant willow tree sat in the center of the square, covered in drooping beads of ice.

"Hengreave is beautiful," I murmured, watching an old man climb up the icy steps into the Temple of Courage.

"It makes me want to visit more human towns." Grae's chest vibrated against my side, our steaming breaths swirling together. "I feel like we're missing half the world."

I was going to respond, but Grae froze, his arm around my shoulder tightening and yanking me to a halt. I looked up to see five men standing in front of us. They wore stone gray cloaks, no hoods or masks. Not Rooks then. I narrowed my eyes at the eldest man with the scraggily gray beard and silvery hair. His eyes flickered golden in the darkness and blood drained from my face.

They were Wolves.

"Hemming," Grae snarled.

"I see you've found your mate." Hemming gave me a smug

smile and I curled my lip at him. "His Majesty has been worried sick about you, my dear. He's sent me to ensure you have safe passage back to Damrienn."

"I'm sure he has," Grae gritted out, dropping his arm and taking a step in front of me.

"This is a pack order, Your Highness."

The men behind Hemming looked like coiled ebarvens ready to strike. My legs grew jittery as I stared into their reflective moonlit eyes.

"Pack orders," Grae muttered. It was the thing wolves said to end a conversation. Nothing mattered more than the will of the pack. Pack orders meant "you lose."

"You must see what this looks like, Grae," said another. I recognized him as the same guard who'd joined Grae in the training rings. "You running off with her, making a bid for Olmdere?"

"What?" I breathed.

"We're going to rescue a member of our pack, Aiden," Grae snarled at his once friend. "One you've all conveniently forgotten."

"And after Maez is freed you'll have a throne there waiting for you, hmm?" Hemming asked. "You planning to usurp your father and take Olmdere for yourself?"

"Grae isn't taking anything. Olmdere belongs to the Gold Wolves," I cut in, sidestepping Grae and baring my teeth.

"Then where is its king to claim it?" Aiden snickered.

"It doesn't need a king," I growled, surprising myself with my own words. Even spending a few days outside of pack life, that much was clear. And once my mind began to pick apart one rule, it began to question them all.

"You've spent too much time around the humans." Hemming laughed, the group chuckling as if I had told a witty joke. "It belongs to the Silver Wolves now, girl."

"You've spent too much time around idiots." I took a step forward, and Grae grabbed my elbow. "And I am not a girl."

"Come home, Grae," Hemming said, ignoring my insult and using Grae's name instead of his title to appeal to his good sense.

"The King understands. He promises to be lenient with you and your mate."

I took in a quavering breath, considering those words. More lenient than what? What would he do to us when he wasn't being lenient?

Grae's fists clenched. "Some arrows can never go back in the quiver, Hemming."

I froze. *Quiver.*

His storming eyes glanced to mine and I knew then that he had remembered the code word I'd told him back in Allesdale. I'd meant it as a joke . . . but now . . . now, I knew we were about to run.

TWENTY-FOUR

THE DOOR TO THE FAR TEMPLE CREAKED OPEN, DRAWING THE attention of the Wolves, and I bolted. Grae raced fast on my heels. I skidded sideways on a patch of ice, and Grae's hand found my side, righting me as we darted down an alleyway.

"Grae, please!" Aiden shouted, his voice far too close. "You'll only make this worse for yourself."

His voice faded away as he cursed something and fell back. I prayed their fancy soldiers' boots would slip on the ice and force them to scramble after us.

The alleyway was crammed with crates and buckets of suspicious-looking substances too frozen to smell. Grae tipped a barrel over and brown slush poured out behind us, turning the already slippery pathway lethal. The closest Wolf, Hemming, went down hard, landing in the frozen refuse. My lip curled in delight, but I didn't stop, not for a second.

Cold air burned my throat, grating down into my straining lungs. I neared the end of the alley, unsure in which direction to turn. I forced my legs faster as I glanced over my shoulder to find three Wolves still behind Grae. The rest had leapt over the frozen slush with ease, using their leader as a stepping stone.

Three? I thought there had been . . .

I collided with the fourth Wolf, yelping as my feet slipped on the ice.

Aiden.

He grabbed my forearms so hard I knew they'd leave a mark. He leered at me with a crooked grin, once courtly and charming, now nothing but feral. Clearly, he thought I was some damsel immobilized simply by his holding me. Which meant he'd seen me in the training rings in Highwick yet hadn't taken heed.

What a fool.

I kneed him hard between the legs, and he barked out a cry of pain. Before he could double over, the Wolf's face whipped to the side at the sound of a loud, meaty thud.

"Don't. Touch. Her." Grae's voice was pure thunder and menace.

I scrambled away from the Wolf's grip as Grae yanked him back by the hair. "Leave him, Grae. Let's go!"

Grae's storming eyes pierced into Aiden's—a look of rage and betrayal. "Were you the one who told them to look here?"

His words dripped with venom, but Aiden didn't flinch, only smiled.

"I figured you couldn't resist bringing your new pet to the hot pools," he snarled, his voice tinged with bitterness. I wasn't sure if he was jealous of my attention or if they'd ever been something more, but that betrayal in his eyes was as clear as the twinkling stars overhead.

The muscles in Grae's jaw flickered as he released Aiden's hair from his grip. "Aid—"

A flicker of motion caught my eye.

"Look out!" I screamed.

It happened so fast. Aiden's hand unsheathed his dagger in the blink of an eye, driving it upward toward Grae's chest. Grae twisted out of the blow, blocking his friend by the forearm. The block made Aiden's knees slip out from under him and he fell . . . straight onto his own blade.

Air whooshed out of me as I stared at that dagger impaled in

the Wolf's gut. Aiden's eyes bugged in disbelief, his mouth opening and closing in soundless gasps.

"Go!" Grae shouted, snapping me from my stupor.

We careened down the empty street. A howl keened through
the night air, and I knew the other Wolves had reached their
friend. A Wolf would survive that wound, I told myself. We didn't
sign our death warrant.

Breathe.

I spotted a high iron fence surrounding a steepled stone
building—the backside of the town square. Grae seemed to follow my train of thought and as I leapt to grab the top of the
gate; his hands found my foot and lifted me. I vaulted the rest of
the way up, swinging my legs over the pointed tips. I landed in
a crouch, starting to run again before I even straightened. Grae
landed behind me.

"Split up! I'll meet you back at the inn!" I shouted loud
enough for the Wolves still on our tails to hear. Grae veered to
the right, jumping over another fence, this one waist high, as I
barreled straight ahead and down the crevice between two temple walls. I turned sideways, my chest and back brushing against
each wall. The walls crushed tighter and I sucked in a breath,
praying the passage didn't narrow further. I was nearly to the
other end when the four remaining Wolves appeared. The one
with the mean scar, Soris, tried to squeeze through but got as far
as one shoulder and had to stop.

"Shit," he growled, turning back to the others. "We've got to
double back. We'll go around."

He gave me one last scowling glare and I couldn't help but
wink at him, thrilled by the rage that spread over his face. Pushing out the far side, I stumbled back into the main square with
the frozen willow tree. I made it three steps down the footpath
before I heard a low whistle. I looked up, seeing Grae leaning out
of a second-story window. How did he get up there so fast?

He beckoned me with his hand and I looked across the vacant square, checking one last time. The Wolves would have to

trek back through that slush-filled alley to get here and by then we would be long gone . . . or so they would think.

I ran two quick circles around the square and down toward another tight alleyway, then carefully doubled back over my footprints in the snow. On silent feet, I jumped up onto the stoop of the temple, leaping over the side and onto the threshold. I smiled down at the powdery, untouched steps—not a single footstep led inside.

Opening the heavy wooden door just a crack, I pushed through the gap and closed it slowly. The stone room was worn with age—columns smoothed by thousands of hands over centuries. Half the wooden pews tilted at odd angles, broken and splintering.

I tiptoed down the aisle to the altar, covered in hundreds of white candles, the wax dripping like frozen rivers off the sides. The only light came from a lone flickering candle in the center of the altar. I hadn't checked which God's symbol covered the threshold in my haste to enter, but now I looked up to the painted ceilings and my cheeks stained red.

Nude paintings, some depicting solitary figures, others the act of lovemaking, covered the frescoed ceilings. The figures wore garlands of flowers around their heads with soft white clouds and songbirds dancing in the pale blue sky—poetic, whimsical, yet primal. I swallowed.

A love temple.

I turned from the altar, my heart still racing from the run, searching for the stairwell. Instead, I found a ladder leaning against an open trapdoor. Human voices echoed on the street, and I rushed to the ladder, scurrying up it. I pulled the folding accordion steps up behind me and gently closed the latch, sealing the second floor. Crouching under the steep, angled beams, I moved to the center where I could stand. I paced toward the front, eyes scanning for Grae.

"Here, little fox," he whispered.

I stepped into a dusty cupboard where Grae peered out the oval window, his back against the far wall, ensuring no one could see him from the street. I tucked in against the other side so the moonlight didn't hit me as I watched the vacant square.

"Did you shut the trapdoor?" Grae murmured.

"Obviously," I said, giving him a look, and he had the grace to look embarrassed at the dumb question.

I looked around the room. Baskets lined the walls, filled with candles, dried lavender, and incenses used in their human ceremonies. Affixed above the doorway was a bronzed piece of art—four naked bodies intertwined, though the way they were carved, it was difficult to tell what sex they were.

"That was a nice touch, the inn thing," Grae murmured, keeping his voice low even though the Silver Wolves were far out of earshot now. "I'm impressed."

"I didn't want them to go searching the wagon or start looking for the others," I whispered, looking back at the shelves. "Of course you picked a love temple to hide in."

Grae tipped his head toward the charcoal sketch nailed to the shelf. "The Goddess of Love and Carnal Desires," he murmured.

The simple drawing depicted the Goddess with a swollen belly and large breasts, one hand on her womb, one lifted to the sky. I wondered if one of the human acolytes had drawn it, something they could look upon with fondness as they worked in the temple.

"Carnal desires," I huffed, looking back out the window. "I'm sorry."

"For what?"

"For driving a wedge between you and your pack." I folded my arms, leaning further into the rough wall. "Aiden seemed like your friend and I—"

"This was a long time coming." Grae crossed his arms in a mirror to my posture. "I wish I had stood up to my father sooner, but I was afraid of what he might do . . ." His hooded eyes regarded me, and I had to bite the inside of my cheek to hold his stare. "But seeing as you're determined to put yourself in danger anyway," he said. "There's nothing holding me back anymore."

I considered those words. He was holding back for me and my safety. There was more there, but something told me I shouldn't push it any further. Not just yet.

His eyes lingered on my face, heat filling them, and the memories of that moment in the pub pulsed through me—how just the feeling of his hand on my knee had made me melt like candle wax. Grae released his arms, balling his hands into fists as he broke our gaze.

I let out a frustrated sigh. The cloying scent of incense and lavender tugged on my desire, probably designed to do exactly that, making me overcome again that building need. The Goddess of Carnal Desires was taunting me.

"What?" Grae asked as I released yet another loud breath.

"Nothing," I said, glancing back at his stunning, sharp features. "It just looked for a second there like you wanted to kiss me."

His eyes were the color of distant fires in the dark night sky, the brown more like a hint of the deepest red. "I had more wicked things on my mind."

"Oh?" I panted, feeling that sweet dizziness cloud my thoughts. "And what made you not act on them?"

"I was thinking." His voice was a predatory growl. "I was wondering how much of me is a man and how much a beast."

"Is that so?"

"Careful," he warned, dimples disappearing as his lips parted. "Don't look at me like that."

"What if I want to?" I didn't sound like myself anymore. A siren's song laced my words, determined to beckon his lips to mine.

"Calla—"

"What if I want you to stop acting like a man and start acting like a beast?"

My words unleashed him. He prowled toward me, his hand wrapping under my jaw as he shoved me against the wall. Before I could gasp, his lips crashed into mine, his chest pinning me in place. My groaning yes was muffled against his lips as his tongue dipped into my mouth in a hot, feverish kiss. His mouth was craving and wild as he plundered my own, his body molding into mine from shoulders to knees so tightly I didn't know where he ended and I began. The muscles in my core fluttered, desperate, as I ground into him, aching for more friction, for more of *him.*

I moaned at the sensations lighting up my body, and his fingertips squeezed my neck tighter. His other hand gripped my hip, clawing into me as he rocked his erection against the seam of my pants. The wanton action set every nerve ending on fire and my whole body pulsed with the promise of release.

Only one more moan and I knew he'd take me, claim me with his whole body the way his mouth claimed me now. I ground into him harder, wanting him to be as burning with desire as I was myself. A deep, guttural sound pulled from Grae's throat, hungry and—in the best way—*angry* and in that moment it felt so right that our first time together would be in a Temple of Carnal Desires.

As if yanked backward by some invisible force, Grae pulled away. I sucked in a sharp breath as the four Wolves ran back out into the square, too lost in my pleasure to hear them coming.

Only four. Aiden was still missing. Heavy shadows cloaked them, the moonlight straining behind a passing cloud.

"Shit," Soris growled. "Nero's going to kill us."

A low rumble echoed out of Grae's chest and I clenched my hands together.

"The King will avenge Aiden," Hemming said. "Grae killed his pack mate. He's not a Silver Wolf anymore."

My heart leapt into my throat. Aiden had died? It was hard to see where his dagger hit him through his many layers, but it must've been the perfect strike to kill him. Grae hadn't delivered that killing blow. Part of me wanted to run out onto the street and scream that it wasn't his fault. He was just defending himself from the attack, defending me. But they'd never believe that. And if they believed Grae killed his pack mate, they'd never forgive it.

Grae stood impossibly still, moments stretching on without

taking a breath. The Wolves followed my swirling footprints to the narrow alleyway that they couldn't fit through and cursed.

"The girl said something about the inn," Hemming said. "We'll check there before we head out. I'd wager they've shifted and are halfway out of town. Check for prints."

The others nodded and they began jogging away. It would've been the smart thing to do, perhaps, to shift. Grae and I were fast in our human forms, but when we shifted, we were some of the fastest Wolves in Aotreas. But doing the smartest thing was predictable, and if they could predict our movements, they'd catch up to us, eventually.

We waited, watching with bated breath as they ran off into the darkness.

I stared at Grae, breathless, as he recoiled from me. My brow furrowed as he stared in horror at his hand. He panted, face bracketing with pain as that hand clenched into a fist and he shook his head. I watched as it dawned on him—he'd lost his pack. He'd lost everything.

I took a step forward and he inched away from me. "I'm so sorry."

"Don't." His voice cracked.

Before I could say anything, he threw open the door and left. I listened to his footsteps marching away and watched as he rushed out into the flurry of snow. With each step, my heart plummeted further.

I couldn't stop the tears that welled in my eyes, my mind turning over all the ways I could've messed this up. When the Wolves tell King Nero, Grae will lose his entire family. In their eyes, he had killed one of his own, the worst of any sin—worse than desertion, or disobedience, or skin chasing. I heard the howl of the Silver Wolves moving out of town and I hung my head. We were safe for another day, but I felt no relief, not as my mate walked away from me.

TWENTY-FIVE

THE MOOD WAS SOMBER AS I APPROACHED THE GROUP. WITH sleepy eyes and slow limbs, they loaded their instruments back into the wagon. I didn't know how long I waited in that temple, giving Grae space and time to process what had just happened. Maybe he blamed me for it, or worse, hated me for it. If he hadn't come after me . . . I clenched my fists, fighting off the gnawing pain in my gut. I needed to speak with him.

"What's going on?" I asked, watching the flurry of movement as they repacked.

"We're leaving tonight," Hector said. He gave me a look that said he knew about the Silver Wolves. Grae must have told him.

"How was the performance?" I asked Ora, trying to push some mirth back into my voice.

"Nothing too exciting," Ora said, passing a leather case to Mina. "Just playing to a dead room of rich humans."

I pressed my lips together, feigning a smile.

"They wouldn't know good music if I smacked them with my bow," Malou added, rubbing her hands together against the chill. "Ora said we needed to head out tonight for some reason."

"We'll sleep on the road," Ora insisted, ushering a tired-looking Mina up the steps. "The oxen know the way. More time for us in Taigoska then."

Malou nodded, darting her eyes from Ora to Hector and back to me.

"Esh. I'll be damned, those waters really are magic," she said, eyes dropping to my chin. I wasn't sure what she suspected, but she shrugged and left it at that.

"I don't know why she won't let you lead her." I twisted toward Navin's voice. He led both oxen between him, Grae a few paces behind. "She's normally comfortable with strangers."

Sadie huffed and Hector nudged her. The humans might not know we were Wolves, but prey animals like oxen probably sensed it.

Grae kept his distance from the large, shaggy animals. From the way he fixed his stare straight ahead, I could tell he was trying not to look at me.

I stepped forward anyway. "Hey, can I talk to you?"

He slowed but didn't stop. "I'm going to ride up front and give Navin a break."

"Okay . . ." My mouth grew dry. "Listen—"

"I'll see you in Taigoska." He stepped around me and my heart sank.

My fingers twitched to reach out for him, to make him listen to me, but there were too many people around. It wasn't the right place to prod at those fresh wounds. Despite that, the fact he wouldn't look me in the eye made me want to crumple to the ground right then and there.

Sadie clapped me on the shoulder. "Come on," she said. "I think we need a drink." She turned toward Navin. "You up for a drink?"

"I'm exhausted," he said with a giant yawn, hefting his harp up the steps. "But have fun."

"Yep," she said, but I saw the hint of disappointment on her face.

"What drinks did you have in mind?" Hector asked, following us into the back seating area. "I don't recall there being anything other than tea on board."

Sadie whipped out a flask from her cloak pocket and wiggled it at her brother.

He guffawed. "We're definitely related."

The others climbed into the upper decks, stowing their instruments and milling about, readying for sleep. I dropped onto the patchwork couch and leaned my head back, looking up at the ceiling. I scrubbed my hand down my face. Ostekke gut me, everything was such a mess.

Sadie sat beside me, kicking her feet up on the low table as Hector lounged across from us.

"Here." She passed me the flask.

I shook my head at her offering. I already felt nauseated enough. She shrugged and took a sip.

Hector watched the others getting ready for bed and muttered, "Are we still on for stealing the nitehock in Taigoska?"

"We have no plans on how to enter the palace undetected," Sadie whispered back, her words rising as the others drifted further away. I scratched a hand up my arm, feeling jittery and unsettled after Grae's dismissal. I knew the siblings were dancing around the Aiden news, and I wondered if they were waiting until the humans were asleep. They carried on their same old spat as if everything hadn't just changed for us—the final nail in the coffin—we could never go home. "Even if we hide under the guise of human servants, you think they'll just let us waltz into the royal apothecary?"

"We could be quick." Hector shucked off his boots and they thudded to the floor. I wanted to interrupt them, wanted to *scream*, but the shock of everything that was unfolding was too much. "In and out. We just need some sort of distraction."

"You're going to get us killed," Sadie hissed.

"And you're going to get Maez killed," Hector snapped back. "How do we get to wherever they're keeping her? Why are you more concerned about stealing nitehock than saving our friend." Sadie twirled her knife like she might stab her brother, but he continued, "You think we can storm the castle on a lake with brute force alone? Sawyn can't be at full power if—"

Ora appeared at the top of the stairs, cutting off Hector's whispered protests.

They had already changed into a thick purple robe. The fabric looked incredibly soft, perfect for the cold Taigosi nights. They cocked their head at us like a curious bird, and I knew they could sense the heightened tension that stormed among the three of us. Ora always seemed to know more than they let on, and I once again wondered how many times this had happened before— stowaways of Galen den' Mora swapping secrets in that very spot. Maybe we weren't even the first Wolves who had hitched a ride . . . I looked past Ora toward the badges swinging above the table, searching for a little Wolf face, but there was none. If a Wolf was hiding on Galen den' Mora, they wouldn't have announced what they were to the humans.

"You night owls enjoy yourselves," they said. "Five hours of playing has us shattered and my mind is halfway in the stars already. Goodnight."

"Goodnight," we replied as Ora pulled the thick velvet curtain across the stairs, giving us some privacy.

Sadie leaned into me, watching the curtain just in case Ora returned. "Grae told us about the unexpected visit."

"It was close," I whispered, reliving the horrifying moment Aiden fell on his blade. "It ended . . . badly."

"I heard them heading out of town," Hector said, keeping his voice low. With our hearing, we could speak at a faint whisper, soft enough that the humans wouldn't be able to eavesdrop through the curtains.

"They nearly took us," I murmured. "That one, Hemming?"

Sadie's lip curled. "I've always wanted to sink my knife into that one."

Hector held open his hands and Sadie chucked him the flask. "He's the king's right hand. I'm surprised he was sent at all. King Nero must be pretty desperate to get to you."

And now he'd be desperate to kill me, just for robbing him of his son. I rubbed the back of my neck, every muscle in me suddenly sore after multiple bouts of running. "He's never going to look at me again," I muttered, more to myself.

"We both know that's not true." Hector twisted and lay down across the far bench.

The wagon shuddered, then jostled to life. I thought about Grae and the long night he'd have riding toward Taigoska.

"How can you be so calm?" I asked, looking between them. "You've lost your pack, your family."

"We knew that the moment we stepped out of the palace." Sadie kicked off her boots and let them tumble to the floor. "Besides, we're not losing family. We're going to rescue family. I know Maez would've severed all ties to the pack to save us, too."

"But Grae and Aiden were friends." Hector tipped his head back into his pillow, slinging his arm across his eyes. "And he is probably drowning in guilt right now for what happened. It's one thing to walk away from the pack, it's another to watch your friend die."

The words punched into my gut. "Yes."

"Give him some time," Sadie said, her knife flicking like the tail of a hissing cat.

As the wagon rocked, my senses reached out to the front of the wagon, trying to feel Grae there. I so desperately wanted to hug him, to throw my arms around him and absorb the grief that must be coursing through him. But he didn't want my comfort. Not yet . . . maybe not ever. And I knew the best way to support him right then was to leave him alone, even if it made my soul feel like it was shredding in two. Was this how he'd felt the day I'd run away? I remembered his pleading voice in my mind, begging me to let him come with me.

Sadie passed me the flask, but I shook my head once more. Smoothing down the legs of my trousers, I stood and stumbled back toward my bunk. My hands reached out to the cabinets above my head, instinctively knowing now where to place them to steady myself should the wagon teeter. I prayed the gentle rumble of wheels over gravel would lull me to sleep . . . but I knew I'd be replaying that evening over and over in my mind.

I ran my hand across the soft mattress of my bunk and frowned. Lying there would feel like a punishment. I rubbed my eye with my palm and let out a long sigh. My shoulders drooped and I turned around, back down the steps, and plopped onto the bench beside Sadie.

Without missing a beat, she slung her arm around me and said, "Have you ever heard the one about the juvleck and the thief?"

I LET OUT A GROAN AS I LIFTED MY HEAD OFF SADIE'S SHOULDER, blinking against the white morning light. The wagon had stopped at some point in the night.

"You're going to have a wickedly sore neck." Sadie chuckled, stretching her arms over her head.

"Thanks for being my pillow," I said, my voice scratchy with sleep. I wiped my face with the back of my hand. "Sorry if I drooled on you."

Sadie shrugged. "No problem."

Hector slept across the bench, his back turned to us and a blanket tucked under his chin. I realized I had a blanket covering me as well.

"Knock, knock." Ora's voice floated from beyond the velvet curtain. "You awake?"

Sadie chucked a pillow at her brother. "We are now."

Hector grumbled, trying to bury his face further into the couch.

Ora pulled back the curtain, already dressed in a heavy velvet shift. They held two steaming mugs and carefully tiptoed down the steps to place them in front of Sadie and me.

"Thank you," I said, lifting the mug and blowing on it.

Ora plopped down on the couch in front of Hector's feet and Hector curled up into a ball, still refusing to wake up.

"I figured you'd need it," Ora said, clasping their hands together. "It seemed like a tough night for everyone."

"It was. We . . ." I had no idea how to explain what had happened in Hengreave. All the revelations of the previous night came flooding back to me.

They held up their hands. "You don't need to explain. Galen den' Mora is always filled with people with stories they'd rather not share."

I glanced down the slender aisle to the chandelier in the galley and the many badges of musicians past. How many of those badges were worn by a person with a sad story to tell? I wondered about it every time I looked at those little embroidered shapes. Who did the bell belong to? Who wore the white rose?

Hundreds of tales lay in the artwork and fabrics from every corner of the continent. Galen den' Mora looked built, repaired, and refurbished by many hands, all with their own unique styles and touches.

"Any plans for today?" Ora asked. "The others are still sleeping."

The life of a traveling troupe. They slept in strange places and kept strange hours. Days would pass with not much to do and then there'd be short bursts of long, arduous performances.

"And Grae?" I asked, trying not to sound too eager.

"He said he needed to go get some things in the markets. He took off a little while back."

My shoulders drooped. "Oh."

"We have an extra day in Taigoska since we traveled through the night," Ora said. "It's a massive city, but I can show you some of my favorite parts if you'd like?"

"A personal tour." I smiled at them, trying to bolster myself from the bitterness of Grae's early-morning departure. "I'd love it."

"Oh, good." Ora rose, smoothing their dress. "It's always more fun seeing the city again through a fresh pair of eyes." Ora gave Hector a playful pat on the shoulder, looking between him and the knife in Sadie's hands. "Are Sleepy and Stabby coming, too?"

"I like you, Ora," Sadie huffed. "Fine, I'll come."

"I'll come, too," Hector grumbled, pushing up onto an elbow. "I need one of those frozen treats to settle my stomach."

"Splendid!"

Malou's sharp voice boomed through the cabin. "Quieter. Please."

The sound of two knocks on the wood came from Mina's bunk, clearly agreeing with her sister.

Ora winked at us and mouthed. "I'll go get my things."

"I WANT THIS FOR BREAKFAST EVERY DAY," HECTOR PROFESSED, holding aloft his cone of shaved ice.

I chuckled, licking my strange dessert on a stick. I twirled the stick again, looking at the sugared frozen cream.

"When I was little, we would bring in a scoop of snow and drizzle syrup over it." I hummed as the sweetness melted on my tongue. "But it was nothing like this."

"One of the many magical things of Taigoska," Ora said, leading us toward the open markets.

Benches and tables sat around a fountain, cascading into a frozen waterfall. Ice sculptures lined the plaza, each one more intricate than the next. I peered at the nearest sculpture—the Goddess of Home and Hearth. The details of her face were so intricate I wondered what tools they used to carve the lips and eyes, so lifelike, I wouldn't have been surprised if she blinked.

The buildings were made of cream-colored stones, several stories high. Colorful signs caught the eye amongst the white and gray. A rainbow of pennants and banners waved along strings tied to a center pole shooting from the top of the fountain, creating a moving ceiling like a canopy of leaves rustling in the wind.

There were stores of every sort, from candy shops to fortune tellers, and it was clear this was the plaza where the humans came for entertainment.

We walked in pairs, Sadie and Hector in front, Ora and I behind. Strolling down the icy paths, we passed a bright purple sign reading *Florist*. I narrowed my eyes, staring into the shop window to see bouquets of delicate paper flowers.

"Sweet Moon." Made in beautiful, vibrant colors, they were styled like roses, cosmos, and lilies.

"A beautiful solution made out of necessity," Ora said. "They even spray them with perfumes, so they smell like fresh flowers."

"If they can't grow flowers here, how do they grow food?" I asked, peering into the bakery window filled with spun sugar treats and spiced fruit buns.

"They grow flowers here, and many crops, actually." Ora pointed to the steeples peeking above the distant rooftops. "The Wolves have these glass houses they use for growing, but the flowers and crops are very expensive. Most humans can't afford them."

We walked past a grocer, the store lined with jars of pickled vegetables and baskets of salted fish.

"I see." It was hard to hide the shame in my voice.

The Wolves only grew and hunted as much as they needed for themselves, feeding even the lowest ranked amongst their pack. And for my entire life, I hadn't questioned it. Wolves took care of their own, and it was the humans' own fault they didn't do the same was how I'd always thought. Never mind that they didn't have the glass houses to grow or enough coin to build one. My naïveté hit me like a slap in the face and, though the logical part of me already understood, I felt even more acutely about how wanting something didn't translate to having something.

"They also trade with the other kingdoms for certain spices and sugars." Ora wrapped their shawl around them, the metal beads clinking together. "It's beautiful, but I wouldn't want to stay in the cold forever." They huffed, their breath coming out in steaming whorls as if to emphasize their point. "There's only so many ice blocks and pickled carrots one can eat."

Sadie laughed, her footsteps lingering at the front door of the swordsmith.

"You don't need any more knives," Hector scoffed, steering his sister away by her elbow.

She frowned. "I was just looking."

"Oh really? Where did you get that?" He pointed to the belt circling her right thigh where a needle-like dagger was sheathed.

"Hengreave," she muttered, and Hector rolled his eyes.

My feet stalled as I spotted a silver and white flag waving in the far distance. Upon it, two swords crossed behind the silhouette of a howling wolf.

"Is that the castle?" I pointed to the flag with the Ice Wolf crest. I could only make out the tallest spire disappearing behind the brick buildings of the human quarter.

Ora paused beside me. "It is."

"I didn't realize Taigoska was so big."

"It's the biggest of all the capital cities," Ora said, following my line of sight. "You need a sleigh to get from one end to the other. I haven't explored the Wolf part of town much though. They only let us down Servants Row to reach the backs of the houses we play in."

Sadie and Hector stilled in front of us, clearly hearing what Ora had said. I wondered if they felt the same pang of guilt, the same unraveling awareness, the longer we spent around humans. When did we stop being their protectors? Hearing all this, it seemed the only monsters humans needed protection from these days were the Wolves themselves.

I glanced around the plaza, searching for a charcoal gray cloak and the tall, muscled prince who had been avoiding me all day. I hated to think Grae was mourning somewhere, punishing himself over what had happened to Aiden. Was he not just devastated, but mad at me, too?

I clenched my fists in my pockets as another terrifying thought speared into my mind: If King Nero disowned Grae, would Briar still be safe? Every second I left her in that castle was a risk. I tried to distract myself with other things, but that undercurrent of fear remained. I needed to get Briar out of Damrienn before she became a hostage. My stomach clenched. Gods, she already was. Our whole lives we'd been used for our kingdom's gold. I wondered if we brought back enough gold, if we could trade it for Briar . . .

I doubted it. King Nero wanted control of Olmdere, but Aiden's death would force his hand. He'd need to win Olmdere through his possession of Briar now, not through Grae. Enemies seemed to be closing in from all sides, and here I was, trapped in my own mind.

"We've played in the castle a few times and it is truly stunning," Ora continued, pulling my attention back to them. "You should come to our performance tomorrow night. We could say you're part of the band."

"Oh, I don't know about that," I murmured, knowing it would be a bad idea even though I wanted to say yes. I bet the ball would be magnificent and it would be the perfect distraction we'd been searching for to acquire the nitehock, but there would be too many Wolf eyes upon us if we weren't behind the scenes, and I couldn't imagine taking the risk.

Sadie and Hector found seats close to the fountain, watching as a little band of brassy horns started to play.

"It's a masquerade," Ora offered, seeming to read the hesitation in my expression. "If you're afraid you might bump into someone you know, like back in Hengreave."

"I'm sorry we had to leave—"

"It wasn't any trouble." Ora held up a hand. Their footsteps slowed, and I looked up into their hazel eyes. "I might seem filled with calm and whimsy, but that was hard won. Not everyone was happy that I chose this life with two hands. I know what it means to need to leave in the middle of the night."

"I wish I felt that way," I whispered, dropping my gaze to my clenched fingers. "That I chose my life with two hands."

"You will when you're ready," Ora said. "And when it's safe

to do so. Not everyone can scream their truths from the rooftops, and that's okay, too."

My eyes guttered. They didn't know how close they were. It was true—I couldn't go around shouting I was a princess of Olmdere or even that I was a Gold Wolf. But there were other truths about myself, too . . .

I looked at Ora, with their perfectly painted lips, neatly trimmed beard, and flowing velvet shift.

"That's a beautiful dress," I murmured instead of the truths in my head.

We wove our way toward the fountain and I admired their rope belt, golden tassels waving in the breeze.

Ora smiled. "You can borrow it sometime if you like."

"Oh, I don't know." I snorted, feeling strange nerves bubbling up in me. "I'm not very appealing in dresses."

"Appealing to who?" Ora cocked their head, their hazel eyes cutting straight through my defenses. "The first person you should be *appealing* to is yourself. You wear the things that make you happy."

I shook my head. "I don't know what that is . . ."

Ora took off their fur-lined hat and plopped it on my head. I smiled, smelling their citrusy floral scent in the fabric. "Maybe it's time to try on a few new hats and see which ones fit."

I had never really considered it. All of Galen den' Mora knew me as someone other than the person I insisted I was in my own head . . . and it seemed they liked me without any other name or label. Just me.

Ora and I joined the others at the table by the fountain, and I kept my jittery hands in my cloak pockets. It felt freeing and confusing all at once. If I gave myself permission to be anything, who would I want to be? No answers jumped immediately to mind, but I knew one thing for certain, though I didn't know what it meant: I didn't want to wear dresses like Briar.

I wanted to wear them like Ora.

TWENTY~SIX

THE MUSIC OF THE HORNS DANCED AROUND THE LIVELY PLAZA as we people-watched. I loved all the rounded fur hats and thick wool cloaks with silver embroidered hems. The Taigosi human garb was a little worn, but exceedingly beautiful. I admired the details on their thick leather belts and the silver hoops they wore in their ears, far more elegant than the humans in Allesdale.

I didn't spot Grae, though I kept searching, and I hoped for the hundredth time that morning that wherever he was, he was okay.

"Navin!" Ora called, flagging down the tall harpist.

Even hunched against the chill, Navin stood a head taller than the shoppers meandering around him. He veered over toward us, winding through the tables and chairs.

Sadie sat up, her slumped posture turning rod straight.

"Join us." Ora gestured to an empty chair.

"I'm off to buy some more resin for the twins," he said, tipping his head toward the end of the plaza. He glanced at Sadie, lips curving up as he looked at her. "Want to come with me?"

"She can't," Hector said before Sadie could reply. "We've got some errands we need to run."

"Oh, okay," Navin replied, rubbing his hands together.

Sadie glared at her brother and back at Navin, jutting her

jaw to the side. "Ora was telling us about this restaurant, the Ice Dragon. Have you heard of it?"

"Yes, I love the food there." Navin's bronze eyes beamed.

"Maybe we could go there for dinner tonight?" she asked, leaning into the table to block Hector. "Just us?"

I leaned back and smirked at Hector's fuming expression.

Navin's eyebrows shot up as his cheeks dimpled. "I'd like that."

"Great." Sadie nodded. "I'll see you tonight."

"See you then." Navin's chest puffed up, the invitation breathing new life into him. He bobbed his chin to the rest of us and headed back into the throng.

"Could you excuse us for a moment?" Hector asked, rising from his chair and tapping his sister on the shoulder.

Ora and I watched the two of them storm off. Hector was cursing something I couldn't hear, flinging his hands in the air, but I knew he was talking about the sign in the third-floor window: *No Skin Chasers.*

I grimaced. "He's protective."

"I can see that." Ora chuckled with a shrug. "Navin's a really nice person and he seems smitten with your friend, but I'm sure I'm missing part of the puzzle."

"Yes," I said with a sigh. A very large piece of the puzzle.

The music stopped and the crowd applauded. Five of the musicians set down their instruments, heading off to the hot cider cart that had just wheeled into the square. Only a lone horn remained, playing a deep, resonant tune. I recognized the Olmderian mining song. "Sa Sortienna"—it meant "above the golden trees." I'd always loved the lyrics. I began mouthing the words, tapping my foot to the sad, slow song.

The musician stopped, lowering his horn. "Do you know the words? Please, sing along." He chuckled, tipping his head toward his bandmates. "They all left me to get a hot drink."

"I'm not a very good singer," I blurted out.

"It'll be fun." Ora nudged me as if it wasn't a big deal to break into song in a public square. "I'll sing, too."

The musician smiled, pursing his lips back to the aperture. My throat went dry as I listened to the intro again.

Ora started singing, a beautiful mezzo, giving me a wink. "*When I leave these caverns, my love, do you know just what I see? Above the golden trees, my love, the same moon shines for me.*"

I took a deep breath and closed my eyes, singing the higher harmony. "*Pray I'll come home, my love, and no monsters steal my gold. But gold or no, my love, pray I return 'fore we grow old . . .*"

The horn crescendoed and my voice grew louder, matching Ora's. My chest vibrated, the sound filling me down to my bones. The song made me ache, each word stretching out into the corners of my heart.

The song was about a couple missing who they were together and hoping they'd be united again. I imagined all those miners singing to their faraway loves, passing the time until they could return home. Each melancholic note rang with that feeling of loneliness. The bittersweetness echoed through me, hope and sorrow singing in equal measure.

Gooseflesh rippled across my skin, the emotions overwhelming my body. The song slowed into its final refrain, and Ora and I along with it. "*Until then, my love, hold on to you and me.*"

Cheering erupted and I whirled to see a small crowd gathered around us. I gaped at them, my cheeks burning. I'd been too focused on the song to notice them.

"Your voice!" Ora beamed, having to shout to me over the applause. "It's so—"

"Beautiful." A man in the crowd stepped forward. He had sharp features and sky-blue eyes. Something about his eerie stillness made my hackles raise.

"I'm Niklas," he said, tipping his fur hat. "The Queen's secretary."

My eyes widened, taking in his perfect clothing—no snow on his jacket, no dirt staining his hems. I narrowed my eyes at him.

He was handsome and elegant, but I didn't think he was a Wolf, merely a well-to-do human in the Queen's employ.

He gave me a crooked smile, clearly thinking my shock was because I was a lowly street performer . . . and not because I was a Wolf. "I know Queen Ingrid would be delighted to have you perform that song for her at the masquerade tomorrow night."

The crowd gasped, applause ringing out again as if it were some great honor to be invited. I let out a stuttering breath, nerves coiling tight in my gut.

Breathe. At least he wasn't a Silver Wolf. At least he didn't know me.

"We're already playing, my Lord." Ora bowed. "We're with Galen den' Mora."

"Splendid," Niklas said with a grin. "Make sure you sing that song for Her Majesty."

"It would be our pleasure." Ora flourished their hand.

Niklas disappeared into the tittering crowd, people giving him a wide berth. The crowd dispersed as the horn players returned.

Ora's face lit up looking at me. "Our little duet will be fun!"

"I can't perform in front of the Queen!" I sputtered. "You can sing the song on your own, can't you?"

"No, no, no," they said. "It's no good as a solo. You must! Please?"

"I-I really don't think that's a good idea," I said. "I almost passed out doing it in front of ten people."

Ora chuckled. "If you close your eyes, it doesn't matter if it's ten or a thousand."

"A thousand?"

They settled their hand on my arm. "It's a masquerade. No one will even see your face."

"Oh, jumping juvlecks." I gulped. "I need to find Grae."

Ora pointed over my shoulder, and I twisted to find a figure at the far end of the plaza. Grae clung to the shadows of the alley, leaning against the wall with his arms crossed. I knew even with his face shadowed in his hood that his dark eyes were staring straight into mine.

I stood, taking a step toward him; his arms fell to his side, and he turned back down the alley. My stomach dropped to my feet. Would he never speak to me again?

I THOUGHT ABOUT HEADING IN THE DIRECTION OF THAT cloaked figure, but I knew Grae wouldn't want me to follow him. He'd heard me sing . . . Maybe he didn't like it? I shook my head, scolding myself for entertaining these thoughts. He needed time, just as Sadie said. My hands clenched in my pockets. How much time did he need?

My mind still whirling, I broke off from Ora to explore the lower east end of Taigoska by myself. The busy markets gave way to quiet older dwellings, beautiful stone architecture, and plaques describing important historical sites.

I stopped at a mosaic of a Wolf with a giant silver serpent in its maw. The inscription below it read *King Joakim Enghdall III, Slayer of the Ebarvens*. This was Queen Ingrid's ancestor—the one credited with ridding Taigoska of the snow snakes. But ebarvens still existed in Taigos, like in the crater outside Hengreave, just pushed to the corners of the kingdom. Still, the humans lit candles upon the altar below his mosaic, a prayer for continued protection. This was the legacy of the Wolves, *my* legacy, but the world was still filled with monsters, Sawyn being one of them.

I stepped into the carved archway of a human temple. Like so many things in Taigoska, the temple was a hidden gem. There was no shrine to the Goddess of Knowledge; instead there were books. The library had towering rows of leather tomes, ladders lining either side, and rows of desks for people to sit and study. The ceilings weren't vaulted and the space wasn't grand, but there was something cozy and lived-in about the worn cushions and the dusty shelves. Stained-glass windows cast spectrums of sacred light around the dim room.

My fingers skimmed the rows, following them to a little nook with a carved crown placard. The shelves were filled with history books, royal lineages, and census scrolls. My eyes landed on the gold lettering down the spine of a burgundy book: *The Sleeping Queen*.

Dizzy, I grabbed the book off the shelf. Of course there would be books written about my mother. She was royalty, one of the most famous figures in all Aotreas. Everyone knew the story of how my father broke her sleeping curse with a kiss. There were songs and plays and children's bedtime stories about the two of them. Still, to stumble across a book about my family . . . With Briar gone, it felt harder than ever to be reminded of their absence.

I took the book over to one of the rickety desks tucked in the corner and sat. I flipped through the yellowing pages, my eyes scanning the detailed borders and drawings surrounding the blocks of text. My eyes snagged on a sentence, and I read it over again:

Sameir Marriel, third child and second son of Their Majesties, King and Queen Marriel.

I flipped over to the next page, but there was no more detail about my father. I read it again. Third child? I never knew my father had any siblings. I knew my mother's side of the family had been killed by Sawyn, along with the rest of the Gold Wolf pack. I also knew my father's parents had passed away before the night of my birth, but siblings? With a sigh, I shoved back from the desk and returned to the nook of royal books. Scanning, I found a book of Olmdere royal lineages: *Wyn dese Olmdelaire*—the kings of Olmdere.

I set the heavy leather-bound tome on top of my mother's story and began flipping toward the end. I got to the last chapter of recent descendants and found the family tree. My stomach lurched when I saw two names above Sameir with an X next to them: Leanna, and below, Sahandr. I had an aunt and uncle that I had never known about.

I turned the page, fingers tracing Leanna's name:

Born under a waning moon, Leanna Marriel, the first child of King and Queen Marriel, was betrothed to Prince Luo of Valta upon her birth. The crimson-haired princess was an accomplished singer and painter. She died of a sudden illness, along with her younger brother, at the age of fifteen.

I turned to Sahandr's page:

Born under a new moon, Sahandr Marriel, the first son and crown prince of Olmdere. He was strong, with excellent sparring and hunting skills. He died of a sudden illness, along with his elder sister, at the age of eight.

Whereas my aunt and uncle's pages were little more than a paragraph, my father's biography took up two whole pages. He was born one year after the death of his siblings. They called him a surprise and blessing. His pages detailed the days and moons of his many accomplishments, his coronation, and his wedding to my mother. And at the very end of the page was the announcement of the birth of his only child, Briar. I don't know why it still stung to see her name there alone.

But it did.

I flipped to Briar's page, the borders only half-drawn and the words hastily written. The halfhearted text made me wonder if the scribe had given up after Sawyn's attack. How the book ended up in a Taigoska library, I had no idea. Perhaps the scribe fled from Olmdere along with so many other humans. Curious, I skimmed over Briar's biography.

Born under a full moon, Briar Marriel, the first child
of King and Queen Marriel, was betrothed to Prince
Graemon of Damrienn upon her birth. Nicknamed the
Crimson Princess for the blood that was spilt on the
night of her birth. Her whereabouts remain unknown
and many believe her dead.

My mouth dropped open. I had always thought they called Briar "the Crimson Princess" because she had red hair, but the moniker originated from something much darker. No one even knew she had red hair, I realized. No one had known her at all except Grae, King Nero, and Vellia.

My fingers trembled over the pages. It was too much. Everyone on these pages was dead or cursed, or both. The only Gold Wolf that still lived never made it into the book to begin with. A book of sons and daughters . . . and then there was me—both and neither. I traced my name over the blank parchment. I existed between the ink and the pages. I existed in the breath after a long-held note. I existed safe in my mother's womb before the world could tell me who I was. And even if the world forgot those silent spaces, those in-betweens, in that moment I knew I had always been entirely whole—that I existed, remembered or not.

I shut both heavy books, the loud thwack echoing in the silence.

I hefted the tomes into my arms and returned to the nook to shelve them. When I turned into the last row of shelves, I smelled the smoky earth scent of Grae before I even saw him. I craned my neck down the stacks, seeing the whipping wool of a cloak. I hastily shoved the books back onto a random shelf and followed, cutting down a narrow row and popping out in front of him.

He halted, hood shifting backward just enough so that I could see his tightly clenched jaw and vexed eyes.

"Is this what we've come to? Tailing me, but also avoiding me?" I asked, leaning back to check again that the library was vacant. "I saw you in the plaza."

"Your performance was beautiful, little fox." The sound of his voice made my body respond with a deep, sorrowful twang. I missed his voice, his smell. I'd been mourning him this past day without knowing it, and now I felt it all rushing into me.

I folded my arms, trying to hide my trembling hands. "And why are you here now?"

"I wanted to make sure you were safe."

"I'm safest when I'm with you." I peered up into his shadowed face, feeling his eyes pierce into me. "Would it really be that bad? To be with me?" I repeated the words he had asked me so many days ago in that tent.

"No, little fox." He reached out and swept a thumb across my cheek. "It wouldn't be bad at all."

I covered his hand with my own, holding his palm to my cheek as I fixed him with my gaze. "Talk to me."

His eyes guttered and his hand pulled away. I let it drop, knowing that I had just touched upon some festering poison within him.

The library door swung open and two humans walked in, shoulders raised against the torrent of snow that followed them in the door. Grae pulled the rim of his hood higher, concealing his face again.

"Talk to me," I pleaded, searching for his eyes in the shadows of his hood.

"Not here." He turned his hood toward the direction of the humans perusing the shelves. His warm hand reached out and threaded his fingers through mine. That gesture meant more to me than he would ever know. I knew he was battling with himself not to pull away from me.

"Come," he said. "I have a place in mind."

TWENTY-SEVEN

"TELL ME YOU SAID NO."

"I couldn't!" I lifted my shoulders. "What was I supposed to say? Tell the Queen I won't perform for her?"

"Yes, that's exactly what you should have said," Grae growled.

I snorted, stomping harder through the deep snow. "That's rich coming from one of the most privileged Wolves in Aotreas."

I squinted against the gale, keeping my head down as we trudged toward the pine forest at the eastern edge of Taigoska.

"You are also one of the most privileged Wolves in Aotreas," he muttered.

"No. I *should* be, but I'm without a kingdom or a pack, remember? That secretary thought I was a human. To him I was a nobody, and I couldn't say no." We broke into the tree line and I sighed with relief. My cheeks tingled with the wind's absence, my nose numb. "Besides, it's a masquerade. No one will see my face anyway, and we were planning on going to steal the nitehock—"

"The *plan* was to stay hidden amongst the human servants," Grae said. "Not parade in front of the entire pack of Ice Wolves. You'd be walking straight into the belly of the beast, Calla."

"Isn't that what we're doing going after Maez?" He didn't reply, so I moved on. "You don't have to come with me," I insisted. "In fact, you and the others *should* stay back in the wagon.

I'll perform, get the nitehock, and get out. The fewer of us in the palace, the better."

"No. We're coming."

"Esh, you are so stubborn," I said, exasperated as I realized I'd used the humans' curse word. "One minute you won't even speak to me. Now you refuse to let me go alone."

"You were never alone. You always had the protection of Sadie and Hector. Or I was close enough to scent you," Grae said.

"That's not creepy at all," I grumbled, stepping into the foot holes Grae's boots left in the snow.

"It's not just about you, little fox. None of us should be alone right now. Not with the Silver Wolves searching for us."

"Okay, fine then, you'll come to the masquerade. You'll stay behind the scenes." I ducked under a heavy pine bough laden with snow. "I'll perform and distract everyone with my glorious performance"—Grae chuckled—"and you'll raid the royal apothecary, and then we'll go."

"That easy, huh?"

"Believe me, I don't want to perform," I muttered. "And the idea of stealing from the Queen makes my stomach hurt. But we need the poison and it's a good ruse, better than any we'd come up with up to this point. And you should've seen Ora's face."

"I don't care about their face."

"I do," I said. "They've been so good to us, and I don't want to disappoint them. I'll probably not be able to get a single note out."

"I doubt that," Grae said, his voice considerably softer as he ambled toward a deep bank of snow. With his sleeve, he swept the snow away, revealing a fallen tree trunk. He perched himself upon it and I joined him. Grae's nose and cheeks were rosy from the chill, his breath coming out in a swirl of steam, but his eyes were filled with fire as he smiled at me. "Your voice is the most moving sound I've ever heard, by the way."

"You're just saying that," I said.

"Not at all, little fox." His cheeks dimpled. "I only say it because it's true. It felt like you were singing straight to my soul."

I tucked a curl behind my frostbitten ear. "I don't know what to say to that."

"You don't need to say anything," Grae said. "I'm just glad you heard it."

I looked up to the pale blue sky peeking between the thick, dark clouds. "Is this another one of your special places?"

"No," Grae murmured, staring up at the heavy pine boughs. "I just knew there wouldn't be many humans all the way out here. There are still ebarvens in these woods." His eyes turned toward me and I could see it all—the fear, the pain.

"What will happen now?" I whispered. "Do you think your father will truly disown you?"

The muscle in Grae's cheek flickered as he bobbed his head. "He'll say it was for the good of the pack, or that he's trying to protect them." He brushed his hair off his forehead, leaning forward onto his knees. "It's amazing the lies we tell ourselves to justify the actions of others."

I could think of so many lies I told myself, about me, about the pack. "What lies do you tell yourself?"

"That I deserved the way my father treated me." Grae hung his head and let out a long breath. "That I could've saved my mother."

Pangs of sorrow carved into me. Grae kept his eyes fixed on the snow. I placed my hand on his back, needing him to feel anchored to me in that moment. *I'm here*, that hand told him, better than my words ever could.

"What happened to her?" I couldn't hide the shake in my voice.

"I wasn't the easiest pup to control. I was stubborn and impulsive, like all good princes should be. But I was going to get a crown for marrying Briar, and that gave me power. So the king used my mother to keep me in line."

I sucked in a sharp breath. "How?"

His eyes remained fixed on his hands. "I think you know how."

The words punched into my chest. "No."

"It was all behind closed doors," he whispered. "But you could see it in public, how hollow she was. She'd try to hide her injuries, but those closest could see them. It happened more often when I was young. I think my father always feared I would try to keep Olmdere for myself once I married Briar instead of joining it with Damrienn. He worried I'd defect from the Silver Wolf pack and start my own." His shoulders dropped. "My father claimed she was sick with *ailments*. He'd justify it in different ways: why she wasn't places or didn't run with the pack. But the rest of the pack whispered about it." Softly—so softly—"And I knew."

"How did she die?" My voice cracked.

"She jumped out her window." Grae's voice was heartbreakingly even. "At least, that's the rumor I'd heard. I hadn't been there that day and the means of death were never divulged, *out of respect to the pack*, they said. But if it had been anything else, they would've said as much."

"Out of respect to the pack," I said, shaking my head. "His hand might've not been on her back, but the king pushed her out that window with his many years of actions."

All the blood drained from my limbs, feeling weightless at the horror of that realization. All these years, I had no clue. My lungs seized, every breath burning up my throat.

"I think she did it to protect me," he whispered. "So my father couldn't use her to hurt me anymore."

My body was covered in pinpricks as my eyes welled. A sharp grief coursed through me.

"By the time I was eight or nine, I was paralyzed by it." He let out a breath through his teeth. "Afraid each of my actions would lead back to my mother in some way."

"Gods." I leaned forward, burying my face in my hands.

I'd shouted at him for not standing up to his father, even called him a coward, when his whole life the people he loved got hurt by it. Defending oneself was a privilege, and Grae was held hostage by his father's power. In the temple, he even said he was afraid of what his father might do . . . but I had never suspected he meant this.

"I was thirteen when she died and my father sent me off to school in Valta to keep me under heel," he whispered. "He probably couldn't think of any other way to keep me in line. But I knew how he could keep me in line still, *who* he could hurt to do it."

His eyes flickered toward me and I swallowed the thick knot in my throat.

"When I asked why you hadn't visited," I whispered, "you said you were suspicious of something and you were afraid of what would happen if your suspicions were true."

All this time. He'd been trying to protect Briar and me by keeping away, afraid we'd take the place of his mother. Is that why he was willing to go through with marrying Briar? My stomach soured. Was that all part of his act to protect us from his father's wrath?

"It's a horrible feeling, watching the life slowly fade from someone's eyes." His deep voice wobbled. "A terrible, helpless feeling . . . and I just stood there."

"You were a child, Grae," I whispered, turning toward the sound of the emotion finally lifting to the surface of his words. "What happened to her is not your fault."

"My father worked very hard to make me believe otherwise." He sniffed and cleared his throat. "It wasn't until she was gone that I realized no matter how obedient I became, no matter how perfect, he'd find a flaw to punish me for."

"You should've never been made to feel like you had to be perfect," I said, sweeping a hand down his back. "You should've been loved as you are. I'm sorry he made you think your only value was in what power you gave to him."

"He wanted me to be strong, but not too strong. Smart, but not smarter than him." Grae's hands trembled. "And when I was too much or too little, he'd hurt her as if my failings were her fault."

The dam broke, tears spilling down his cheeks. At the first streak of tears, I moved, dropping to my knees in the snow and wrapping my arms around him. He dropped his head onto my shoulder as I held him, pressing my cool cheek into his warm neck.

"I should've done more to save her." His pained words were muffled in the fabric of my cloak. His fingers clung to me like he was falling from a cliff; I held him tighter, tunneling deep into a place of calm—the anchor in his storm.

"There's nothing you could've done, Grae," I whispered as his fingertips pressed in tighter. "Don't torture yourself. She wouldn't have wanted that for you."

Tears burned down my cheeks as I absorbed his sorrow, feeling it as keenly as my own. My knees soaked in melted snow and I didn't budge. I would freeze into the ice and not let him go. I'd weather any storm to ease that festering pain.

"The scars on your back . . . ," I murmured against his skin. "That was him, wasn't it?"

"A lesson." Grae's voice broke. "He wouldn't let me shift or heal. A reminder of who was truly in charge."

"He feared your power even then," I said, angry and confident at this idea. "Afraid of all you could be if he lifted you up, so instead he pushed you down. He was neither a good father nor a good king."

I slid one hand to his neck, holding him against my shoulder.

"When I saw Hemming . . . when he said my father would be *lenient* with you . . ." Grae took a shuddering breath. "I tried. I was willing to make terrible choices to keep you safe. But when he said that, I knew you could never be a part of his pack. I knew I finally had a chance to protect the one I loved."

He'd feared for me. It made all his actions suddenly so clear—his silence, his avoidance, even that amber necklace. I'd never realized it was his father he was trying to protect me from, rather than protect himself. No wonder he didn't speak up that day in King Nero's office. The more attached he seemed to me, the more danger he put me in.

That fear and pain was a living thing brimming to the surface now.

I pulled back just enough to rest my forehead to his, wiping his tear-stained cheeks. "You don't ever need to fear what your father will do to me," I promised him, wiping my thumbs across his cheeks. "You said it yourself. I am strong."

"Yes," he said with a halfhearted smile. "But the people I care about the deepest are always in the most danger, and I would burn Damrienn to the ground before watching that life fade from your eyes." I stared deeply into his red-rimmed eyes, so raw, so vulnerable. "I can't—"

He choked on his words, and I held his face up, making him look at me.

"I won't ever leave you like that," I promised. "Wherever we are going in this life, Grae, we will go there together. You and me. Always. And I will tear the throat out of anyone who tries to take me from you." My voice dropped into a lethal snarl. "I am stronger than your fears. And if I ever step foot in Damrienn again, I'll make damn sure the King knows he can't use me to hurt you. His words and actions will never declaw me. I'll always bite back."

His eyes welled and he nodded. Leaning back, he scooped me up from where I knelt before him and pulled me onto his lap. I tucked my head into the crook of his neck, holding him as he wrung out his sorrow. I wished I could undo all that had been done, but at least I could assure him it would never happen again. I wouldn't go quietly out of this life. I'd fight with every ounce of my being. For Grae, for Briar, for Galen den' Mora, but most of all, for me. No more hiding in the shadows. I would burn brilliantly for however long I had.

"Thank the Gods," he murmured, dusting the snow off my knees. "You are a fearsome creature, little fox, and I'm so grateful for it. I don't know how we're going to rescue Maez or deal with my father or defeat Sawyn, but from now on, we figure it out together. No more running off"—he gave me a knowing look—"and no more hiding away. However long we have, we will spend it together."

I brushed a soft kiss to his cold lips and murmured against his mouth, "The moon knew we needed each other, better than I ever understood, and now I know I was meant to be yours just as you were meant to be mine."

Those claiming words felt greater than any vow, and as Grae's lips met mine, I felt that promise fulfilled deep in my soul. It felt just like the moonlight bursting from the center of my chest. It cracked me open, all the raw parts of me opening up as we deepened our kiss. Everything felt suddenly greater—the depths of my sorrows, the highs of my joy, and the loudest note that sang through the chorus of emotions was that of belonging. I'd deny it no longer. I belonged with him, now and forever.

TWENTY~EIGHT

WE STROLLED BACK THROUGH TAIGOSKA AS NEW PEOPLE. GRAE'S
warm arm enveloped my shoulders, his cloak a blanket at my
back, and my hand wrapped around his waist. I still felt raw
from his confessions in the forest. I'd thought I knew him, but his
life had been harder than I'd ever known. But that's because we
had been apart.

No more.

We ambled through the human quarter, through twisting
roads and colorful shops, until we spotted a familiar figure.

Sadie stared into a storefront window with a look of trepidation on her face. As we neared, I spotted the sign proclaiming the
shop a "boutique"—little bottles and palettes of rouge displayed
in the window.

"What is she—"

"I'm going to talk to her," I whispered to Grae, silencing him.
"I'll meet you back at the wagon?"

He darted a wary look to Sadie and back to me. "I'll be with
her—I'll be fine." Grae relented. He kissed the top of my head
and released his arm from around my shoulders.

"I'll see you soon," he said. He took one step away from
me, and I grabbed his elbow, making him halt. I lifted onto my

toes and planted a soft kiss on his lips. With a satisfied hum, he opened his eyes and smiled down at me.

"Be safe, little fox," he murmured and carried on down the road.

I watched him walking away, my heart fluttering like the hem of his cloak. I stood beside Sadie, staring into the shop window. She eyed the delicate golden necklaces and baskets of kohl, and I knew she was thinking of her date with Navin that evening.

"Have you come to lecture me, too?" Sadie muttered in her usual bitter tone. "Do you think I'm a fool for disobeying pack rules?"

"I don't." Her hooded eyes found my reflection in the glass. "We were taught to never question the rules. And now that we're here in Taigoska, disobeying one, it feels like we're ready to question them all."

"I always felt proud to be a Silver Wolf." Sadie folded her arms. "I knew we had our problems—King Nero, the worst of them—but it still felt right. Loyalty. Honor." She bunched up her shoulders as a flurry of snow blustered down the street. "Now, it all feels wrong."

"I wonder sometimes how I never questioned it all before. I suppose I did in the back of my mind, but . . ." I looked up at the curling cursive letters above the door. "That's a human thing—questioning it all. It's not what Wolves are supposed to do."

The bell to the storefront jingled and a human walked out, carrying a pastel bag in her hand. She gave us a sideways look and darted across the street.

Sadie huffed, watching the human rush away from us. Even without knowing we were Wolves, I'm sure we looked intimidating in our dark clothes with our sharp features and predatory stillness.

"We don't fit in with the humans, but don't want to fit in with the Wolves, either," she groused.

"Why are you here, Sadie?" I turned to her. "Why this shop?"

"I don't know," she hissed, scowling at the baskets of perfumed oils. "I wanted to look pretty or something for my dinner with Navin."

I smirked at her and her scowl deepened. "Pretty or something?"

"Whatever," she mumbled.

"I'm not making fun of you," I quickly corrected. "I'm commiserating. Gods, I think I understand better than anyone."

Sadie glanced at me. "You do?"

"I understood how I was meant to look, *who* I was meant to be, but deciding for myself is . . ."

"Scary," Sadie whispered, looking back into the window.

"Two Wolves scared to enter a boutique." A giggle escaped my lips at the ridiculousness of the situation.

Sadie grinned. "More comfortable with daggers than rouge."

"To be clear, you don't need any of this, Sadie, if you don't want it." I waved at the window. "Navin only has eyes for you, just as you are."

"I know," she said. "But it's frightening to think about."

"What?"

"Who would I be if I could be anything?" She pinned me with a look and my eyes began to well, even as I laughed at it all.

"I think I understand that better than anyone."

Her brows pinched together as she looked at my smile and tears. "You okay?"

"If Briar were here, I'd know how to dress. But if I could be anything? I wouldn't just be the forgotten Gold Wolf or Briar's twin or even Grae's mate." The thoughts were still spinning within me and I was too afraid to pin them down or make sense of them.

Sadie hummed in agreement, as if she could make sense of all the words that I couldn't. "In a pack, we are told exactly where we rank and what that means for us: how we can act, who we can love, how much we can dream for. Before now we only existed as one part of a bigger beast," she said. "But now as individuals . . ." She blew out a long breath.

"They'd have never allowed it," I said. "We were all just pawns in Nero's own game."

"If we defeat Sawyn, it won't matter what anyone else says," Sadie said with fierce confidence. "You can claim that kingdom and make your own rules if we win."

"We?"

She shrugged. "Hector and I talked about it. After we rescue Maez, we're coming with you. We made ourselves targets the second we left with Grae. Either you win or we die, so we might as well help you." She grinned, shuffling her feet closer to the window to escape the gale of icy wind. "In your kingdom, will you let humans and Wolves be together?"

I hadn't thought about it before then—that I might be able to make decisions that would affect other people like her, but the word came tumbling out of my mouth. "Yes."

Sadie pulled out her dagger and held open her palm. "Then I pledge my sword to you." She slit her hand and held it out to me. "My future ruler and regent."

"You're so morbid," I muttered.

"The word is 'sanguine.'" She smirked. "But yes, always."

I took out my knife and did the same, knowing that this was a declaration to myself as well. I thought to Grae, to our confessions in the forest. It was time I showed him all I was willing to fight for.

Vellia's voice whispered back into my mind: *Whatever it is you want from this life, Calla, I hope you have the stubbornness to take it.*

No more silent submission. I would be the ruler of Olmdere or I'd die trying.

"I accept." I shook her hand, our blood oath tying us together to whatever end. "Welcome, Sadie Rauxtide, Knight of Olmdere."

We both balled our cut hands into fists, turning back to the shop window.

"I'm freezing my tail off. Do you want to go inside?" I asked. Sadie nodded. "Celebrating your knighthood by perfume shopping." I guffawed, shaking my head.

"I think I'm going to like your court, Your Majesty." Sadie laughed, holding open the door for me. "Don't drip blood on the carpet."

WHEN SADIE AND I RETURNED TO THE WAGON, SPIRITS BUOYED, only Ora was there. Sitting at the kitchen table, they had needles held between their clenched, ruby red lips and pieces of fabric strewn across the table all around them.

"Oh good," they said, their eyes landing on me. "I was doing some mending of the costumes for the performance, now that you're going to be a little star."

Sadie leaned into me and muttered, "What does that mean?"

"I'll explain later," I replied.

"I'm going to go sit up front and sharpen my knives," she said, clapping me on the back and then lifting her bag of makeup, "and try not to stab myself in the eye with this kohl stuff."

"Have fun," I said as she crunched back down the icy steps toward the front of Galen den' Mora. I raked my snowy boots across the grating before shucking them off and adding them to the pile of drying shoes by the door. Warmth greeted my cold nose and cheeks, the smell of cinnamon lingering in the air as I sidled down the narrow corridor to where Ora sat.

"So . . . ," they said, spreading out different fabrics: satins, beads, feathers, velvets in every hue of the rainbow. "What do we think?"

What did I think? I took in all the different options with a shake of my head. "I'll be honest, I'd half-forgotten about the performance with everything else that's going on." The moment in the forest with Grae still echoed through me, contending with Sadie's new oath for pride of place in my mind. I clenched my too-long sleeve around my cut palm.

"Masquerade." Ora tossed the word around, tapping their fingers across the different materials as if summoning a spell. "Dark and sleek, bright and fun, glittery and elegant . . . What kind of performer are you going to be? What do you want to wear tonight?"

I blinked down at the fabric and two completely different answers leapt instantly into my mind, canceling out my decision before I could even speak it. Why was this so hard for me? Why couldn't I just pick one? These answers shouldn't feel like a knife twisting in my gut, forcing me to reflect on everything that I am.

That nagging feeling came back again, the one that had been growing in me for days since Malou first asked my favorite color, since I first admired Ora's wardrobe, since I first started asking questions of myself that I'd never asked before. But now, I knew it was so much more than colors and clothing, it was the rudderless searching part of *me* that felt . . . clashing. At war.

There was the person I positioned myself as, the one I showed to everyone: the shadow, the warrior, the one I felt I *needed* to be. I knew how she dressed, what she wore, not because she liked it but because it made sense for the person I created her to be . . .

But then there was this other person, someone freer and more vibrant, someone who was beginning to claim more and more space in my mind, and they were starting to shout to be heard over the sound of who I was supposed to be.

"I don't know how to pick," I murmured, that inner voice screaming at me for the cowardly answer. "I'll wear whatever you think is best, okay?"

Ora clasped their hands together, seemingly reading the silences between my words as readily as they heard my words themselves. "I told you before: it all starts with what appeals to *you*. It shouldn't matter what *I'd* want you to wear," they pushed, ever so gently. "I can't tell you who you are."

"Who am I?" I wasn't sure if I was asking them or myself, but the words shook out of me regardless, that shouting growing louder in my mind. I balled my fists, wanting to punch one through the wall.

Ora took the needles out of their mouth and stuck them back into a giant ball of felted wool. Standing, they walked over to my side of the bench and sat back down, the action making my eyes well. It was so careful, so tender, it made me feel like they saw under all my layers: the frustration, the realization, the grief, and release, all the words so close to being spoken and yet tucked down so deep.

"Who are you, love?" Ora asked the question with such gentle warmth, finally giving me the courage to turn toward the thoughts that had been gnawing at me.

From the moment I met Ora, it felt like a missing piece was placed in the puzzle of my mind. No, I remembered what I had first thought. A key in a lock that fit, but I wasn't sure if it would open. There was this restless agitation in me that had no name . . . but now, knowing that there were actually people who thought how I thought, who felt how I felt, who eschewed the confines of constructs that never fit them, it made that key start turning. And now, being put on the spot and asked that question, knowing such endless kindness waited patiently for my answer beside me, I felt the tumblers finally click. I could deny it no longer.

A tear slid down my cheek and Ora kept radiating that calm warmth, seemingly knowing that strange sort of joyful release that was washing through me.

"I was always searching outside of myself to find who I was— for someone else to tell me." My voice cracked and I took a shaky breath. "How could I find out there something that was always within me? I shouldn't have been searching, I should've been digging. I was buried there all along."

Ora's lips pressed together to keep from smiling. "And who have you unearthed?"

"I don't know how to describe it, but I've never felt more certain of anything." The words were on the tip of my tongue and I took a steadying breath. "I-I just don't know that woman is the right word for what I am. I've always had one foot outside of it, felt further away from that name than others somehow. It's not who I am, nor who I want to be." I felt lighter and lighter as the words tumbled out, speaking my deepest confession aloud for the first time. "I like my body better when I don't have to be *her*. I like my voice, my clothing, my personality . . . I like *me* better. It feels like the most honest thing I could be—both a part of and outside of—and moving through everything in between, and yet, I don't have a word for it . . ."

"And yet I understand." Ora put their hand on my forearm and more tears slipped down my cheeks.

"Gods, I can't stop crying today." I sniffed, wiping my eyes. "These aren't sad tears."

"I know," they said. "If anything, you seem relieved."

"I am." I still couldn't believe the words came out of my mouth. Shock coursed through me. But Ora, of all people, seemed to be someone who wouldn't judge me for it. "It felt good to say that out loud even if I don't know exactly what it means. I know who I am, even if I don't have a word for it."

"A part of, outside of, and moving in between . . ." Ora cocked their head at me. "I think in Olmdere you'd say 'merem.'"

I tossed the word around in my head. In Olmdere, humans had words for man and woman, words for those who were both and those who were neither, and then there was *merem*. It meant "with the river." I loved that. With the river—flowing, carving its own path. That river was taking me further away from all the things I was told I should be. It was the language of my people, and yet, not my word. Wolves spoke in only black and white, but I was now filled with every color.

"I like merem. I'm still just me, just Calla, but . . ." I shook my head.

The confession I was saving for Grae came spilling out to Ora instead, but they seemed like the right person to tell, a safe person, one who would understand me without me having the words myself. I thanked the Moon that I met Ora, that they opened me up to the possibility that I could exist beyond what I was forced to be. I took a shuddering breath. Maybe it would be easier to say a second time to Grae now that I'd said it aloud once. "Maybe one day I won't have to contort myself to make sense anymore."

"Maybe you'll be the one to change that for yourself," Ora said. "And for others, too."

"Maybe," I whispered.

Maybe one day Wolves would also use these words for people who flowed between man and woman, for people who existed outside either, and for people who were all of them at once. It wasn't the Wolf way and I'd never questioned choosing something for myself before that wasn't solely for the good of the pack. Wolves clung to tradition and, for some reason, I'd thought those traditions would keep us safe. Yet as soon as I stepped outside of that world, I realized how hollow it all was. It wasn't for safety. It was for power.

And not *my* power.

"I'm glad you told me." Ora nudged my shoulder with their own. "It feels good to claim who you are with two hands, doesn't it?"

Another tear slid down my cheek. "Yes."

Sadie stumbled in the back doorway, still sharpening a knife. "It's colder than an ostekke's co—" She looked up and spotted my tears, her brows furrowing in confusion.

"Stuck 'em with a pin," Ora said, covering for me as they gathered the fabric from across the table. And I noted how easily they danced around the word "her" when addressing me, giving me the space and freedom to figure that part out still. "Sorry songbird," they added with a wink.

I swiped at my tears with my sleeve, the way Ora addressed me making them fall heavier.

"It's been a long day," I mumbled. "I think I'm still hungover."

"Now *that* I understand," Sadie said, collapsing into one of the couches.

The words I was afraid to whisper even into my own mind hung in the air now.

Ora picked up their sewing again, sitting beside me smiling to themself. Such a small quiet moment, and yet everything felt like it was tearing apart and being put back together again. All the gray was now the brightest color, running faster than my Wolf through my mind. The peace I felt between the warring parts of myself just because they saw me. All of me. And they understood.

And with one simple word, merem, Ora mended a broken part of me, too.

I TOSSED AND TURNED, UNABLE TO FIND SLEEP. I'D LISTENED TO Sadie and Navin stumbling back at a late hour from their date, the happy hushed voices telling me they'd had a good time. Finally, I relented. I dragged back the curtain to my bunk and climbed out, knowing where I was going before my feet even touched the floor.

At the far end of the wagon, I climbed the notched footholds in the cabinetry and peeked at the netting that hung close to the canvas ceiling. A stretch of translucent fabric filled a hole cut in the roof in a makeshift skylight. The netting bowed in the center, holding Grae.

He stared straight up at the roof inches above him. "Couldn't sleep?"

"No," I whispered, crawling onto the taut netting. My body dipped down toward Grae's, our sides pressing together. "Is this where you're sleeping?"

"I figured it would be better than the couches," he murmured. "Night owls and early risers alike would want to use that space."

"You could come bunk with me," I said, and he turned his head to look at me.

His expression was soft, sleep taming his normally serious features. He nodded but didn't reply, looking back at the starry sky through the window.

"Did you ever think we'd end up here?" I whispered.

"In a wagon filled with human musicians?"

I nudged him with my elbow and he looked at me again. "All the adventures you used to tell me . . . now we're living one."

"I hope to have many more adventures with you." He swept

his hand up my arm, his fingers idly tracing my neck and lips. "All those years apart broke me, little fox."

"I wish I could've been there for you." I looked up into his sorrowful eyes. "I'm here now."

"I still can't believe it sometimes," he murmured. "You're here. You're safe from him."

I ached at those words. After knowing what happened to his mother, I no longer wondered why he was willing to go along with any of his father's requests. I wrapped my hand around his waist and tucked my head into his shoulder. The warmth of his body tugged me toward sleep, the lull I'd struggled to find alone so easy to find wrapped in his arms.

Grae kissed the top of my head, his voice cracking as his arms tightened around me. "I was so afraid of loving you."

I lifted my head, my mouth finding his in a soft, sleepy kiss. "You don't have to be afraid anymore." I knew they were the words he so desperately needed to hear, and I meant them with every ounce of my being. My lips skimmed his stubbled cheek. "I've never felt stronger."

I rested my head back on Grae's shoulder as I thought about the conversation Ora and I had that day—of who I'd unearthed.

Merem. One little word had made everything open up—a calm, steady assurance washing over me. Every choice that had wavered suddenly felt clear. I didn't need to lessen myself any longer. I wouldn't make myself smaller in order to fit into the Wolf world. It was such a brand-new thought, and yet ancient, inevitable, my brain racing toward this change and slowly easing into it all at once.

I glanced up to find Grae's eyes closed, his breathing slow and steady. He shifted me closer in his sleep, his smoky forest scent enveloping me. Another quiet moment would come, I promised myself, and when it did he would hear me and understand. I closed my eyes, forcing away the swirling nerves. For now, we both needed to rest with our mate by our sides.

TWENTY~NINE

"I CAN BARELY SEE IN THIS THING. WHAT IF WE'RE ATTACKED?"
Hector snapped, adjusting his mask for the hundredth time.

"No one will recognize us." Sadie kicked her brother in the shin. She wore a matching simple silver mask, studded with pearlescent beads.

Ora had procured the masks for us from one of their costume boxes. There seemed to be a treasure trove of ensembles for every possible occasion. We wore the masks in the sleigh as we rode to the palace on the off chance anyone was around who would recognize Grae. The rest of Galen den' Mora split up into two more sleighs to fit their instruments, and the Wolves followed in our own sleigh.

I glanced at Grae to find him already looking back at me. He wore a black mask with twisting midnight horns that made his cheekbones and jawline seem even sharper.

"Why would the Silver Wolves be at an Ice Wolf masquerade?" Sadie tipped her head to Grae. "We have a tentative relationship with them at the best of times."

"She's right," Grae said. "I doubt my father garnered an invitation, and sending his scouts would be most unwelcome. Queen Ingrid already hates my father."

"Why?" I asked, wiping my sleeve on the fogged glass and

peering out onto the pristine streets of the Wolf quarter. "I mean, not that I blame her."

Grae pointed out the window at three black-cloaked figures marching down the street. Rooks. I watched them patrol down the perfectly shoveled paths and past the glittering white buildings carved in the phases of the moon. Whereas the human quarter was filled with color, the Wolf quarter was nothing but black, gray, and white. It was tasteful and cold, no sign of personality to denote which Wolf family lived in which home.

"Ingrid let Sawyn's Rooks into Taigos pretty quickly after her razing of Olmdere," Grae said. "She didn't even try to push back, maybe out of fear of the sorceress, I don't know. The Rooks occasionally bleed over the border into Damrienn, causing trouble, but my father pushes them back into Taigos."

"I'm sure your father had something to say about her breaking off her engagement to Luo, too," Hector said.

My eyes darted to Hector. "Luo?"

"She was betrothed to the King of Valta for a time," Hector replied. "The second princess to shirk him."

"He must be a real delight," Sadie snarked.

"What happened?" I asked, thinking of my own possible engagement with his brother.

Hector shrugged. "When Ingrid started letting the Rooks into her borders, she cut off her alliance with Valta. The kingdoms still trade, though, so it couldn't have been that uncivilized."

"Of course, my father hated that." Grae snorted. "If the other kingdoms accepted princesses as heirs, then Briar or Calla could claim the throne of Olmdere and threaten his grab for it."

"I can hear him prattling on about pack tradition now," Sadie scoffed. "Funny how he was only sanctimonious when it came to a kingdom with gold mines."

The group chuckled, but the sound was tinged with bitterness.

I watched as Sadie flexed her hand. She hadn't shifted so the scar would remain, and I looked down at my own hand.

Grae must have caught all this, because he said, "I still can't believe you let Sadie pledge her blade to you before me." He lifted my hand and kissed the thin wound across my palm. His hot breath made the hair on my arms stand on end. "I'm supposed to be your mate."

"You are my mate," I said, the words filling me with heat—a claiming of sorts every time they were uttered. "And she is my knight. She offered and I accepted."

"So you're really going to do it, take Olmdere's throne?" Hector asked, pursing his lips.

"Only if we can get this nitehock and kill Sawyn with it. But if by some miracle we do, then . . . "I glanced at Grae. We hadn't discussed this—what our future would be.

Grae threaded his fingers through mine. "The Queen of Olmdere," he said, lifting my hand and softly kissing my knuckles. "And I shall be your consort."

"What? Not King?" Sadie gaped. "You'd give up your Silver crown and the Gold crown beside hers?"

"Damrienn holds no happy memories for me." He squeezed my hand and the memory of all he told me that day in the woods flashed into my mind. "And Olmdere isn't mine to claim. It should be a Gold Wolf on the throne, just as Ingrid is on hers."

I swallowed, tracing his masked face with my eyes. As a man and as my mate, by Wolf law, he had the right to all that was mine . . . and he'd just promised he wouldn't take it. He'd do the hard things because they were the right things. It was the last piece, that little question still hanging over me, and now, I knew for certain that there was nothing holding me back from this bond.

"This is all well and good, if you can find a way to rescue Maez and defeat Sawyn." Sadie looked between us. "And so far, the plan consists of us riding into the castle with a bunch of musicians and then hoping for the best?"

"That's why we're here now, isn't it?" I asked, turning to her brother. "With the nitehock we might actually have a fighting chance to rescue Maez."

"Sawyn will be too busy panicking about her failing powers to stop us rescuing Maez," Hector said. "I promise."

"I need another promise from you," I said, looking at the two siblings. "Once you get Maez, you two need to take her and flee."

"And leave you two behind?" Sadie's eyebrows shot up.

The sleigh turned a tight corner and we all pitched to the left. "You need to get Maez back to Damrienn. She needs to break Briar's curse."

"But wouldn't killing Sawyn also break Briar's curse?" Hector asked. "Surely five Wolves against her is better than two. And with her magic rendered useless by the nitehock, it would be the perfect time to strike, possibly the *only* time to strike."

"This is why we need the poison. We need to think like assassins, not warriors."

"We could dress up as servants. One of us could get close enough to slit her throat as a backup plan if the nitehock fails," Grae said. I shuddered to think what would happen if the nitehock failed. It was our best plan by a long shot, but Grae was right, it couldn't be our only plan.

"I could hide up in the rafters with a bow?" Sadie suggested. "I saw a shop with some nice ones in the human quarter."

"All of them," I said, lifting my chin. Poisoned, slit throat, shot with a bow and arrow. "We need to try every way. If one fails, the others will be there to take its place. She might catch one, but not all three." I adjusted the ribbon that held my mask to my face. It was a scarlet mask, covered in delicate lace, a plume of red feathers bursting from the top corner.

"There's still time," Grae said. "We'll figure it out."

"We're going to have to." I loosed a slow breath. "Turning back is a death sentence."

"Going forward feels a lot like one, too," Hector muttered.

"All the more reason for tonight to go off without a hitch." Sadie gave her brother a look, his expression lightening at the reminder of the plan he himself had concocted.

"Thank you for coming on this journey with me," I said.

"You've put yourselves in the thick of it to save your friend, to help her and my sister, to help me and my people. It's more than any royal should ask for."

"No, it's not," Sadie replied, giving me a grin. "We're your pack, Your Majesty.

"Packs stick together."

WITH LOW BEAMS AND A FROZEN EARTH FLOOR, THE BUILDING appeared to be old stables, now used as a changing room for human entertainers. We'd been left to dress while Galen den' Mora began their performance in the great hall. Their music floated through the high open windows and into the stables. I had seven songs to get ready and then I was expected to sing. My stomach clenched. I was about to sing for a pack of Ice Wolves.

I stared at my warped reflection in the mirror propped against a splintering gate. Ora had outdone themself. I'd given them a brief rundown of how I wanted the outfit to feel, and they'd taken it from there.

They had left a flowing garnet ensemble for me hanging on a tack hook. Fawn trousers hugged my legs, the hem of the dress cut short at the front and trailing in a train of bloodred feathers at the back. Feathers created epaulettes on the shoulders, matching the feathers in my mask, and the front of the dress was double-breasted with carved golden buttons. Black-heeled boots completed the outfit, making me look both carnival-like and military in styling, an odd combination that made me feel strange yet powerful.

A little note on the garment bag read *Za Faunique.* The Phoenix.

That's what I felt like then—reborn into something else—neither solely masculine nor feminine, but both. This outfit was only further confirmation that Ora understood my raw confession back in the wagon. They'd taken my truth and turned it into something beautiful and strong.

"It's nice, this."

I jumped at the sound of Grae's voice, my curls bouncing off my shoulders as I turned to find him leaning against the door-frame.

"What is?"

His cheeks dimpled. "You seeing yourself the way I've always seen you."

I turned back to my reflection. "You see me covered in red feathers?" I gave a mocking twirl, the train fanning across the frozen ground.

"No." Grae chuckled, pushing off the doorframe. His fingers lifted, tracing the line of my mask to the shell of my ear, making my skin tingle in the wake of his touch. "I see you like every other person is in the shadows and the moonlight only shines on you."

My hand lifted, gripping around Grae's fingers. In my heeled boots, I barely had to lift to meet his eye line. "And you are like every sound in a room going quiet until I can only hear your song."

He grinned, arms enveloping me as he bridged the last distance between us. His kiss lit up every corner of my body, rushing through me like a river after a rainstorm. I slung my arms around his neck, leaning into his solid chest, tasting him with my tongue.

The only light. The only song.

"Calla!" Sadie hissed, her sharp words forcing us apart. "You're on. Let's go."

"Shit," I cursed, having completely forgotten why we were there in the first place.

Grae chuckled, releasing me. "Have fun, little fox."

Hector appeared beside his sister, his eyebrows raised. "You're going to miss your cue."

"It was my fault," Grae said. "Wait." He halted me by the crook of my arm and wiped a thumb down the corner of my mouth.

I had forgotten I'd painted my lips red. Grae's lips were smudged scarlet as well. I gave him a mischievous grin, turning and following Sadie toward the main hall.

"Hector found the apothecary's room," she whispered, her voice barely audible as we rushed down the hall. "It's a floor above, unguarded. We should only need a few minutes. Make it good, songbird, and there will be no eyes upon us."

"No pressure, then?" I muttered, lifting my heavy feather train so I could walk faster.

"Not much," Sadie taunted. "Just the fate of your kingdom hanging in the balance. Nothing too big."

"Thanks," I snorted and she clapped me on the shoulder.

Reaching for the gilded side door, her hand stilled on the handle. "Of all the Wolf rulers I ever thought I would follow, I thank the moon that it is you."

My breath hitched, humbled by her words, and I simply nodded to her, afraid that any more words might lead to tears.

The music up ahead slowed and I knew the last song was finishing and then it would be my turn. Somehow, whatever butterflies existed in the pit of my stomach had vanished. The feathers fluttered along my shoulders as I rolled them back and strode through the opening door. My smile widened. I felt like I was flying.

THE VAST HALL GLITTERED WITH GILDED CHANDELIERS, DRIPping crystal candelabras, and mirror-lined walls. The clamorous banter dropped to a hushed din as I skirted through the side door, trying to embody the power of my bright red costume. A sea of masks tracked me as I approached the quartet tucked in the corner.

"You look magnificent," Ora whispered as I took my place on the golden pedestal in front of them.

I bowed deeply to the Queen standing in the center of the crowd.

Queen Ingrid had white-blond hair arranged atop her head, her silver and gold crown spearing toward the sky like rays of sunlight. Her voluminous icy blue dress belled so wide around her that the doting courtiers circling her were beyond arm's reach. I couldn't make out her eyes in the shadows of her diamond-studded mask, but I knew she was watching me from the curious cock of her head as she fanned herself.

I wished Briar were there. She might've never wanted to be a queen, but she would've loved to come to a ball like this—to wear fine gowns, to dance among royal Wolf family, to relish the long evenings that stretched out to dawn. She might never get a chance.

Not unless I made this count, right here, right now.

The hall was so crammed with masked faces that I couldn't see the far doors. Was the Ice Wolf pack this large? Unless Queen Ingrid invited Wolves from other realms to her soiree . . . It seemed unlikely that any of them were human.

Malou's bow tapped me on the calf and the crowd tittered. I glanced to the side and saw her frowning up at me.

Oh Gods, I'd missed my cue—too mesmerized by the giant crowd and opulent room.

The strings swelled again and this time I began to sing. Ora accompanied me, though their voice was considerably softer than the day before in the plaza.

The crowd was supposed to dance and chat while I sang, but first they joked about my miscue, and now every partygoer stood still, watching me like I was a famous opera singer. My heart pounded in my ears, but I forced my voice louder, praying it didn't wobble.

From the corner of my eye, I spotted Grae's twisted black mask. He was tucked in the corner, barely visible behind a white marble pillar, but knowing he watched strengthened my voice. I gave him a warning look. Even with his mask, it was dangerous for him to be out here.

When I hit my final note, the crowd burst into applause and I dropped into a bow, humbled by their ovation.

"Encore, encore!" they cheered.

They began calling out the titles of songs, many I hadn't heard before, requests I didn't know. My brows pinched together as my eyes darted from one voice to the next.

Queen Ingrid took a decisive step forward and said, "Do 'The Sleeping Queen.' Everyone knows that one."

My stomach dropped. "The Sleeping Queen," the song about my mother. I glanced to where Grae leaned against the wall. How could I get myself out of this? I couldn't tell if it was a trick of the light, but Grae seemed to nod his head, an infinitesimal movement. The way Queen Ingrid requested it left no room to refute. I clasped my hands together and bobbed my head to her.

The musicians began the faster refrain. It was a happy tune, a tale of true love triumphing in the face of unbeatable odds. Gratefully, the crowd broke apart and began to dance as I sang, spurred on by the jolly melodies. But the joy of my mother's tale felt horribly hollow to me. She didn't have her happy ending, and her daughter had befallen the same fate, and this time Sawyn was wise enough not to leave her mate around to break the curse.

They were gone. My family was gone. My kingdom was in ruin. Our people, like Navin, suffered at the hands of a sorceress. And here I was singing a merry tune about a love story whose true ending was one of death and grief. If my mother's soul had a song, it wouldn't be this one.

A knot formed in my throat and I wasn't sure if I would make it to the end. My body felt impossibly light. This wasn't just a story to me anymore, but I couldn't let this Wolf pack know it. Why would a human cry over the sad fate of the Gold Wolves?

My voice began to rasp, but with the crowd now diverted back to the dancing and the instruments nearly drowning me out, it didn't matter so much. I wondered if the troupe did it on purpose, or if they were simply lost in the song, but I was grateful.

Each wooden note felt harder than the last. I didn't know if I could do it, if I could reach the last line and sing about my parents' "happy" ending. How could I form those words? Sweat broke out along my brow, my stomach dropping as I realized I might reveal my secret right then and there in front of hundreds of Wolves.

Keep going, I prayed, but the words were sandpaper against my windpipe. It all came crashing down on me in this one sweet song. Fear gripped me—the lights blinding, the final words choking in my throat and, in my panic, my eyes found Grae.

As if hearing my plea, he pushed off from the marble column and strode toward me. As the last notes died on my lips, he grabbed me and kissed me.

The crowd laughed and cheered, delighted by the seemingly playful act of a partygoer interrupting the song. The kiss pushed all other thoughts to the recesses of my mind, and I finally found my breath again. Grae's lips lingered, his wide body shielding mine from onlookers. For that one brief moment, it was as if the rest of the room disappeared and only he and I existed.

"I've got you," he whispered, his warm breath making my lips tingle.

As the applause died down, I was reminded of the audience and took another steadying breath. Grae threaded his fingers through mine and led me back into the corridor. Galen den' Mora had already moved on to a new jaunty tune.

Grae cupped my cheek. "You were wonderful, little fox."

"I don't know what overcame me," I breathed. "I've heard that song a million times before—heard it just recently, in fact—but something about actually singing my parents' love song in front of an entire pack of Ice Wolves . . ."

"Your parents' story had only ever been that—a story. But the closer we creep to Olmdere, the more real it becomes."

"From the moment Sawyn cursed Briar, it became real." I wiped my clammy hand across the back of my neck. "Remembering her on that stone tomb only reminds me that their story didn't end like that song, no happily ever afters for them."

"They had many years of happiness together, though," Grae said. "Some would trade a lifetime for those years they spent together. Their lives were more than just their endings."

I found Grae's eyes in the shadows of his mask and I knew he was thinking of his mother, too. "Yes."

Grae's eyes smoldered as he wrapped his hand around my waist and gathered me to him. "You can't come to a ball and not have a dance with me." He looked at the snow-covered broom leaning against the wall. "Though this isn't quite what I had imagined."

"Me either." I let out a soft laugh, looking up into his beaming eyes shadowed by his fiendish mask. "Though I think this might be more appropriate for our first dance."

"You belong in the center of every room, Calla," Grae murmured, eyes dropping to my lips. "But yes, selfishly, I like having you all to myself right now."

He began moving me in a simple box step, gliding me around the tight space. So often I had to practice being the lead dance partner with Briar. It felt good to be guided around the floor for once. The beautiful melody filled me as Grae twirled us around.

He sighed. "I'll never forget that moment, the sound of your voice, the way you looked."

"You have a beautiful voice, little songbird." We both jolted

THIRTY

THE EMPTY HALLWAYS ECHOED WITH THE SOUND OF MY RAGGED breath.

"Where are we going?" I whispered as Grae shouldered open a little door to a courtyard. The sound of strings echoed up the tall stone walls. Golden light filtered from a high-arched window, a sliver of chandelier peeking through the glass. We were so close to the ballroom and yet we felt a world away.

I lifted my train with my free hand and stepped into the dusting of snow. Crates and buckets lined the far wall, probably from the overflowing kitchens. We hadn't seen much of the castle on our ride through the back entrance, just the tips of the white needle-like spires above a towering white wall of snow. I was certain the front entrance would be grand, but humans didn't enter that way.

The far door had the symbol of a Wolf and the Taigosi words *Da Lothien Ostrosko*. It roughly meant "hospitality closet," where Wolves could find clothing if they traveled to the palace on all four paws. How well the Wolves treated their own kind . . . how poorly they treated everyone else.

"Thank you," I said to Grae, releasing his hand and leaning against the cold white stone. The coolness soothed the torrent of emotion swirling inside me.

apart at the sound of the smooth, warm tone. "It reminds me of someone I knew long ago."

We stared through the open doorway as Queen Ingrid sauntered toward us. Her hoop skirts squeezed through the archway as she waved her feathered fan along her décolletage.

"Hello, Graemon," she said with a quirk of her lips. She lifted her chin in Wolf greeting and tapped her fan closed against her lace-covered hands. "Not a very convincing disguise, I must say."

I straightened, wishing I had more than just my knife in my boot. Grae took a step closer to me as he bowed, and I did the same.

From this close, I could see the streaks of silver in Queen Ingrid's white-blond hair, the minute lines around her mouth and neck, the only indications of her age.

"Your Majesty," Grae muttered.

"That was a delightful little act you put on in there. And who is this phoenix you kissed?" She cast her cold eyes toward me. "What's your name?"

"Calla," I whispered, dipping my head in a half-bow again.

Queen Ingrid sniffed the air as if she could discern who I was from scent alone. Her pale eyebrows popped up above the line of her mask. "Is this the mate I've been hearing whispers about?" Grae took a step closer as she pointed her fan at me. "Take off your mask."

"I—"

"Let me see the face of Graemon's mate," the Queen insisted.

With shaking hands, I reached back and untied the ribbon around my head, letting my mask fall into my hands. I looked up at the Queen. For a moment, time seemed to stand still, her pale eyes boring into mine, until I thought she might laugh or sneer or call me ugly, unworthy of Grae.

"Moonlit curses," she whispered instead, her eyes roving my face. "Your mate isn't another Silver Wolf, is it? I know a Gold Wolf when I see one."

"How did you know?" Grae's jacket sleeve brushed against mine, his shoulders raising like a hound ready to bolt.

"And not just any Gold Wolf," she said, ignoring the question. She cocked her head, letting out a cackle. "I'm impressed you managed to keep this a secret, Graemon. A Marriel? How?"

"What makes you think I'm a Marriel?" I rasped as she prowled a step closer.

"Because you are your mother and father combined. You've got your father's green eyes." She scanned me from head to toe, reading my lineage etched into every feature. "And nose. You have Rose's hair, though, and stature. I suppose those who knew them best are long gone, but anyone who remembered the King and Queen of Olmdere could see them in you in a heartbeat."

The feathers on my shoulders fluttered as my chest rose and fell. She had cut to the core of us in a single passing glance. I had always thought Briar took more after our parents—that she looked like the truer Marriel. But with one discerning look, the Ice Wolf Queen had figured it out.

"A secret child, what a scandal!" She seemed delighted, as if this bit of juicy gossip didn't affect our entire lives.

"We're not the only court with secret children," I muttered through clenched teeth. "We've just been through Hengreave."

"You mean my pathetic half-brother?" Queen Ingrid flashed her white canines. "If he could shift, he'd be battling down my door demanding the throne right now." She shook her head, waving off the notion. "Men.

"Anyway, every family has its dramas, even the Marriels. So maybe don't be so quick to bandy gossip about royals so readily, right, Calla?"

My brow furrowed.

"Oh, you don't know." The Queen smirked. "I'm sure Sawyn will enlighten you."

"Why have you allied with her?" Grae demanded.

The side door opened and a servant bustled out, pausing

when they saw the Queen . . . No, not a servant at all, but Hector. He bowed quickly, acting as if he'd stumbled out the wrong door, and darted back inside. As he left, he patted his coat pocket twice, a gesture that would go unnoticed by the Queen but told us he had the nitehock.

"Perhaps I see things in a way you do not," Queen Ingrid mused, pursing her lips, and my muscles eased the tiniest bit that her assessing eyes hadn't seen Hector for what he was, too.

"You let her Rooks run wild through your kingdom," Grae said, pulling her focus back to him.

"The Rooks are indeed welcome in my court." Queen Ingrid gestured around the dimly lit space. "They leave the Ice Wolves alone and make Luo think twice about claiming Taigos as his own."

"Why would he do that?"

"Because I ended our engagement with no other explanation than I simply wanted to." Queen Ingrid grinned like a snow cat. "And that is tantamount to breaking a contract in pack terms. Luo wants his cut of Taigos." She lifted her chin, straightening her crown as she did. "And I am disinclined to give it to him."

"This would all be fixed by allowing first children to claim their thrones, regardless of their gender," I said.

"Perhaps. But that isn't the case, is it? So be careful, Princess," Queen Ingrid said. "You're speaking more like a sorceress than a Wolf."

I shook my head. "I am a Wolf, therefore I'm speaking like a Wolf," I snapped. "Just perhaps we've been letting the wrong Wolves decide what is and isn't for the good of their packs for too long."

"I like your mate, Graemon." Queen Ingrid winked at him. "She's stunning. You don't deserve her."

"I know," Grae replied instantly.

The rumble of his voice made my toes curl in my boots.

"I've been hearing some wicked whispers from Damrienn.

Your father's Wolves were at my doorstep only two nights ago, looking for you and her. I wondered if you'd show up at my doorstep."

They'd come to Taigos after Aiden's death? Not straight back to Damrienn? My eyes widened as I wondered if they'd told Queen Ingrid that Grae had killed him. Perhaps we wouldn't be walking out of this castle after all.

Grae clenched his fists. "What did they say?"

"You don't know?" She practically bubbled with the thought of being the one to tell him. "You're no longer the heir to Damrienn. Your father has declared you and your mate traitors."

I sucked in a sharp breath. "He really did it."

"He's named Hemming's son, Evres, as his heir and put out a bounty of a thousand gold griftas to whoever returns Maez safely."

"So *now* he cares about Maez?" I asked.

"He could care less about her, I'm sure. He wouldn't even care about your kingdom at all, Princess, if it wasn't filled with unclaimed gold. Nero has always maneuvered himself for more power. It's why he brokered his marriage with the Valtan Princess after her failed engagement." Grae's lip curled at the Queen's word. "He probably thinks if they return Maez, he can carry on with his plans. Perhaps he thinks she's easier to control, too." She pursed her lips at Grae, shrugging. "How convenient he has another Gold Wolf in his possession who happens to be her mate."

I gritted my teeth. *In his possession.*

"Don't worry." She waved her laced-covered hand. "I told the Silver Wolves I heard rumors of you turning southward, that you cut down the Stormcrest Ranges to Valta."

"Why?"

"Because I despise Nero Claudius and I don't like Silver Wolves in my kingdom," she sneered. "More, I won't let *any* man say what goes on in Taigos, *ever*. I won't alert the Rooks that you are here, either." Queen Ingrid looked between us. "Payment for your song. If you decide to stay here, that promise will carry. But if you cross into Olmdere, you're on your own."

I clasped my hands together, hanging my head. We wouldn't end up in a dungeon tonight. "Thank you."

"You are most welcome in my court, Calla Marriel." Queen Ingrid bowed her head back to me. "I suppose you are, too, Graemon, now that you are not Nero's puppet anymore. I wish you luck."

And then the Queen of the Ice Wolves left to return to her party as we both stood there, stunned.

THIRTY-ONE

THE SOUND OF THE CURTAIN RINGS SLIDING BACK ROUSED ME from my slumber. Sleep had claimed me from the moment my head hit the pillow. I had changed into my chemise and scrubbed the paint off my face with frantic haste, leaving my phoenix costume hanging on the hook by the kitchen cupboards. I understood now why Galen den' Mora kept such strange hours. My body was exhausted and I'd only sung two songs. After the run-in with Queen Ingrid, I was eager to get out of Taigoska, too, despite her promise to protect us. I didn't doubt she would try, but I couldn't be sure she'd succeed, and hiding here would still mean Briar was in danger. No, now that Hector has the nitehock, the world opened up for us. We might actually be able to defeat Sawyn.

Grae's warmth seeped into me as I breathed in his comforting scent. His familiar bonfires and rainstorms encircled me, but also the crisp smell of snow that clung to his hair. Even in his human form, his scent was imprinted on my mind now, as if our bond somehow connected us in every possible way. I sighed, savoring that scent, so uniquely him. I didn't shuffle backward to give him space, letting him wrap his arm around me and gather me into his chest.

Navin had taken the nightshift driving the oxen out of town

and Sadie offered to ride along with him. We plodded out of the city at a slow, lumbering pace. Apart from the rumble of the wagon wheels, the rest of the cabin was quiet, not a single clink of teacups or shuffle of boots. How late had Grae stayed up before coming to bed with me?

He brushed a soft kiss against my mouth and breathed me in.

"Do I smell like lilies in the summer sunshine?" I whispered against his lips.

"Yes." His chest rumbled against mine as he kissed me again. "It's intoxicating."

His smell did the same thing to me. That heady earth and smoke made my heart race, rousing me from the depths of slumber. I deepened our kiss, tracing my tongue along Grae's bottom lip until he opened for me. A low groan reverberated in his throat.

Grae's chest rose and fell against mine. "What mischief are you up to, little fox?"

"Nothing," I murmured as I hooked my leg over his hip, tilting myself closer against him.

His fingers traced up my knee, pushing up the hem of my nightdress until they reached my bare backside.

Grae groaned. "Are you trying to kill me?"

I grinned, rocking myself against his hardening length.

"What do you want, little fox?" Grae's hand circled lower, slowly curving around my thigh, and I writhed against him, trying to get his fingers closer.

This. I'd always wanted this. Us.

My wanton voice sounded foreign to me. "I want you."

There was no shyness, no embarrassment, not with Grae. With him, one moment just rolled into the next, no questioning it. We were inevitable.

"Gods, promise me at the next stop we'll find time away from this bloody group." His chuckle morphed into a growl as I ground against him. His hand stilled my hip. "Not here," he whispered. "I told you what will happen the first time I have you."

I pulled my swollen lips away from his, trying to find his eyes in the darkness. "You promised to make me moan so loud even the Moon Goddess would hear."

"Yes." The word hissed out between his clenched teeth. His fingers began circling again. "And I mean it. But I think you need a little taste now."

"Desperately," I panted, arching as his fingers skimmed the hair between my legs.

Grae's lips found my ear as he whispered. "This is just a glimmer of the way I'm going to make you feel."

My nipples peaked against his chest as his finger slid into a teasing glide, drifting up my folds and parting my warm, wet flesh. Grae nibbled on my ear, and I moaned into the pillow as his fingers found the tight bundle of my clit. Every muscle in my body tightened as he slowly circled that throbbing button. He slid his fingers up and down again, coating me in my own wet heat.

His voice was nothing but feral as he growled, "You're so ready for me, aren't you?"

"Gods," I moaned, tipping my hips into his fingers as he continued his maddening slow circles. My inner muscles flickered, desperate to be filled, as I begged, "More."

The pad of his fingertip circled at the entrance to my thrumming core, waiting as I writhed.

"Yes," I mewled, my voice louder than I had intended.

His lips left my ear, finding my mouth as he dipped his finger inside of me. His kiss absorbed my moan, muffling the sweet, lustful sounds he wrung out of me as he slowly slid his finger in and out. He added a second finger, stretching me wider and deeper than I'd never felt before. His thumb continued to circle my clit as his fingers curled inside me, massaging my inner walls in a way that made my eyes roll back.

I ground my hips into his fingers, my body taking over as I chased that sensation building within me—a precipice I'd only ever reached with my own hands . . . and never, ever like this. Grae's fingers strummed through my body like he was playing the sweetest song. The rhythm of his fingers matched the circling of his thumb, thrusting faster as my movements became wilder. With every breath, I climbed higher, my body becoming light and dizzy as every inch of me homed in on those fingers.

Higher and higher, that buzzing grew until Grae wrapped his other hand around my neck, holding my mouth to his as my soft sounds turned to deeper moans. I was so close. With one more pump of his fingers, my climax blasted through me, shattering shards of white-hot bliss through every muscle in my body. Grae's chest vibrated against mine as he absorbed my hot moans of pleasure, his fingers wringing out each little note as I clenched around him again and again, riding his hand and chasing that euphoria. My sounds ebbed to heavy panting breaths and his lips finally released me, his fingers slowly sliding out and finding my back again.

"That . . . was," I breathed, my face flushing as my body echoed with pleasure.

"Barely the beginning," Grae promised, his swollen lips brushing a soft kiss into my hair. "Tomorrow. Promise me we'll find someplace, just us."

"Tomorrow," I said, tucking my face into the crook of his neck. The heaviness of sleep tugged on me again as my heart slowed. A smile twisted my lips. I couldn't believe we just did that, and, in the same exact breath, nothing had felt more right—as if our bodies were finally acknowledging what we'd known all along in our souls: we were meant to be one.

"EVERYBODY OUT!"

The shout made me jolt. Grae's arms tightened around me before he even opened his eyes.

"Shit," Hector growled. "Rooks."

The sound of curtains sliding open filled the cabin. I rolled out of the bunk after Grae and quickly grabbed my undergarments and leathers. I jumped them up over my thighs, buckling them as shouts rang out.

"We're at a road stop," Navin said, throwing a shirt over his head. He must've swapped driving with Ora in the wee hours of the morning.

My eyes widened at his surprisingly muscled torso and then darted to Sadie, who was gawking at him from her bunk. I tried to hide my smirk. When the hem of his tunic reached his belt and his muscles were off display, she began flicking her throwing knife again.

"What happens at a road stop?" Hector asked.

Mina and Malou sat around the kitchen table, already dressed. The narrow galley made it hard for everyone to gather. I spotted the swaying strands of badges hanging from the chandelier, looking patchier and sparser than when last I'd checked. Had some fallen off during the ride?

Grae stepped in front of me, blocking my line of sight to cover me while I changed my shirt. I chuckled. People were frantically getting shoes on and grabbing weapons. No one was looking at me.

"If we're lucky, they'll just ask for money and send us on our way," Malou said.

"And if we're not lucky?" Sadie asked.

"Then one of us might get a black eye or our stuff stolen," she muttered, biting her thumbnail as she eyed us. "But with you lot here, who knows?"

"Everybody out!" a voice boomed again. Solid thwacks knocked down the side of the wagon. The unsettling sound pushed everyone to dress faster.

"Just be calm," Navin said, ushering us to the back ladder. "It'll be fine."

"That's what you said last time," Malou muttered. She and Mina clambered over the couches and down the ladder.

I followed behind her, Grae's hand on the small of my back, wondering what had happened last time. The bright sunlight was blinding against the freshly fallen snow. The heavy shadows and low angle of the sun told me it was still early morning. Only the smallest flashes of color peeked out from the frozen surroundings. We had entered another narrow pass on our descent toward Olmdere. A watchtower sat on the hill above us, looking like a lighthouse in a sea of snow.

Four Rooks stood beside the wagon, only their eyes visible above their covered mouths and noses. Ora stood beside the oxen, watching as we climbed out. The only one dressed for the weather, they wore a fur hat and thick indigo cloak. We barely had time to put on shoes, as we stumbled out in tunics and trousers. The chill bit into my skin and my arms instinctively wrapped around me as I trudged out into the ankle-deep snow.

"Where are you heading?" the front Rook asked Ora. His black cape whipped behind him, sounding like the flapping of a bird's wings. He nodded to two of his comrades and they broke off to search the wagon.

"Olmdere, my Lord," Ora said, taking off their hat and brushing back their curls as they bowed slightly to the Rook. "We are Galen den' Mora. We are going to perform at Her Majesty's celebrations."

Her Majesty. The words made acid rise up my throat.

"You're all musicians?" The Rook's hood turned as he assessed our lineup. He twirled his hand scythe around his pointer finger, brandishing his steel claws for all to see.

"Yes, musicians and crew," Ora murmured.

The Rook walked down the line of us, looking each of us up and down. Mina clenched her sister's hand as the Rook paused in front of her.

"What's your name?" he asked her.

Her gray eyes grew impossibly wide as she signed her name back to him.

"Mina," Malou interpreted for her and in that moment the twins looked so different I wondered how I could've ever mixed them up. Malou was sharp and fierce. Mina was gentle and shy.

Both were beautiful and talented, but never once had I seen that wide-eyed fear of Mina's expression on Malou's face, nor the gruff distaste in Malou's pinched mouth on Mina's.

The Rook arched his brow. "A musician who can't hear?"

"She can hear," Malou said, her tone tipping the balance from sharp to mean. "There's more than one reason to use the language of signs."

The Rook twisted toward her so quickly it made her rock back on her heels. He twirled his hand scythe again and Malou had the good sense to stay quiet.

He snickered at her surprise, but kept walking, apparently satisfied with her reply. I kept my gaze downcast, watching as his boots appeared before mine.

"And your name?" I knew he was asking me without looking up.

I wasn't sure if it was better to lie or not. Now that people knew about King Nero's renouncement of Grae, maybe they'd know my name, too.

"Vellia," I said.

"Vellia what?" the Rook asked, tilting his head so his eyes pierced into me from under his heavy brow.

Grae sidestepped closer to me.

"Vellia Sortienna, my Lord," I said, bowing my head. *Vellia of the Golden Trees.* It had been the first word that popped into my mind. "I'm a singer."

"You've probably heard of our little songbird from Queen Ingrid's masquerade?" Ora flourished their hand toward me. "It was the talk of Taigos afterward."

"I'm not much of a music-lover," he said with a spit. But the Rook didn't move for the longest time after that. With each passing moment, my pulse grew louder, wondering if he recognized me somehow.

Finally, he spoke. "All right, it'll be ten crovers to pass the border."

"*Ten?*" Ora exclaimed. "Borders are normally one."

"We're charging per person nowadays," the Rook said, turning toward Ora. "And extra for you lot wasting our time."

Ora looked like they might protest, but Grae grabbed the coin purse off his belt.

"Here." He hastily chucked it at the silent Rook waiting behind his commander.

The Rook looked at the heavy bag of coins, tossing it up and down in his hands. He nodded to his commander, clearly more than ten crovers inside. The other Rooks disembarked the wagon, shaking their heads at him—they'd found nothing.

Navin's eyes narrowed, assessing each of the Rooks, though their covered mouths and deep hoods made it hard to discern their features. I knew he was searching for his brother again. I wondered if his heart leapt into his throat every time he saw these cloaked figures—if he hoped that, this time, he'd finally find his family member.

"Safe travels," the head Rook said, gesturing to his comrades with his hand scythe. They all turned toward the thin trail back up to the lookout.

Mina nudged Hector when he didn't move and he turned to follow the rest.

We filed back into the lower seating area, dragging snow across the rough hessian mat. We crammed into the couches and took off our boots, leaving them to dry along the back grate.

"That was stressful," Sadie said, resting her woolen socks on the low table in a mirror to Navin. Their trousers just touched each other and I noticed the little smile that played on Navin's lips at the action.

"At least now we're in Olmdere," Hector said.

"No, actually we're not." Malou snorted. "We've got another day's descent before we reach the border."

Hector's brows dropped. "But didn't we just pay a border tithe?"

"One of many." Malou crossed her arms and leaned back against the patchwork couch. "We'll be paying greedy Rooks at least two more times before we get into Olmdere, and then, who knows. There might be roadblocks in every village."

"There aren't," Navin said, and everyone's eyes darted to him. "There aren't enough travelers passing through, and those that travel within Olmdere have no money to extort."

I grimaced. My parents probably had provided for the humans better than Sawyn, but still, I couldn't help but wonder how well the humans could've lived under their reign. I thought to Taigoska, to the city separated into human and Wolf quarters, how we entered the back of the palaces and how the guests at the ball were all Wolves. I was confronted once again by how each city, each kingdom, comprised two different worlds—different words and Gods and customs, different lives lived and different futures attainable. And I felt it more keenly than ever how I wished the world blended every color and not just black and white. What if I wanted to pray to the Goddess of Courage? What if I wanted to exist beyond the names and words given to me on the day of my birth? What if I wanted to be not a woman but merem?

Guilt burned through me. I hadn't considered it before. I had dreamed of reviving Olmdere, of reestablishing the Gold Wolf pack, of even doing away with the restrictions between humans and wolves . . . but how much had I actually considered changing things in a substantive way? Where were the humans in these daydreams of grandeur?

"How long until the next roadblock you reckon?" Hector asked.

"Midday, probably," Malou said with a shrug. "We'll stop in the little village there. Water the oxen and switch drivers. We should be getting close to the border by nightfall."

The wagon lurched back to life, rocking us all backward. We continued our slow plodding descent down the icy switchback roads.

"There's a great spot along the border for stargazing," Navin said, nudging Sadie with his calf. "Maybe you want to check it out?"

"I need breakfast," Hector groused as the group snickered, shooting up from the couch. "Who wants tea?"

"I'll help you," I said. Grae's hand squeezed my hip as I rose.

I looked down at him, seeing the fire still burning in his hooded eyes. I gave him a little nod. We'd find our own spot tonight and he'd fulfill those promises that filled me with instant yearning. I felt dizzy and flushed as I climbed the ladder after Hector to the blackened box stove. It overwhelmed me how much I needed that connection. Everything was storming around me, but Grae was my anchor, my constant. After twenty long years, I'd be in my homeland again. I'd uphold the promises my ancestors made to the humans. I'd rid their kingdom of monsters, starting with the sorceress.

THIRTY-TWO

THE SNOW GAVE WAY TO THICK CLOUDS AND THE SCENT OF spring rain. In the late evening, we'd rolled into the half-deserted border town of Durid. I yanked the hood of my cloak lower as Grae and I darted hand in hand, sheltering under the next roof.

"I don't think there will be much stargazing tonight," Grae shouted to be heard above the sound of pouring rain.

With the thick cloud cover, the night had swiftly claimed the day. Where there should've been a sunset, it already appeared as darkest night.

"Sadie didn't look too concerned when they left." I chuckled, thinking of the look on her face when she and Navin ran off just like we were doing now.

Most of Galen den' Mora chose to stay in the wagon, hiding from the deluge. I'd hoped to get a peek of Olmdere from this vantage point, but we could barely see two feet in front of us. From what little I could gather of Durid, it seemed like a midsize town with modest thatched-roof homes around the outskirts and taller stone edifices in the center. The largest forge appeared to be abandoned, the parapets crumbling and the windows overgrown with ivy.

"Where are we going?" Grae called as I yanked on his hand, pulling him back into the rainstorm. Our boots splashed through deep puddles, mud flying around us as we darted toward the fortress. My clothes were soaked to the skin, but I didn't care. In that moment, with just Grae and me and the roar of rain, I felt giddy and light.

We reached the outer wall of the ruins and climbed over the rubble. I tore back the vines obscuring the doorway and stumbled into the shadowed room. Grae's hand clenched around mine, keeping me upright as my feet wobbled over the loose stone. My eyes strained. A human would probably see nothing but darkness, but, even in this form, I could see the outlines of shapes.

I panted, wiping my wet hair off my forehead as I surveyed the space. Shrubs and weeds had reclaimed the floor, growing from the dirty cracks in the paving stones. Cobwebs covered the ceiling and only a few scraps of wood remained.

"What is this place?" I released Grae's hand and ventured further into the room. I held out my hands in front of me as I walked, my eyes working to see through the gloom.

"A ruin of some sort," Grae breathed, wiping a hand down his wet face. "A human temple maybe?"

He followed after me as I found my way to a curving stairwell. Rivers of water ran down the moss-covered steps, the heavy rain misted from the caved-in ceiling to the right. I got up two stairs before Grae caught my hand.

"I feel like one misstep and this entire thing will crumble," he said, pulling me down a stair so that I was the same height as him.

I slid my hands up his chest and around his neck. Fingers dipping into his drenched hair, I laughed. "You might as well have jumped into a lake."

"I was lured into the rain by this beautiful creature. It's not my fault I was bewitched." His hands slipped between the folds of my cloak and circled my waist.

"I wanted to be alone with you," I whispered.

His lips found mine, enveloping me in a warm, soft kiss. His mouth skimmed up to my ear. "This is far from the crackling fire and a warm bed I'd imagined for our first time together."

"What is this wolfish obsession with firsts?" I rolled my eyes. "The third time can be in a nice warm bed, or the fifth." Grae's lips twisted into a wicked smirk. I waved a hand up and down my tunic and leathers. "Do I look like some dainty, soft-hearted damsel?"

"No." He took a step closer, his cloak brushing against the fabric of my tunic. His breath danced across my cheek as he leaned into me. I sucked in a sharp breath as his teeth tested the flesh below my ear. "You look like my mate."

"If we waited for everything to be perfect, we might never have each other." My fingernails pressed into his neck. "Besides, we are Wolves. We don't need fires and beds."

Grae responded with his tongue replacing his teeth, making me arch my head back further.

"I knew I shouldn't have given you that little taste," he murmured, his hot breath in my ear making my skin ripple with goosebumps. "Now you're ravenous."

"Yes," I groaned through clenched teeth. The rain poured so loud throughout the cavernous space, I was certain no one could hear me.

"What do you want, mischievous little fox?" Grae's hand strayed from my hip, moving around to cup my ass. "Tell me and I'll give it to you."

"I want you." My lips parted as I panted, "I want you inside of me."

Grae groaned as his fingers pressed in tighter and then he released me. His hands made quick work of unclasping his cloak and he threw it down on the stairs behind me. I grinned as he hastened to unclasp mine and did the same, layering the stone steps in our thick wool cloaks.

"You have no idea how badly I've wanted to hear that," he growled.

His lips crashed into mine, pulling my bottom lip between his teeth and sucking until I moaned. He guided me backward and I perched myself on the crumbling stone steps. Grae prowled over me, holding himself up as his hips nestled between my thighs. The friction of our leathers made me squirm, and he tilted his hips, rubbing his hard length against me even more directly. I already felt so light that I might've tipped over the edge from anticipation alone.

"Since the moment you crashed into me in Allesdale," he groaned, rocking against me as his teeth found my neck again, "I've been wanting to claim you as mine in every way. You'd claimed my heart so many years before that, but it was then that I knew for certain. You are mine."

My tongue slid against his in a hot, deep kiss. My hips matched his rhythm as I chased that throbbing desire building within me.

"And you are *mine*."

He took my hand and put it against his erection straining against his trousers. "Is this what you want, little fox?" Grae's voice was low and husky.

"Enough teasing," I growled against his mouth, giving a squeeze to show he wasn't the only one in control. "Take your clothes off."

Grae sucked in a breath. "Yes, Your Majesty."

I fumbled with the buttons of my trousers as Grae unbuckled his belt.

"Grae!" a voice boomed through the darkness.

Our hands both stilled. It was Hector.

"Fucking Gods," Grae muttered, dropping his head. "I'll gut him myself."

"Grae!" Hector screamed again, and the panic in his voice sobered us. "They've taken her."

I snatched the cloaks as Grae ran to the sound of Hector's voice. "Taken who?"

"Sadie and Navin, they've taken her and—"

"The Rooks?"

"No," Hector wheezed, bending over and sucking in heavy breaths. "Silver Wolves."

"Shit," I spat. "Do you think Queen Ingrid lied to us about what she told them?"

"I don't know." Grae shook his head, turning back to Hector. "Where have they taken them?"

"I heard her screaming," he rasped, his eyes wide and haunted. "They were headed west toward the other side of town. I think they're still here looking for us."

"We need to get back to the wagon and get our weapons," I said, already moving toward the crumbled entryway. "We're going to have to kill them."

Hector and Grae's footsteps halted.

"You know it's true." I whirled on them. "They took Sadie! If they return without us, they will be killed for failing. If they return with us, *we* will be killed. Do you see any other way?"

The two of them looked at each other, knowing I spoke the truth.

"I know it's your pack—"

"*This* is our pack now," Hector cut in. "Sadie and I chose you, Calla." He stepped in front of me, stalling my movement. "Which is why you should stay behind."

"Absolutely not," I scoffed, shoving him to the side.

They followed me into the rain.

"You're the future queen," Hector shouted, darting after me. "You're the *future* for all of us. Let Grae and me go."

I whirled back at him, pointing my finger into his face. "Firstly, Grae is my mate and if he is killed, I die, too," I shouted, watching Hector retreat a step at the force of my words. "Secondly, Sadie pledged her sword to me and I refuse to sit back when I know I could fight. This is the queen I'm going to be, Hector. This is the future you signed up for. Get used to it."

I felt the claiming in those words—a sudden clarity of who I was, of who I wanted to be. I was going to be at the front of the pack, not hiding behind it. I would lead with my kingdom, not rule over them. Splashing through the sodden streets, I dashed back toward the wagon. This was what I wanted out of life, and I was finally stubborn enough to take it.

WE STORMED INTO THE WAGON AND TOWARD THE BUNKS, NOT stopping as the others stared at us. I grabbed my dagger, riffling in my pack for my belt.

"Esh," Malou cursed, looking us up and down.

"What is going on?" Ora rose from the couch. "Is everyone okay?"

"We can handle it," Hector said, strapping a belt of knives to his thigh.

Within seconds we were all armed to the teeth, our glinting weapons strapped to our sodden clothes.

"Sadie, Navin, are they okay?" Ora asked, eyeing the fire in our eyes.

"They will be," I said with quiet menace.

"Where are they?" Malou asked. "Where are you going?"

"Look," Grae said, climbing down the ladder. "There are things about us we can't tell you and—"

"Things?" Malou cocked her head. "Besides you lot being Wolves, you mean?"

We all froze at the casualness of her tone.

"Mal," Ora chastised, giving Malou a stern look.

My eyebrows shot up as I looked between Malou, Mina, and Ora. "You *knew*?"

"Of course we knew." Mina snorted. "We know Wolves when we see them."

My mouth opened and closed as I blinked at them.

Ora gave me a grin and shrugged. "We suspected when we first met you and, of course, your bruises disappearing after you snuck off that day. That was clearly Wolf magic." They glanced at Grae. "Also, Grae, or Graham, as you introduced yourself and just as quickly forgot." They rolled their eyes as if we had all instantly forgotten the name. "Someone with a similar name and an eerie likeness to the Damrienn prince?"

"We're not dumb," Malou said, concluding the thought for Ora. She unfolded a piece of paper from her pocket and laid it on the table. "We found this tacked up outside the stables today, confirming our suspicions."

I stared at Grae's likeness on the yellowing paper and up to the words: WANTED. Graemon Claudius. Traitor to the crown of Damrienn.

"You saw this and you let us stay?" I asked quizzically.

"How many times must we tell you? People find Galen den' Mora for all sorts of reasons. In truth, it has a knack for finding those in need," Ora said. "I suspected you needed a safe place and so we provided it."

I let out a chortle of disbelief. It was an unfathomable kindness for humans to knowingly harbor Wolves.

"The Silver Wolves have Sadie and Navin," Hector said, cutting to the point. He shifted his weight back and forth, clearly eager to get moving.

"Aren't they your pack?" Malou asked.

"Not since we disobeyed King Nero and followed Grae, no." Hector snarled, a full Wolf snarl, and Mina gasped. "Look, we can explain later, but I'm sure they're still in town looking for the rest of us. You need to hide and we need to get to them before they try to get answers out of Sadie."

"Gods," Malou cursed, touching her fingers to her forehead in prayer. "We'll come with you."

"No." I held up my hand. "It's too dangerous."

"We want to help," Ora insisted. "Let us."

"Navin and Sadie are our friends, too," Mina signed.

"We might not be good with weapons, but we can create a distraction," Malou said with a wink. "Never trust a fiddle player around a pack of matches."

Grae and Hector looked at me, waiting for me to make the final decision.

"Okay, fine." I relented. "You can create a diversion. But if a Wolf is anywhere near, you run, got it?"

"Yes," Malou said, leaping up and snatching her cloak off the back hook.

I looked at Ora as the others readied. They were the one I felt the most guilty for misleading. I hated to admit how close I'd become to Ora. They revealed a world to me I didn't know existed. They opened up parts of my soul, too, and their disappointment would've shattered me. "I'm sorry I didn't tell you."

Ora took a step toward me and placed a hand on my arm, the gentleness making me want to crumble. "Wolf or no, Calla, you're a good person," they said. "I'm glad you see that humans can be good people, too."

"Talk later," Hector snapped, breaking our shared moment.

For all his bickering with Sadie, it was clear how much he cared for her, how panicked he was that she could be hurt. He looked ready to fight a whole pack by himself to protect her, and I realized my own feelings weren't too far off that. We plunged back into the rainstorm, planning as we ran. What a strange group we were—humans and Wolves, running into danger together, to save our friends.

And yet maybe it wasn't so strange—or, at least, shouldn't be. If I got my throne, I'd make sure this was the way of Olmdere, at least.

Fur or skin, it didn't matter. When someone we loved was in danger, we fought back.

THIRTY-THREE

A LONE CANDLE LIT THE WINDOW, SIGNALING THE WOLVES'
presence at the far end of town. We crept through the outer
streets, wading through calf-deep puddles to keep to the shadows. The rainstorm had eased to a fine mist that coated our faces
as we prowled closer. The others broke off to the building across
the street while Grae, Hector, and I snuck around the back.

I pointed a finger up to the darkened window next to the
illuminated one. Grae crouched and put out his hands to give
me a boost. He vaulted me upward with ease, and I hooked my
elbows around the open window ledge. The rotten wood groaned
as I anchored my leg and swung myself inside. I paused, listening to the low, mean growls of men talking in the adjacent room.
I peeked out the window and gave Grae a nod. He took a step
backward and then ran, leaping up to the window ledge and
swinging himself inside in one swift movement.

I couldn't help but roll my eyes at his act of stealth and
strength. The Gods were taunting me with this gorgeous Wolf.
Hector appeared through the window before I could tell Grae as
much, snapping our mission back into focus.

We tiptoed to the far wall, where flickers of candlelight
flashed through the splintering boards. I pressed my eye to the
widest gap, fighting the urge to gasp as I spotted Sadie sitting in

the corner. Her wrists and ankles were bound, her face swollen and bloodied. Navin sat in mirror to her, panting as he rested his head against the wall.

Four Wolves loomed over them. Hemming, Soris, and the two others whose names I'd never bothered to learn. They were the same height as Hemming, but younger and leaner, looking the same age as me. They'd be the easiest to take down. Get them first and then we'd have a better chance against the others.

"Where are they, Sadie?" Hemming asked, storming up to her and smacking her in the face.

She didn't answer and Hemming booted her in the gut. Sadie cried out, and Hector unsheathed the dagger on his hip.

Grae stayed his hand. "Wait for the signal," he signed, and I was grateful to Mina I'd learned enough to understand. Our voices would carry too well through the splintering walls.

"We can take them," Hector signed back.

"Yes, but they might kill one of them before we fight our way in," I signed. I frowned at Hector. If anyone died, it would be my responsibility. If I was going to take the throne of Olmdere, every death, every loss, would be mine to bear. "We need to draw them out. I promise—this will work. Wait for the signal."

Hector's muscles went as tight as a bow string, but he stayed put.

"I don't know!" Sadie sobbed. "I ran off with the human. I broke off from them in Taigos. I don't know where they are."

"I've known you since you were a pup." Hemming spat at her. "Your parents would be so disappointed you turned into a bloody skin chaser—even more so than disobeying your King. But here's the thing: I don't believe you. You think I'd accept you abandoned your pack for a human? You think I'm that stupid? Fine then. I know what will get you to talk."

He whirled on Navin and kicked him so hard on the jaw that Navin's eyes rolled back.

"Stop!" Sadie screamed. "Gods! Stop!"

Blood trickled from Navin's temple as he blinked vacantly,

trying to stay conscious. There would be no shifting for him, no magical healing. If they injured Navin badly enough, he wouldn't survive his wounds.

"Hmm—maybe she does love this human piece of filth—"

"Hemming," Soris growled, tipping his chin to the window above Navin's head. "We've got a problem."

Orange light flashed through the window.

"I guess we don't have to find them after all." Hemming chuckled, rubbing his hands together. "I knew they'd be foolish enough to try to save you, you lying bitch." He turned to the two wolves behind him. "You two go find them. Bring them back here."

The two younger Wolves darted to the door at his command.

"Do you think they'll be able to take Grae?" Soris asked, looking in the direction they left.

"Grae is a good enough fighter, sure—I should know," Hemming huffed. "I was the one who first put a sword in his hand. But him and Hector against Ax and Fedic? Against *my* boys? Not a chance."

"A proud father of many strong boys. I thought you were already at the top of the heap, Hem," Soris said with a low chuckle. "But look at you now. Your eldest is Nero's heir. Evres will take Olmdere and you'll have the wealth of two kingdoms at your fingertips."

Grae's fists clenched by his side.

Soris's eyes stayed fixed on the far wall. "And Grae's mate? Do you think they'll find her, too?"

"She was trained to protect the Crimson Princess, but she's never been battle-tested." Hemming shrugged.

I shook my head, realizing I was still a nameless Wolf to them. King Nero wouldn't tell anyone I was a Marriel, especially not after disowning Grae. My name would only legitimize Grae's claim to Olmdere.

"Grae would never let his mate come along into battle," Soris jeered. "She's probably hiding in a hole somewhere." Grae and I exchanged glances. I winked at him and his cheeks dimpled, his canines flashing.

"No matter," Hemming said. "When we kill Grae, she'll die, too."

A predatory rumble shook from Hector's throat at the threat. They were no longer planning on bringing us back for judgment. The orders must've changed the moment Aiden died. These Wolf guards were now assassins.

The sound of the two young Wolves' footsteps faded away and Grae looked between us, signing, "Ready?"

Hector was all but coiled, waiting for that one word that would unleash him. I unsheathed my dagger and nodded. I took one last steadying breath and we crept out the doorway and into the hall. Grae stood in front of the shut door behind which Sadie and Navin were waiting. He tipped his chin up to the ceiling and Hector and I followed suit, our last prayer to the Moon Goddess, before his boot slammed into the door.

Splinters flew as the door snapped clean off its rusty hinges. The three of us barreled into the room, Grae aiming for Hemming as I turned toward Soris. With the element of surprise, I was able to slice across his bicep before he could grab his sword. He growled, jumping back from my next swing. I felt the whoosh of air just in time to duck under Hemming's swinging fist as Grae kicked him backward.

"You." Hemming seethed at me.

"I'm sorry to disappoint you, Hemming," I said, choking up on the grip of my dagger. "But I don't hide from a fight."

"Then it will be more fun to kill you."

With a bellowing shout, he shoved off the wall and charged forward. Grae intercepted him, forcing him to pivot to block the blow. Soris ran toward me, trying to use his dominating size to overpower me. But muscle and brawn only won a battle when combined with speed and tact. And the way he barreled toward me made it easy to sidestep and trip him.

He collided with the wall, barely having time to lift his hands to shield his face. His hand snaked out and snatched my ankle, yanking me to the ground. The air knocked out of my lungs as I slammed into the wood, my skull bouncing off the floorboards. With my neck craned back, I saw an upside-down Hector and Grae circling around Hemming. Despite it being two on one, Hemming was holding his own. His fist collided with Hector's side and Grae just had time to dart out of the strike of his blade before attacking again. The chaos of their battle was cut short as Soris yanked me forward, grappling to pin me to the ground.

I bucked my hips, headbutting him square in the nose with enough force to hear it crunch. Using the whole weight of my body, I shoved him onto his back, thrusting my dagger down but hitting nothing but floorboard as Soris rolled to the side. I lurched back, scrambling to my feet and setting distance between us again. My chest heaved as I squared off with Soris, but before Soris charged at me, he pivoted and kicked out Grae's foot, Grae's attention too trained on Hemming.

Sadie growled as she struggled against her bindings in the corner, flailing across the floor to free herself, shredding at the ropes with her teeth. I felt her frustration but didn't have time to help her at the moment.

Instead I shot forward, attacking with my dagger again as I heard the awful bark and thud of Hector hitting the floor, the *shing* of metal clashing. Sadie screamed her brother's name. Fear roiled in me that, even as I kept my eyes trained on Soris, Grae and Hector might be losing their battle against Hemming. Soris shoved me backward and charged at me again. This time, I held for a split second longer before spinning, using my momentum to drive Soris's skull into the wall.

Whether the impact rendered him unconscious or not, it didn't matter. I whirled, following through with my dagger and stabbing him between his shoulder blades. I knew from his wet gasp that I had pierced his lung. He flopped to the ground as Grae's dagger clattered to my feet. I spun just in time to see Grae's bloodied face hit the floor. He crawled forward toward his weapon as Hector tried to hold off Hemming solo. King Nero's right hand had proven why he'd claimed the title—his fighting prowess evident in his relatively unscathed features while he rained his wrath upon Hector's brutalized body.

Blood dripped from the corner of Hector's lip, one eye so swollen it was nearly shut. He swayed on his feet, his guard lowered—an easy target. Grae scrambled to his feet and we launched forward in unison, but we were too many strides away.

I screamed as Hemming took the final step in toward Hector, ready to stab him in the gut.

Hemming's eyes bugged. He went utterly still, taking an unseeing step forward, then teetered over. He dropped to the ground, revealing the knife through the back of his neck. Sadie leaned against the wall, staring at the throwing knife imbedded in her victim. Her binding lay discarded at her feet, her wrists bleeding from where she'd thrashed against the rope.

Hector stared from Hemming's lifeless body and back at his sister, frozen in shock as if still waiting for Hemming's blade to sink into his belly. Then he moved. In two strides, he grabbed his sister and pulled her into a fierce hug.

"Thank the Gods." His voice cracked, the veins in his hands popping out as he crushed her into his chest.

Grae untied Navin, slinging his arm over his shoulder and helping him to stand. Navin swayed, barely clinging to consciousness.

"You need to get him out of here," I said to Sadie. "Let us handle the other two. We'll meet you at the wagon."

"I want to fight," Sadie growled.

"You already have," I said, pointing to Hemming and then back at her bruised face. "But both of you are seriously injured." I took a step toward her. "You can fight for me another day."

She held my stare for a moment before pulling me into a swift hug. "Thank you for coming for me, Your Majesty."

"Your Majesty?" Navin asked as Sadie ducked under his other arm, taking his weight from Grae.

"I'll explain back at the wagon," Sadie said, leading him hobbling out the door. She looked back at Hector. "Can you fight?"

Hector wiped the blood from his face with his sleeve and spat onto the ground. "I'm fine," he lied. Half of his face was turning purple, but he rolled his shoulders and bounced on his toes like he was ready to jump into a sparring ring again.

Sadie shot a look at me. "Be careful."

With that, Sadie and Navin disappeared down the long hallway, heading toward the back exit. The rest of us turned toward the stairwell and thundered out onto the street. The fire the others started now consumed half a building. I looked around for them, seeing their three cloaked figures huddled in a doorway.

Malou touched her hood in proud greeting.

"Thank you," I signed to them. "Now get back to the wagon. Sadie and Navin need you."

They nodded and scampered off into the shadows as the two Wolves circled around the corner. They scanned the burning building up and down, looking for the perpetrator.

"I have an idea," I whispered, looking over my shoulder at Hector. "You go around to the back door of that building."

He looked at the towering inferno and back at me. "What?"

"Go to the back. Keep the door open and wait for my command," I instructed.

"Oh Gods," he muttered, checking the shadows before running across the muddy street.

I turned to Grae. "Do you trust me?"

He grabbed me around the waist and planted a fiery kiss on my lips. "Always."

The moment his lips left mine, I let out a loud whistle that carried through the night. The two Wolves swiveled from the burning building.

I flashed a wicked grin. "Are you runts looking for us?" I taunted as they began darting toward us.

"Remember," Grae said, a bit of worry in his voice. "I said I trust you—"

I almost laughed as I ducked left down the lane between the rundown buildings. Mud flew through the air as our boots squelched down the street. I slowed my pace, wanting them to keep us within sight. Turning right down the back of the building, I waited until I heard them behind us and then turned right again.

I led them in a wild circling chase around the far building and back toward the burning one, buying Hector enough time to reach the back and drawing the Wolves away from the fleeing humans.

As I raced toward the burning building, I sent up a prayer to the Moon Goddess and leapt across the crackling threshold. Grae stayed hot on my heels, following me into the blaze. The layout of the building was the same as the one across the street, two stairwells at either end of a long hallway. It looked like it had been some sort of mill before it had been abandoned. The bottom floor was filled with wooden tables and piles of scrap fabric that exploded into bright bursts of flame.

I dashed up the stairwell, choking on smoke as we climbed. My eyes stung as I blinked through the haze to see, sure enough, the two Silver Wolves had followed us inside.

They pulled their tunics up around their noses. One elbowed his comrade and pointed up to us at the top of the stairs as we bolted again, down the long hallway. I tipped over a flaming barrel behind us, slowing down the Wolves's chase. Kicking over a table, Grae created a burning blockade as we reached the far stairs. The flames consumed the stairwell, far worse than in the front. Smoke scorched my lungs and I hesitated before I felt Grae's hand on the small of my back. He shouted something, but I couldn't hear it over the hissing cracks of the floorboards combusting beneath our feet.

I shielded my face with my hands, screwing my eyes shut as I forced my feet onward, racing down the stairs through the wall of flames to where I knew the open doorway led back out to fresh air. For a terrifying moment, I felt nothing but scorching heat and the roar of fire and then the cool, fresh air hit my face again. Grae tumbled into the mud beside me.

I fell to my knees screaming, "Now!"

Hector slammed the door behind us, moving a heavy rain barrel in front of the smoking door. Steam hissed along the wet wood.

A patch of fabric on my elbow still flamed and I smacked it, stamping out the fire. I looked at Grae's soot-covered face, his hair white with ash. He doubled over coughing, his hands splayed in the mud. The panic gripped me so tightly I wasn't sure if I was injured. My clothes seemed mostly intact. My hands were blackened with smoke. My lungs ached, but I was alive. I thanked the Gods for the rain and our drenched clothes. They had probably saved our lives.

The back door thudded, the boards creaking, but the rain barrel kept it from budging. Fists pounded wildly on the door, one last desperate attempt to break out of their fiery death, and then they ceased. I wondered if they would try for the front door. I knew, in my heart, they'd never make it.

I retched, heaving acid into the muck. My throat burned with smoke and bile. Grae spat into the mud, hacking up the smoke from his lungs.

"We killed them," I wheezed, my words deep and scratchy. I felt the heavy cloak of shame, the inky dark of my choices, and I knew if I leaned into it just the slightest bit more, dark magic would be there staring back at me. I'd led those Wolves into that trap—a gruesome, painfully horrible trap—to save my friends, my kingdom, and myself . . . but I knew only the thinnest seam separated me from the darkness. A part of me thought to move toward it, to gain what it offered if it meant saving more of those I loved, but then Grae was near me, checking me for wounds, and that was all I needed to push away from the darkness, allowing myself to feel the punishing grief of my decision.

"Holy fucking Gods," Hector said, collapsing into the mud beside us and burying his head in his hands. "I think we've just started a war."

THIRTY-FOUR

WE GATHERED AROUND THE KITCHEN TABLE, PULLING UP EXTRA stools and crates to sit on. My body felt numb, weightless, as we stared vacantly at each other. The horror of what had just happened whispered across our expressions.

Mina passed Hector a glass of water, then signed, "Are you okay?"

"I don't think any of us will ever be okay with what just happened." Ora handed me a wet cloth and fell into the empty seat beside me. "But that doesn't mean it wasn't necessary."

"If you shift?" Navin dabbed ointment on Sadie's busted lip. "You'll heal, right?"

"Yes." She grimaced, swatting his hand away and snatching the vial. "At least faster than you."

"Why don't you all shift now?" Ora's frown deepened, each person looking worse than the last.

"Four Wolves in a moving wagon?" Grae pulled his hair back into a high knot. "That would be a very bad idea."

Malou had braved the storm to keep us rolling out of town. Others would go investigate the fire, and when they found the bodies, rumors would spread.

"We never saw the Silver Wolves," I said, making eye contact with each of the group. Each shuddering breath burned down my throat. "They were attacked by Rooks. We played no part in it."

They all nodded in wary agreement. I scrubbed the wet cloth over my face and neck, pulling myself out of shock and back into my body. The sounds of those fists pounding against that burning door would haunt me forever. I'd led them to their deaths, and it was somehow so much worse than stabbing them in a fair fight . . .

"The secrets of Galen den' Mora stay with her," Ora murmured, lifting a trembling mug of tea to their lips.

"I never thought I'd see the day when Wolves risked their tails for humans," Navin said, bowing his head to Grae and me. "Thank you for saving me."

"It should have always been that way." I scrubbed the dirt from my knuckles. "Wolves swore to protect humans. I'm sorry that got lost somewhere along the way."

Sadie threaded her arm through Navin's. A strange, dumbfounding feeling settled in my gut. Our expressions oscillated between terror and giddiness. We'd saved them and we'd survived.

"We shouldn't be sitting in wet clothes on your chairs," I said, feeling the damp fabric on my seat.

"You almost died!" Ora exclaimed. "I'm just glad you're safe. You could smell like a wet dog for all I care." They sucked in a sharp breath, placing a hand on my forearm. "I'm so sorry. Is that offensive?"

I snorted. "We *do* smell like wet dogs. It's fine." I pursed my lips. "I appreciate you taking us in."

"Who exactly are you?" Mina asked, toeing my boot from under the table to get my attention. "These three are Silver Wolves . . . but who are you?"

I glanced at Grae and he bobbed his chin, a silent conversation passing between us. They'd helped us so many times. We could trust them.

"My name is Calla Marriel," I said, and the humans gasped,

and though it was clear they probably didn't need the last part, I finished, "I'm a Gold Wolf, twin of the Crimson Princess."

"Another Marriel child?" Ora gulped. "How?"

"It was my mother's dying secret," I said. "A faery granted her dying wish to protect us until Briar's wedding day." Grae threaded his fingers through mine. "King Nero said it would be safer to keep me a secret as well, one less target for Sawyn, but now we know he just wanted one less Marriel standing in his way of claiming Olmdere for himself."

"That's awful," Ora said.

"You have no idea," Hector replied, leaning his head back and staring up at the canvas ceiling.

"So you're going to challenge Sawyn for your family's throne?" Navin asked.

"First, we need to rescue my sister's mate, Maez. We need to find a way of getting Briar out of Damrienn, too. Every day we leave her there is a threat." I squeezed Grae's hand. "She's King Nero's last bargaining chip, and I know he will use it however he can."

Ora fiddled with their golden rings. "So, what's our plan?"

"We will leave you at the first town in Olmdere," I said. "I don't want to drag you into this anymore than I already have."

"You didn't hear me correctly. What is *our* plan. Does it look like we're being dragged?" Ora huffed. "We want to help you."

"Sawyn destroyed my family." We all turned to Navin's rasping voice. His right eye had swollen shut, purpling all the way up to his temple. His ear was so swollen with fluid it had completely lost its shape and I wondered if he could hear out of it. "I want to help."

"I'm sorry for what happened to your homeland." I swallowed, looking into his one open bronze eye. "I don't know that my parents treated your family any better . . . and I'm sorry."

"I don't quite remember myself, but that's irrelevant. What matters is what you plan to do going forward." Navin pursed his swollen lips. "Olmdere needs a ruler to lead us out of this darkness. I'd rather it be you than her. And if I can help, I will."

My gut clenched. It wasn't exactly a roaring endorsement, but it was more than I'd expect.

"I can see the guilt of your ancestor's actions running through you," Navin said. "If you dedicate your reign to righting their wrongs, then the people will follow you, too."

Sadie leaned her head into his shoulder.

"I think I will need some human advisers to keep me in line, should you like the position?"

Sadie's eyes widened at me as Navin kissed the top of her head, a rare smile appearing on her face.

"I'll think about it," he said.

"Hear, hear," Ora said, raising their mug and pausing. "We're going to need some stronger drinks."

We all chuckled. I glanced around the muddied and bruised group. We'd narrowly escaped the jaws of death and even more battles lay ahead.

"Good. I doubt I'll sleep tonight," I said. "Tomorrow we'll be in Olmdere."

"What are we going to do about that?" Hector tapped his finger on the wanted poster sitting in the center of the table. "These were all over town. I'd imagine the Rooks at the border will have them, too."

"You could hide in the wagon," Ora offered.

"And if they search it and find me, you'll all be imprisoned." Grae shook his head. "I can't risk that. I'll pass through on foot."

"There is no passing through on foot," Navin warned. "The Sevelde forest is filled with Rooks and booby traps. And being caught is a fate worse than death. The only way in or out is under."

My mouth dropped open. "Through the mines?"

"But that is not without its risks, either." Navin's eyes grew haunted. "Though maybe for Wolves it won't be as treacherous."

"So we'll split up and meet you on the other side," I said, cutting Grae off with a look. "I swear to the Gods if you suggest I stay behind, I'll throttle you."

Grae's lips twisted. "I wouldn't dare."

"We'll come, too," Sadie rasped, leaning forward.

She was met with a chorus of nos.

"You look one bad sleep away from death," Navin insisted, pulling her in closer. "There's not a whisper of you two deserting, nor Calla for that matter. Only Grae."

"Why?"

"Maybe they want us to flip?" Hector picked at his dirt-stained fingers. "Maybe they're hoping we'll turn him in?"

"Well then, he's an idiot," Sadie growled. She looked at me. "Will you be okay?"

"We'll be fine," I assured her. "We'll meet you in the capital. It'll be easier for us to travel on four paws anyway."

"Okay," she said tentatively.

"You two should shift once you pass through the border," Grae said. "We'll need all the strength we can get when we reach Olmdere."

"I can't believe it," Navin said, shaking the hair out of his eyes. "We're finally going home."

"Home." My chest tightened as I nodded at him. "I've never known the true feeling of it." Grae released my hand to wrap his arm around my shoulders. "But right now, here with you all, I think I'm beginning to understand."

"I'll drink to that," Ora said, returning with two bottles and an assortment of teacups dangling from their fingers. They made quick work of passing them out and we raised our chipped teacups to one another.

"To the Gold Wolf pack," Hector said, winking at me.

"No." I shook my head. "No more packs." I lifted my teacup higher. "To the Golden Court. To our family."

They cheered as our cups clinked together and we swigged back our wine. I thought the Silver Wolves would make me feel this sense of belonging, but instead I found it in the back of a wagon with mud-stained human musicians and chipped teacups. And I would fight the Moon Goddess herself to protect that feeling of finally being home.

THE FIRST THING I SAW OF OLMDERE WAS THE GOLDEN TREES, the leaves of every hue from honey to amber to rust. A perpetual autumn blanketed the Sevelde forest despite the humid summer air that made my ringlets coil tighter. Beyond the marigold canopy and peeling white bark, the undulating hillsides of Olmdere waited for me . . . but first we'd have to cross the border.

The air was fresh, the sweet damp scent of earth after a rainstorm. We stopped at the edge of a forest, finding a creek that had turned into a rushing river from the storms. We were all in desperate need of a wash. As I stepped my bare foot into the cool water, I wondered if the ashes from the fires washed downhill in the water swirling around my ankles. The stories of Taigos and the villages above us flowed downstream to where I now stood.

The twisting river provided us each with a spot of privacy to disrobe and bathe. Laughter fluttered downstream as the rest washed away the horrors of the past day.

I sat on the river stones, hugging my legs to my chest and watching the slow eddies of water twine through the forest. The current pushed at my back, spurring me forward toward my kingdom, my destiny. Merem. With the river. That is who I was in my soul.

Twittering birds sang in the trees, their voices nothing like the ones I was used to. The forests of Olmdere even sounded different. The mine below these golden trees was my ancestors' dying wish. As a child, it seemed glorious and cunning to wish for such a thing. I'd been proud of my kingdom's wealth, as if it had anything to do with me. But I gave no thought to who mined the gold. Now that I was prepared to venture below ground, it was all I could think of.

I tipped my head back into the water and smoothed my hair

off my face. I knew Grae would be watching me through the dense underbrush. He took his position one turn away from me, a guard on watch after all we had been through. We'd split with the rest of the group here, the border only an hour north.

My throat was still raw, my eyes still stung, and angry blisters had broken out on my fingers and cheeks. Once we shifted, they'd be gone, but first we had to go through the mines. I considered shifting for a brief moment then, but I knew it would be too dangerous with humans so close by. My Wolf would want to run, want to hunt, and with my mate so close by, *other* desires might supersede my good sense. Even in Wolf form, though, running through Sevelde was a dangerous idea, which was why we needed to go under it. I scrubbed a rag down my arms and over the back of my neck. At least there would be no towns tonight. It seemed every town we entered was more treacherous than the last.

"Rolling out in twenty minutes." Navin's deep voice easily carried through the forest.

"Aye," the group echoed back.

With a final scrub, I wrung out my rag and stood. Droplets traced down my skin as I snatched my fresh garments off a low-hanging branch. As I yanked my tunic over my head, I spotted a flicker of light in the water. Narrowing my eyes, I walked along the bank, trying to discern what it was. A fish scale? A coin?

I bunched my trouser legs over my calves and waded back into the stream. Stooping, I reached for the object and pulled up a glimmering rock—a solid piece of gold.

I gasped, turning the nugget over in my hands. It glinted, catching the beams of dappled sunlight. Legend said the ore in the earth was what turned the trees gold. The wealth of my kingdom came from this very place. It was what drove King Nero to uphold Briar's engagement. Whoever controlled the gold mines of Olmdere controlled Aotreas. But Sawyn had never reopened the mines after my parents' slaughter. She had left them dormant, boarded them up so that only fleeing humans dared navigate them. Apparently a sorceress of her power didn't need coins.

I reached for another flickering piece of gold in the murky water, feeling around the river stones and silt. I grasped the smooth, rounded rock and lifted it up. But what appeared in my hands wasn't a rock at all—it was a jawbone.

A shriek caught in my throat as I stumbled backward, falling onto the mossy shore. The bone dropped back into the water with a splash, and I stared at the spot it had landed as if it might jump back out at me. What had happened to that person? Did that jawbone belong to someone fleeing Olmdere, trying to chance the Sevelde forest over the mines? Had they made it all the way to the other side only to fall at the border?

My mouth dried to sand. We were bathing in a river of golden bones.

The greed for gold warred with the desperate need to survive in this haunted place. A thousand stories could be told by this river alone, and I was a part of its legacy now.

If things went right, though, I could also be part of its future. A future where this could never happen again.

"Calla?" Grae called through the trees.

"I'm fine," I lied, standing and dusting the moss off my fresh clothes.

I took one more look at the unmarked grave, certain I was headed in the right direction. I never wanted my kingdom to feel that desperation ever again.

I followed Grae up the deer trail toward the entrance to the mines. He put his hand on my arm and I halted, looking up to see Navin kneeling at the entrance, Sadie beside him. The dark tunnel into the earth was covered in timber, boarded shut apart from one narrow gap where the boards had been pried free. Trinkets lay strewn in front of Navin—necklaces, pieces of clothing, and little whittled figurines. My heart sank. It was a makeshift memorial to all those who didn't make it out the other side.

"Be safe," Hector said from behind us. "Don't do anything heroic."

"We'll try," I said, giving him a hug.

The rest of Galen den' Mora ambled up from the creek, and one by one we said our farewells. I hugged Ora last.

"Here," they said, pulling something out of their pocket.

"You made me a badge!" I looked down at the rusty red embroidered fox's face trimmed in golden thread.

Ora smirked. "You're one of us now, Your Majesty."

"Just Calla," I corrected, giving a mocking frown. "*Always* just Calla with all of you, please. And thank you. For everything."

"I'll hang on to it for you until you return," Ora said, tucking the badge back into their pocket.

I chuckled. "I see what you're doing."

"You'd lose it in your Wolf form." Ora shrugged as their lips quirked. "And if it gives you more reason to return, then so be it."

My eyes welled and I gave them another swift hug. "Take care of the others."

"I will."

I turned toward the mine and Grae stepped up beside me, rolling his shoulders.

"Ready to go home?"

I took a steadying breath and nodded. "Let's go."

THIRTY-FIVE

SHADOWS CONSUMED THE TUNNEL, A THICK INKY BLACKNESS like swimming in the dead of night. Little offshoots disappeared into nothingness. Pits? Caverns? I couldn't tell.

We navigated by the light of our two stubby candles. Our footsteps resounded across the spherical walls and deep into the belly of the mountain. Dripping stalactites flecked with gold glimmered along the roughly hewn walls. We descended a steep, unending trail for an hour before the ground started to even out.

How many more hours to reach the other side?

I held my candle up to the splintering beam above my head and read the Olmderian carving: *The only way out is under.* Wax dripped over my fingers, but I couldn't feel the sting, not as my limbs shuddered. I stepped under the eerie omen, wondering again how many people died in this place.

"This wasn't exactly the evening I had planned for us, little fox," Grae grumbled, kicking something to the side. It clattered against the wall and dropped into a cavern. I didn't want to know.

"Haunted mine shafts not in your plans?" I muttered, sticking close behind him.

"No, but the forests on the other side lead out to the eastern fjords." He wiped a curtain of cobwebs away. "With any luck, we'll be running to them by nightfall."

I spotted a heart carved into the wall. The tunnels were covered in names and prayers etched into the pale stone. "Sa Sortienna" sang into my mind. The song originated in these very caverns. Those sorrowful notes bled from each stone, the whole mine feeling exactly like the ballad.

"Careful," Grae said, skidding to a halt.

I peered around him to a crack in the tunnel floor. It led to a gaping precipice bisecting the path.

"Hold my hand." Grae swapped his candle to his far hand and grabbed my sweaty palm.

Pressing his back to the wall, he shuffled out onto the narrow bit of path clinging to the wall. I twisted sideways, looking down to the black abyss. The tips of my boots hung over the ledge as I shuffled on my heels. There was nothing to grab on to. If this tiny strip of earth gave out under my heels, we'd plummet. And, judging by the distant echoes of rubble falling into the pit, it was a long fall.

Grae reached the far side of the chasm and I leapt the rest of the distance to him. His arm yanked me upright as my legs wobbled. There were hollow caverns all around us. At any moment, the ground could give out from under us.

A skittering sound made our heads snap to the right.

"Dear Moon, let it be a squirrel," I muttered, raising my candle higher. I didn't spot any movement, only inch-wide holes in the rock. "Or a mole."

"Let's keep moving," Grae said. "The sooner we get out of this bloody place, the better."

"Agreed." I lowered my hand as candlelight glinted off the shimmering pieces of ore. "If the souls who dwell in this gilded tomb knew who I was . . ."

Grae stepped around an overturned cart. "This was not your wish, little fox. Or your doing."

Bugs scuttled across rotten slabs of wood.

"But would I have even questioned it—this place—if I had grown up in a castle?" I clutched my candle tighter. "If I grew up in silks and tiaras, would I have ever wondered about the humans mining our gold?"

"Who knows who we could have been," Grae whispered, the candlelight dancing in his eyes. "But I'm grateful for who you've become." He whispered the words as if they were meant only for himself.

The path narrowed, sloping downward as the tunnel pressed to shoulder width. All at once, the ceiling disappeared, opening into a massive cavern. Darkness stretched out from all sides, the air cooler. I held my candle higher, but every direction ended in shadow.

"Gods," Grae cursed.

Two lengths of waist-high rope stretched out toward the other side. The path below our feet became so narrow we had to step one foot in front of the other. My stomach lurched as Grae stepped out onto the thin land bridge, and I swallowed back the bile rising in my throat.

I gripped the rough rope with my free hand and stepped out after him, praying the other side wasn't too far in the distance. The sound of our heavy breaths cut through the eerie quiet. Each step made my legs feel lighter until I was shaking so badly I thought I might fall.

"Nearly there," Grae whispered as I inched forward.

Little clicks and chitters sounded along the stone. My hand gripped the rope tighter, splintering hessian into my palm. Something scuttled over the back of my hand and I yelped, waving my candle wildly in its direction.

"What was that?" I hissed as Grae turned toward me.

"Calla, don't move," he commanded.

"Oh Gods, what?" I didn't obey, glancing down at my shoulder.

A centipede-like creature skittered over my shoulder and I

screamed, dropping my candle to flick it to the ground. My candle disappeared into the abyss and I stomped on the creature. Losing my balance, I nearly toppled over the ledge. Arms wheeling, Grae grabbed me and pulled me against him.

"Curse the fucking Moon, I said don't move," he muttered, holding me tighter.

"That's the worst thing you could say if you want someone to stay still," I growled.

He huffed, lowering his candle to the squished insect.

"What is that thing?" It was longer than a centipede, with a scorpion-like tail and beetley eyes. I toed it and a long thin thread trailed out of its face. It curled out like a cracking whip.

I retched. "Is that a tongue?"

"It's a juvleck," Grae said.

My eyes widened. "Like the ones painted in your castle?"

"Yes."

"But I thought they were bigger than Wolves," I gasped.

More chittering sounds echoed up the walls.

Grae gripped my hand. "Keep moving."

He picked up the pace, hastening to the hole in the rock that led to the other side. The ground below us trembled as the scratching sounds grew louder.

"Oh Gods, oh Gods," I cursed, moving faster as gooseflesh rippled across my arms. I knew, though, the Gods had forgotten this place a long time ago.

The sound of air whipping sounded to the right and a thick, sticky tongue wrapped around the rope.

"Run!" Grae shouted.

We bolted as the rope barrier to the right fell. The squeaking, clicking sounds grew louder as the full-grown juvleck mounted the bridge. It moved with incredible speed, lashing toward us.

"Why didn't we bring our weapons again?" I screamed, dashing away from the sound. I felt the air move at my back and shrieked as the stinger landed against the rock beside me.

Grae leapt into the tunnel, whirling to grab my arm. The

snap of a whip rent the air and then I felt it—that sticky hot rope coiled around my ankle, burning into me like candle wax.

It yanked and I screamed.

My feet fell out from under me as I toppled over the edge. Grae's hand slipped up my arm and tightened around my wrist.

Flailing, I kicked against my bound ankle, grinding my heel into the juvleck's tongue until it released me with a shriek. Thrown off balance by the loss of tension my weight had caused, the juvleck's shrieks faded as it dropped into the abyss.

I dangled by one arm, staring up at Grae. His candle flickered beside his feet as he bent and grabbed my belt with his free hand. He hoisted me up and we collapsed through the tunnel. I panted on top of him, our noses touching.

Light filtered into the room, enough to see his storming, fearful eyes. I crashed my lips to his, our mouths colliding in a rough, burning kiss. His arms tightened around me as he breathed me in. My tongue swept into his mouth. A fervent need overcame me as my heart thundered, my fear being replaced with heat.

Good sense finally reached me and I broke our kiss, looking around the anteroom. The tunnel caved in up ahead, and I searched for the source of light. Above the pile of rubble was a sliver of sunlight, a crack in the earth.

"We'll have to go up," I wheezed.

With trembling limbs, I climbed up toward the crevice. The ground shuddered again and scree fell from the ceiling.

"Go!" Grae shouted as the air whooshed again.

Another whip-like tongue shot out, wrapping around Grae's throat. The juvleck scuttled into the tunnel, its giant scaled body taking up the entire entryway. It loomed over Grae, its spindly legs pinning him to the floor as its tongue squeezed the life out of him.

Without thinking, I grabbed a rock and leapt. I landed on the armored scales of the juvleck's back. It thrashed, trying to buck me off as I smashed the rock into the back of its head. It released an ear-splitting cry but didn't let go of Grae. I slammed the rock down again and again, battering its tough shell. It wailed, writhing to the side and crashing me into the wall. Pain stabbed through my shoulder, but I didn't stop. With one final cracking blow, the juvleck dropped, its legs giving out, throwing me forward.

I scrambled for Grae, unwrapping the lifeless juvleck's tongue from his neck. He gasped, sucking in air as his bloodshot eyes bugged. Angry red blisters ringed his neck.

I helped him to his feet and pushed him up toward the crack in the earth. He barely squeezed through, shoulders scraping against the stone as he pulled himself into the sunlight, but I was sure nothing in Aotreas would keep him from getting out of this tunnel because I felt the same way. He reached down for me and pulled me up after him.

I collapsed on top of him once again, my chest heaving. The air was fresh with the salty brine floating in the breeze. We'd made it to the ocean.

"Are you okay?" I traced my hand around Grae's bruised neck. He nodded but couldn't speak, each breath a rasping wheeze. I grimaced as I tried to lift my smashed arm. "We need to shift."

Grae's hands shook as he reached for the hem of his tunic.

I stopped him. "Shift. Shred your clothes," I instructed. "We'll leave them behind anyway."

He screwed his eyes shut, clothes ripping as he morphed into his glorious Silver Wolf. He shook the scraps of fabric from his fur and I sighed, knowing he'd be all right.

"Never again." I looked into his gleaming Wolf eyes. How had Navin survived that place? How had anyone? "No more gold will ever come from that mine. No more people should have to face those beasts."

I took one last look at that ominous crack in the earth and shifted into a Wolf.

～

RED AND GOLD TREES COVERED THE LAND, STRETCHING OUT TO the craggy fjords and crashing ocean waves. Pillars of smoke rose from little villages that stretched across the vast peninsula. The capital was a distant red dot on the horizon. Even from Sevelde, I could see the red stones, the entire city a deep burgundy. The rushing river below my paws ran all the way to the capital, twisting through smaller towns and ending in a vast and glorious lake. Gold and red spires shot up from the center of the lake— the palace. From the mountains of Taigos, all the way to Sawyn's door, that eerie river ran the entire length of my entire kingdom.

"Eager to run through the forests of your homeland, little fox?" Grae asked in my mind, racing after me as I thundered through the forest. "Or eager for something else?"

"All of it."

His voice turned husky. "All of it."

He chased after me, nipping at my heels. I heard his chuckle echo in my mind as he ran faster, an unburdened howl splitting the air. I howled in response to the sound of my mate as I chased him through the dark forest.

The sun set beyond the far hills as we kicked up leaves, thundering through the night. The further we ran eastward, the sparser the forest became as the roaring of waves replaced the sound of crickets and hooting owls. Grae slowed to a stop as we reached the cliffs. Far below, the moonlight gleamed off the choppy ocean waves. Sprays of mist floated up from the waves crashing into the rock. The salty scent mingled with the earthy loam. I howled to the moon again, overcome by the sweeping views.

I took off, racing around the fjords, dipping inland and back out to the sea. Golden leaves danced in the breeze above us as the waves crashed, sea foam flying into the air. I ran and ran, the sweet song of Olmdere filling my veins with the same molten gold. We'd made it out the other side.

I was home.

I chased that crescent moon along the cliffs until my muscles burned and my soul hummed. The moonlight called to me along with the ocean waves, begging to touch my skin, and, with a final leap, I shifted back into my human form. I held my hands skyward, my toes sinking into moss, salty air coating my skin.

Panting deep breaths of sea air, I felt reborn, as if the land was claiming me as much as I claimed it. I tipped my chin up toward the moon, feeling her bless me and welcome me home.

With a final sigh, I dropped my hands and turned to find a Silver Wolf watching me from the shadows. Grae's golden eyes beamed through the darkness, and I suddenly realized I was standing naked before him.

I fought the urge to cover myself. Not here. Not with the moon on my skin and the sea at my back. I took a step forward, then another, toward that Wolf and his hypnotic golden eyes.

Grae prowled forward, his growl rumbling through me and straight to my core.

I stepped back, leaning against a tree trunk that twisted sideways against the winds. My heart pounded as I let him stalk toward me. I felt each step of his paws echoing through my body. When he was a hair's breadth away, he shifted, golden eyes morphing to dark umber, smooth muscles and sharp jawline replacing his silver fur. My lips parted at the intensity of his stare and the sight of the rest of him. His chest brushed against my peaked nipples with every heaving breath and I could feel him hard and ready against my belly.

My throat no longer stung, my blisters gone and my shoulder healed. My many wounds from the mines and the fire before that were now blissfully absent. Grae's own smooth bonfire scent finally replaced the stench of smoke in my hair. My heart and mind and soul still felt their stings, though, and there was only one thing that could ever heal me of that.

His eyes drifted from my lips to search my eyes. "It was always you," he rumbled, and his words made heat pool between my legs. "My mate."

His rough hand skimmed up my hip, my belly, and to my breast, sweeping his thumb across my nipple. I arched into the sensation as I held his wanton stare.

"Should we keep moving?" he asked. "The others . . ."

"Right now, there are no others. Just you and me, Grae."

We'd already outrun the wagon at nearly double the pace. If we kept going, we'd be waiting like sitting ducks in the city. No. We had time, and more importantly, my soul needed this moment as much as my body. I needed Grae's body to fulfill all the truths I already knew in my heart.

"How badly do you want me to make you mine?" I asked as his other hand settled on my hip and his lips skimmed up to my ear. My breathing hitched at the movement. "Tell me."

"You were the only one I ever wanted, the only part that felt right." He trembled as I traced my fingers along the muscles of his back. "Always."

Grae pulled away to look into my eyes. I permitted my hands to roam further down his back and over his firm ass, urging his hips to press into me.

He let out a groaning breath and kissed me as I rocked against him. The same way I had in the love temple and the ruins but now there was nothing between us but the sweet bliss of his skin against my own. His lips sent tingles throughout my body, the warmth of his skin, the fire of his kisses, the anticipation of what was to come making my legs shake.

Grae pushed his knee between my legs, propping me up with his hard thigh as he deepened our kiss. I ground myself against him, spreading my damp heat over his leg, coating him in my scent, showing him how ready I was for him, as a moan escaped my lips.

"Gods, you're so wet," he groaned, his lips leaving mine to trail down to my breast.

His mouth closed around my nipple, tugging on it, and I writhed, uncaring as the rough bark of the tree bit into my back. He circled his tongue around my taut bud and tested the sensitive flesh with his teeth. The sensation sent lightning bolts of pleasure straight to my throbbing clit and I squirmed against him, aching to be touched.

"You feel so good, little fox," he murmured, reading my body like an open book. He dropped to crouch between my legs. "But how do you taste?"

I sucked in a breath as he hooked my leg over his shoulder. My knee clenched into his muscled back, hanging on for dear life, the anticipation making me shake more wildly than the wind-tousled golden leaves above my head.

Grae's lips traced the flesh of my inner thigh, his tongue trailing my ocean-sprayed skin closer to my pulsing bundle of nerves. I slung my arm over a low branch, bracing myself, my fingers gripping the bark so tight I thought it might snap. I panted— waiting, waiting, *waiting, Gods damn it!*—as his breath tickled the hairs between my legs. Every sensation in my body was tipped on a knife's edge.

His tongue slid over the very place I needed it to be and I cried out, the feeling so overwhelming that my standing leg buckled. I would have fallen, but I knew I wouldn't, knew Grae was right there, slinging my other knee over his shoulder, putting me at his complete mercy as he pinned my hips to the tree. His tongue slid over me again and my fingers gripped the bark tighter, my arms straining as a deep guttural moan cut above the roar of the waves. Grae's tongue circled me faster, lapping at my clit, each brush of his wet mouth ringing out feral sounds. He hummed his pleasure against me; the vibrations pushing me higher. My thighs clamped around his head, gripping him tight as I rode his mouth. The building pressure made me squirm, but he held me still, feasting on me as the ocean mist swirled around us.

Grae worked my thrumming, swollen clit with skill, again and again, pulling every mewling sound from me I didn't even know I could make. His lashing strokes turned frenzied, the growling vibrations of his mouth sending me toppling over the precipice. Before I could prepare myself, a euphoric scream escaped me as my body jerked. My hips bucked as I came against Grae's mouth. His tongue slowed but didn't stop, working me until my soaked inner walls stopped clenching and my muscles released.

Grae grabbed my hips, guiding me downward onto his lap and holding me against him. I dropped my damp forehead to his shoulder, taking deep gulps of cool air as his fingers traced lovingly up and down my spine. Never had I been so high, so soaring, the echoes of my release pulsing through me like a heartbeat.

His mouth found mine and I tasted myself on his tongue. Warmth seeped from his skin as my hand dropped between us. Wrapping my hand around his silky, thick length, I stroked him up and down. His eyelids drooped as he groaned against my mouth, his breath more jagged with each pump of my hand.

"Look at me," I said, and his eyes snapped open. I held him with my own eyes, and the desire I saw there was mixed with adoration and wonder as I rose up on my knees and positioned him at my entrance. He swallowed, face flushed, mouth parted in an O as he steadied my hips. I waited there, breathless, gazing into his eyes. How long had I dreamed of this moment, of being with him, of having him inside of me, of being joined in a way that I'd fantasized about for years?

"I love you, Calla," he whispered, brushing his lips against mine. "I always have."

I lowered myself an inch, stretching as he filled me. I let out a ragged breath. "I love you, too."

I lowered myself further, pain building along with the pleasure until I was fully seated, the gasp that came from me echoed in his groan. We stayed like that, staring into each other's eyes, feeling the joining that we'd already felt in our souls. I felt filled and fused to Grae in every possible way, my heart stretching wider as my body did the same.

Our chests rose and fell together, that open, raw look in his eyes enough to start that wanton yearning building within me again. My breath hitched, and Grae's lips met mine, his tongue sliding across my bottom lip. I rocked my hips, a testing movement, seeing how he slid along my inner walls, making each nerve ending light up, and we both moaned.

Grae cupped the back of my neck and guided me backward, laying me onto the mossy forest floor. My legs hooked up around his hips as he propped himself above me. His eyes scanned my face as he slowly pulled himself halfway out and glided back in. My eyes fluttered as I let out a breathy moan, a brief soreness tinting the salacious building within me.

His eyebrows knitted together, searching my face. "Are you hurt?"

"No," I panted, shaking my heads. "A little, but, Gods, I don't want you to stop."

His cheeks dimpled as he pulled out of me, licking his thumb and circling my throbbing clit again. I moaned louder, the warm press of his thumb enough to make my muscles ease and my pussy even wetter. He pushed back inside me, that slow, delicious friction setting me on fire. His lips devoured mine as he repeated the movement. Over and over, that slow tortuous movement lit up every inch of my body until I couldn't take that relentless building anymore. I needed my release and I needed him to give it to me.

My fingers clawed down his back as my heels dug into his ass, spurring him to move faster, letting him know with my body that I needed more. His hips moved in rolling thrusts, a little faster and deeper each time, testing me as his dark hair fell into his eyes. His arm muscles strained beside my head as he looked down at me.

"It feels so good inside of you," he groaned. "Sweet Moon, Calla. It feels so good."

"Grae," I moaned, my body clenching around him at his name, echoing his own desire as he hit a spot inside me that made my eyes flutter closed. I tilted my hips, his cock hitting that spot again and again. I clawed down his back, desperately hanging on as he drove into me, chasing me toward my release.

My sounds grew more clipped, my breathing faster, each

noise a little higher than the last. "I love the way you fuck me." The words were a desperate confession that made Grae pump into me faster, the slick sounds of our bodies filling the night air.

"Oh Gods, oh Gods," I moaned louder as he thrust deeper, hitting that perfect spot within me that set me ablaze. And I knew then that there would never be enough of this, never enough of him. We were one soul, one body, one deliciously sweet pleasure growing between us.

White-hot yearning consumed me as I rocked my hips, riding him as he thrust into me. His mouth dropped back to my breast, sucking and swirling around my tight nipple, making me arch. The sensations were too much, my body vibrating like a plucked string. His teeth tested my nipple right as he thrust into me hard. My sounds turned to screams as I called out, "Grae!" so loud the Moon surely heard and my climax tore through me, so massive, so world-bending, so much more consuming than I ever knew was possible.

I had no name, no body, no history beyond this moment. I was a symphony of pure pleasure.

My vision clouded to nothing but stars, my muscles clenching and releasing around him, working him to his own release. With two more frenzied pumps, Grae barked out a cry and followed me, tumbling over the edge, coming inside of me. His body twitched against me as the sounds of our release intertwined, his slick torso collapsing on top of mine as our muscles continued to echo where we joined.

His chest rose and fell against me as mist pricked against our skin. He rolled to his side and pulled me against him, his arms folding around me. I rested my burning cheek against his chest. His hand swept slowly up and down my back as I closed my eyes. We weren't two separate beings anymore. I felt it shift into place with the same certainty I shifted into my Wolf. We were two notes in the same song, two destinies of the same fate, two bodies with the same soul.

THIRTY-SIX

HIS SOFT LIPS TRACED MY TEMPLE. SONGBIRDS CHORUSED IN the early-morning light. The roiling ocean waves had settled into a hushed melody, slowly sweeping over the rocks and back again.

"We need to get going," Grae murmured into my hair.

"No," I rasped, my voice scratchy with sleep. I stubbornly curled further into him, slinging my leg and arm around him as if that would hold him in place.

My cheek bounced against his chest as he laughed. It was a beautiful sound, one that filled me with pride because I knew it was hard won. Seldom did I get to hear his genuine laughter, not since we were young. A chuckle, a snicker, perhaps, but that gorgeously open timbre of his laughter filled me with golden light.

"We've got to find Galen den' Mora in the city," Grae said with another kiss to my head. "Destiny awaits, little fox."

"Destiny can wait one more hour," I grumbled.

We'd barely slept. The night had stretched on oscillating between running in our Wolf forms and stopping for unbounded bursts of passion. We got closer and closer to the city through the night, but every time I thought it was sated, my desire would surge in me anew. Every time I shifted I wanted to be marked with Grae's scent, claimed by him again. Grae learned every inch of my body just as I learned his—along with all the ways we could make each other come undone. We collapsed outside the city just before the dawn, the need for sleep finally demanding to be heard. I wasn't sure if it was the newness or the excitement that my deepest wish had come to pass, but I seemed endlessly ready for him, even now in the quiet of the morning.

My hand traced idly up his bare thigh and his arm tightened around me.

"Calla," he warned. "Hector will start looking for us soon."

I let out a frustrated sigh and stayed my wandering hand. "Hector is probably all the way in the capital. He'd have a lot of woods to scour before finding us."

Nothing held me back now—my fingers found Grae's skin whenever they felt called to touch him. I hadn't realized how much I needed to be touched, to feel his warm skin and soft kisses and whispered breaths, that buzzing sensation of skin against skin that slowed my pulse and calmed my mind.

"When will we be able to do this again?" My lips skimmed over the dusting of black hair on his chest.

"I don't know," he murmured as his hands circled my back. "But if it's more than a day, I may combust."

"Agreed," I said with a breathy chuckle.

Grae gathered me to him, kissing the top of my head one more time. "It feels wrong to let you go."

I tipped my head up and kissed him. "Then don't let me go."

Grae twisted to his side and my leg hitched higher over his hip. He let out a frustrated groan. "You are making it very hard to do the sensible thing right now, little fox."

I brushed a lock of his black hair behind his ear. "Where are we going to find clothes?"

Our clothes from the day before were shredded to pieces and reeked of juvleck. We wouldn't be turning back for them.

"Clearly you didn't spend much time gallivanting off in your youth." Grae's cheeks dimpled. "Maez, Hector, Sadie, and I used to nick them from humans' clotheslines. I'd send a bag of silver to whoever we stole from, but, yeah, we were wolflings then."

"I've done that once," I protested. "When I was running . . ."

The words died on my lips. *When I was running from you.*

"Ah yes." Grae's hand slowed its sweeping circles down my back. "We found your discarded clothes in the woods. When I realized you'd doubled back to lose us"—his hand stopped—"something broke in me. I knew then you weren't just trying to get to Maez, you were trying to leave us behind, too."

"I thought you'd drag me back to Highwick." I settled my head back against his chest. "I thought a lot of things . . . that I was doing what was right for my pack. That Briar's marriage was the only way to save Olmdere. That you were going to *be* with her."

Grae's chest vibrated below my cheek as he snarled. His voice was low and quiet. "I thought going along with the arrangement would keep you safe, both of you. But I never intended to be with her like that."

His confessions in the snow flashed into my mind—about his childhood, about his mother. "I understand that now."

"But you defied my father. You left even though you knew what it would cost you." He sighed. "You're braver than me, little fox."

"Or more stubborn."

"That too." He chuckled, his hand resuming its circles down my spine. "I'm glad you ran. I'm glad you fought. You made me rise up to meet you and I'm stronger for it. I won't tiptoe around my father and his tyranny anymore."

"I know you won't." I stroked a hand down his stubbled jaw-line, gazing up into his eyes. "And I won't let him hurt you, either."

I watched the power of my words land as his eyes bracketed with pain. He needed to know it wasn't his burden to carry alone. Just as he was determined to protect me, I'd protect him. That is who we'd be together.

"When we take Olmdere," I said, "we'll need to act quickly—send messengers and promise your father mountains of gold in exchange for Briar's safe return. We can't go back to Damrienn."

"Agreed."

"Like Queen Ingrid, I'll take my parents' throne, not through you, but of my own birthright."

I knew Briar would be proud of me in that moment. She had never wanted to be Queen; she went along with it to protect us, to save our people. But she didn't have to brave that title now. I would take that place and grant her the life she'd always wanted. I felt so certain of it now. I was the Marriel who was meant to rule.

"You will make a fierce and beautiful queen." Grae brushed a soft kiss against my lips. "You are the ruler Olmdere needs."

My lips silenced him as they covered his mouth in soft, lavishing kisses. I breathed in his scent as I deepened our kiss. He grunted as the tip of my tongue brushed his, lifting one hand to cup the back of my neck, the other trailing down to cup my ass. I rolled my hips against him, feeling him harden against me.

With nothing between us, I reached down and positioned him between my legs, making him groan. He pushed into me slowly as our sleepy hands roved each other's bodies.

My breath hitched and my eyelids drooped at the feeling of him inching deeper inside me. The sensation that had been foreign to me the night before now felt so familiar, so right. I tilted my hips, finding that sweet spot inside me that made my toes curl. He gripped my waist tighter and rolled his hips, his mouth parting against mine as he groaned. Gods, that sound, that silenced groan, that hint of a growl that disappeared into a heaving breath. I could come from that sound alone, knowing how I made him feel, and it made my core flutter around him.

I pushed on his shoulder, rolling him onto his back and keeping him buried inside of me. His hands found my hips as I stared down into his lust-filled eyes and parted lips. I lifted and lowered slowly, feeling every spot inside me that he touched. One of his hands drifted from my hip to my pulsing clit and began circling me.

I moaned, my nipples tightening as I rode him faster, grinding into his fingers as I chased my release, knowing now exactly how to take my pleasure from him as well as I knew how to give it. He thrust up, my breasts bouncing as I met each of his pumps, our rhythm growing frenzied. I clawed my fingers down his chest, trying to fight that maddening pull within me, like the heavy rip of waves pulling back out to sea.

He thrust deeper, bucking me up and down, as his fingers circled my clit faster. I cried out as my climax roared through me, shuddering ecstasy from the crown of my head to the tip of my toes. Grae groaned, that glorious sound heightening my pleasure, as his breathing faltered and he came inside of me. I rode him through those rolling waves of pleasure, wringing out the last of our releases, before finally collapsing onto his sweaty chest.

I traced slow kisses over his collarbone, a wicked grin on my face. "Now we can go."

WE RAN ANOTHER HOUR NORTH, OUR WOLVES EASILY CLOSING the distance to the Olmderian capital. We stuck to the eastern forests that wove around the fjords before cutting inland toward the city and the towering castle in the center of the lake. Farmhouses appeared through the trees, and we shifted back into human form.

My bare feet padded across the mossy forest floor. I brushed my hair over my shoulder and glanced back at Grae. The claw marks down his chest were gone, but the heat in his eyes remained, along with the clear evidence of his arousal.

I smirked, shaking my head. "We need to find you some clothes."

His proud grin was all Wolf.

My hands trailed over the underbrush, and I paused at a bush covered in crimson berries. Serilberries. I popped a few ripe ones in my mouth. They were very sour raw, usually cooked with honey, but the zing on my tastebuds woke me up and freshened my mouth.

They were used for flavoring recipes and in many medicines, too. All the known spots to forage serilberries in Allesdale were picked clean each season . . . but out here, far from any town, little red fruits filled the bush. They would probably be a worthy payment for whoever we took clothes from. I snapped five branches laden with berries and kept walking with the bouquet in my hands.

Another half hour down the trail, we finally passed a house with washing on the line—trousers, tunics, dresses, and aprons. I had no clue if the sizes were right, but they'd have to do. We heard people talking in the barn, but it was obscured from view by the house and I prayed no one would walk around the bend.

We approached the garden hedge, crouching and peeking over the untrimmed shrubs.

Grae glanced sideways at me, a mischievous grin curving his lips as if we were children playing a prank. "Ready?"

I gave a quick nod and we darted out to the clothesline, snatching a bundle of garments. I dropped three serilberry branches as payment and darted back to cover.

I threw on a tunic that hung down to my knees and stepped into the trousers. They were far too big on me, even with my wide hips and large thighs, so I threaded the tunic through the belt loops and tied the ends in a knot. They were also far too long and I had to roll the hem up seven times before my feet poked out of the fabric.

Grae, on the other hand, was nearly bursting out of his clothes. His muscled arms and shoulders stretched the fabric at the seams until gaps of his golden-brown skin peeked through the stitching. He'd also snagged a tattered cloak off the line, and, clasped around his neck, it only hung to his knee. At least the hood would be deep enough to hide his face. If Rooks were looking for him on the road, they'd be looking in the capital, too.

I shook my head. We were a sorry-looking pair, but it would have to do. We'd find Galen den' Mora in the city and get our proper clothes and weapons back.

I glanced one more time at the farmhouse, thinking of the life Briar had always dreamed of—the cottage by the river, the vegetable patch. She and Maez could run through the forests and howl to the moon. I sighed. I just had to defeat a sorceress first. But that life she had daydreamed of pushed me forward, winding back into the forest. We needed those dreams, those bright futures, as much as we needed the sobering truth of the past behind us. Both the hope for the future and pain of the past gave us something to fight for.

Grae walked beside me, taking my hand without looking and giving it a squeeze. The red and gold city peeked above the tree line and I picked up the pace, feeling drawn toward the capital as if pulled by a rope around my waist.

The trees parted and the capital appeared. The city of my birth, a home I couldn't remember, and yet, I knew this place somehow. Grae pulled the hood of his cloak up, hiding his face in shadow as people meandered the cobbled streets. My eyes trailed the wide river that cut through the city, dropping in little waterfalls down to the dark blue lake. Long white boats ferried out toward the palace, crimson pennants waving from their bows. The castle was stark against the dark lake, brilliant shades of red and gold shimmering like the sun in a cloudless sky.

It was the most beautiful place I'd ever seen. Vellia's drawing didn't do it justice. My feet walked the worn, smooth cobbles, navigating toward the markets where Galen den' Mora would be parked. Without thought, I seemed to steer us in the right direction, as if something in my blood recognized this place. A strange familiarity tugged in my chest. The windmills and flower gardens, the town squares and city stables, the glinting gold-flecked stones—I knew them somehow. The smell of freshly baked bread and twittering birds all spoke deep into my soul, like a favorite tune, but with forgotten words, a painting with the edges faded and blurred. But even if I didn't remember her, Olmdere City remembered me.

THIRTY-SEVEN

WE DIDN'T FIND GALEN DEN' MORA IN THE CITY SQUARE OR IN the open markets that teemed with people in the corner of town. We decided to meander the stalls while we waited for that massive wagon to come rolling past. Wolves ran faster than oxen could walk and I knew they might be hours behind us still.

We wound through the markets, searching for better clothing and a vendor willing to trade for serilberries. A stall owner peeked up at me over their book, eyeing my clothes and frowning. Trinkets filled every corner of their haberdashery stall. Ribbons hung from the canvas ceiling, baskets of gold buttons lined the tables, and bolts of gauzy fabric leaned against the wall. I gave a half-smile and kept walking.

I paused at a table of herbs, wondering if, after all our travels, Hector still had that vial of nitehock in his possession.

The merchant perked up as we stopped. "What can I get for you?" He lifted a basket of dried lavender to me, raising his brows. "Something aromatic?"

"I'm looking for a particular seed," I said, squinting at him.

Recognition dawned on his face. He lifted his chin and swallowed, peeking right and left. "You're not from the capital, are you?"

"We've traveled for the celebrations," Grae said in a smooth tone as he picked up a sprig of rosemary and twirled it in his hands. "A party is the perfect distraction for all manner of misdeeds."

The merchant wiped a hand over his sweaty brow. "You wouldn't be the first to try such . . . misdeeds." He lifted a basket from below the table and offered it out to us. "What makes you think you will succeed?"

I examined the brown paper packets, different flowers sketched on each one. Flicking through the basket to the very back, I found the drawing of nitehock flowers, their petals bursting out like stars.

"How much?" I asked, lifting the packet as the merchant wiped his rag down his face.

"If you say you're using it for what I think you are, then it's free," he muttered. "But you didn't get it from me."

I held his pale gaze. "Thank you."

"I'll pray to all the Gods you have better luck than the last."

"It doesn't seem as bad here as I was expecting." Grae looked up and down the market stalls. "Why risk this? Why help us?"

"It's what you don't see." The merchant scowled. "Aye, the bricks are flecked in gold, but what good is that for an empty hearth and silent table?" He sat back on his stool, throwing his rag on the table. "That witch turned my eldest two boys into Rooks. When they left, our whole family fell apart."

"Her enchantments are strong," I said, trying to sound reassuring.

"Enchantments?" The merchant furrowed his brow.

"Her compulsions," I replied. "How she convinces them to join her guard."

The merchant let out a bitter bellow. "The Rooks are not enchanted, ma'am. They volunteered."

I sucked in a sharp breath, pain stabbing into my ribs. "What?"

"You thought Sawyn enchanted the Rooks to join her army?"

He shook his head. "I suppose her poisonous promises are enchantment enough. But she has pulled people to her side without any incantations at all."

"That can't be." I felt the blood drain from my face as my heart pounded in my ears.

Sorcerers could cast all manner of spells, like how Sawyn hypnotized Briar . . . and yet when I remembered the Rooks we encountered on the road, I realized they didn't have that eerie green glow in their eyes. They didn't seem vacant and hollow husks. They had shrewd and cunning eyes, vicious but aware. How had I not put that together? How could I have assumed they were under her spell? But I knew why I had made such assumptions: the truth was so much worse. They had willingly followed her. Siding with Sawyn had been their *choice*.

"Some said Sawyn was our savior. Others said we should kill her." The merchant crossed his arms and glared at us. "I've lost a lot of people I loved, even though they're still alive."

"Why didn't you follow her like your sons?" I tried to steady my breath, dropping the serilberries on the table even though he didn't ask for payment.

"She shut down the mines, so many people without a job." He shook his head. "The strongest were conscripted to become Rooks. They could've said no, but then there'd be no money to send home, and after Sawyn's wrath during her search for the Crimson Princess, the towns were left with nothing. Fields lay fallow, people fleeing across the border being chased by their very own family members, so many lives torn apart . . ." He picked up another packet of seeds and flipped it around in his hands. "Our options were three: side with Sawyn, starve, or flee. I could never celebrate such a ruler, but neither shall I dissent. I'm not a Rook, but I'm not against her either, if anyone were to ask. Some people still rely on me to put food on the table. My choices are not only my own."

I let out a shuddering breath. "I pray one day your choices and the ones that serve your family are no longer at odds."

He clenched his jaw, releasing a world-weary sigh. "If you're successful, maybe I will live to see that day."

I pocketed the nitehock seeds and turned from him without so much as a farewell. The sights and smells of the market soured upon his words. The abundance and life that seemed to thrive in the capital was a hollow facade.

I saw it now on each face I passed—that weariness of people broken by the reign of Sawyn. Their silence was their only vote of confidence for the sorceress, but enough to keep her in power. What good would a mob of humans be against her dark magic, anyway? Some had to support her . . . but some *chose* to support her, too.

I ducked past the rows of hanging tapestries, twining through the tables, and halted, throwing out my arm to stop Grae from stepping any closer.

A line of Rooks marched down the thoroughfare. People scattered to give them a wide berth. I watched the sea of black parade through the streets like a swarm of ants.

"We may well be able to cut the head off the snake," I said, clenching the seeds in my pocket. "But it will start a battle, not finish it." My chest rose and fell, the sounds of the market rising louder. Each one of those Rooks was a member of my kingdom, someone's family. It would've been so much easier if they'd been under a spell. "How many of my people will I have to kill to save the others?"

"Calla?" Grae's voice was muffled, far away above the roaring in my ears.

I barely felt Grae's hand touch the small of my back as he led me through the markets. How many people would I have to kill? How many lives would be lost before my righteousness didn't justify it anymore? We moved down an alleyway, away from the crowds, but heat still burned my cheeks. Grae shouldered open a rickety door and pulled me inside.

My eyes darted around the room, unseeing, as he rested me against the shut door.

"Breathe," he commanded.

I choked on each breath, gulping, but no air filled my lungs. I stared up at the dusty rafters, feeling the fiery panic scorch my skin.

Would I lose my soul trying to do the right thing? Would darkness claim me just as it had Sawyn? I took a shallow, shuddering breath, noticing the space at last. It appeared to be a grain store, little more than a cupboard, with bags lining the walls and a set of scales sitting on a wood table.

Grae's cool hand on my cheek made me jump. "Breathe, Calla." He rested his cool forehead on mine.

My lungs expanded. One breath, then two. The panic slowly ebbed.

"They're not under her spell," I whispered.

"I thought they were as well." Grae held my gaze. "But our plan remains the same. We rescue Maez, we kill Sawyn, and we pay off Damrienn to get Briar." Grae breathed along with me, his own rhythm slowing mine. "Once your sister is safe, we will come up with a plan to deal with any Rooks still loyal to their fallen queen. Give them some time to realize they're on the wrong side. You'll feed the villages and reunite their families . . . they'll see you're a better ruler."

I wrapped my arms around his back, feeling the connection that pulled me back into myself. "It's a start."

"We don't need to fix the entire world tomorrow," Grae whispered, brushing his lips against mine. "You don't need to control every flame. Tomorrow is the spark that will set it all ablaze."

My lips crashed into his, needing the comfort of his promise. His tongue met mine as he rumbled a pleasurable hum. The rush of panic morphed into the rush of desire. I would set it all ablaze.

His hands found my ass and hoisted me up. I hooked my legs around his hips as he pinned me back against the wall. My chest heaved against his, wanton desire burning through me.

My lips found his ear as my hand slid down his torso. "I need you inside me. Now."

He growled against my mouth, spinning me and dropping me onto the worktable. I chuckled at the fervor with which he untied my tunic. I gripped the edge of the table as he yanked my trousers so he didn't pull me off with them. His eyes filled with predatory heat as he scrambled to free himself and stepped back toward me. I dropped to the floor, spinning around to grab the far edge of the table, ready for him. A feral snarl escaped him as he watched me spread my legs. He prowled forward, gripping my hip and lining himself up.

He thrust inside me, filling me to the hilt, and I gasped as the sensation sent bolts of desire shooting throughout my body. He moaned, pulling out and thrusting in again. I held the table tighter, the rickety wood thudding with each wild pump. He reached around, his fingers finding my throbbing clit and circling it as he drove deep into me. Everything else faded to the recesses of my mind as my body homed in on that feeling building between my legs, unable to tell where he ended and I began. I pressed my cheek against the table, groaning at the crazed rhythm of him moving inside me.

The sound snapped his leash and Grae pulled out of me, spinning me around and lifting my ass onto the worktable. His hands hooked behind my knees and he yanked me toward him. I wrapped my hand around his cock and guided him back to my entrance. His fingers gripped my chin, making me look him in the eyes as he slowly pushed back into me. My mouth dropped open further with every inch as I watched his pupils dilate until only the tiniest rim of dark brown ringed the inky black.

"Whatever happens tomorrow," he breathed, his voice rough with desire as he filled me, "whether we have a hundred years or one more day—we will face this world together."

"Yes."

He slowly inched out of me and rolled his hips in taunting

thrusts. My eyelids grew heavy as my head dropped back. I tipped my hips, finding the perfect angle. His fingertips dug into my ass as he picked up the pace. Each thrust pushed me higher, his throaty groans making my skin ripple with gooseflesh and flooding my core.

I dug my heels into his hard backside, making him pump harder, needing him to fuck away every anxious thought. He pushed me down, so I lay across the table, one hand gripping the far edge as the other held my ass in place. His hard, rapid thrusts made the whole table rattle as my moans grew more desperate. My fingers clawed down his arms as he pushed me higher still, his hands digging into my flesh as he struggled to hang on. He pounded into me, again and again, hitting that spot that made my eyes roll back. With a final scream, my body spasmed, clenching around his cock as pleasure flowed through me in crashing waves. Grae growled my name, battling my tight channel as he tipped over the edge, his jerky thrusts ringing out my final rolling waves of ecstasy. My muscles flickered and my skin tingled as if I was being pricked with a thousand tiny raindrops.

The stars slowly faded from my vision as Grae collapsed on top of me.

"That may be my favorite way to calm the mind." I chuckled, a satisfied smile pulling on my lips.

He laughed, kissing my sweaty temple. "I love you."

"I love you, too." I traced his jawline and he turned his lips into my palm. "And whether we have a hundred years or one more day, that will never change."

MY MISCHIEVOUS LAUGH LIFTED ABOVE THE CLAMOR. I squeezed Grae's hand as he led me back through the bustling markets. "I can't believe we just did that."

We surveyed the markets, searching for the traveling musicians, but Galen den' Mora had still not arrived. The space was crowded now. Afternoon travelers filled the rows, many heading downhill toward the boats to be ferried across the lake. My stomach tightened again, the moment of reprieve from my panic wiped away by the sight of the revelers.

They were celebrating Sawyn's victory.

I told myself it was only because they felt compelled to attend, or they needed the food and coin that surely would be abundant at the festivities. But what if they were dancing and cheering over the demise of my sister just because they wanted to?

"As soon as this is over." Grae wiped a stray lock of hair off his sweat-stained brow, still carefree in the aftermath of our stolen moment. "We are finding a room with a gloriously big bed." His chest puffed up with wolflike pride.

"A bed?" I flashed him a cheeky smirk. "That would be new."

Grae stopped so suddenly I almost crashed into his back. I craned my neck around him to see the merchant from earlier speaking to a Rook. My heart dropped into my boots as I spotted the merchant holding a rectangle of yellowing paper—Grae's Wanted poster. His head lifted and his eyes bugged wide as he saw us and pointed.

"Shit," we cursed in unison.

As Rooks swarmed the streets, we whirled and ran. We bolted down the rows of tables, fleeing under hanging walls of fabric and tipping baskets of produce. Shouts rang out behind us. We stumbled out onto the road and the Rooks converged from every side, corralling us toward the high red stone walls of the market.

I grabbed a reed out of a toppled merchant's basket and swung it into the first Rook. He lashed out with his scythe, hooking the reed and snapping it in half. His arm swung wide, though, opening up his body. It was careless and lazy, his fighting skills clearly not sharpened over many years. Had Sawyn just given them weapons and uniforms, and left them to their own devices? Perhaps these were new recruits. Perhaps she thought the fear of seeing a pack of Rooks alone would keep people in line.

My attacker tried to repeat the same move, and I let him, knowing his back swing would move his scythe far out of range. I waited until he was wide open again and then took a step into him, stabbing the snapped reed straight through his throat.

He let out a wet, sickening gasp. I didn't even flinch, my mind already thinking of the next Rook to my right. I knew it would churn in my mind later. *Later.* First, I had to survive.

The next blade narrowly avoided my side as I swung and struck the Rook's wrist with my fist. His scythe began to slip from his fingers and he lowered to snatch it, exposing his back to me. I drove the reed down between his neck and shoulder blade, a shallow puncture, before I hit bone. It wasn't a killing blow, but the Rook fell to his knees in pain, one less to worry about.

Retreating another step, I collided with Grae's back. We circled, back-to-back, sizing up the tornado of black capes. There were at least a dozen of them now and more spilling over the hillside. They seemed to seep from every crack and crevice in the city, an endless army of obsidian feathers and iron claws.

It was too many. Even with our Wolf strength and speed, we wouldn't win this fight.

Bodies circled our boots, a gory barrier between us and the encroaching Rooks. Scarlet rivers of blood flowed down toward the drains, and I wondered if tomorrow the lake would turn the rusty red of dried blood.

The bustling market was silent now, apart from the rushing of feet away from the square. A few stragglers stole one last look over their shoulders before they disappeared, fleeing the carnage as more Rooks rushed into the street.

The jostle of Rooks pushed one forward, within striking distance. I ducked under his blow and kicked out his knee, making him drop. I stabbed my makeshift blade into his shoulder, blood spraying into my eyes. He screamed, scrambling backward as the rest of the Rooks held a tight circle around us.

"Enough!" a shout echoed all around us, ricocheting off the stone and booming in my mind.

I spun, trying to find the location of that voice. Static filled the air, my curls lifting skyward as dread pooled in my gut.

A bolt of green lightning shot across the sky, cracking into the stone walls and spraying debris across us.

"Sawyn." I breathed as the ground dropped out from under me. My stomach lurched into my throat as I fell, bracing for a landing that never came.

THIRTY-EIGHT

THE CRUSHING PAIN IN MY SKULL MADE ME GRIMACE AS I PEEKED through slitted eyes. My shoulders ached as I tried to pull them forward, only to find cold steel biting into my wrists. Chains rattled as I dropped my head forward. I sucked in a painful breath through my scratchy throat. I twisted my head, lightning shooting from my neck down into my shoulder blades. How long had I been left in this position?

My tailbone ached as I adjusted my seat on the cold, wet stones. A gaping pit in the corner reeked of foul odors, drips of water from the ceiling falling far down into the rotten drain. A lone torch flickered through the rusting iron door. The attack in the market came flooding back to me—Sawyn. I was in her dungeon.

I was in *my* dungeon.

I scanned frantically for Grae, but I was alone in my cell.

Or maybe not. A smooth voice floated from beyond the shadows. "Who are you?"

She stepped forward, walking straight through the iron door as if it were a cloud of smoke. With pale skin and sharp green eyes, she looked just as menacing as that night in Damrienn.

Sawyn.

Her red hair was pulled back in a tight braid, and she wore a flowing black dress that pooled at her feet and was cinched at the waist by a gold belt holding a thin sword. A high cuff around her neck and a golden crown atop her head made her hold her chin high even as she stared down at me.

She pursed her red-stained lips. "You're the servant girl from Damrienn, the one I couldn't kill." Her eyes dipped to the low neckline of my too-large tunic and she flashed her white teeth. "You should've kept that protection stone."

I spat at her feet, eliciting from her a mirthless laugh that grated against my skin.

"But you're not a human at all, are you?" She took another step forward and crouched in front of me. Her movements were flowing and slow, her lilting words so at odds with her sharp features. "I should've seen it before. Those dark curls and bowed lips. You look so much like your mother."

I sucked in a sharp breath, pulling against my restraints.

"I had wondered why this victory felt hollow," Sawyn said, looking at the palms of her hands as if divining the future. "And now I know. There was one more Gold Wolf untamed. A twin." Her lip curled. "I should have guessed."

"Release Maez and Grae." I panted. "They have nothing to do with this."

"You give orders like your father, too." Sawyn's eyes slid to mine, the same shade of green. "I don't know who this Maez is, though . . . oh, you mean that Silver Wolf? I could care less about her. I only kept her to draw out the last of the Wolves who dared to challenge me and make Nero think twice about mining my gold. Instead, I caught another princess." She flashed a toothy, too-white smile. "Do you think Nero will lift a hand to rescue his son now that he's declared him a traitor? His bounty for his niece is all for show. Your sister wouldn't be the first time two females were mates, though royalty has never honored such a bond. Not even the most powerful of magics can supersede the will of arrogant kings consumed with hoarding their power and protecting royal bloodlines. I think Nero would rather sire a few more heirs with some poor young female from his pack in the comfort of his castle than cross into my borders now." She picked a cobweb off her sleeve with a vicious grin. "Not even my gold can tempt him anymore."

"So what? This is all just to aggravate Nero?"

"Hardly."

"Then why? Why did you do all of this?" I shook my head. "I never understood. In all the stories, it never made sense. Why Olmdere? Did you only want a crown?"

"I wanted *my* crown." Sawyn stood, dusting her hand down her skirts. "I know you were raised in a foreign kingdom with a foreign tongue, judging by your accent, but do you know what Sawyn means?"

My brow furrowed. I hadn't considered her name before. "It's Olmderian. *Sa Wyn*." Why hadn't I pronounced it that way before? "It means *above kings*."

"A more fitting name than the one I was given," she said. "I chose it for myself."

My heart thundered in my chest. "What was your name before?"

Sawyn's green eyes gleamed, a wicked smile spreading across her face. "Leanna," she said. "Leanna Marriel."

Leanna Marriel.

"Impossible," I wheezed. "I saw the books in Taigos. Leanna died."

"I clearly didn't die," she sneered. "I transformed. Evolved beyond that which they made me to be."

"No . . ."

"Look at me," Sawyn said, waving her hand at her face and down her body. "Who do I remind you of?"

I scanned her—the shape of her face and nose, the color of her hair. "Briar."

"The Marriel line was strong with the Crimson Princess." Sawyn brushed her dark red braid over her shoulder. "They used to call me that, too, once upon a time, though for very different reasons." Her sharp green eyes bored into me. The same eyes as mine. "You take more after Rose. A beauty, no doubt, but nothing like royalty."

She stared off at the wall as if staring through time. There were similarities, for sure, but that also made it feel uncanny to be looking at her. She should've looked decades older, but she seemed no older than Briar and me, her true age no doubt hidden by her magic. No wonder she was so unconcerned with her successors. Her dark magic would make her age at a snail's pace, and I'm guessing she wouldn't even care at that point.

"Who was it that made you turn toward dark magic?" I whispered, bile rising in my throat. "Who did you kill?"

She arched her narrow brow. "I've killed many people."

"But there had to have been a first. A sorceress is created through death magic," I said, wincing as I swallowed. "When you cursed my mother, you were already a sorceress, which means you killed someone before . . ." My eyes widened as I thought back to that dusty tome in Taigos. The day Leanna died, another died, too. "You killed your brother, didn't you?"

She tried to hide her surprise, but I saw it there for a split second—the widening of her eyes, her mouth going slack. How many decades had it been since anyone asked her about this? Since she had even thought about it herself? Did she believe her violent beginnings were lost to time?

"Very good, Princess. I'm somewhat impressed, considering how little you seem to know about your own family."

"And whose fault is that?" I asked with as much venom as I could muster.

"Touché," she said with what seemed to be genuine humor. "Yes, my darling brother's blood was my gateway to this power. I was about to turn sixteen—they were going to send me off to Valta, a country I'd never seen, to marry a man I'd never met." Sawyn clasped her hands together, staring out the high window at a sliver of blue sky. Her voice was tinged with her own venom as she stared back through time. "Sahandr had to die. Then my parents couldn't ship their only heir off to the Onyx Wolves." She rolled her shoulders back, her posture belying the rage in her eyes. "But they didn't see it that way. They said they could sire more pups, have more sons. They tried to kill me for what I'd done to him." Her chest rose and fell faster. "And so I disappeared, faked my death, bided my time while I honed my new powers. I thought sorcery would enslave me to its dark magic, but it was what set me free."

A draft blew in, the breeze tousling the wisps of scarlet hair around her temples. The crazed look on her face seemed equally filled with wrath and joy.

"And then my father was born," I murmured.

"I had hoped Sameir would be a better man than our father. When my parents died, I went to him, asked him to hand over what was rightfully mine, but he refused."

"What did you expect? You killed his brother!" I cried, my restraints biting into my wrists. "And you turned into a sorceress! Wolves swore to rid the world of dark magic. Why would he honor the claim of a sorceress *and* an oath breaker, family or not?"

"Because the crown should've been *mine*," she seethed, her eyes darkening as static charged the air. "He usurped *my* throne." Flashes of green lightning skittered across the ceiling. "Which means *my* will should have been pack law, and I above such accusations. But no one saw it that way. No one thought a mere woman could be anything but a depository for another Wolf's pups. And so I showed him just how wrong he—and everyone else—was. You know the story, of course. I believe there are some lovely songs about it."

I thought about trying to sing at Queen Ingrid's palace, and how much it had devastated me then. Now, though, I found it oddly gave me strength, because I *did* know the story—the one Grae pointed out to me wasn't all darkness and death. Her jibe missing its mark, I asked instead, "Why didn't you just kill my parents back then?"

"I did something far better." A grin stretched her thin red

lips. "I knew she'd awaken—I wasn't an idiot to think they weren't actually true loves. But that wasn't the real curse."

"What—what do you mean?"

Sawyn's delight was almost palpable in the rancid cell. "I didn't curse Rose, I cursed Rose's *womb*. That it—and all that were born from it—would never again produce a male heir." I gasped, my pulse pounding in my ears, and she continued, savoring my shock. I wondered how long she'd been holding this in, waiting for the day to finally tell someone just how brilliantly evil she was, even as she said, "Then Sameir would know my pain. I thought he'd bow to my power, beg me to undo what I'd done, but he didn't. Rather, I made him a hero. Those putrid stories and ballads of their love spread into every corner of Aotreas, and when the arrangement with Damrienn was announced, I knew then my error. Instead of my brother mourning his legacy, he would give it to Nero. He'd rather forfeit everything he had to a foreigner than a woman."

"In the stories . . ." I took another shuddering breath. "They said on the night of our birth you demanded our father bow to you. He said you'd never be queen."

Sawyn smiled. "He was obviously wrong."

"Why didn't you kill Briar in Damrienn?" The image of her splayed red hair across that tomb flashed in my mind—the same red hair as the sorceress who cursed her.

"Because mine will be a long life, and I wouldn't want to deprive it of entertainment. No, I wanted to see Nero mourn all he had lost and scramble for a way to fix it. I wanted him to come crawling to my kingdom begging for the Crimson Princess's mate and see me on my throne and know he'd never have it." Her eyes flashed as lightning crackled. "That is the thing with these arrogant kings. More will just keep coming to take their place. Lessons must be learned. New rules written. I make them understand in the only language they know: through power, through blood, through taking." The hair on my arms lifted in the charged air. "But then *you* came along."

"Apologies for ruining your revenge," I said. "I was trying to get mine."

She cackled a sharp laugh. "We are not so different, you and I."

"We are nothing alike," I hissed.

"It would make it easier to believe that, wouldn't it, niece?" She peered at me under her arched brow. "We are wild-hearted and sure-footed and bound to this land, more Queen than Wolf." Her cheeks dimpled as the blow of her words landed. "Laces itch and ribbons grate. We are not frail or simpering like your sister. We are not the puppets for a king's glory. We shall know our own glory."

The air crackled, vibrant bolts of green brightening the room, almost as if she couldn't contain her magic in her own excitement.

"Is it glorious to know your people are fleeing and dying?" I pushed back. "That they'd risk that quick death to not slowly starve? What of the gold mines?"

"They flee because they don't trust me as queen," she hissed.

"I wonder why? Maybe it's because you're a murderer!"

"Ah." She grinned. "But you're a murderer, too, aren't you, niece? I saw you in the markets, cutting down my Rooks without batting an eye. The only thing that separates you and me is that you think you're right."

"The difference is I feel remorse," I panted, feeling her magic zap across my skin as if being summoned by my words. "I feel the horror of what I did and feel sorry for it, rather than succumb to it. I deny the darkness's pull. I push it away and you turn toward it."

"Such speeches for such a young Wolf. But you don't know what you're talking about, yet again. Dark magic *saved* me," she said. "And it will save many more Wolf daughters still."

"Like Queen Ingrid?"

"Ingrid broke the system." Sawyn's eyes crinkled. "She risked war with Valta to stand her ground and fight for her rightful crown. It's worked for now, but it will only be so long before another king—or even a Wolf in her own court—turns on her. I've been nudging her toward dark magic for years. One day she'll see it's the only way to a different, better world."

"I, too, want a different world," I whispered, shaking my head. "A world beyond everything we've been told we had to be."

"Exactly!" she exclaimed, as if we had somehow found common ground. "It is a pity you are mated to the Prince of Damrienn." Sawyn adjusted her crown. "I would've liked to keep you around."

"Why can't you?"

"Because Damrienn is poison, just like the rest of them. And I will not have it in Olmdere." Her eyes narrowed. "And more, Nero needs to learn. After all he's done, this is a lesson he *will* remember. I won't rest until every Wolf kingdom is ruled by their rightful heirs."

"Grae is not like his father," I pleaded. "I'd gut King Nero myself if given half the chance."

"If we are so in agreement, what makes you think you have more right to Olmdere than me?" Sawyn hummed.

"Because you aren't doing your duty as Queen."

"Excuse me? I am fully in control—"

"You let your people starve," I growled. "*Our* people. You let them die, pitted them against each other, threatened and tortured them. You may have had a claim to be heir, but you squandered it when you abdicated your responsibility to your people."

"Humans," she spat.

I yanked against my chains, snarling at her. "So you pity the daughters of kings, but have no sympathy for the people who actually make up your kingdom?"

"Wolves are the natural-born leaders. Humans are weak in both mind and body, nothing more than ants under our boots," she hissed. "They knelt before the Wolf kings because they couldn't drive out the monsters themselves. They are barely worth the grain to feed them. They let this world be what it is, and they wouldn't lift a finger to save you."

"You're wrong."

She cocked her head. "Then where are your precious humans now, hm?"

"They're waiting."

Sawyn snorted. "Just as they've waited for hundreds of years. Because nothing changes!"

"You can't expect anyone to fight when they don't even know when their next meal is." My chest heaved. "But they would if they weren't trying to survive."

"Then they haven't tried hard enough to save themselves, and it still proves my point."

"The dark magic has rotted your heart, Sawyn, if you think you can pick and choose in such a way." My eyes and throat burned as her green magic filled my veins. "You hate the Wolves for what they've done. You hate the humans for what they are," I snarled. "You let thousands of people suffer, and the only one you care for is yourself.

"You're selfish. And you are alone."

Her final tether snapped as she whirled on me, balling her hands into fists. "*I have suffered!*"

"And you've punished innocent people for it," I spat back.

"I *will* save the Wolf daughters," she seethed.

"That is meaningless unless you care about human daughters, too," I gritted out. "Are you the last cause that's important? Once your battle is won, all that suffering evaporates into thin air? No, you're lessening your pain only by putting it on others. That isn't a victory at all. It's nothing but cowardice."

"You know *nothing* of bravery. You know *nothing* of the decisions I've had to make in order to survive—"

"In order for *you* to survive! Don't you hear yourself? You are the queen who cares nothing about her people. How are the humans supposed to survive?"

"They get by. I called them ants before, but they're more like roaches, no? They keep popping up." She laughed at the analogy, a tinge of madness apparent in her voice. "Humans are dangerous when given too much hope. They'd threaten our very way of life." She curled her lip, unknowing that she only cascaded her pain down onto those she still had power over. Kings crushed queens, queens crushed humans, and everyone's suffering only compounded. "You are such a disappointment, girl, that you can't see clearly what would happen if we let them off their leashes."

"Don't call me girl," I raged. Now that I had claimed my true self, that word grated against my skin, the irritation it caused before increased tenfold. I'd spent so long being silent about it, letting each time I was called "girl" chip away at me a little more, and I wasn't going to take it anymore, especially not from Sawyn. "That is not what I am."

Sawyn rolled her eyes. "You want to be a man so you can have everything to yourself, don't you?"

"No, not a man, either." I shifted my knees under me, trying to take the strain off my arms. "Something else. *Merem*. That's who I am."

"You've spent too much time with the humans." Sawyn waved off my words. "That is their short-lived nonsense speaking. Those aren't our words."

"And you've spent too little time with them! Maybe we should be more like the humans."

Sawyn's head whipped toward me. "Skin chaser."

"Those *are* our words—and aren't the insult you think. Less separates us than you would believe." I saw it in her eyes—she thought I was crazy, so certain that she was right. Disbelief warred against her rage.

"Just one look at you and I know exactly what you are," she seethed. "You think your made-up words can deceive me?"

"I have been deceiving everyone, including myself, my whole life," I shouted, spittle flying from my mouth as I raged, not only against her but every person who ever made me feel lesser than.

"No more. You choose to see what your closed little mind tells you. But I'm done trying to make sense to people like you. I'm finally now being honest."

"And what does your prince think of this ridiculousness, merem?" Her eyes widened when I didn't respond. "Oh, you haven't told him, have you?" Her lips curved up in an evil grin. "Shall we ask him?"

THIRTY-NINE

SHE TWISTED HER HAND UPWARD, BOLTS OF GREEN LIGHTNING shooting skyward, and a thump sounded to my left. Grae appeared in front of me, doubled over and gasping wet breaths. One eye was bruised shut, his lip busted open. When he spotted me, he let out a cry of relief, crawling toward me and wrapping me in his arms. A sob escaped my lips as I dropped my head onto his shoulder.

"Tell him, Calla." Sawyn's voice cut short our relief.

"Are you okay?" Grae whispered, searching my face and body for injuries. I nodded against him and he sighed.

"Tell him what you think you are," Sawyn taunted.

"What?" Grae pulled back, his worried eyes meeting mine.

"I was going to tell you." I clenched my jaw, staring past him at Sawyn, hating that this was how the conversation would play out. "But at first I didn't know how to explain it and . . . and then there were more pressing things, but I was going to—"

"Go on." Sawyn's face filled with wicked delight as she waited for me to speak. I knew from her catlike grin that she thought I was about to humiliate myself . . . but that arrogance, that certainty, only bolstered me to speak. Let me show her how a real Wolf acted, because as confident as she was, *I* was certain of my mate.

"This is the first time I've been away from Briar," I said, steeling myself with a deep breath. "And it's the first time I've seen myself as someone other than her twin. Someone other than a Wolf. Someone who existed outside of my title and pack. I always felt as if I'd been cast in the wrong role, one that never quite fit me, but I could never put my finger on why. I thought maybe it was because I was never meant to be a shadow, but it was so much more."

Grae's arms stayed folded around me as I spoke, his eyebrows knitting together in concern.

"And then I met Ora, and I realized there was someone within me under the layers of self-doubt and agitation . . . and then it all made sense. I think you've seen it within me on this trip already. Maybe you've seen it within me my entire life, before either of us could understand. It slowly grew within me and struck me like lightning all at once," I whispered, shaking my head in disbelief. "Daggers and jackets, dresses and kohl, man and woman and beyond. I exist somewhere, flowing in between them. And I thought I'd have to break myself down into little pieces to make it fit me, that I'd have to deny one part of myself to choose another, but I don't." My voice wobbled. "I am a whole person always, flowing, carving my own path."

Grae's arms tightened around me. "Yes," he murmured softly into my hair.

I began to pull away from him, but Grae held me tight to him, looking down into my eyes. "Ora had a human word for it—merem. With the river. That feels like what I am."

Tears welled in my eyes as I claimed that word for myself again, relief and joy washing through me even in the confines of a dungeon. And now I'd said it to my mate. He finally got to know all of me. This was a power Sawyn would never know—the confidence I had that Grae would love me unconditionally.

"Ha! He's speechless!" Sawyn cackled, misreading how our bond was growing even stronger. "He thinks you're crazy too, *girl*. Why would you think any Wolf would want you if you don't want to be his woman—"

Grae grabbed my cheeks, pulling my lips to his, the action silencing Sawyn. Tears streamed down my cheeks as he kissed me, slow and deep.

He lifted his lips an inch from mine to speak. "I only ever wanted you, little fox." His chest rumbled against me. "I've seen the beauty and strength in every side of you, even before it had a name, and I know all the things that you are were meant to be mine. You're my partner, my person, my mate."

A dizzying, soaring feeling washed through me as he wiped my tears. He wrapped his arm around my rib cage and squeezed me against his muscled chest. His lips enveloped mine, a promise of all he said, a sweet burning kiss that skittered down to my toes.

"I love you," he murmured across my mouth. "You're *my* merem." The word on his lips made a soft cry escape mine.

I pressed my salt-stained lips together as more tears spilled down my cheeks. "I love you, too."

"You can't be serious," Sawyn hissed, snapping her fingers. "Disgusting."

Grae flew across the room and I screamed as he hit the grate, stopping inches from falling into the open drain.

"You two would erase the Wolf way of life if you could," she sneered. "You spit on your ancestors' graves with these human words. But *I* will make it better. My reign will be magnificent." She turned over her hands one more time, straightening her emerald ring. "Unfortunately, you won't live long enough to see it."

"You don't have to do this, Sawyn." I yanked against my chains. "This is your last chance."

"Your spirit is admirable, *girl*. Most entertaining." Sawyn huffed. She cut a glance at the gurgling drain. "But I have celebrations to attend, a victory to claim. Goodbye, niece—may our ancestors shun you in the afterlife."

She vanished, leaving sparks of dark magic in her wake. A swirling rumble echoed up the black pit in the corner. Grae scuttled away from the hole, watching in rapt terror.

"What in the Moon's name is that?" But we didn't have time for an answer before a black tentacle slithered up from the abyss.

"That can't be." I watched in horror as another obsidian tentacle snaked up from the pit, probing the wet stones, searching for its prey.

"An ostekke." Grae's eyes darted around the room, looking for a weapon.

"I thought they were all dead," I hissed, gaping as a third tentacle suctioned to the wall.

The tip of the slimy limb reached Grae's bare foot, and he drove his heel down, stomping on it. A keening wail split the rotten air as black water burbled up the pit and sloshed over the edges. The ostekke withdrew only an inch and then shot forward, grabbing Grae around the forearm and yanking him off his feet.

I screamed as he crashed into the slippery stone, his free arm barely catching him before his face hit the floor. Grae frantically clawed and punched the corded limb, but the monster wouldn't release him. The ostekke pulled again, yanking its victim toward the hole and a watery death in the lake below. I thrashed the skin of my wrists raw, the stinging adding to the pain in my shoulder joints, but to no effect.

"Grae!" The soles of my feet slipped on the cold stone, trying to reach my mate.

My scream seemed to split the ostekke's attention. Its second tentacle shot out toward me, slithering around my shoulder. Its grip was so tight, suckers pulling painfully on my skin. In desperation, I twisted my head and sunk my teeth into the slimy flesh. Hot goo burst into my mouth and I gagged as the foul mucus coated my tongue.

The creature shrieked, recoiling so rapidly its tentacle ripped through the chains. My arm dropped and my body lurched forward, hanging from my one tethered arm. The pain shot through me, calling forward my Wolf, and with one blinding jolt I shifted, my forearm slipping free of its shackle as I dropped onto four paws.

Grae groaned, lifting a hand to clutch his head as the beast released him. Relief flooded through me, and as his eyes landed on me, he shifted, too, his Wolf being beckoned by my own.

His paws scrambled toward me when another unearthly wail burbled from the pit. Five limbs emerged, shooting wildly across the room, tearing stone from the walls and twisting the iron door.

Grae ducked under the thick, flailing limbs as one wrapped around my barrel chest. My paws slid across the slick floor but I was held in place by the beast. A snarl escaped my maw as I twisted to and fro. The air whooshed out of me—my howl dying on my lips—as the muscled tentacle constricted. My ribs stabbed with pain under the crushing weight.

Grae raced over, biting into the limb around my chest, tearing into it with his teeth. Yellow mucus rained down through my fur, but one tentacle was instantly replaced by another. No matter how Grae attacked, the beast wouldn't release me.

We worked in unison, twisting and snapping, biting and shredding. Something in the way we growled and attacked felt primal, ancient—the same way my ancestors battled these monsters centuries ago. But my ancestors battled the ostekke as a pack, and Grae and I were only two. Another tentacle lashed out and wrapped around my center again and I yelped. How many fucking tentacles did an ostekke have?

"Hang on!" Grae shouted into my mind, whirling toward the warped and twisted iron door. He leapt over one tentacle and ducked under another, lying belly down on the ground to crawl under the gap in the gnarled door. His human form would've never made it, but his Wolf squeezed through.

I tried to swallow and winced. It felt like a blade being dragged down the back of my throat.

The ostekke pulled, but I had no air to yowl. Another tentacle wrapped around my front leg and yanked so hard I was certain my leg was about to pop out of its socket. Grae reemerged with the torch clenched between his snarling teeth, leaping over to me and holding the flame to the beast's mucus-covered skin. One tentacle retracted, only to instantly be replaced by another around my neck. I felt the blood vessels bursting in my eyes as I choked, desperately trying to get a purchase on the slippery floor.

As Grae moved to burn it again, he was knocked to the ground, a flailing limb sweeping out his feet. My eyes spotted, even in this form I could barely hang on to consciousness against the brutal, unending wrath of the ostekke. The monster grabbed Grae by one front paw and one back, yanking in opposite directions until his screams stabbed through me.

A muffled shout came from the end of the hall as four Rooks appeared beyond the door. One booted down the twisted iron grate as another charged into the fray, holding aloft an unlit lantern. Swinging, they smashed it against the wall, oil dripping onto the wet stone. They threw it into the pit while another Rook grabbed the discarded torch and lit the oil. The flame trailed down toward the abyss, and then—

The room erupted, fire shooting in a scorching beam upwards, singing my fur. The tentacle around my neck released and I turned my face from the white-hot blaze. A sickening squeaking and popping filled the putrid air as the flames turned from white to red. With a final flash, the bright light faded back to darkness.

My limbs finally freed, I collapsed to the ground, my head lolling onto the boots of the nearest Rook. I looked up into those hazel eyes, instantly recognizing them.

"Calla?" Ora asked, cocking their head at me.

I whined, my tail thumping on the stone as Ora surveyed my Wolf form with an appreciative smile. My chest rose and fell, my mouth open and panting from the exhaustion of battle.

Ora pulled their face covering down and grinned. "Well, that was a bit more dramatic than we had planned."

Relief flooded through me as I glanced at the other three—Hector, Sadie, and Navin.

With a groan, Grae sat up and shifted, leaning his naked form against the far wall. "You have no idea how good it is to see you."

I shifted in mirror to him, hugging my legs to my chest and sighing as my body healed along with the transition. Without the torchlight, the room was cast in heavy shadows, and even then, now was not the time to be concerned with modesty.

"You killed an ostekke," I said to Ora, staring down at the severed strands of burnt flesh.

Grae chuckled, wiping his hair off his face. "I thought it was the Wolves who were supposed to save humans from monsters."

"Humans can be heroes, too, when given half a chance." Ora found my cheek and cupped it through the darkness. "We can save each other."

"Thank you." I stood and searched the shadowed room. "Where are the others?"

"The party," Navin said, pointing to the ceiling. "The plan is in motion, Your Majesty." He gave me a wink at the title.

Grae stumbled over to me, half-covering my naked body with his own in a way that made me want to roll my eyes. We were so covered in shadows and burnt ostekke goo you could barely make out our figures anyway. Ora seemed to get the hint though and removed the cloak from their Rook uniform and tossed it to me. Hector did the same for Grae, and my mate and I stood shoulder to shoulder as we stared, bemused at our rescuers.

"What plan is in motion?" I asked, eyeing each of them.

Navin stepped forward and held out a dagger to me. My dagger. The one Vellia had made for me. My fingers traced the gilded etchings of the Gold Wolf crest. Sadie and Hector tipped their chins toward the sky as I took it.

Navin placed his hand over his heart and bowed his head in an act of reverence. "The plan to take your throne, Your Majesty."

~

THE OTHERS DISCARDED THEIR ROOK UNIFORMS AS THEY walked, leaving a trail of black along the tiled floor. The dungeons gave way to gilded opulence, flowing in Olmdere's patron colors of burgundy and gold. By the time we reached the ground floor, Ora was dressed in their performance uniform once more, Sadie and Hector along with them. I couldn't help but smile at the fanciful silver toggles and ballooned brocade trousers. Sadie cut me a look, daring me to comment on it, and I pressed my lips together.

I tried to take in the castle—*my* castle—as we rushed toward the grand hall. The gold-flecked stone shimmered in the midday light, the rooms accented with cream and black. Detailed reliefs covered the walls along with portraits of Wolves in gilded frames. I wondered which Wolf was my father as I passed portrait after portrait of the Olmderian kings. I wondered which room would have been mine. I was born under this roof. This was my very first home.

"This way," Navin whispered, leading us into an anteroom filled with bustling performers.

Jugglers and bards, fire dancers and minstrels, all crammed around the warped mirrors painting their faces and unpacking their trunks. No one paid us any mind, even though Grae and I looked like a monster had nearly eaten us. Maybe they thought the Rook capes were costumes? Maybe we were actors in a play? Whatever they assumed, they were too busy dressing themselves to notice.

"Here," Ora said, passing us two crimson robes, painted in spirals of gold. They grabbed a glass bottle off the countertop and misted floral perfume all around us until we were practically drowning in it. "This should cover the worst of the smell."

We hastily dressed, shuffling toward the screen against the far wall. A tapestry wove across the window, obscuring the grand hall from view. Navin pressed his face to the sheet of stretched fabric and I followed, gasping as I saw the throne room through the gaps in the weave.

The grand hall was warmer and richer than the halls of Taigos and Damrienn. Six golden chandeliers hung from the ceiling, shaped like stag's antlers, a candle atop every point. The wood-accented wall trimmings reminded me of the cabin I grew up in, though much grander, and I realized Vellia had put nods to our kingdom in every corner of our home. Long burgundy banners hung on either side of a dais, and upon that dais was a carved-wood throne.

Sawyn surveyed the festivities with a crooked grin, sitting upon my father's throne. She held a piece of paper between her pointer and middle finger, tapping the edge of the paper along the armrest.

I scanned over the festivities, searching. The room was filled with entertainers; the walls lined with chattering Rooks. They all stood casually, not guards at attention but attendees to the party. There seemed to be no other Wolves in attendance . . . apart from one.

I gasped as my eyes landed upon Maez. She sat on the steps of the dais, an iron collar around her neck, chained to the throne. The collar was flush against her skin—too tight for her to shift forms without snapping her neck. I wondered if she'd been tempted to try, but if she tried and failed, her death would mean the death of her mate, too. She was filthy, her hair matted and her face stained with grime. In the weeks she'd been gone, she'd withered away, looking weaker and leaner than the muscular Wolf I'd seen in Damrienn. Her eyes were hollow as she stared straight down at the floor.

"Are you enjoying your victory?" Sawyn called, and the Rooks echoed a booming reply. They raised their goblets to her, pulling down their masks to swig down their drinks.

"This is the world we have won together!" Sawyn's shouts were met with more cheers.

I choked down my anger at her fake words. They were cheering for a false savior and in turn were just pawns for her own glory. Yet her praise seemed to be enchantment enough for them. Ply them with drinks and good food, tell them her victory was theirs, and they'd fight for her, die for her, and I could see why that was enough.

She glanced one more time at the piece of paper in her hand and crumpled it into a ball, throwing it onto the floor, bored.

"King Nero thinks he can threaten me with his possession of the Crimson Princess. He thinks he's still powerful." Her predatory smile made her teeth gleam. Her Rooks jeered at her words, spitting and cursing King Nero's name. Sawyn held up her hand and the Rooks silenced instantly. "Worry not. King Nero couldn't see the many cracks in his threats." Her fingers twirled, green lightning zapping between her thumb and fingers. "But that's because he knows nothing of true power."

She flicked her hand upward and bolts of lightning zapped across the room. The crowd gasped as a body appeared out of thin air, tumbling to the foot of the dais.

"Let's see Nero get her now."

Cheers erupted and my heart cracked as recognition bloomed.

Lying at the base of the steps was Briar.

FORTY

MAEZ'S SCREAM TORE ABOVE THE CHEERING—A DEEP, SHARP wail. She bolted forward, only to be yanked back by her collar, inches from reaching her mate. She scrambled forward again, reaching out her hand to try to grab Briar's sleeve. Her fingertips skimmed the fabric, but she couldn't grasp it.

"Pathetic." Sawyn grinned as the Rooks erupted in laughter.

But I didn't see anything pathetic about Maez's attempts, and the only thing keeping me from doing the same was Grae's grip on my arm and his soft, steadying words in my ear. For all that, I couldn't tear my eyes away from my twin's limp body. Her hair covered her face, her lifeless arms splayed at odd angles, her skirts askew. A river of white lace trailed out toward the quintet of musicians who'd resumed their lively jig. The merriment made me want to howl with rage.

I spotted Malou's dark hair and gray eyes at last, weaving through the crowd. She held aloft a golden tray with a single bejeweled goblet in its center. In the tan garb of the royal servants, I'd almost missed her. One arm tucked behind her back and her head bowed. Her eyes darted to the tapestry where we stood and gave us a wink. My stomach lurched as she stepped up from the dais, curtsying as she proffered the goblet to Sawyn.

"It's time," Ora said from beside me, placing a hand on my numb shoulder.

I pulled my head away to look at our gathering group.

"Please tell me you brought more weapons?" Grae asked Hector.

Sadie opened her puffy costume jacket to reveal her fighting leathers. Armed to the teeth, each belt and buckle was strapped with knives and daggers. "Take your pick."

"*Esh*," Navin cursed at the armory hanging from the lining of her coat.

"Gods, I love you." My heart raced as I took another throwing knife and paring knife from her belt to accompany my dagger.

I turned to Ora, gesturing to the busy room of performers behind me. "We need to get as many people out of here as possible. Sawyn will think nothing of the human casualties. When the fighting breaks out, you need to lead people to safety."

"The people who are here want to be here, Your Majesty." Ora pulled the fox badge out of their pocket and passed it to me. "Look for the badges."

I furrowed my brow as I swept my thumb over the little fox face. "Look for the badges?"

Ora nodded, taking my shoulders and turning me toward the woven screen. "Do you like this song?"

"Why are you asking me that now?"

"Just tell me."

I strained to focus on the strings above the sound of clamorous banter. It was quick-paced but melodic, a hint of sorrow amongst the sweeping crescendoes, trailing upward in a way that made my heart swell.

"It's beautiful," I whispered. "Who wrote it?"

"I did," Ora said, pulling my gaze back to them. "This is Calla's song. This is how I think of you." I took in a shuddering breath as my eyes welled and Ora cupped my cheeks again. "You are not alone, Your Majesty. Look for the badges—"

A deafening crack of lightning shot through the air and everyone jolted.

"It's time," Grae said, grabbing me and pulling me into a burning kiss. His storming eyes met mine. "Let's go save your sister."

"Let's go claim my crown."

My lips collided with his in one more desperate kiss before I grabbed the hilt of my dagger and plunged through the doorway.

WHAT I SAW WHEN I DARTED INTO THE GRAND HALL MADE MY heart tumble. In a single breath, chaos had erupted around us. Screams and clangs of metal against metal echoed across the vaulted ceilings. A wall of obsidian cloaks blocked our path to the dais. My eyes flew to Malou, pinned to the wall, glowing green light circling her as she clawed at her throat.

"You try to poison me? *Me?*" Sawyn raged, squeezing her hand through the air as Malou's eyes rolled back. The same chokehold that would've killed me in Damrienn were it not for Grae's protection stone.

I raced forward, only to be met by a wall of Rooks. Mina darted out through the crowd, brandishing a fallen Rook's scythe. The normally mousy twin looked ferocious, slashing at Sawyn. The sorceress gaped down at the split fabric of her dress.

"Curse the Gods," she snarled. "More twins."

Her free hand shot out and Mina flew across the room, slamming into the wall beside her sister.

I ducked at the whoosh of air, nearly caught off guard from watching Sawyn's attack. But I was, above all else, a warrior, and my fist cracked into the Rook's nose, blooding pouring from his face covering. He tried to swing at me again, slipping on his own blood and landing hard on his knees. I didn't pause, slicing my blade straight across his neck, grateful for the time and training that made my body move without thought. It was a dance, the

Rooks only knowing a few steps, and I always knew their next move. Not only that, I was dancing to *my* song. I yanked my blade from a Rook's neck, whirling toward another three. Their eyes narrowed as they charged me, pushing me back into Sadie and Grae.

Grae ducked under careless swings, Sadie and I right behind him. He let three Rooks slip past him, funneling them toward us as we cut them down. I lost sight of Navin and Ora as they plunged into the fray. The swarm of black feathers blocked from sight the wall where Mina and Malou were pinned. They weren't skillful, but there were so damn many.

I choked up on the hilt of my dagger, waiting as Grae sparred with the Rook closer to me. When his back turned, I swiped my blade, catching only the fabric of his cloak, but it was enough to make him whirl toward me. Mistake. The second his head turned, Grae lurched forward, wrapping his arm around the Rook's neck. He locked his wrist with his other arm, choking the attacker as his eyes bugged, turning bright red. He clawed at Grae's muscled arm, easily holding his prey. His eyes rolled back and his body drooped. Grae released him, letting him fall to the floor.

For each soldier we cut down, two more appeared. Like the ostekke's tentacles, the endless onslaught pushed us back, and fear coiled in my gut. Their sheer numbers might still overwhelm our superior skill. I tried to keep my focus on one at a time, knowing if I lifted my head the odds would feel insurmountable. I needed to get to the dais. Briar was mere feet away. We were so close. We just needed to keep going.

A thud sounded and I looked to see Sadie's right hook land on her attacker's temple. He fell limp to the floor as the sound of more footsteps rushed through the hall. She turned toward her next attacker, and he booted her in the gut. Stumbling backward, she grabbed her dagger from her oversized coat. She advanced, raising it only to be met by the block of a sword, but it wasn't a Rook holding the blade . . . it was Navin.

Sadie's eyes flew wide as she stared past their warring blades and into his bronze gaze.

"Stop," Navin whispered, his chest heaving as he pushed the Rook behind him.

The Rook shrunk, his shoulders deflating as if relieved to have Navin's protection.

I surveyed the Rook behind Navin, the same height as him with the same bronze eyes, and, even with the rest of his face obscured, I knew it was his brother.

"This is him then? Your brother?" Sadie growled, dropping her dagger and easily shoving Navin backward into his sibling. "He just tried to kill me!" Navin opened his mouth, but no words came out. "I see." She took a shuddering breath, hiding it behind a snarl, but I could see the pain lancing through her worse than any slice of a blade. "I should've known you wouldn't pick me."

"Sadie, please—" Navin pleaded, taking another step toward her, and she shoved him again. He tumbled backward into his brother, both of them falling to the floor.

It was a stark reminder that she was a Wolf, easily overpowering him not only from fighting skill but also from sheer Wolf strength. She twisted toward me, pain bracketing her expression as she shoved me toward a gap in the wall of soldiers.

"Go," she urged. Even as her voice cracked, she turned toward the next Rooks, black capes swarming her once more. "Help the twins. I'll deal with this lot," she added, and I knew it was the closest that she'd get to saying she was okay.

I nodded, spotting another opening in the line of attackers. I seized it, bolting toward the dais. My shoulder cracked into an entertainer and I threw out my hands to catch them. My thumb skimmed over their collar as I steadied them and my mouth fell open. I stared at the embroidered raindrop—the same one I'd seen hanging above the dinner table in Galen den' Mora. Was this its original owner? My eyes darted from the badge to meet their dark eyes. They gave me a wink and plunged back into the fray.

Look for the badges.

I was beginning to think Ora might be the most amazing person I'd ever met.

The music bolstered me as I scrambled up to the dais, barreling into the back of Sawyn. The sorceress fell forward but caught herself before slipping to the ground. As her hands fell, the twins plummeted to the floor. I screamed at the sickening crack of Malou's head against the stone. Mina curled into a ball, groaning. I wanted to run to their aid, but I was under the full focus of the green-eyed sorceress.

"You!" Sawyn seethed, spinning toward me.

She stumbled forward, her breathing thick. She threw out her hands toward me as if to cast her magic, but little more than sparks flickered around her hands. She repeated the gesture and fewer sparks sputtered from her fingertips. I grinned. The nite-hock Malou had given her was working.

She narrowed her hateful eyes at me. "You think I need my magic to defeat you?" Unsheathing the thin sword at her hip, she smirked. "I shouldn't have let the ostekke have you when I could've finished you myself."

She swung, and I blocked, locking my arms to hold my guard. I shoved her back, twisting under her attacking arm and swiping her side with my dagger. She ducked out of my blow, her sword carrying on the momentum of her strike. The edge collided with my forearm and I barked out a cry of pain as the blade pierced my skin.

"You've severely underestimated me, girl." Sawyn cackled at the shock on my face as she bested me at every attack and battle tactic I knew. All my training, I assumed Sawyn would rely solely on her magic, and now I was facing that miscalculation at the tip of her blade.

Two Rooks ran up the steps to aide their queen. With a quick back spin, I unleashed my throwing knife into the eye socket of one, and the other . . . Sawyn grabbed him and stabbed a dagger into his belly and booted him back down the steps.

"She's mine, fool," Sawyn snarled, booting the bleeding Rook back down the steps. "No one gets between a Wolf and her prey. Speaking of," our blades locked and she took the moment to casually look me up and down as if she had all the time in the world even as screams and sobs echoed through the throne room around us, "Why haven't you shifted? Not Wolf enough, you bloody skin chaser?"

I shoved her back and took a swift sidestep to avoid the swipe of her blade. My steel met her own, slamming into her cross guard as I growled, "I've spent too many hours sharpening this blade to end you with my teeth."

I lunged forward, catching her side. I wasn't sure if I caught skin or only fabric but Sawyn's eyes flared at me as her green magic sputtered, trying and failing to protect her. A flicker of betrayal flashed in her eyes as she glanced from the slashed fabric at her waist to me. "Everything I've done would've benefited you, too, you ungrateful bitch."

"Including killing my family?" I asked with disdain.

She didn't have an answer for that.

Fast as a snake, she struck again, and I barely had time to block her blow. My arms buckled. A messy block. My hand flew wide and I darted backward, knowing she'd take advantage of my exposed side. I twisted again, using the momentum to yank my paring knife off my belt and drive it into her bicep. She growled, grabbing my wrist and twisting until the knife clattered free. She kicked it off the dais, scowling at the blood seeping from her arm.

"I thought you had plans for that dagger?" She lashed out with maddening speed. Again and again. I tried to find another opening in her defenses.

"I have more plans than just that," I said, retreating a step, then another, leading her back toward the throne until I could drop into it. "I have plans to take my rightful place right here. I have plans to steal back everything you have taken from my kingdom."

I knew it would infuriate her enough—seeing me on that

throne—to take that final step, the one I'd been slowly goading and guiding her to take with all my feigned blows and seemingly faulty footwork. And when she did, Maez was there. A chain looped around Sawyn's neck and Maez yanked it tight, making the sorceress's eyes bulge from her skull. I didn't hesitate, driving up with my golden blade and plunging it into Sawyn's gut.

"This is for Olmdere. And this," I said, twisting my dagger until blood poured from her wound. "This is for all the Wolves like me too afraid to claim their true selves because of people like you. We fear your hate no longer." I twisted the knife again as Sawyn choked on her own blood. "And this is for all of the humans you tried to crush under your boot."

Sawyn's sword clattered to the ground and her bloodshot eyes welled, brimming over with heedless tears. Maez let her drop, crouching over Sawyn and grabbing the keys to her collar out of the sorceress's pocket.

Maez wheezed as her collar crashed to the floor and, without a pause, she rushed down the dais to Briar. Her muddy hands brushed Briar's hair out of her eyes. She bent down so tenderly, clutching Briar's lifeless face, and whispered, "Please work."

Tears slipped down her cheek as she kissed Briar, tracing clean trails through the grime. I held my breath, waiting, hoping. Maez's arms shook as she kept her lips planted on Briar's, a desperate cry coming from their joined lips. My heart punched into my ribs, watching for signs of life.

"Wake up, wake up." She chanted it like a prayer. "Please," she sobbed.

Briar's finger twitched and a howl escaped my lips as she lifted her hand to Maez's cheek. The room seemed to pause, a collective gasp rising up as Briar's eyes fluttered open. In another blink, they returned to the melee. Performers mobbed the Rooks, overtaking them three to one—far more musicians, jugglers, bards, and acrobats than the feathered obsidian guards. It hadn't seemed like that even moments before, my focus naturally drifting to the formidable guards, but now that I surveyed them all individually, there were hundreds of human performers entering the fray.

They were a whorl of colorful costumes and detailing and . . . My eyes widened when I spotted them.

Badges.

A sea of badges, every color of the rainbow, filled the hall. The same ones I'd seen hanging above the kitchen table in Galen den' Mora. The ones I'd noticed missing before. There was the blue songbird and there was the crescent moon. In the corner was the red candle and at the back door was the white rose. My hands trembled and my chest heaved. They'd come. The humans had come to defeat Sawyn. They'd come to help Ora, to help *me*.

Rooks began tearing off their uniforms, dropping to their knees and raising their hands in surrender. Their hand scythes clattered to the ground; their loyalties so easily turned.

I took a step forward toward my sister, and a hand grabbed my ankle. I scowled down at the bloodied fingers and then up at Sawyn's pale face. Blood dripped from her mouth as she coughed. With the wound in her gut and the poison coursing through her veins, no magic would cure her. Even shifting was beyond her now. Hers was the face of someone in their final moments, but there was no fear in her eyes, only pure wrath.

Standing before the throne of my ancestors, I crouched down to Sawyn.

"Do you know who won this battle?" I whispered, my lips curving up at the anger and hate in her eyes. "The humans. If you'd only seen their true power, you could've been here to lead this better world."

"You fool." She panted ragged wet breaths, blood trailing from her mouth and nose. "You're turning your back on your own kind. You're giving away your power to those sheep."

"I'm gaining so much more than you could ever know. You feared losing power so much that you cut off everyone who would've helped you attain it." Sawyn reached for her sword, but I stepped on the blade and slid it out of her pawing grasp.

"You were a one-Wolf kingdom, *Sa-wyn*, so consumed with being above everyone that you ended up with no one but yourself. That's why all this felt so hollow, like something was missing." I waved my arms around the grand hall. "The things that separate us and the humans are so much smaller than you would choose to believe."

"People." Sawyn's eyelids began to flutter, the poison flooding her veins as blood pooled around her. She screwed her eyes shut as if summoning the strength to take her last breath. "Let's see your *powerful* humans save you from this."

She threw out her hand and a loud crack shook the ground, pulsing through the air. A flash of bright green light made me shield my eyes . . . and then silence.

Sawyn's hand dropped and I stared at her lifeless body, her flash of dark magic draining the last of her life force. Her lifeless eyes looked to the ceiling, her hateful smile going slack.

The sounds warped around me, the air bending and twisting before my eyes, and I heard distant muffled screams. My brow dropped heavy over my eyes as I tried to take a deep breath. My legs went out from under me and my knees cracked onto the stone, and that's when I smelled it—burning flesh. I stared down at the singed hole in my tunic, my mind trying to make sense of it. I couldn't feel anything, not my fingers, nor the hole in my chest where Sawyn's lighting struck.

Someone screamed my name and suddenly Grae was in front of me, his eyes wide with horror. I couldn't feel his hands as they clutched my cheeks. His panicked gaze roved my body. My name was on his lips, but I couldn't hear it.

"My sweet Calla," a warm voice whispered into my mind, a voice so familiar.

My eyes flitted from Grae's panicked face, over his shoulder to where Vellia stood. She wore her sage-green dress and matching kerchief around her silver hair. The air warped and billowed around her as if she floated on an invisible wind.

"Vellia." My mouth formed the words, but no sound escaped.

Grae looked to where the faery stood, his expression cracking from panic to utter despair.

"I've come to grant your wish, my love," Vellia said with a soft smile.

I tried to suck in a breath. My chest shuddered as my numb trembling fingers swiped the tears from Grae's cheeks. I licked my lips, trying to summon the will to speak.

"These people, *our* people," I whispered to him, "need you."

"No." His eyes pleaded with me.

A wet rattle escaped my throat as I looked to Vellia. "I wish to sever this mating bond so that Grae may live without me. Save him."

"No!" Grae sobbed, gripping my face tighter. "Calla, no, don't. I can't go on without you. Please, no."

"May our people be led into a better future," I prayed. "May they know peace. May the humans of Olmdere thrive."

"Don't leave me." He pressed his wet lips to mine. "Please."

"I love you," I whispered onto his lips, feeling the inevitability of this choice, the peace of my decision.

Vellia's voice filled me as golden light swirled around us and that cold numbness within me morphed to warmth.

"That was the right wish, my love," she whispered.

People gasped as warm, brilliant sunlight flooded through me. I kept my lips on Grae's, the perfect end, as I let that sunlight consume me and felt myself fade away.

FORTY-ONE

GOLDEN LIGHT FLASHED BEHIND MY EYELIDS AND I SQUINTED them open. Calloused fingers stroked my temple, brushing my hair off my face. I peered up into Grae's soft eyes, bright daylight circling his head like a halo.

"Hello, little fox."

"This must be the sweetest dream," I murmured, my lips pulling into a smile.

All at once, it came flooding back to me, and I bolted upright. My head swirled as Grae caught my shoulders and guided me back onto the silk pillow. The soft mattress hugged my curves. The room smelled clean and floral, like lemon and honeysuckle, a cool summer's breeze wafting in through an open window.

"Easy," Grae said.

"I'm alive." My brows pinched together. "I'm alive?"

His hand smoothed down the sleeve of my chemise, emotions choking his voice as he whispered, "You're alive. You're safe."

"I don't understand. Vellia . . . my dying wish . . ." My eyes darted across the ceiling as though the answers were written in the rafters.

I touched the center of my chest, where Sawyn's magic speared straight through me. Unbuttoning my chemise to my belly, I gasped. The blackened hole was now smooth skin the color of molten ore. The scars radiated out in rivers of gold from the center of my chest like a bursting sun.

"How?" I trailed a finger over them, expecting them to be cold and smooth, but they only felt like skin, and I wondered if they were golden all the way into my bones.

"Your wish. *May our people be led into a better future. May they know peace.*" Grae's voice wobbled and he lowered onto his elbow, stroking a hand down my cheek as pain raked through his expression. The same look that I saw as I felt my soul leaving my body as he watched me die.

"I heard Vellia's voice," I whispered, threading my arm around his side and pulling his torso against me. "She said it was the right wish."

"It's you, Calla." Grae lay down, gathering me against his hard chest. "You are the one who will lead the people to a better future. The only way it could be fulfilled was if you lived."

Mouth agape, I shook my head, and I wondered if that tricky faery had twisted the truth of my wish out of her love for me. Was *I* truly the key to Olmdere's future? "I made that wish for you—"

His lips silenced me with a kiss. I pulled him tighter, filled with the assurance that I was indeed alive again as his mouth enveloped mine.

Grae's lips skimmed across my jaw and up to my ear. "And in doing so, made it for all of us."

I swallowed the burning knot in my throat. "Gods, that's too much for anyone to bear. I—" His lips met mine again and I laughed. "Are you going to kiss me every time I worry?"

"If it works." He grinned, breathing in my hair just as he had done that day back in Allesdale.

"A bonfire after a rainstorm," I whispered.

"What?"

"That's what you smell like to me." I traced one of his dimples and down the curve of his jaw. "I never told you."

I sighed, taking in the room. Gauzy curtains billowed on the summer's breeze. Beyond the open windows, the dark lake swirled.

The turquoise river that rushed through the city battled with the dark water, creating whorls of blue and black as if the lake itself was fighting off the dark magic in its murky waters. I wondered if, now that the ostekke was dead, the lake would turn clear once more.

"We're in the castle still," I murmured, surveying the red velvet curtains and golden chandeliers.

"We're in *your* castle," Grae corrected.

"Briar?" I bolted upright again. "Where is she? Is she okay?"

"Gods, you're going to be the death of me," Grae growled, catching me as I leapt to my feet and my legs crumpled under me. "Could you please rest for one day? You just died!"

"But I'm not dead, am I? I need to see her." I wobbled on shaking feet over to the upholstered chair.

"See who?" Maez asked.

My head whipped to the side to see Briar and Maez entering from the arched anteroom.

I ran to my sister, but she was faster, racing to me and sweeping me up into her arms. She squeezed me so tightly she might've cracked a rib, but I didn't care. She was awake.

"You saved me, Cal," Briar said. Her voice strained and I realized I was squeezing her just as tightly. I eased my grip on her and she laughed. "Or should I say, Your Majesty?"

"I don't know if I'm ready for that," I huffed. "Not from you, at least. But I'm glad I won't be in this alone."

"We're not going anywhere." Briar released me, her eyes dipping to the golden lines snaking above the neckline of my nightdress. "I spotted a nice patch of land just outside the city. Perfect for a farmhouse."

I laughed, in my mind already imagining the house she'd build—whimsical and colorful, a garden of every hue of the rainbow, just like the cabin we were raised in.

"It's so good to see you awake," I whispered, releasing her to rub a lock of her crimson hair between my fingers.

"It's all she can seem to do now," Maez said, stepping beside Briar and slinging her arm over her shoulders.

Briar cut Maez a look. "I've slept plenty the last few weeks, thank you."

I could tell this was an ongoing point of contention between them. Shaking her head, Briar smirked and leaned into her mate.

Maez looked at me, her eyes softening. "I'm so sorry about your friend."

I looked between her and Briar, all at once remembering the battle in the grand hall.

I whirled to Grae, my chest tightening. "Malou?"

He nodded. The sound of her head cracking on stone, the vision of her lifeless body . . . they'd live in me always. The joy of reuniting with Briar instantly turned to sorrow as tears welled in my eyes. She had died helping me.

"The others?"

"They're okay. Well, all except Mina."

Tears started falling as I thought of losing not only my friend, but practically feeling her sister's pain. Grae circled his arm around my waist and pulled me back to sit on the bed beside him. "She's surrounded by those who love her. She'll heal." I looked at him, uncertain. "She *will*. We all will. When you made your wish, you filled with this bright golden light and then it snapped, shattering out into millions of pieces. Any Rooks left in doubt of your sovereignty laid down their weapons then and there. Your wish proved you were meant to lead Olmdere."

"I may have been saved in order to rule, but not alone." I shook my head, looking to Maez and Briar. "No one should have complete power like that. I will not be like Sawyn. I will not be above anyone else."

"Sa-wyn," Briar tossed the words in her mind. Recognition dawning on her face.

I huffed. "There's so much I need to tell you."

WITH EACH STEP OUT TOWARD THE FJORDS, MY HEART SANK. I clutched the bouquet of the last summer flowers tighter. Navin sang a deep, slow song as Ora accompanied him, playing Malou's fiddle. Mina knelt at the edge of the cliff, holding the urn of her twin's ashes.

We listened to Malou's song carry out over the misty air as her ashes scattered on the breeze. Her song was lively and mischievous, sharp yet warm, just as she had been. And it felt like the most fitting way to say goodbye to her—listening to her song played on her own instrument, her ashes swirling on the currents as if dancing to the tune.

Mina's shoulders drooped as she hung her head and crumpled around the empty urn. Hector was the first to reach her, kneeling beside Mina and taking her hand. That tenderness coming from him, of all people, made my tears fall heavier. He'd been the most wary of humans, but I knew in that moment he didn't think of anything but his fallen friend. We weren't the same people we'd been weeks ago on that first day in the wagon together. Little had we known we were the beginnings of the Golden Court.

Briar shuffled to my side and wrapped her arm around me. I dropped my head onto her shoulder, crushing the flowers in my hand against her back. Watching someone mourn their twin . . . it was a fate I had narrowly avoided myself.

Days had passed and still the sight of her dropping to the stairs of the dais jolted me awake at night. Grae would hold me through the nightmares with his calm, steady presence. I didn't know how long it would be before the panic would ease, but I had faith it would. There was so much to do now, but so many more reasons to do it.

I gave my sister one last squeeze and turned to the sheer drop. Grae followed a step beside me as I reached the edge and knelt. He dropped to his knees beside me as, one by one, the rest of the group did the same. Dozens of mourners lined the ledge, many former Galen den' Mora musicians staying to pay their respects.

As Ora came to kneel, the group began to sing. The human prayer carried on the wind, the chorus of voices eddying along the briny breeze. I didn't know the words, but I hummed along, as did Grae. The need to mourn Malou with music felt the only way. A hot tear slipped down my cheek. I knew I'd feel the responsibility for her passing for the rest of my life. It lit a fire in my veins to protect the humans of my kingdom, to not have to carry the deaths of any more of them on my shoulders than I already did. I'd live to fulfill my own dying wish: *May the humans of Olmdere thrive.* Every day, I pledged to make good on that promise, and Mina was planning on sticking around to make sure I did.

The final notes of the song died on the wind, and Mina's fingers tightened around Malou's flame badge. Hector pulled her into his shoulder, dropping his lips to the crown of her head.

I sniffed and dropped my bouquet over the edge, whispering my goodbye to Malou before rising. Most of the mourners drifted back through the forest toward the capital, but our little group remained. Oxen lowed as Galen den' Mora sat proudly on the hillside, the golden forest lit by the setting sun behind it. Ora dallied at the back of the wagon, hugging Sadie.

"Are you sure you don't want to stay?" I asked Ora one last time.

Ora smiled, shaking their head. "I'll always be a part of your court, love, no matter how far I roam. But this music must be shared, you know? And there are so many who need us," they said, pointing to the wagon.

Sorrow pierced through me, though I knew this day would come. Galen den' Mora wasn't meant to stay in one place. It would continue to travel as it had always done, but I still didn't want to say goodbye.

The group clustered together, exchanging hugs and farewells, apart from Mina and Hector, who still knelt on the cliff's edge.

I spotted Navin at the edge of the clearing, wringing his hands together as he watched us. His eyes scanning the group for Sadie as he ambled over. Lifting his hand, he took a step toward her and she turned away, following the rest of the mourners into the forest. Navin's hand hovered in the air as if he could reach through time and space to pull her back to him, but he didn't follow.

I understood why he saved his brother's life and I also understood why Sadie hated him for it. Navin's brother had been attacking her, trying to kill her just as much as she was trying to kill him, and it was not his brother's scythe that Navin had stopped. He hadn't intervened to protect her, probably because he knew she was far more likely to win.

Navin looked at me with pained eyes and mouthed, "I'm sorry." He turned back toward the forest before I could reply. As I watched him disappear into the shadows of the golden trees, I wondered if he'd stay in Olmdere and reconnect with his family. Ora would be rolling Galen den' Mora out of town alone.

Ora watched Mina and Hector, clutching a hand to their chest as if feeling the sorrow blooming there.

"We'll give her your love," I promised Ora, glancing from Mina to them.

"She knows she already has it," they said with a sad half-smile. "I couldn't be leaving her in better hands. I know I'll see you again soon." Ora wrapped me in a warm hug. "Until then, be well. Be you."

I nodded, swallowing back more tears.

Ora took a fabric-wrapped parcel out of their pocket and handed it to Grae. "That thing you asked me for."

I quirked my brow at Grae, but he didn't reply, simply nodding and pocketing the fabric.

The wind whipped our hair and cupped our ears as we waved to Ora. The wagon slowly disappeared into the golden forest, and I knew my fox badge would be swinging above the dining table along with the rest of them. It had been the first place that truly felt like home.

Grae slung his arm over my shoulders and I leaned into his warm side. I'd let that feeling guide me as I rebuilt Olmdere—a place where my people felt that same belonging.

FORTY-TWO

THE CRISP AIR SWIRLED AROUND US, PROMISING THE COMING autumn. Dappled sunlight streamed through the swaying branches of the golden oak tree. I leaned into Grae, listening to his steady heartbeat beneath my cheek.

Water rushed from the river below, spilling into the turquoise lake. The color had brightened from its murky black since the ostekke's death. Humans were swimming in it again, delighting in the warm waters, baked for months by the hot summer sun.

I plucked a leaf off the branch and twirled it by the stem.

Grae kissed my temple. "What are you thinking about?"

I let the leaf fall, floating through the air down into the river. My eyes followed the golden speck as the river carried it away.

"This may be my new favorite tree," I whispered.

"Mine too," he murmured, sweeping my hair behind my ear.

My sleeveless linen dress billowed with the breeze. I loved the flow of the fabric on the hot summer's day. Claiming the word "merem" had freed me. I wore the clothes that made me happy and I lived as the person I knew I was.

Mina was the first human appointed to my council, along with the town leaders from each of the five counties. A parcel had arrived from Queen Ingrid the day after Sawyn's death—a silver and diamond tiara, a gift from the Ice Wolf pack congratulating my victory. Sawyn's body was barely burned and the Taigosi queen was already politicking. I had sent the tiara back, along with a bag of gold from my treasury, asking Queen Ingrid to supply its worth in grain and produce instead. Sure enough, five massive wagons rolled into the capital the following week, one for each county, enough to fill their bellies twice over while the rebuild began.

The laughter of children splashing in the lake carried uphill.

I closed my eyes. "Gods, I would give anything to protect that sound."

"You have." Grae's voice dropped to a low rumble as his arms tightened around me. "And you will. We all will."

I craned my neck back to look into his warm eyes, his cheeks dimpling even as he took in my worried expression.

"There is so much to do—towns to rebuild, fields to sow . . ." I released a slow breath. "The war with Damrienn hasn't even begun."

My mind flashed to the haggard-looking face of the Damrienn messenger who had arrived that morning. King Nero demanded we yield Olmdere to him or ready for war. I knew he'd do it and yet the actuality of it stole my breath away. I'd barely taken my place on my throne and already I needed to defend it.

"He has to get through Taigos to march his armies here and Ingrid hates him almost as much as we do. We have time." Grae swept his calloused hand down my bare arm. "For now, your people are safe."

I shook my head. "You will be at war with your own father."

"*You* are my family." He searched my face and reached into his pocket, his fist clenching around something. "You are my everything, little fox."

He opened his palm to reveal a gold ring holding a large amber stone ringed with diamonds.

"Is this—"

"Your protection stone." Grae smiled.

My eyebrows shot up. "You kept it all this time?"

"I gave it to Ora to turn into a ring." He looked down at the ring, the diamonds casting spectrums of glittering light all around us. He chuckled. "Though in hindsight it would've been better to hang on to it, had I known how many monsters we'd encounter. I'd planned on giving it to you before the siege, but . . ."

"It's beautiful," I whispered. "Are you—are you proposing to me?"

"Poorly, it seems," he huffed, flashing that charming grin. "I am already yours in every way. You are the merem of my heart. Be mine? Marry me?"

My heart cracked open at those words, a smile splitting across my face as I nodded. "Yes."

Grae slid the ring onto my finger and pulled my face to his. We could barely contain our smiles long enough to kiss. Joy rushed through me like I'd never known. Here in this golden tree, with the river rushing below me, and the sounds of my kingdom finally at peace, I knew I didn't have to dig any deeper to find who I was or where I wanted to be. Grae's arm threaded around me and pulled me tighter against him.

My eyes fell to the rushing turquoise water—the same river that flowed down from the mountains of Taigos and over the gold mines of Sevelde, the life force of Olmdere, the history of war and prosperity carved through the land. The fight was only beginning, but I finally knew what I was fighting for—for all of us, those who struggled to be all the things they felt inside, those who didn't yet know how to carve their own path. I knew then that my reign would be like this river, forging ahead, finding my own way until everything flowed into the stillness and beauty of the lake at my back. The Golden Court would rise like a river after a rainstorm and all our enemies will be washed away.

DRAMATIS PERSONAE

PEOPLE

CALLA MARRIEL: Gold Wolf, twin to Briar, child of the late King and Queen of Olmdere

BRIAR MARRIEL: Gold Wolf, twin to Calla, Crown Princess, child of the late King and Queen of Olmdere

GRAE CLAUDIUS: Silver Wolf, Crown Prince of Damrienn

NERO CLAUDIUS: Silver Wolf, King of Damrienn

MAEZ CLAUDIUS: Silver Wolf, cousin to Grae and niece to the king, one of Grae's royal guard

SADIE RAUXTIDE: Silver Wolf, sister to Hector, one of Grae's royal guard

HECTOR RAUXTIDE: Silver Wolf, brother to Sadie, one of Grae's royal guard

ORA: human, leader of Galen den' Mora musical troupe

NAVIN: human, part of Galen den' Mora

MINA: human, twin to Malou, part of Galen den' Mora

MALOU: human, twin to Mina, part of Galen den' Mora

SAWYN: sorceress who killed the king and queen of Olmdere and now controls the kingdom

ROOKS: soldiers of Sawyn's army

INGRID ENGDAHL: queen of the Ice Wolves

LUO YASSINE: king of the Onyx Wolves, older brother to Taidei

TAIDEI YASSINE: prince of the Onyx Wolves, younger brother to Luo

COURTS

OLMDERE (CAPITAL: OLMDERE CITY): home to humans and the Gold Wolf pack

DAMRIENN (CAPITAL: HIGHWICK): home to humans and the Silver Wolf pack

TAIGOS (CAPITAL: TAIGOSKA): home to humans and the Ice Wolf pack

VALTA (CAPITAL: RIKESH): home to humans and the Onyx Wolf pack

ACKNOWLEDGMENTS

THANK YOU TO ALL MY AMAZING QUEER READERS AND OUR allies for embracing (*and excitedly demanding?*) more types of queer fantasy stories. I hope you feel seen and welcomed into the world of high fantasy!

Thank you to my Mountaineers for celebrating my books both online and out in the world. You are the most amazing group of readers, and I'm honored to share these stories with you! *The best mountains to climb are fictional ones xx.*

Thank you to all of my family for supporting and encouraging me to pursue the career of my dreams. To my husband and children: I adore the life we've built together and love you endlessly.

Thank you to all of my amazing patrons for making this novel possible! I love creating worlds with you! A very special thank you to my fae and royal fae patrons: Jaime, Linda, Nicole, Leslie, Marissa, Traci, Amy, Ciara, Drea, Hannah, Kelly, Maggie, Mandy, Mariah, Sarah, Shanda, and Virginia. Your support means so much to me! I can't wait to take you on more fantasy adventures!

To my writer friends: thank you for lifting me up through the writing of this book and on my author journey. I am so grateful to have you in my corner cheering me on, guiding me, and helping me find my own way!

Thank you to my book wifey, Kate, for all of your support and for the amazing job you do formatting my gorgeous novellas, designing merch, and keeping the A.K. shop running! Thank you to Sabrina for keeping Team A.K. going. I so appreciate all of the work you do!

Thank you to my amazing agent, Jessica Watterson at SDLA, for championing my stories and for supporting me through this wild journey of publishing. I love working with you and look forward to many more bookish adventures in the future!

Thank you to the whole Harper Voyager team all over the world. It has been a pleasure working with you all on this new series. Thank you to my amazing team for championing this book and supporting diverse stories. A big thank you to my editor, David Pomerico, and to Natasha Bardon, for helping make this story the best it can be!

Lastly, thank you to my fur babies, Ziggy, Bruno, and Timmy, for saving me in the anxious moments of getting this book out into the world.

We hope you enjoyed the first installment of
The Golden Court trilogy. Want more romance and magic?
Turn the page for a sneak peek at the fifth and final book in the
Five Crowns of Okrith series . . .

THE
AMETHYST KINGDOM

Coming Summer 2024 from Harper Voyager
wherever books are sold

THE AMETHYST KINGDOM

CARYS DIDN'T GET FAR FROM THE DINING COMMONS, HER STEW-
ing anger making her pace outside the doors.

Back and forth. Back and forth.

Gods, she needed to end this. Leaning against the stone archway, she listened as the competitors finished their lunch, paying
particular attention to the footsteps of the people shuffling from
the dining commons and into the hallway.

When she had last seen Ersan, neither of them had been particularly adept at fighting. But Carys had developed her fighting
prowess in her years of being a soldier in Hale's army. She only
prayed that Ersan had continued on his highborn trajectory and
hadn't invested in his swordsmanship. His wooden leg would
surely hinder him in the melee too. At least then the first competition would excise him from her life again.

She listened eagerly for the tap of Ersan's cane. When it came,
she took a deep breath, waiting for Ersan to pass her narrow hiding
space between the main entryway and the side corridor.

When Ersan passed, her hand shot out, grabbing him by the
collar of his shirt and yanking him into the narrow corridor. She
hoped it would leave a bruise on his back as she slammed him

hard against the carved wood. In the blink of an eye, her knife was unsheathed from her belt, and she stabbed it into the beam a hair's breadth from Ersan's head.

Those dark eyes didn't so much as flinch, as if he'd expected this exact situation to unfold.

"Hello, love," Ersan said with a wink.

"Stop telling people I'm your Fated," Carys seethed, ignoring his cavalier greeting.

"This seems a bit like the kind of intimidation Councilor Elwyn warned us against, no?" His smile was taunting, only incensing her further as his eyes shifted to the dagger beside his temple. "Are you nearing your cycle then? You were always particularly murderous around that time—"

She yanked him off the column and smashed him back into it again, hoping every nodule along the carved wood would leave bruises down his spine. Gods, it would feel good to impale her knife into his guts and twist. She pinned him with a venomous look. "I'm not joking! Stop saying we're Fated!"

His scent hit her like a crashing wave, like Arboan clay and blossoming snowflowers and sunshine over the ocean. He smelled like every good memory that now filled her with grief. It made her fist clench tighter in his starched, white shirt. He'd taken every moment of joy. He'd taken everything from her. And she still didn't really understand why.

"But it's the truth. You are my Fated." Ersan's midnight eyes twinkled against his lashes, so thick that from a distance they seemed lined with kohl. His face was still all the same sharp lines, but his strong jaw was now covered in dark stubble all the way up to his defined cheekbones. His straight black hair was just long enough to be pulled back into a low knot at the nape of his neck, and stray strands fell across his thick black brows. "Why should I lie to anyone about it?"

"If you weren't here, you wouldn't have to lie. And you shouldn't be here at all," Carys gritted out, yanking her knife free and clenching it in her hand. She debated holding it against his golden brown skin, wondering how good it might feel to draw blood. "You just couldn't stay gone, could you?"

"You think I'm here for *you*?" Ersan chuckled, his mouth quirking with cruel amusement. "You truly have a sense of entitlement, don't you? Carys, I'm here the same as any contender. I'm here for a crown."

"What about Arboa?"

Ersan shrugged. "Collam will make an excellent Lord."

"Collam?" Carys asked incredulously. They couldn't be speaking of the same boy. Ersan's younger brother was a gentle, artistic soul. He was a painter and a philosopher, not a politician. Carys hated that when everything had imploded between her and Ersan, she'd lost Collam too. She hated thinking that the boy missed her and their inside jokes and games. She'd abandoned him in some ways . . .

She cleared her throat. It wasn't her fault. Ersan had kept the most important of secrets from her and had never bothered to explain himself in all the years since. Carys pulled Ersan closer only to shove him back again, banging his head into the beam and rattling his broad shoulders.

He only laughed, the sound grating against Carys and making her clench her jaw. He couldn't even let her have the satisfaction of rattling him a little bit.

"Still got that fire, Car," he said, his eyes trailing down to her mouth. "And it still makes you blind."

Before she could respond, he released his cane and his hand shot out to her wrist that held her knife, immobilizing the weapon. He shoved off the beam, using his size and muscle to pivot Carys so quickly it felt like magic. In another breath, he had her chest pinned to the stone wall across the narrow hallway. He held her knife in one hand and her braid in the other, tugging on her rope of hair and making her stretch up on her tiptoes to arch her head back.

Clearly, she'd been wrong about the hindrance of his leg, and her hopes of his easy removal from the strength competition were now dashed.

His warm breath found its way to her pointed ear. "Do you still like this?" he rasped in a husky lover's whisper.

Carys's stomach flipped and her duplicitous core clenched even as fire filled her veins. "No."

His soft breath brushed against the shell of her ear. "You liar." His nose grazed up her neck. "You think all this perfume in your hair can hide your true scent from me?" He leaned in, his chest pinning her harder, until the rough stone bit into her skin and her body pulsed with traitorous desire. "I know you, *Fated*."

Carys's fingertips dug into the stone, fighting the urge to relent, to lean into his touch. She knew exactly how it would feel—how deft his fingers would be, how skilled his mouth. But then the pain and heartbreak flooded back into her, dousing her desire and filling her with an inky black rage.

"You don't know me anymore," she said, shoving backward and using the hilt of her sheathed sword to shove into Ersan's groin—a trick she'd learned from Bri. He pivoted just in time, but she managed to knock him hard in the hip anyway. Without the stability of his cane, he stumbled backward a step. In one smooth movement, she twisted his wrist and snatched back her knife, sheathing it and storming away before Ersan could grab her again.

Carys tsked at the surprise she'd seen on Ersan's face. Clearly, he didn't know her anymore at all. She'd been a working soldier for the last several years, training with the most elite warriors in all the realm. She'd always been a good fighter, but now she had the experience to know how to outmaneuver an opponent with not only brawn but intellect. The Carys Ersan once knew had died the same day as her father. Ersan might be a trained fighter, but Carys was a *warrior*, and she'd never surrender to him, nor would she ever forgive him for the truths he'd kept from her.

"Go back to your flowers, Lord of Arboa," Carys called over her shoulder, swishing her hips just to taunt him further. "You will never be anyone's King, least of all mine."

ABOUT THE AUTHOR

A.K. MULFORD is a bestselling fantasy author and former wildlife biologist who swapped rehabilitating monkeys for writing novels. She/They are inspired to create diverse stories that transport readers to new realms, making them fall in love with fantasy for the first time, or all over again. She now lives in Australia with her husband and two young human primates, creating lovable fantasy characters and making ridiculous TikToks.

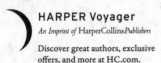